THE DAILY GRIND

BOOK 5

THE DAILY GRIND

BOOK 5

ARGUS

Podium

Podium

BOOK 5

CHAPTER 1

It felt appropriate that his day started with a loose end. That was just the kind of life James had been living lately. All loose ends, no conclusions. Maybe that was just how life was supposed to be, when you were actually following up on every opportunity, and also maybe a wizard. James didn't know.

Actually, he didn't know a lot of stuff. And he was fine admitting it, too. There was always more to learn, and that was the human condition. Or whatever word they'd need to use now that human wasn't the only option. Regardless of what terminology they eventually settled on that would include their camraconda friends, it wouldn't change that James had just learned something unpleasant.

"What?" he heard himself say.

The word was half incredulous, half honestly confused. It came out of James's mouth as he was talking to Lua, going over the potential risks of any enemy agents still operating, and how easy it would or wouldn't be to put lives back on track. He'd been really honestly sympathetic to the fact that Lua had now had her life upended by dungeon bullshit *twice*, which was impressive on its own. Some people hadn't survived once. Wanting to help, he'd told her that if she felt like she was doing actual good work at the high school, she could head back there whenever she was ready. Which was extra important, for the bonus reason that they really, really needed to keep an eye on that dungeon.

Which was when James had learned they were closing the school.

He scratched at the back of his head. "I mean, I guess we did fill their parking lot with bullets. And a couple corpses. And kids *do* keep going missing there . . ." he admitted, starting to rationalize the news, before Lua cut him off.

"No, no. Not . . . well, not *entirely* because of that. Sadly. It's the pandemic, not the dungeon," she informed him.

"Sorry, the what now?" James blinked.

Lua raised her eyebrows, reeling back a bit. "The pandemic? COVID-19? Someone brought it off a cruise ship and went through Washington before they came home to Forest Grove. Now it's in the state, and people are worried."

"No, wait." James shook his head. "I'm sorry, I don't . . . there's a pandemic?"

"Yes?" Lua's voice was mostly concern at this point. "Is there something wrong? Did you get your memory wiped by evil coffee again?"

"First off, that has never happened, as far as I know. Second, don't speak ill of our lord and savior, coffee," James chastised her. "But seriously, no, I just had no idea there was a plague happening. How bad is it? They're closing schools?! That's nuts!"

Lua eyed him suspiciously. "This has been on the news for *months*," she said. "Anyway, the closure isn't slated until a couple weeks from now. They haven't announced it yet."

"Okay. Okay, holy shit." James rolled his knuckles on his forehead as he leaned against the table. "Alright! Not sure what we'll do about it, but we'll get on it, I guess?"

"What?" Now it was Lua's turn to be perplexed.

"There's an outbreak of an I-am-assuming-deadly disease," James said, using his mildly sarcastic explanation voice. "That seems like the thing we're here to deal with. So we're on it. The Order, that is. We'll figure something out."

". . . How . . . ?" Lua's suspicion was palpable.

"No idea. Containment, maybe? Cure, if we can leverage some

virology orbs? We'll see. It's just in a couple places, right? We've got a little time." He shrugged. "If nothing else, we could make an informorph that does gene sequencing, probably. *Maybe?* Maybe not accidentally make a small and unstable god this time."

"What?!"

"Yeah, it's been a busy month. Are you seriously surprised I haven't had time for the news? I haven't even had time to play video games, and people keep recommending *Control* to me, for some reason." James groaned as his sore muscles and bruises protested him standing up. Augmented human or not, he'd been through the wringer the last few days, and there wasn't a single member of the Order that wasn't also feeling some amount of pain and bone-deep exhaustion. "Anyway. Go talk to . . . I'm gonna say Deb. She's our resident medical expert so far. Tell her I'd like her to start drawing up a plan for it. I've gotta go buy furniture."

James stumbled over the cafeteria bench as he left. He wouldn't miss these things one bit. He'd spent a month and a half griping about the hard seats and threatening everyone with beanbag chairs, and today he aimed to make good on that. Secretly, he'd been hoping JP or maybe Alex would have already upgraded the room just to get him to shut up. But they hadn't, and now he had free time, and a company debit card, and it was his time to shine.

He'd even budgeted for a big truck. And with that thought in mind, James made his way to the parking lot, thoughts of better chairs only marginally overshadowed by concern about how the hell he was supposed to punch out a pandemic.

The R&D basement—really just the research basement, as they didn't do much development—felt like it was holding its collective breath. Everyone was in a loose circle around the shellaxy play area, which now also contained a few iLipedes, including Lily. About five minutes earlier, she'd finished her analysis of the latest copied green orb, the one that Anesh had brought them after the minor Office delve that had happened a few days ago. Once everyone had gotten a chance to look at the screen, or the whiteboard where Reed had copied the text up at the top, they'd moved away to make their own notes on folded pieces of paper.

They'd also all tossed ten bucks into someone's hat on a desk nearby.

Honestly, it wasn't very much about the money. The group of scholars, programmers, and lucky guessers who dwelt in the basement and were collectively called Research were all actually paid pretty well. It had been a long time since Reed had worried about money in any serious way. So, betting on their iLipede interpretation skills was really more about bragging rights than the actual cash.

This time, it was Virgil who acknowledged the tossing of the last wager into the hat and cracked the orb. And it was *only* cracking with greens. As far as they knew, totems required either blood or death, and absorbing or making life was *right* out, given how the green orbs seemed to universally come from creatures that were under direct dungeon operation, and also very lethal.

[+1.2 Skill Ranks : Programming—C++]

[Local Area Shift : +3 Couches]

". . . I don't . . ." said someone in the silent group after Virgil announced the upgrade. "I don't understand."

Reed glanced at the board where he'd copied Lily's reading on the orb. "Power Unit Type : Authority. Operation Time : 102 hrs/1K. Contains traces of : Comfort, Space, Leather."

"Nik, go find where the new couches spawned," Reed called out to one of his minions. He looked down at the array of wagers in front of him, the gambling skill in his core spinning up as he analyzed the odds. "Alright, points to whoever said 'an arbitrary number of furnishings.' Good call there."

They waited around for a bit before Nikhail ran back into the room. "Found 'em!" he panted out, leaning on one of the desks and not paying attention as a nervous researcher carefully moved an experiment away from his hand. "They . . . *hoof* . . . they're all in little alcoves that didn't exist before. One's upstairs, the other two are down here."

"Score, free couches," someone cheered, and the group joined them in amused celebration.

"Alright! A split between whoever said 'arbitrary furniture' and whoever said 'extradimensional seating.' *No* points for whoever wrote, and I'm quoting here, 'new basement open parenthesis sex dungeon close parenthesis.'" Reed looked up, unamused. "No," he restated, eying the cracked grins from the people who appreciated the joke more. He leveled an accusatory finger around the room. "Noooo."

"No what?" James asked from behind him.

The voice caught Reed off-guard, and he spun around, dropping the hat of money back onto the desk. He shuffled quickly to cover it up, and saluted their leader almost by reflex. A few other people in the crowd mimicked the gesture, and Reed pretended not to notice James wincing. "No to an idea on what an orb would do," he informed James. He cleared his throat, then asked, "What can we help you with?"

"You guys are *allowed* to put dumb bets on orbs, you know," James told him, leaning around to eye the hat of money, ignoring the sheepish blushes on some of his staff's faces. "I'm just here to ask if you had any progress reports on the candy thing. Oh, and also to ask why there's a couch intersecting with the kitchen. I brought back a bunch of beanbags and now I feel one-upped."

Reed studiously avoided eye contact. "Ah." He cleared his throat again, buying time. "It's a green orb that adds couches."

"Is this more testing on identifier keywords?" James asked. "Where does Anesh store the backups of orbs? I don't think we'll be making more of that one, but I want couches for my apartment."

"That sounds like an abuse of executive power," Virgil chimed in semi-sarcastically from his desk, where the smoky wisps of green dust had already dissipated.

James exercised his executive power to briefly and awkwardly flip him off. "I fought the laser computer, I get the couches!" he declared, in a sentence that would have given a confusion headache to any uninitiated civilian that heard it. "Anyway. Reed, candy?"

It was one of several projects that Research was working on. Reed, specifically, in this case. They were starting to diverge into specializations, and while it was cool to have someone who wanted to be a dominionologist, or a dungeon linguist, it was more often than not starting to lead to people being laser-focused on their own specific pet projects, leaving Reed to do the grunt work of tracking data, compiling statistics, and trying to answer whatever question James came down here with this week.

"Candy," he repeated, trying to not show his frustration. "It might do something, yeah." He led James over to his computer while everyone else dispersed to their own workspaces and set Lily up with a new green orb. Pulling up a spreadsheet on the laptop, and desperately hoping the leader of his magical order didn't judge him for his anime desktop wallpaper, Reed started pointing out numbers. "So, here's the list of delvers. We've been trying to track candy eaten now, as well as everything else that we *try* to monitor. The key word here is try, because the more stuff we're watching for, the less convenient it is for people, and the less accurate information we get."

"That makes sense. How many things are you guys actually following?" James asked, narrowing his eyes to focus on the petite letters on the spreadsheet.

"Orbs used, absorbed. General physical stats like height and weight, for medical reasons. Kills. Delves, time spent inside. Candy, now." Reed shrugged. "Lots of stuff. A lot of it inherited from Anesh's system, but I'm trying to keep it all in one place."

"And?" James prompted.

"And I can make charts. Look." He clicked a few times, and brought up a graph comparing two downward-trending lines.

"... I'm not gonna lie to you, I can't really read charts that well at a glance. What am I looking at?" James asked.

"Well, the blue line with big chunky changes is the number of delvers that have different numbers of blue orbs absorbed. The spikier orange line is the amount of candy eaten." Reed traced the two lines. "So, they both have similar profiles, basically showing that more candy means more orbs; but the thing is, we have kind of a low sample size. Blue absorption *also* trends upward with kills, and with total value of owned vehicles."

James tilted his head so far to the side his neck cracked. "Sorry, the what?"

"It's a correlation versus causation thing. Do you want me to explain . . ." Reed cut off as he caught the tight-lipped frown James was giving him.

James sighed. "I know what correlation is. I was more wondering why we know how expensive people's cars are."

"I don't actually know, JP just had a spreadsheet for it on the server, so I added it to this," Reed admitted. "Um . . . anyway, I guess this is just me telling you that the candy *might* be creating some kind of metaphysical bond between the people eating it and the Office, but it also might be doing nothing. None of the ones we've done tests on act any differently than normal candy, too."

James considered that information for a moment before something occurred to him. "I've never had the time to actually ask this before, but does any dungeon tech really show up as different under a microscope or anything?"

"Yes, actually!" Reed excitedly replied. Any sense of nervous worry at talking to the leader of their operation whisked away as he started to get into the groove of one of his own passion projects. "The materials externally mimic mundane compositions, but *actually* are artificially uniform, and have a *very* different method of radiation refraction compared to things that aren't essentially built out of orbs! I'm waiting for Rufus or Ganesh or one of the camracondas to have some free time, because I suspect that we'll find that Life follows similar rules, with created matter adhering to—"

"I'm gonna stop you there," James said, raising a hand. He had a small smile on his face, which helped put Reed at ease, but he still needed to cut the conversation short. "I've got a *lot* more that I'm curious about now, especially since I think this means you could speed-identify magic pencils. But I've got a hell of a headache today, and I'm having trouble following. Do you mind if we have a group briefing about this sometime tomorrow? I'm not gonna allow you PowerPoint privileges, but I know there's other people who'd like to know this."

Reed blinked, then cleared his throat again. "Oh," he said, at first dejected, before he realized that James wasn't just ignoring his work. "Oh! Yeah, sure! Um . . . I'll be here all day?"

"Great," James told him with a nod, which was instantly followed by a lip-biting wince. "Ugh. Okay. Well, keep up the good work. Also, Lily dinged halfway through this chat, so she's got some good speed on those greens. Good luck on your next wager," he said, turning to leave. James was halfway down the hall back to the elevator when he called back over his shoulder, "And thanks for the couch!"

The collective basement research team waited patiently until they heard the elevator doors close, before Reed pulled thirty bucks out of the hat. "Alright, who had 'James not annoyed at result'?" he called out.

". . . And that's all from this week's special guest!" Sarah spoke cheerfully into her microphone, her voice pitched by an uncanny instinct for what picked up cleanly on audio equipment. "James, thanks for talking to us about the haunted attic. Everyone, thanks for listening. This has been the Order of Endless Rooms news update for Wednesday, March eleventh! So long, and remember: if you're thinking of petting the cat in the basement? Don't!"

She leaned back from the desk, reaching over to hit the *stop record* button with an exaggerated arm motion, then used the movement to pitch herself backward, flopping her whole body over both chairs on this side of James's desk.

They were using his office because it was actually the only place in the entire Lair that was a sort of private enclosed space and also didn't have concrete walls.

"So, question for ya," James asked, as he started to unplug his own microphone and pack away the recording equipment.

"Fire away, mon capitan!" Sarah exclaimed from her entirely uncomfortable bed.

James rolled his eyes. "If you salute me too, I'm putting our friendship on hiatus. But no, I was wondering if the podcast counts as a product."

"A . . . oh! For the value?" Sarah sat up, tapping her chin with a stylishly painted fingernail. "Dunno! What adds value, anyway?"

"The orb . . ."

"No, I mean, what could increase the value of an audio file, you dingus!" Sarah swatted at him, missing by a country mile. "Like, would it add outro music?"

"That'd be cool. But I dunno either." James clipped the microphone case shut, nearly knocking the recording laptop off the cramped surface of his desk. "Ugh. We need to get you a dedicated studio room."

"We could use one of the basement rooms." Sarah shrugged. "It's not like the audio quality is that important for a fifteen-minute rapid fire update."

If there was one thing that was constantly, almost daily, impressive to James, it was Sarah's ability to cram words, meaning, emotion, and a pervasive sense of upbeat optimism into tiny spaces of conversation. Putting her in charge of her own podcast idea and giving her free rein to do it however she wanted had been probably the best idea James had ever enacted. It was instantly something their members were interested in, and a great way for everyone to keep up on the big and small happenings around the Order and the Lair, from random members of the support group who were only loosely affiliated with the Order to the core group of hardened delvers. *Everyone* liked Sarah, and no matter who she brought in to talk with her, she found a way to get that person to open up, share something useful, and do it at her energetic pace. Also, she managed to say "Order of Endless Rooms" without it sounding unnatural.

James had settled on the name in a moment of what he felt was excellent High Fantasy Worldbuilding. He'd shared it with Alanna, and almost instantly felt like he'd made a mistake. Saying it had felt . . . rocky. Like he was a kid playing at having a Real Adult Job, miming those business-words that he knew how to say, but not how to use. He'd wanted to take it back, and just call them the Northwest Delvers Association or something that sounded practical and solid, but of course, it was far too late. Alanna had loved the name, immediately shared it with Anesh and Sarah, and it was a snowball from there. No take backs.

So, it was nice that Sarah could make it sound smooth. And James did realize that eventually, he'd be saying it with the same cadence; like he meant it, like he didn't have to *try* so hard.

Today's podcast had covered everything from the list of programs currently brewing in the basement on the odd little emerald chips, to the update on the green orbs in effect, to the current available numbers on blues and oranges for anyone wanting to absorb a new tool, and finally, to the "special guest." Today it had been James, there to get everyone caught up on the Attic—or as much as was possible in five minutes. Sarah had almost instantly named it Clutter Ascent; James hadn't protested. He knew he'd never beat that even if he had a week to think. So he just focused on talking about how they were going to be opening it up to volunteers for constant exploration.

In other words, the podcast covered a *lot*, and it usually aired every few days, too.

"I feel like . . ." James framed his words with his hands as he replied to Sarah's mildly self-depreciating comment. "Hm. How to say this. I think you're making something cool?"

Sarah gave him a thumbs-up. "Thanks! What does that have to do with sound quality?"

He shushed her. "The show is cool, it's obviously useful to us as an organization, and people like you. So I guess my point is, you deserve good sound quality, and you're important."

"Aaw! Thank you!" Sarah basked in the praise. Then her face turned slightly more serious. "So, how are we gonna do the Clutter runs? High roll gets to go in?"

"I've heard worse ideas. Good luck getting it by Karen." James sighed.

"I don't get why—" Sarah's gregariously worded complaint about Karen's stuffy behavior was cut off by a rapping knock on the door, followed shortly by Alanna not waiting for a response, pushing it open, and sticking half her frame through the gap.

"Hey!" Sarah greeted her, not even bothering to finish the less-than-charitable thought she'd been about to express.

"Yo." Alanna waved at them. Her face was flushed, a thin sheen of sweat on her skin.

"How's camraconda practice going?" James asked, carefully maneuvering his way around the cramped interior of his personal workspace as he tried to coil cables up properly.

"Not bad!" Alanna grinned. "Did you know that their basilisk thing is actually really goddamn hard to explain? I didn't! And I still don't care!"

"So, Research had some questions for ya, eh?" James pursed his lips and nodded knowingly. "You know, I feel like giving them their own basement to work in is creating a very . . . let's say 'unique' subculture in the Order. I kinda want to talk to JP about it, but I worry that he's gonna play devil's advocate for the whole thing, and I won't learn whether or not it's actually a good idea."

"Don't you literally have leadership skills?" Sarah accused him. "Use your HR powers! Divine the truth!"

"I've never heard anyone be that excited about HR before," Alanna groused. "Anyway, before this gets too off-track, have you seen Anesh? I need him for a thing, and I can't find either of him."

James suspected, correctly, that this was a further attempt by Alanna to try to form one of the Attic bonds with Anesh. For some reason, the skulljack hive mind trick actively stopped bonds from forming; maybe because the bonds considered the member persons to be a single individual at that point, and you can't form a bond with yourself. But whatever logic they were operating on, the two of them hadn't unlocked anything during the Status Quo assault, or anytime since. And Alanna was taking it as an excuse to really just spend more time with Anesh, which was honestly good for the two of them anyway, in James's opinion.

He loved his partners, and he liked seeing them together too. Also, if they unlocked a bond that let them share food or nutrition or something, he could stop trying to appease both of them at once with his cooking. He *loved his partners*, he reiterated in his head, but they could be *absurdly* picky eaters sometimes.

Right now, though, he got to deliver awkward news. "He's on a date," James told Alanna. "That math tutor girl he had coffee with . . . last week?"

"Oh! Good for him!" She blinked in surprise before grinning. "Does he know it's a date?" she asked James coyly.

"He hasn't a clue," James replied.

Sarah looked between the two of them. "Um . . . you know it doesn't count if . . ."

"We know," James and Alanna echoed together, amused. James continued, "It's just more fun this way. Also, I think they might actually legitimately just be friends; we're teasing, mostly."

"We should make sure she's not a spy, though. Hey, can I borrow the glasses that show affiliation?" Alanna cracked the door open wider, shuffling her feet around the camraconda napping on the floor in front of James's office like a technorganic speed bump.

"Why do I feel like you have some ulterior motive in mind?" James asked, and Alanna didn't need her magic empathy boost to know he was being sarcastic.

She still feigned innocence. "No?" She coughed into her hand. "I mean, I admit, I'm kinda curious how some members show up . . ."

"They don't work on reflections," Sarah chimed in with a cheeky grin.

"Dammit." Alanna snapped her fingers.

"Also, I think Nate still has them," James informed her.

"Dammit!" This time Alanna rolled her eyes, throwing her hands up to the ceiling. "James, you can't give the best counterintelligence tool we have to the *one person who we know is spying on us!*" she informed him. Loudly.

"It's fine, we're totally gonna make a copy or five of it next week. It's in the production queue, right after the rest of the hearts we owe that doctor." James shrugged. "Also, I trust Nate."

Alanna growled at him lightly. "I'm still mad about this. I'll go with your judgment, but I don't like it. Nate shouldn't have lied to us."

James couldn't really disagree with that. "I mean, yeah, okay. I'm not happy about the whole thing. And I admit that I am suspicious now that there's recording devices in my office. But on the other hand, we have an emerald working on an anti-spyware program that'll probably cripple the entire concept of malware for a year or two. That's kinda cool."

"We could have done that without being spied upon," Sarah pointed out, shifting herself out of her chair and standing up, her laptop having finished saving everything that needed saving.

"Also, thanks for making me worry about bugs now. Cool," Alanna muttered. "Anyway, I'm gonna go relax. Text me if Anesh comes by."

"'Kay. Love you!" James called after his partner as she turned to leave, half-tripping over the still-immobile camraconda under her feet.

Sarah eyed him with a little worry, though her voice didn't betray it. "You're taking the spy thing pretty well, honestly."

"Eh." James waved it off. "So, you wanna know my weird moon logic on this?" he asked.

"Sure!" Sarah laughed a little at his phrasing. "Hit me."

James held up three fingers. "When Curious told me about the people that were after us, she listed three categories. Angry, curious, and the specific threat of Status Quo." He ticked down one finger. "Status Quo is as good as dead; the individual agents left alive may be problems, but not on the scale of the whole organization." The second finger closed into his palm. "I'm pretty sure the curious ones referred to the kids, who have already 'found us.'" He put down the last finger. "And I'm almost certain the angry one is the police detective, who is still on the fence as to whether or not I'm a serial killer."

"So . . . you're not worried because . . ."

"Because a nascent god didn't list the FBI as people who were looking for me." James shrugged. "Far as I can tell, Nate's here because our behavior and spending patterns were suspicious, and the FBI wanted to know if we were a domestic terror group. We aren't; they probably don't care."

"There is no doinking way it's that easy. Also, didn't you impersonate the FBI, like, exactly while standing in front of him?" Sarah accused.

"I did! I did do that. Yes . . ." James trailed off sheepishly. "Ahem. Well."

"You ding-dong. I'm telling on you," Sarah concluded with a little nod, crossing her arms on her chest.

James quirked an eyebrow. "What?"

"Yes. Telling!" Sarah confirmed with another little nod.

"Telling . . . whomst?" James asked, a little worried to hear the answer.

"Anyone who listens to the podcast!" Sarah announced.

James wanted to argue, but honestly, outing their chef as a government agent actually seemed like the kind of casual, non-threatening revenge that he felt perfectly fit the minor frustration he was trying to play off under the guise of being a chill dude. He thought about it a little more before he decided on the most elegant way to make sure Sarah followed through on her "threat."

"Oh yeah? I *dare* you," he said, the two of them grinning at each other like idiot kids until they couldn't hold in the laughter anymore.

Later that evening, James sat almost by himself, dialing number after number from his contacts list.

None of them answered.

His parents' cell phones, their home number, his sister, his aunt . . . he didn't have that many family members, but still, they didn't pick up.

They hadn't picked up for a while. Since before the Order had realized what Status Quo was doing. His family had been snatched away while he fooled around in the dungeons.

The worst part, he thought, as he tried to search for any Facebook profiles with their names, was that he honestly didn't *care* that much.

Oh, sure, he didn't want his parents dead. He really did love them; his mom had been . . . *was* . . . a fine enough person. And his dad had been the reason James had turned out the way he did, which could really be good or bad depending on how depressed he was feeling on any particular day. Same with his sister. She was an annoying pain in the ass, but that absolutely did not mean she should be murdered by the shadowy agents of a secret cabal.

But James wasn't Anesh or Alanna. Anesh, who lost his parents that he *really* loved. Or Alanna, who worked so hard to provide a better life for her younger sisters. James just . . . wouldn't really miss what he'd lost, that much.

But that didn't stop this little ritual.

"There is *something*," Secret said, orbiting James as he ran one last search. "It is a hidden thing. I can see the hiding, and the intent, but it left no trail. I do not believe this was an infomorph like myself; nothing alive, just a weapon, perhaps?" His orbit was methodical and precise, a swift and meaningful coiling around James's seated form during this very focused search. "Yes. Something is being hidden, not just from you. But that is all I can say for now."

"Well," James sighed, slumping back and pushing the keyboard away. "It's a start." He glanced over at the folded piece of paper on his desk; the little handwritten note bearing the short list of the handful of skill orbs his sister had snapped before vanishing from his life forever. "One step at a time, eh?"

"Eh, indeed," Secret agreed, slowing to lazy loops before settling his snout on James's shoulder. "We will find the trail. I swear," he said.

James reached up to pet along the ridge of one of his eyes, careful not to poke the semi-corporeal infomorph anywhere sensitive. "I know, buddy. I know. I just . . . hurt. And I was hoping at least this one we could clear up easily in a few days."

"Have hurts ever worked that way?" Secret asked, seeming to be earnest in his ignorance.

James snorted. "Not a goddamn once," he said bitterly.

Early spring sunlight clawed its way through the mildly opaque high windows that surrounded the ex-warehouse space that made up the Order's combination cafeteria-gym-and-lounge area. The oncoming summer months were doing that thing they always did to James: gradually appearing while he was busy sleeping through sunrises and staying up until 4 a.m., only to be met with his absolute shock when suddenly there was warm weather and the smell of new greenery.

"Okay, so." James was sitting down with Deb and Alex, eschewing the normal environment of his cramped office for the much more pleasant sensation of holding an official meeting while sprawled haphazardly on a beanbag chair. "Bring me up to speed. What are our options?"

The two women exchanged a look. The kind where they idly gnawed on their lips, raised their eyebrows, and tried to nonverbally decide who was going to tell James that he was an idiot. Or at the very least, perhaps *misinformed* about the nature of a given issue.

"Okay," Deb echoed James's words. "So." She leaned her elbows onto the low coffee table the beanbags were piled around, shifting uncomfortably to try to make hers behave more like a chair. "Here's the thing: we don't really have a lot of options. Like, at all."

Alex took up the pause in the conversation. "Yeah, um, I looked into some of the WHO and CDC stuff on it. A global pandemic is *way* outside our ability to seriously impact." James's face fell as they explained, and Alex quickly tried to apologize. "I'm sorry! It's just . . . we don't have the manpower! Or the resources!"

"Ah, I'm not that surprised, honestly." James sighed deeply. "I just figured that we had enough magic bullshit here to help *somehow*."

"Thing is, a lot of our magic is very personal." Deb spread her hands in front of her. "Skill orbs are a large percentage of it, and they're basically all instantly ruled out. And yes, that *does* include medical ones. I know you've started thinking of me as the team doctor, but you should know there's at least three other people walking around who have high-level immunology, biology, or surgery orbs. I'm pretty sure someone knows how to do an organ transplant, not that we're planning to test that. And *none of that is helpful*, because applying those toward large-scale help requires you join or form a large-scale organization. We don't have the numbers to make one, and we certainly can't deploy people to join others because they're going to have bizarre gaps in credentials."

James nodded. "Okay, I get that. So, what about the other chunk of magic?" A second later, he added another question, asking, "And how much of your time did I waste with this? I'm sorry, I coulda probably checked a lot of this myself when I had time."

"We all know you don't have the time," Alex told him, giving him a scrunched-up stare that involved a rapid shake of her head and her mouth curled into half an incredulous frown.

Deb continued. "I also have an orb for logistics, and another for city planning, which both made this a lot easier. See, that's another thing that sorta complicates this. Every time you bring back a new batch of yellows from a delve, we roll the dice on people completely changing specializations. And for now, we can handle it, because we need *everything*. But when it comes to large-scale problems like this, it does make it hard to come up with systemic answers." Deb matched James's sigh. "I'm a better programmer and living computer wrangler than a nurse these days. And that feels weird! But I'm also *still a nurse*, you know? It's a weird feeling. And also this part isn't relevant."

James gave her a reassuring smile. "I mean, it's actually fascinating, though. So, no options for helping the world?"

"Well, I'm not gonna say that. We have a couple small-scale possibilities, and one big one that I can think of," Deb said.

"Okay, hit me."

"The iLipedes," Alex stated. "We have a few so far, and they've all got pretty specific but really strong scouter abilities. So if . . ."

"Apps," James corrected, sipping at his drink.

Alex rolled her eyes at that. "I'm not calling them that, it's weird. They're alive. Anyway. If we can find or maybe breed one? Dunno if that's an option, we've never seen iLipede *eggs* or anything like that. Anyway, if we find one that can track medical history, or even just scan people, that'd let us get an advantage on a local scale."

"Local being statewide," Deb provided. "That is, if we're okay copying it. Which is a big if, when we could be copying anything else."

"We actually do have one that creates a social network that displays what I think are 'most relevant' connections to people," James mused. "It's around here somewhere. I'm willing to bet that being infected with a potentially deadly disease counts."

Deb nodded. "Maybe. Maybe not to everyone. Magic items from the Office are weird and always feel like they've got terms and conditions, you know? But any tool like that would let us track infection vectors, limit exposure, and keep it at least 'more under control.' Even if just for our . . . our group here. It sounds like so far the spread is limited, but it is *not* something to be taken lightly. I've got five or six skills screaming that this is a threat, and it's a bizarre feeling."

"You have medical dangersense?" James asked, curious. He'd been wondering if enough orbs in one area would start to compound to something more than the sum of their parts. Or maybe if humans just sometimes had magical powers anyway. This could go either way, or it could just be that Deb had a bad feeling, which was far more likely.

"I don't . . . know what that means exactly. So, yes?" Deb glanced at the younger woman next to her who nodded in agreement. "Okay. Yes."

"So, what's the other option?" James asked, trying to move forward. "What's the big option?"

"We find a yellow for medical knowledge, copy it *a lot*, and just pour a truck full of the things into whatever building is working on vaccines or whatever." Alex sounded positively gleeful as she presented their plan. "Like get a cement mixer and back it up to their window and just *pouuuuuur . . .*" She made a hand motion that didn't really look like pouring anything to James, but he got the intent.

Deb had the good grace to look sheepish. "My assistant is exaggerating," she claimed, mostly accurately, as she tried to silence Alex by shoving her back into the beanbag. "But yes, accelerating human medical knowledge by providing the tools to upgrade researchers to the people whose job is to safeguard the health of the population of Earth seems like a good idea."

"I like this plan. What other resources can we offer them?" James inquired, already racking his brain for the answer. "Money? What does the WHO operate on?"

"Four billion dollars. Annually."

"Not money, then!" James cheerily backed off on that option. "Um . . . test . . . subjects? No. Space? No, probably . . . well, maybe an extradimensional virology lab? Containment if something goes wrong?"

Deb held a finger up to her lips before answering. "I do see what you're going for. But no, that's not going to help. It would take years to verify if most of what we have to offer is even *safe*. It's not useful, short-term. Or even long-term, especially. A lot of our magic is just not actually worth it."

"Orbs it is then, I guess." James hummed. "Is there, and I ask this mostly to any economics or logistics orbs in the room, any chance at all that this helps my long-term goal of harming the pharmaceutical industry's stranglehold on useful innovation?"

Deb and Alex shared that *look* again. That look that both passively and actively asked the question of why this particular question was happening; why they hadn't sent someone else to field this while they got actual work done. But the look only lasted briefly, before

Deb gave an acknowledging tilt of her shoulder. It actually was kind of a fair question, and taking power away from major medical companies without removing the skill and innovation they controlled would be, in general, sort of great for humanity.

"No," Deb told him. "But not because of the reasons you're probably thinking. The thing is, people who do good independent work tend to get hired to do that same work for lots of money. You'd need to do a lot more to break the 'stranglehold' you're talking about. But even then? What's being controlled is access to the innovation, not whether or not it's happening. You shouldn't be mad that new drugs aren't being made, because they are. You should be mad at the extortion in the pricing."

"Oh! Okay, I can be mad at that," James told her with a chipper nod. "But seriously, this is a big help. And thanks for your time. Keeping up on a dozen things is making it hard for me to actually *do* stuff like this, so I get it, and I appreciate it." The other two stood up, only one of them slipping backward into the beanbag before finding her footing. Deb scowled at the additional seating while James pretended he wasn't chuckling. "Hey, on the way out, can you stick your head in the kitchen and ask if I can borrow Nate's new assistants? I need to talk to the kids about . . . fuck, everything, I guess." He massaged his forehead. "All I do these days is give people bad news," James muttered.

Deb tapped Alex on the shoulder, ushering her out ahead. "I'll let them know. You want me to get them to bring you food or anything?"

"Yeah, sure, deliver some bad news to Nate too. Share it around," James joked. "But yes, thank you. I haven't eaten in a while."

"Hey," Deb said quietly, starting to back away from the table but not yet turning around. James looked up as her tone caught his attention. "We're still with you, you know? You're not on your own. Just keep doing what you're doing, and we'll be here to help."

"'Here to help' is what I want on my tombstone," James told her. "Maybe if the Order survives my untimely demise, it can get big enough to actually do good."

At that, Deb finally gave into the sarcastic voice in her head. "If you don't think you've done good so far, I don't think dying is gonna change your mood," she shot his way, pivoting on the ball of her foot and striding to catch up to Alex; off to take care of one of the dozen tasks that needed doing today.

"Touché," James muttered morosely as she left. The conversation had been productive, and left him with at least part of a plan that he'd text to Anesh later, but overall . . .

They weren't big enough. They weren't strong enough. Twenty, thirty, forty people, it didn't matter. They were a tiny fish in a massive ocean of humanity. Even counting the camracondas, which doubled their numbers, doubled their problems right along with it. Added new sweeping issues they'd have to tackle eventually about potential discrimination, interspecies accessibility, and other stuff James couldn't even imagine to plan for right now.

They needed more. More reach, more options, more manpower. More personal abilities, more bizarre dungeon loot that recontextualized society by just being a weird pen or something.

James shook his head. He was half daydreaming, half mentally rambling, and half letting his depression wreak havoc with his mood today.

It'd work out, he thought, as Nate brought him two kids that wouldn't stop hanging around the Lair, and two slices of pizza to go with them. They'd do this the same way they always did. The same way he'd dealt with the Office, the Attic, the school, the police, the company, the infomorphs, the prisoners . . .

One step at a time.

A thought jostled in James's brain. He pulled out his phone, and went to make a note: *Talk to Theo about the company.* But he found it was already there. He made the note again as he started on a mouthful of pizza, while a pair of high schoolers tried to pretend they were too cool to enjoy beanbag chairs.

One step at a time.

CHAPTER 2

When James woke up, he was almost surprised to be in his own bed.

It was the same king-sized monstrosity it had always been, although an observer who knew what to look for now would be able to see the stratified patterns of blankets and sheets that denoted the increased number of people who called it theirs. It took up the majority of the floor space of the master bedroom, and with parts of Anesh's room across the hall given up to computer desks and dressers and things, the only other stuff left in here was mostly James's original furniture.

The window had a blackout curtain, so he didn't know what time it was, but he did know he'd slept for a *while*. He had that feeling in his bones and muscles; the kind he used to get after a delve where he had to jog a little too much, but which had gradually been pushed back as his body hardened into something a little more athletic. That old feeling had, James realized with a stretch, never really gone away. He'd just kind of gotten used to being covered in bruises and aches. But something about the last week had left him . . . tired.

Maybe it was blood loss. He *had* been shot a few times. Nonlethally, but still, that wasn't something that just went away. Or maybe it was just how overwhelmed he felt.

James had been sort of arbitrarily designated the "leader" of the Order, mostly by virtue of everyone having this weird idea of owing him a life debt or something. Hell, before his own idea of what they should be, there *was* no Order. The organization had almost gone through auto-genesis, with only minimal input from James himself. He'd known he didn't want to call it a guild, he'd known they were there to help people, and he'd known that the dungeons were worth exploring. And that had been enough; still was, really. Almost.

But he didn't actually have any leadership skills. And not even magical ones, either. Despite the fact that he had an orb about leadership, and a business degree that was nominally about the same topic, James had no *experience* leading. He could say the words that made people listen, but he knew, on a deep level, that he just didn't deserve the respect and authority that he'd had foisted upon him.

This feeling, James was aware, was called imposter syndrome. And it was how his brain chemistry lied to him; especially when he'd just woken up, or right when he was trying to sleep. So he took a few long breaths, screamed lightly into his pillow, and shoved the feeling of inadequacy aside for the moment.

It helped. But it didn't change that he still felt completely overwhelmed.

He started running down his mental checklist of problems. Three dungeons, one new, one familiar but still strange, one evil. Two adversaries, one broken and maybe gone, one the goddamn FBI. One new species to integrate into society. He paused in his thinking; this was sounding a little too much like a Christmas song, and it was only early March.

But those were the big problems. Then there were the *small* problems, which somehow still required his attention.

The basement operation of Research had things they wanted to talk about. A few of the people who were becoming permanent delvers wanted permission to build a shooting range. Harvey had questions for him about exactly what level of secrecy they should be aiming for. James *still* hadn't officially quit his day job. There was a dead body in their basement being kept frozen under a religious vigil by a camraconda high priestess, and James probably had to deal with that at some point. Also, his boyfriend was on edge and angry lately, for a variety of legitimate reasons, lashing out at random things, and James really needed to get into the Lair and *talk to him* before Anesh could make another daring escape. Oh, and he had his searching pseudo-ritual with Secret. And at some point, it would probably be a good idea to actually *talk to Nate* about him being an agent of the federal government.

James curled up under the blankets. Maybe he'd sleep in today.

He entertained that thought for about six minutes before he got bored and overheated under his blankets, groaned, and rolled out of bed, thumping against the carpet on his elbows as he just let himself drop. Yeah, it was a lot. Yeah, he didn't know where to start. And yeah, James had a serious problem with anxiety taking over when he felt overwhelmed.

But Anesh and Alanna were already up and doing things, and he actually cared about the people he had obligations to, and even better, he could *delegate* now.

And as a bonus, he thought as he checked the time on his phone, he was right on time to pet a dog on the way out the door.

James pulled into the parking lot of the Lair, powered by mundane coffee and arcane sleep transfer from Sarah, who *had* decided to stay in bed another four hours. This power was addictive, and despite being zero-sum they were already enjoying abusing it. Still, James had a hard time worrying about that when his brain felt lit up with electrical potential.

"Okay, let's get one thing out of the way early." He let the words roll easily off his tongue. "We're stretching what budget we have, and I'm not getting JP to cash out his weird investment portfolio for a hundred-k-plus construction project on a building we don't own." James was addressing Simon and the other James, who still mystically resisted an easy reference nickname. "Get a membership at a gun club, I know there's a decent one over in Sherwood that my dad used to go to . . ." James choked on the sentence as he realized what he'd just said, but shook it off. Today was not a morose day, dammit. "We don't need and can't afford our own gun range even if it is in a magical basement."

Simon and his James sighed in unison, and James realized that the two were currently wearing skulljack braids, probably connected to each other through the building's *very* impressive Wi-Fi. The braids weren't really braids exactly, just a cluster of cables and a secured microcontroller or two that enabled anyone with a skulljack to access wireless internet with their brain. Which meant, if you were like Simon and James, and seemed to have formed a dedicated relationship around sharing your brain with someone else, you wore them a lot.

The two didn't argue with James about the lack of new construction, though. Enough actual fights had shown them a losing battle when they saw it. And James was pretty reasonable about saying no anyway.

James had just let the door to the Lair close behind him when he stopped, had a thought like a bolt of lightning, and poked his head back out into the parking lot's early spring sunshine.

"What are you two doing?" he asked the duo suspiciously.

Simon and his James, with one motion, looked down at the polished four-foot lengths of dark wood in their hands, currently crossed between the two of them in the middle of intercepting each other's strikes, and then back at James. "Practicing?" they said together. "Anesh asked us to. We're testing how much a skill rank is worth, to see if an orb is worth copying a million times."

A million was an exaggeration, but only because of the time frame and limited number of copies they could make. James was aware of the idea of having an armory of sorts, and while the project was absolutely working out just fine without James's input, he still kept up on it.

The general idea was that they should have a box of upgrades in various flavors that could be easily copied with the ritual overhead projector in Officium Mundi. The kind of thing that could be used to bootstrap a new member of the Order into someone at least a little bit better equipped for delving, until they could get their own unique abilities. So far, they had the purple orb for memory, a red orb for courage, and a trio of yellows for running, trauma response, and apparently now quarterstaves. Alanna wanted to add a book from the Sewer, James wanted to add a gun bracelet, and Anesh wanted to add Ganesh, though all of those were still being planned around.

Except the last one, because Ganesh had said no. Or at least, protested in the way the little drone could without being able to speak.

James peered at the two men for a second, then around at the rest of the parking lot. Then up the slope to where the main road was almost visible from the parking lot. Then back to them, with their skulljacks and all-too-perfectly-timed movements, swinging weapons around in the middle of the day.

"Go practice in the back lot, guys," he said, ducking back inside.

Shaking his head, James got about halfway toward the kitchen, and his fated meeting with Nate, before he was caught by Alanna and interrupted.

"Hey, have you seen Secret?" she asked him as they stopped to chat in the cramped hallway, near where a plush leather couch was set into a little alcove in the wall. There was a camraconda made mostly of seafoam-green cables curled up on it asleep, and the space around had been decorated with some of the pieces of art they'd brought with them out of their tower refuge.

"Yes!" James replied cheerfully.

Alanna let him sit there with the goofy grin on his face for about fifteen seconds before she snorted a laugh, smiled, and corrected herself to, "Tell me where the godsnake is, you wiseass."

Still grinning back, James relented. "He's with Lua at the high school. Since we don't have a lot of time to keep eyes on it before it gets *shut down I guess,* she's guiding him through in incorporeal form to do a sweep for any antimemes we missed." James threw his hands in the air in frustration before dropping them back to his sides. "Also,

I think he'd resent being called a god-anything. Why, you need him for something?"

"Nah, just concerned." Alanna shrugged. "Also, yeah, the shutdown thing is . . . That came outta nowhere. I've been slacking on keeping up with world events, clearly. Which is *bad*. Can't let the dungeon make me uninformed."

"Arguably, you're one of the most informed," James pointed out. "But I get what you mean. I had to get Alex and Deb to do a logistical breakdown for me of why we cannot punch an outbreak."

"It's a pandemic now!" Alanna informed him with grim cheer. "Also, actually, wait, is that why Alex has been here all night?"

"What?" James raised his eyebrows.

Alanna nodded, clicking her tongue. "Yeah, she's been 'doing research' for the last twenty hours or so. I guess she's trying to impress you. Or kill a virus."

"I would be perfectly impressed if she'd get some sleep." James sighed and leaned against the edge of the alcove. "Can you tell her to do that? I need to go talk to Nate."

Smiling with a full row of teeth, Alanna replied, "Oh yes, I can tell her. Honestly, that kind of dedication is kinda hot. Maybe I'll keep her."

"Ask first," James scolded his partner. He paused a second, then followed up with a curious question. "Actually, hang on, are you bisexual? I never actually *asked*, I've just been coasting through our relationship and relying on constant existential dread and combat scenarios to keep all the awkward conversations away."

Alanna ruffled his hair affectionately. "Awww, that's an adorably terrible idea!" she said, and both of them laughed. There was something about today that had put them in a similarly snarky good mood; maybe it was seeing the noon sun for the first time in what felt like months. "And I dunno. All my normal relationships failed horribly, and so far the only thing that's worked out has been literally dragging the people I like into bed. What sexuality is that?"

"Alanna, that's not a sexuality, that's . . . that's not even a thing. That's either incredibly lucky, or assault, depending?" James massaged the oncoming headache out of his forehead. "Your relationship model is just being some kind of emotional bulldozer."

"I like that!" She laughed, beaming. "Anyway. Go talk to your rogue agent. I'll catch up with you later. We need to talk about—"

"Lots of things, I know!" James cut her off, already striding away down the hall. "I have a list! It's so long!" he griped, only half serious as he heard Alanna's laughter chime behind him as the two parted ways.

He shook his head in amusement as he moved through the cafeteria space. There were a few people here eating, or just relaxing on the beanbag chairs. James was increasingly pleased to see that the camraconda population was continuing to integrate pretty well into the Order. He knew it wasn't a good indicator of how the world at large would handle them, but it was nice to see the serpent people sharing tables, food, conversation, and in one case a magazine, with the other delvers.

His brain had automatically labeled the camracondas as delvers, despite knowing most of them weren't. But still. Enough of them had participated in the Status Quo raid, and several more still had expressed interest in joining teams when they explored the Attic and school, that James just kind of assumed that the whole population had been folded into the Order proper.

At this point, he thought with a rough sense of humor, about ninety-five percent of his people were rescues. He really needed to recruit more to balance that out. They couldn't count on just saving people with compatible ideologies forever.

James winced as he realized what he was doing. Then he added *recruiting* to his mental checklist.

He pushed open the double doors of the kitchen, taking only half a second to glance over at the left-hand wall. There was a sink, an ice machine, one set of normal coffee brewers, one coffee machine that would boost your mental acuity, and farther back, a nice little horseshoe-shaped stainless steel counter for prep space. This was all pretty mundane kitchen stuff. But even with his constant exposure to weird spatial distortions, James still gave it a suspicious eye as he tried to figure out where the hell the couch on the other side of the wall *was*.

"Greet you." A digital voice pulled James's attention over to the counter in the middle of the room, over by the back wall where the door to the walk-in sat. A camraconda, probably perched on a stool James couldn't see, was at the counter. It spoke through the speakers in a harness on its side, connected through a cord and an adapter to the skulljack it had been gifted by the Order. In its mouth it held a long-bladed kitchen knife, the speakers letting its speech be unimpeded by having its fangs clamped around the handle of the object. It was slicing cucumbers. It was also doing a startlingly precise job given its restrictions, using fairly accurate twists of its long body to bring the knife down on the unsuspecting vegetables.

"Hey, James," Dave said from next to the camraconda. He was dealing with a tray of thin bowls, arranging in them elegant piles of leafy greens, sliced vegetables, and chopped meat and cheese. Chef's salads; the kind of thing Nate liked to have a dozen of on hand for when people came in and wanted something for lunch on short notice. "What's up?"

"Well, first off, I'm gonna process that I now know how a snake would hold a knife," James said. "I wasn't expecting this."

"I prepare," the camraconda stated, and James detected a hint of pride in the words, especially with how it rose up to full height as it spoke. "Much to learn. Much cutting."

James nodded. "Okay, yeah, that's pretty much the perfect attitude for a prep cook."

"That's what Nate said, too," Dave told him. "Also, since you're probably here for him, he's out back smoking."

"Eh. I can talk, if either of you need anything?" James prompted. Instantly, he noticed, the camraconda broke eye contact and looked away. It was a behavior that was becoming annoyingly familiar, and it happened every time he offered to talk, or to help. "Oh, stop that." He rolled his eyes as he chastised the camraconda. "You just got a radically different life, world, and probably destiny if that's a thing. It's okay to *ask me questions*. I've got enough people around here acting like they owe me their lives," he muttered. Dave turned to his work partner and patiently shrugged, but the serpent just went back to making short, precise cuts to the vegetable in front of him on the cutting board. "Alright. No rush, just remember I am literally here to help. Dave, how're you? How's Pendragon doing?"

Dave pursed his lips as he added crumbled egg to a series of the dishes. "She's . . . okay. Took some damage in the fight, and it's hard to repair. She doesn't really heal that fast, and we got shot at a lot."

"Yeah." James blew out a breath, noticing the camraconda nodding in agreement, and the population of the kitchen shared a quiet moment together as they composed themselves. "Well, same thing to you, yeah? Lemme know if you need anything," James said as he walked through the center of the kitchen, heading through the dish pit toward the back door. "I'm gonna go harass Nate. You guys have fun."

James turned away as the two nodded at him, and pretended not to hear their soft conversation as they tried to figure out how to adapt a salute to the camracondas, seeing as the snakes lacked any kind of *hands* to work with.

His smile faded as he approached the back door. He didn't really know what to expect from this conversation. But still. He felt good. The day was shaping up. And before his anxiety could give him a heart attack, he pushed the door open and stepped out onto the patio.

Nate was mercifully stubbing out his cigarette when James joined him in the break area. He was sitting on a wooden bench braced against the wall, with a nice view of the line of trees and plants that made up the barrier between their parking lot and the building next to them. It wasn't a warm day, exactly, but the weather was such that neither of them were cold in short-sleeved shirts.

James stood there for a while, leaning against the closed door, looking out at the brief interlude of nature. He realized, suddenly, that he didn't know what to *say*.

This man had put his life on the line to fight with him, because he believed it was right. Because he trusted James. Because he'd seen some of the magic in the world, and maybe wanted to hang on to that.

But he wasn't some random chef; he was an agent. He was a very *specific* chef, whose job was to spend time with the Order and report back to a government that none of them really trusted that much. The news cast everything he did in a suspicious light. Did he fight to maintain his cover? Did anything he'd said to James mean a damn? And, knowing all that, did it make even the smallest bit of sense why James *still trusted him?*

"So . . ." James started, clearing his throat.

"You need someone better on security," Nate cut in. His voice was gruff, blunt, and utterly unhostile. It was the same voice he used to tell people how to make killer potatoes, or the proper way to scrub a pan. "Harvey's a good person, and he's the wrong person for this. You need someone who's at least a little bit of a bastard."

"Not sure that fits our developing culture," James admitted with a shrug.

Nate spat to the side, flicking his cigarette butt into a coffee can filled with the things. "You'd be surprised," he said. "Lots of people with the skills have a change of heart."

James didn't reply for a while. He let himself be distracted by someone pulling their car around to the back lot before he found the words he wanted to respond with. "Is that what you've got going on?" he asked.

"That's better," Nate said approvingly. "Be more direct. Good leadership skill."

"Nice deflection," James scoffed. "Seriously, though. Can you just tell me what's going on in your head?" He looked at Nate, and realized in that moment that this burly tattooed jackass was actually *embarrassed*. Or at least, something like it. James pressed on in the silence. "You gave me advice after we killed those first agents. You said, you told me, that I should trust myself when it came to making a better world." James leveled an almost accusatory finger at him. "Was that a lie?"

"Nah," Nate said, tilting his head back to let the bald dome rest against the building's siding. "Nah, that's real. Everyone's heard the recording between you and their boss by this point. Those guys . . . you know, my team, the side I'm supposed to be on, we've done some nasty shit? But no one *ever* just shrugged off feeding kids into the machine like that." He looked over at James. "Your instincts were right. Fuck 'em. World's better off without."

James realized, again, that Nate had tried to deflect. This one was a lot more subtle, though, and it would have worked if James wasn't himself a practiced master of deflecting from uncomfortable subjects. "So what're you thinking *now?*" he asked. "You're still here. You're just gonna go back to making salads and spying on us?"

No one said anything for a while. Overhead, a helicopter buzzed by. Birds chirped. Traffic gave a low background roar from the road. The clack of wood signaled Simon and James were still training in the parking lot. The sun glimmered, waiting for summer.

"No," Nate said, pushing himself forward on the bench. "No. I quit."

"What?" James looked around in surprise. "Wait, what?"

"Here," Nate said, reaching into his apron pocket and procuring a pair of glasses, which he handed to James. "I should give you these back. Hell of a tool, massive invasion of privacy, but no one ever cares about that."

"I kinda care about that," James argued.

"I know. It's part of why I quit," Nate told him.

"I don't . . . Okay. Yeah, okay." James tried to clear the lump out of his throat. "Wow. Shit. We'll need to hire a new chef."

Nate blinked. Then started laughing. His laugh was a throaty wheeze, smoker's lungs fighting with a powerful voice. "Oh! Fuck, no! I meant I quit my other job!" he corrected. "I wasn't kidding when I said we'd done some *nasty* shit. But you? You haven't." Nate stood, brushing off pine needles from where they'd collected on the bench and his slacks. "And maybe you won't, either. You've got a better world in mind, kid. I'd like to see it," he said, pushing past James to walk back into the kitchen.

The door closed with a heavy crash, reminding James that they needed to get that door frame fixed, but also jolting him out of his puzzled stupor. Nate had just . . . quit?

James looked down at the glasses in his hand, then brought them up to his eyes. He wasn't kidding when he'd said he kind of cared about the privacy thing. But he felt like Nate having literally been spying on them for a month or two balanced it all out. So he only felt a little guilty as he looked at through the lenses at the back of the chef walking back toward the stockroom.

Nate Marselli. Unaffiliated.

The last word showed for only a heartbeat before James made his decision, and then it changed, the word fractaling into a new shape as James chose to trust his ally.

Nate Marselli. Order of Endless Rooms.

Knight.

"I don't mean to be a wanker about it," Anesh was saying, "but it doesn't mean much."

James let out a guttural *ugggh* sound from the driver's seat. "Come onnnnnn," he complained. "It was dramatic, useful, kind of cute—don't tell Nate I said that last part—and it's just kind of a solid win. Why can't he just be on our side?"

Anesh glanced up from his phone, trying to make eye contact with James, who studiously focused on the road, even if they weren't actually moving at the moment. "Because that situation sounds like *exactly* how I'd bait you into believing something if I needed to. A sudden windfall with a dramatic twist? James, it's your aesthetic. Your vibe. Your . . . I don't know, something else Americans say."

James answered reflexively. "My oeuvre. Okay, *fair*, but . . ."

"Also, there's too many ways around the glasses, if you know what they do. And Nate *does* know what they do." The last words were a bit harsh coming out of Anesh's mouth.

James withered behind the wheel. "I wanted to trust him," he said. "Wait, I still do! This proves nothing!"

Affecting a very stilted American accent, Anesh made mouths with his hands and held a mock conversation. "'Nate, you're sacked!' 'Oh no, now what will I do?' 'Well, if you need a hobby, how about spying on a group of rogue wizards?' 'Great idea, not-boss!'" He glowered at James. "See? Easy."

"Would that actually work? Like, I feel like they'd have to actually, you know, take him off payroll and close out his retirement account, right?" James let his curiosity take over for his shame as he got caught up on the mechanics of the glasses. "There was also no formal induction into the Order, either, so that means they know about intent. Or maybe 'membership' is a fluid concept sometimes . . ."

Anesh tapped him on the forehead. "Getting off topic. Also, the line's moving."

They were in a drive-thru. It was well past time for both of them to eat, and ambushing his boyfriend with the offer of a burger had been enough to get James in the door for a conversation. Better yet, the drive-thru was moving comically slowly, so they had plenty of time to talk.

"Alright," James admitted. "I concede that we shouldn't just pretend he's done a total conversion to Team Us." He held up a finger. "But! I still want to give him a chance. Besides, if he's spying on us, then the worst case scenario is that the FBI knows that . . . hm . . ."

Anesh raised his eyebrows, having to put a lot of effort into not grinning as James trailed off. "No, no, go on. I wanna hear this. Knows *what?*"

"Okay, so, it took me about twelve seconds to realize that maybe we've done some crimes."

"Some," Anesh flatly uttered.

"Many crimes," James relented. He sighed. "In my defense, they were all good ideas at the time. I guess I just hope it works out. But you're right, we should have a plan for if it doesn't."

"That's all I ask," Anesh said, letting the conversation drift off and going back to tapping on his phone.

James waited for the car to inch another space forward in line, which was about five minutes or so, before he tried to shift the conversation to his original goal.

"So . . . how're you?"

There were times in his life where James felt like he was nothing more than a passive observer, watching some horrifyingly incompetent version of himself making absolutely impossible mistakes. In those times, in the split seconds between the words, he usually wanted to slap that version of himself. Right now, he really, *really* wanted to slap that version of himself.

Anesh barely glanced up. "I'm fine," he said without much emotion.

James closed his eyes, breathed in through his nose, and took a second to hope he wasn't making a bigger mistake. "No you're not, man," he said, worry in his voice. "And everyone's noticed, too. Alanna's worried. *I'm* worried. And you know if *I've* noticed, that means something's gone catastrophically wrong. Please tell me what's up?" James pleaded with his partner.

With a tired sigh, Anesh tilted his phone down a bit. He glanced over at James, and was mildly surprised to see his boyfriend looking at him with sad eyes. He sighed again, letting out a resigned huff of air as he looked away. "I'm . . . okay," he said, and James knew he didn't mean he was okay. Just that he was collecting his thoughts. "Okay. You know there's several me. Or at least, there were."

"One week cooldown, right?" James asked. "Also, I still don't know how to handle a copy of you dying. I'll be honest, it still hurts."

"Yeah. Well." Anesh's voice was a riot of bitterness. "Good thing you don't have to this time."

James blinked, not understanding. "What?"

"I knew. We knew. The other copies and myself. We knew which ones we were. Are." Anesh met James's eyes, and James saw he was almost in tears. "I know you've got these grand transhumanist beliefs, about how a person is their thoughts and that's that, and I thought I shared them, but *I'm dead!* The original me has been dead since Status Quo tried to turn me into a magic item factory or whatever. It's just . . . copies. Now. Just spares." Anesh sniffed, rubbing at his eyes. "It's kind of bothering me." He tried to smile, but his voice cracked halfway through the sentence.

"I . . . aw, shit," James stuttered. "But you're all synced up. You have the same orb upgrades. You *know* you're the same."

"I want to," Anesh whispered.

James didn't know what to say. Didn't know if there was anything *to* say. He reached over, taking Anesh's shaking hand in his own freshly scarred palm, and tried to impose some kind of comfort on his boyfriend. Warmth fed through skin contact, and they sat there together, trying to wish everything better. But there wasn't a magic spell to banish existential dread, or trauma.

They both started as the car behind them honked. James pulled forward. Both of them were thinking it was going to be wildly awkward when they had to order.

"We need to get a therapist," James offered, his heart recovered just enough to try to be light.

"We have Lua. And Sarah, too," Anesh pointed out.

James hummed. "They're too close to us. We need someone who's an outsider."

"You do understand that our lives are insane, right?" Anesh said with a wet chuckle.

"All the more reason to get professional help." James grinned back. "Now. What kind of burger do you want? They have one made of *beans*."

"I'm mostly vegetarian already and somehow you made that sound weird."

James leaned over to give Anesh a kiss. "It's my job and my calling," he admitted, before rolling down the window to order. Existential dread or otherwise, neither hunger nor drive-thru lines waited for mortal man.

"I'm confiscating this," James told the chastised-looking camraconda and mongausse duo that were currently sitting before him. He was holding up a pencil; lacquered blue wooden exterior, dull tip, and currently the cause of his headache.

His headache had started when he'd walked in the door and Magneto had bounded by, being trailed by a quartet of broken tree branches, the natural wood whipping through the air as it raced after the dog-shaped magnetic distortion. James was prepared to make some kind of quip about how normally it was the dog that chased the sticks, before the headache had appeared.

Specifically, the headache started when one of the branches had clipped James in the forehead, knocking him on his ass and spilling his french fries.

The culprit, beyond just the two nonhuman members of the Order that were screwing around with weird magical effects in the front lobby, was this pencil. It magnetized wood. That was something James was having trouble wrapping his brain around, but that might have just been because he hadn't gotten to his stash of ibuprofen yet and his forehead ached.

"You can keep the sticks," James told them, and the two perked up. The camraconda was one of the smaller ones, and while that didn't really mean much given how dungeon life tended to work, this was one of the ones that was more childish in demeanor. Despite all being roughly the same age, and all having enough knowledge to more or less function, each camraconda had a different emotional maturity about them that really came into focus in moments like this.

Deep in his soul, some part of James's parenting instincts kicked into action. "But play outside!" he said with a firm tone. Then he paused. "No, wait! Play . . . goddammit," he muttered, rubbing at his chin. "We need more space. Okay, use the back lot. Try to get in James and Simon's way if they're still out there. They could use a challenge, okay?"

The two entities nodded excitedly at him. James gave a small smile and a sigh as they raced off, a couple of the pieces of wood from the pile jerking into motion to follow them through the air as the mongausse's field clipped them.

He pocketed the pencil. This would absolutely come in handy later. He'd just have to figure out how once his painkillers and his lunch kicked in.

"History isn't real!" JP slammed a paper down on James's desk, his flat palm and splayed fingers making a satisfying slap as they hit the wood surface.

James eyed JP around the burger he held between his teeth, holding the food in place as he looked back down to where JP's hand held the document pinned. He took a bite. Chewed. Slowly. Swallowed, set the burger back down on the wrapper he was using for a plate, and looked up at JP with disappointment. "Half an inch to the left and your fake history would have splattered my ranch sauce across the room," he chastised.

JP tilted his nose up. "Truth waits for no sauce."

"Sure, but you could at least *aim* your . . . Okay, nevermind. History. What about it?" James tried to get a read on the document JP was now leaning on.

"Oh, this is nothing," JP admitted, folding up the sheet of paper and shoving it into a jacket pocket. "I just wanted to make an entrance." He brushed aside James's incredulous look. "So, I've been thinking about Status Quo."

"As have most people, yes," James dryly commented.

"Sure. They've been covering up magic stuff for a *long* time, though. Their documentation dates back *ninety years*." JP emphasized the time frame, hard. "So, in that time, do you think that maybe there might have been one or two teams just a little bit like ours?"

"Fuck, that's way longer than I expected," James admitted. "And yeah. If you mean ideologically, sure. The man upstairs seemed to think it was always groups of three, so they may never have encountered anyone *quite* like us. But people who think like we do, sure. Probably also people who want to rule the world or some dumb shit."

JP frantically waved his hands in the air. "Exactly!" he exploded. "Ninety years of dungeons, delvers, cover-ups, purges, and after-action reports that read like action movie plots!" he exclaimed. "And not a single one of those things made it into the history books!"

"Wait, not one?" James frowned, eyebrows pulling together in thought. "He basically flat-out admitted Nike harvests product from a dungeon. There must be other things that're 'real' but kind of sterilized. Right?"

"Sure, but no *magic*," JP reiterated. "No mention of delvers being involved in any major political or social movements, no mentions of weird coincidences or near-supernatural events. History, 'normal' history, is *totally barren* of this kind of stuff after about the early 1900s. Which means it *must* be fake."

"I'm not following." James rubbed his temple. "Do you mean the Status Quo reports also bear out that there was no weird shit going on? Or do they talk about stopping people from using magic to cause large-scale changes?"

JP settled himself into one of the chairs on the other side of James's desk, and James groaned internally. He just wanted to eat lunch. "No, see, that's the thing. They don't have any records of it either! Not 'surviving' ones, at any rate. They seem to purge them fairly frequently, which is incredibly disrespectful to me as I play at being an archeologist. So my *theory* is that we're in a simulated copy of the real world, where history is identical, and the 'records' of magic are only surface deep—"

"Get the hell out of my office. I'm eating," James cut him off suddenly, his voice projecting the sound of an entire TED Talk's lecture hall rolling its eyes at once.

"No, no! It makes sense! I actually wanna hire someone to be a dedicated researcher on this. I think there's something bigger out there, that's either been actively preventing magic from propagating to the public, or that such an effect isn't required because the universe is *new*, and magic is a new addition. So what I'm—"

"No," James cut him off again. "Nope. No. I actually have a sign up somewhere that says *no simulationist philosophy in this building.* No." He pointed accusingly at JP. "I will admit the history thing is weird, but that mostly just means that the only people succeeding are *exceptionally* good at stealth. Or that there was some kind of quiet war, and the winners rewrote the history books. It's an understood fact that we don't know the full extent of the events of even the Great Depression, and that was fairly recent on a global time scale. But I *refuse* to entertain the idea that we are but a dream within a dream."

JP deflated briefly, before opening his mouth with a curious look on his face. "We don't know what happened during the Great Depression?"

"Not really." James shrugged. "Lots of missing documents. Tons of people just kind of vanished. Widespread famine, obviously, but also a lot of unsolved murders and things like whole families just disappearing. Also, a pretty improbable prison break happened during that time. Cool stuff, in retrospect, but probably an awful time to live in."

"I should look into this," JP murmured, standing up.

"Yes. Go do that. Let me eat my lunch." James ushered him out of his office. "And please don't end up making diagrams out of red string and newspaper clippings. We're running out of display boards for things like that."

"I'll add it to the budget," JP idly acknowledged James without actually addressing the real problem. He exited the office head down, deep in thought, and left James with a mounting headache.

James looked down at his burger. Pushed it aside, and pulled his keyboard a bit closer. Tried multiple times to compose a group message that didn't sound crazy, even by Order standards. Eventually gave up, then messaged Alanna and Anesh to talk to JP about history.

Maybe his friend was right. Maybe things were wrong. Or maybe the adventurers and heroes of the past had some secrets the Order could yet unearth, and put to use.

Only one way to find out.

After lunch, obviously.

As James walked through the front of the building, passing the half dozen camracondas lounging around out here, he wondered for the first time how often outsiders came up to the windows, peeked in to see what this place was, and got stared down by a security serpent.

It couldn't be zero, right? The camracondas had been here for a couple of weeks now. And given that schools were cutting off early for the year, there were probably roving gangs of feral high schoolers poking around anything and everything that they shouldn't be. James would have to ask Harvey about it; they had a security system after all, and actual non-alive cameras around the building. Though at this point, Harvey was drawing on people's time to act as sentries, too. No one had really signed up to be a security guard, but it was a job that needed doing until they were sure no one from Status Quo would be seeking vengeance.

There were actually a lot of jobs around the Lair that just needed doing. Places required maintenance. Upkeep. Even just basic cleaning. And while James was perfectly willing to scrub a bathroom, it was much nicer that they were working on a system to make sure things got done without someone having to ever exasperatedly throw up their hands and declare that they would do it themselves.

"We should get curtains," James muttered to himself as he looked back at the front window, mentally restocking his to-do list that he'd been steadily checking off through the day. He had a few more things to deal with before he planned to go home and just do something *fun*—and also not life-threatening—for a while, and this next one was one of the trickier tasks for the day.

He rehearsed in his head on the elevator ride down.

The camracondas had brought with them as much of their nascent culture as they could. Their art, their relationships, their personalities. And also their religion. And that, awkwardly, included the sentinel vigil of the body of the original human woman who'd created the place they had called sanctuary. That body was now *in James's basement,* and while he wanted to respect their culture and their right to self-determination, he also felt a very real need to figure out who she'd been, and especially if she had any surviving family.

"I understand your beliefs are important to you . . . no, too condescending. Your vigil is important but . . . no, no, that just sounds dismissive. Don't use the but. Um . . . your culture is unique and I don't want to trample it . . . *interfere with it* . . . but . . . goddammit, saying 'but' sounds awful and I do it on reflex." James slapped his hands to his face and let out a muffled *uggggggh* sound, cutting off almost instantly as he heard the elevator ding. "Something about . . . trust . . . no."

The elevator doors opened. James stepped out, nodding to the camraconda coiled next to the elevator, one of the more stalwart guards of the high priestess. His name, as James had overheard it, was Cold-Wind-Friction, which sounded cool. His job was to act as a messenger and stand-in when the high priestess needed to talk to people, or sleep.

Camracondas did need to sleep, James had recently learned from Deb. They didn't need quite as much as a human, but they sure *liked* it though. Deb had also admitted that they might actually need *exactly* as much as a human, but were lying to seem more useful or to fit schedules, which, if true, James absolutely wanted them to stop doing immediately.

"I'm here to talk to . . ." James stopped, then looked around the space he'd stepped into.

The camracondas had a set-aside section of the vault for their practice until a more suitable spot could be obtained; probably through green shenanigans. The vault was on the other side of the Research part of the second basement. Where the first basement was tight hallways and small concrete rooms, like it was plucked from an office building or something, the second basement was more of an open area. It had one hallway at the start that led either left to the bathrooms or right to curve around into the main open floor space.

While the basement itself was "more open," it was still a basement. And that spot getting off the elevator was a landing designed for efficiency, not aesthetics.

Which is why it was *weird* that the space was now *much* more open. The area stretched up twenty feet or so, there was a domed ceiling with arched wrought iron, and ten feet overhead, a similarly iron railing jutted out of the mezzanine that looked down over the elevator doors. A tight spiral staircase in the corner led up to the overlooking walkway.

The materials were almost the same as the rest of the basement; concrete and pipe, but also a different color stone in places, and the darker wrought iron. But it had a certain elegance to it. And the whole thing was lit by strings of colored Christmas lights, with more currently being hung up by someone on the upper balcony.

"Sorry!" Alanna called down to him. "This one was my fault!"

"Why?" James called back. "What was wrong with our cramped, dark, artless hallway—okay, I'll shut up." She bellowed a laugh in return, and even the camraconda gave a stuttering hiss, his people's version of showing humor.

"Green orb," Alanna called down. "Already recorded in the database. Plus one balcony."

"Is this one of the ones that Anesh copied?" James asked. "Because I can see that getting out of hand *fast*. Like, we'll be more dungeon geometry than building, after a few of those."

Alanna rattled her colorful light bushels at him. "It'd look awesome! But no, this was one of mine, and since we don't have the time or resources to copy *every* orb, especially when they're the big ones, I figured I'd fire it off. It . . . I mean, it's not *bad* . . ." She sounded kind of dejected.

"It looks awesome. Maybe we can get some art commissioned for the ceiling. Go all Sistine Chapel in here." James grinned at her in the dim light. "Anyway, I've got a meeting."

"Have fun!" She waved as he let Cold-Wind-Friction guide him through to the vault.

Neither James nor the camraconda said anything as they moved, simply keeping to a companionable silence. Some—a lot, really—of the camracondas were, James was noticing, behaving a lot like the people they'd originally rescued from monster-Karen almost half a year ago. Respectful, bordering on reverent. It wasn't actually very fun for James, or for some of the other delvers. Though it *had* led to an uptick in the humans he'd saved treating him more like a person, now that they got a taste of their own medicine.

Stopping just inside the vault, James turned to address the spiritual leader of the camracondas. She—and she did currently identify as female—was still adorned with many of the artistic trappings of her position. Though whether they were of religious significance or just personal taste, James still didn't know. Behind her, on the wall of the vault, the desk panels carved with the history of the camraconda people were on display. An anthropologist would have a field day with camraconda culture.

"Greetings." The digital voice came smoothly out of the Bluetooth speaker concealed somewhere in the priestess's adornments. She didn't look up from her charge; a woman's body, lying in repose on a low metal table. Wounds still fresh as the day she died.

He'd tried to come up with something elegant to say as an opener, but this scene tugged at his heart every time he saw it. Anything even distantly related to planning for this conversation fled James's head. "Hey," he said softly. "I . . ."

He trailed off. What did you say to someone when you wanted to disrupt their main cultural pillar? It was a tricky question. It was an *impossible* question. And as he tried to find the words to do so, he came to a realization. He was going about this all wrong; he was trying to form this as an argument, instead of just asking and listening. James leaned forward, dropping himself down to the floor in front of the table. He noticed, as he folded his legs under him, Cold-Wind-Friction tensing up behind him when he got a little too close to the body on the table, but James didn't move any closer. He just sat.

"This woman," James said. "How do you feel about her?" he asked the priestess, waving an open palm at the dead woman.

"She saves us," the camraconda replied, almost right away. Her digital voice stopped, as if that was the only thing there was to say about it. The most important thing; and it very well might be to them. James thought about it, and wondered if the tense was intentional.

He nodded, leaning his chin on an arm propped up on his knee. "Do you ever wonder who she was?" he asked her.

"Always," the priestess replied, shifting her tail in a way that didn't move her gaze away from the body. "Like thinking she has kindness. Bravery. Think she is like me. Or Frequency-of-Sunlight. Or Buried-Under-Blankets. Like us. Worthy." The camraconda's digital voice was turned quieter as she spoke, which James took to be either contemplation or reverence.

"She is strong," Cold-Wind-Friction said behind him, adding his own words to the answer.

James took a deep breath, and then let it out. "You know, I came down here without really having a plan, so I'm just gonna ask this. Would you like us to try to find out who she was?" He made as much eye contact with the priestess as her vigil would allow. "She might still have family, or friends out there. People might know her. I wanted to ask permission to search her for an ID, maybe put a picture of her up or hire a private detective or something." He sighed. "But . . . I can't tell you that she will have been the person you believe she was. And I also don't want to force it, because she . . . well, she's been in your care for a long time."

The camracondas were quiet for a while as they thought about it. And while they did, James sat, and thought about the dead woman. Who had she been, before her life had intersected with the Office? He hoped she'd been someone worthy of these people.

Eventually, just as his legs were starting to get sore from the position he was in, Cold-Wind-Friction spoke up, moving up toward the table and the corpse. "She had strength," he said. His head and singular camera eye pivoted up to look at James and the priestess in turn. "Before does not change the end."

"She possessed family?" The word *family* wasn't one the priestess had ever really said before, though she knew what it meant, in theory. Her people were her family. They were important, all of them.

"She might have," James answered.

"They should know she is strong," the priestess said. "That we love her for what she did."

The words hung heavy in the air. James felt tears on the edges of his eyes. He steadied himself with a breath. "Okay," he said, moving to a kneeling position. "I'm gonna see if she has a wallet, and we'll go from there. We have more resources and tools than I ever really expected. We'll find something."

"I will tell others," Cold-Wind-Friction said, and the priestess made a hissing assent at him.

He and James moved back to the elevator in silence. This time, everyone could see the contemplative look on his face, and no one in Research bugged him.

Anesh caught him right before he went home, plopping a folder of printed paper into his inbox just as James was trying to find his keys in the mess that was his desk.

"Hey! I'm heading out. Gonna go sit alone and watch YouTube for a couple hours." James said the words with an almost palpable relish. "When're you gonna be home?"

"Later. I've got a lot of stuff to do, and I'm feeling a lot better now." The *thanks* was silent, but still there. Anesh tapped the folder. "We got a final count of all the stuff from Status Quo. The tools they were using, anyway. There might be more hidden in the boxes of documents or something, who knows. Their organization is utter and complete bollocks."

James perked up. "Oh! With the list of what they all do?" He cracked open the folder, and started peeking at it. "Yesssss," he hissed out, impersonating a camraconda himself. "This is gonna be so useful."

"Yeah. We've got notes on the 'messages' these things give, too. It lists ability name, level, progress, cooldown, stored charges, and then any conditions at the end. Like the automatic activation for the shields." Anesh shook his head mournfully. "I feel like they could have killed all of us without trying if they'd turned off the autopilot."

"Any news on how they kept the gear invisible?" James asked.

Anesh clicked his tongue in consternation. "None. But there isn't much variety in the objects, so we have a full list of abilities already. None of them do it; it must have been something else."

"Bah," James griped. "Well, this is still gonna be huge for us. I can't wait to play around with some of these. But later! I need downtime now! Been doing stuff *all day!*"

With a soft smile, Anesh stepped around the desk and gave his boyfriend a reassuring hug, warm arms enfolding James, who leaned into the affection. "Yeah you have. Go home, decompress. Alanna and I'll be back in a few hours and we can hang out, or just leave you to catch up on podcasts or whatever it is you do."

"Mostly watch YouTube video essays about professional wrestling," James admitted, pocketing his escaped car keys and breaking the hug as he held the office door open for Anesh to go out first.

"Why?" Anesh asked with abrupt confusion. "Do you . . . like . . . wrestling? I feel like I would have, and should have, noticed this."

"Nah, I just like hearing people talk about it," James admitted. "It's just cool to kind of vicariously pick up a passion for something. Like a hobby, but with less footwork."

Anesh chuckled. "You're impossible."

"I'm busy! I don't have time for wrestling!" James countered. "Besides . . . huh?" He trailed off as his phone buzzed. It was always worth checking, because at this point in his life, only two people texted him, and if it was the Order's chat server, then it was either someone asking him something directly or a message from the Emergency Notification channel.

When he saw Anesh pulling his own phone out, and Sarah doing the same from where she was just walking in through the door, James felt his heart tense up.

It was a message from Lua. *SCHOOL OPEN. EIGHT MISSING. TEN MINUTES AGO.*

James's phone started ringing in his hand. Loudly.

He looked up at Anesh. "Go get whatever might slip past the weapon restriction on the school. Grab everyone who's available. Volunteers for combat!" James pivoted around the room, catching the eyes of the handful of humans and camracondas here. There'd be more in the back, someone on the roof, plenty of people in the basement. "Civilians in danger! Move!"

He answered the phone.

"James!" Lua's voice sounded over the other end, panicked.

"I know!" he barked. "We're moving! Where's the breach right now, and how many people are in the school?"

"It's in an equipment shed on the field!" Lua told him, voice wavering. "I don't understand! I don't know why so many students went in!" She was well and truly panicking.

James spoke calmly and firmly. "We're on the way," he said as he started to stalk toward the front doors. "Don't go in. Meet us out front. Have Secret keep an eye on the breach. We'll be there in ten minutes."

"James, the police are here," Lua sobbed. "They're yelling, and half of them have their guns out. I can't do this again," she gasped out.

"Just hang on," James said. "I need to move, now. We'll be there soon." He hung up without waiting for a response. Looked up from his phone.

Alanna was already there, along with a half dozen other humans and three camracondas. James briefly considered asking Pendragon if he could pilot her and use her as a troop transport again, but that was a *little* beyond the scope of this one.

"What's the plan?" Alanna asked.

"The usual," James said, a strained joke in his tone. "Swoop in, kick ass, save lives."

"Can we make *that* our motto?" Alanna said with a quirked eyebrow.

"Let's give it a few more times before we commit to it," James quipped back. "Sarah!" He called her name, and tossed his friend who could manipulate magnetic fields an unpolished blue pencil from his pocket. "Here! Have fun! Everyone else, I hope you read the briefing on the school; grab anyone else who's ready, and get in the vans. We leave in five minutes when Anesh comes up."

James stood in the eye of a storm of motion. Humans and snakes and a few other things besides burst into action. Grabbing backup, helping camracondas into armor, pulling the excluded weaponry out of their emergency action kits, piling into vans. James took a deep breath, only half paying attention, trusting his people to make this work.

His first thought was they need to do drills for this sort of thing, if it was going to be happening often enough that it could be their motto.

His second thought was that it was a shame they'd had to use their prepared thermobaric explosive on Status Quo. It'd be another week or so before he'd have the option of blowing up the school sewers.

But oh, boy, was he feeling that hot anger that made him want to level the entire place.

He hoped this time they'd be fast enough. That they'd be strong enough. That it'd all work out okay.

Because if it didn't, he was going to embezzle enough Order funds to rent a backhoe, and tear the whole high school down, brick by brick, and make sure this never happened again.

CHAPTER 3

James drove the van, doing his best impression of someone who had left traffic laws far behind, while in the rear compartment, Sarah did her best to recap the briefing for everyone who hadn't read it.

"The school dungeon, which we're tagging as the Akashic Sewer . . ."

"Are we?" James muttered quietly enough not to interrupt her shouted words. He liked the ring of it, and he wasn't so petty that he couldn't admit when someone beat him to coming up with a cool name for things.

". . . is awful." Sarah finished her sentence over James's thoughts. "Almost no light, seems to be intentionally dirty, possibly dangerously so, and the majority of Life has been bug- or rat-based." She rattled off points like she'd memorized them, and James idly wondered if she was reading the operations manual off her phone. "Last time, the tunnel removed certain items from people, suspected things that aren't allowed in schools, blah blah blah, we already did this part . . ."

He almost laughed from up in the driver's seat. They *had* already done that part; James had listed things that had been removed from them, and it was gratifying to have everyone sort of blandly repeat, "So, things you can't take into school. Got it." Even though he'd avoided saying those exact words.

They didn't know if that was true, exactly, and making assumptions about a place as obviously hostile as this one seemed like a potentially lethal plan. But so far, it seemed to be the way this worked.

They'd grabbed anything that might make it past the filter and could be used to keep them alive. Keys were a big one; they knew those worked, along with the little keychain lights on them which were now a standard feature for members of the Order. They'd kind of had to accept that, eventually, they were gonna end up somewhere dark and horrible, so having backup light sources was a given. Sporting equipment; there were a couple baseball bats in the Lair, though James made a note to get more if this worked. They also had a few dangerous office supplies adapted as best as possible into weapons: the pen that vaporized things, a pad of sticky notes that paralyzed things they were attached to, a binder that could trip people. Nothing serious. Nothing nearly on the level of just having a gun.

They also had a laptop that should be suitable for school use. They'd even uninstalled Minesweeper off it.

"The Sewer has eight current known attempted victims!" Sarah was saying as James took them down the side street that led to the school's rear parking lot. "Our goal is to get in, kill *anything* that doesn't instantly identify as passive, and get out!" There was a wave of concerned voices from the back, organic and digital, at that statement.

Alanna's voice cut through. "The doors are gated by kills," she said. "If any of you missed the first briefing, that's how the dungeon coerces students into killing each other to escape." Silence followed that statement. "Yeah. So kill everything that moves and isn't a person. And if possible, actually focus killing hits into as few people as possible. We need our own exit."

"We're here," James shouted back from the driver's seat as he slowed them down to take the turn. They weren't in such a rush that he needed to bruise his whole coterie before they even got there. "Everyone ready?"

They absolutely were not. Neither this group, nor the follow-up squad in the second van behind them, felt ready. They'd felt more ready going to fight actual humans with guns. Here, they didn't even have body armor. Just leather coats at most.

A couple of the camracondas had their armor on, just in case that worked. But most of them actually also had "jackets" on. They were an emergent fashion statement that came out of the fact that a lot of the camracondas were artists, a lot of them were *bored*, and the Order had a comically large stash of coats in the basement. Usually they had the arms cut away, but some of them used the sleeves with notches in them to secure the garments. They were an awkward design, made for creatures without arms or shoulders, and intended to be able to be put on without too much help. Some of them were quite stylish. Whether they were going to hold up in battle was up in the air.

"Cops," Alanna said, pointing as she poked her head up through the gap between the cargo space in the back and the two upholstered seats in the front.

"I see 'em," James grimly acknowledged. Two police cars, both with the lights on, both at an angle, blocking off the road to the parking lot and the rest of the building. Farther up, near the roundabout in front of the school, a pair of yellow school buses idled their engines, and a third police SUV was flipped over onto its side. "Well, shit." A pair of uniformed officers stood behind the barricading cars, watching the school, one speaking into a radio. "Let's get this over with." James sighed, slowing the vehicle to a stop.

The officers had already turned and had their hands on the grips of their sidearms as James pulled the van up. One of them was walking toward them, hand held up in a clear *stop* gesture, which James mostly ignored. He threw the vehicle into park, and with a quick motion, hopped out of the driver's side door.

"Sir, get out of here!" the officer was saying. Yelling, really. "Get back in your fucking vehicle!"

"No!" James yelled back cheerfully. "We need to get through! Please move!"

When the other officer turned, and both of them actually drew their weapons, James realized he probably could have phrased that better. When other people started hopping out of the back of the van, the cops got *really* edgy, backing up against their cars, one of them screaming into the radio for backup.

"Guys, we just need to get through. I'm with . . ." James started to say.

He was cut off by another uniformed officer rapidly crossing the front lawn from where it looked like another police car was blocking the parking lot's exit. James recognized him quickly as not-detective-anymore Madden, as the man opened dialogue by shouting, "You!" at the top of his lungs at James.

"Sergeant, we're in a hurry . . ." Alanna started to say in a polite, low-pitched tone. The kind that James recognized as what you'd use for a wounded animal.

Ex-detective Dave Madden started shooting. Mostly at James, but it was kind of a moot point after the other two officers, operating on twitch reflexes, did the same.

The standard police-issue Glock 22 held fifteen rounds, and could fire those rounds about as fast as someone could pull the trigger. It took roughly five seconds for all three cops to unload their weapons in James's direction, and a few more seconds for them to start fumbling for reloads.

James stood there, luminous grid of argent light burning lines into the retinas of anyone looking directly at him, as the bullets slammed into the bracer shield projected around him and surrendered their kinetic energy to whatever bullshit blood magic powered the thing.

Halfway through pulling out a fresh magazine, one of the officers that *wasn't* Madden noticed. Jaw hanging half open, he elbowed the second man at his side, who was already staring, gun held loosely in his hands.

"Look," James said, rubbing a finger behind his ringing ear. He looked around, trying to appear as casual as possible as he assessed how many bullets had just hit the windshield of his brand-new used van. "We're in a hurry. If you could . . ."

"What the fuck . . ." came from one of the cops.

"This is your fault!" He caught the words, bellowed by Madden, who had slammed a full load of bullets back into his gun and was now leveling it at James's head from maybe ten feet away. Behind the van, the few knights who had gotten out already stayed where they were, waiting for either the situation to diffuse, or for Alanna to start putting the police in headlocks. "I knew it! You did this!" Madden fired again, just a single bullet this time, like he needed to test it.

It didn't work; the bracer's shield was absurdly potent against whatever it was set to, and nine-millimeter rounds were never going to make it through. They did deplete the charges, though, which James mentally eyed with some worry. The shoot-out had depleted a *lot* of charges, overall. But not as many as it should have if his math on the guns was right, which he decided to wait until later to find unsettling for a different reason.

James eyed Madden, vaguely wondering why more cops hadn't shown up in response to the shooting. "Look," he said. "I tried to tell you. I tried to point you in the right direction. You didn't fucking believe me. Stop fucking shooting at me, you asshole." He turned to the other two officers, who were still looking on the fence about whether they should try shooting again. Though the blatant display of magic kind of had them tilted toward *maybe not*, and James could see their hesitation. "Hi. Let's try this again," James said, stepping forward, and internally snorting as the cops took a step back from him. "James Lyle. *FBI.* We need to get into the building."

"He's lying!" Madden screamed, face bright red, eyes wild. He still held his gun, and was starting to turn toward his fellow officers. "He knows! He did this! Shoot him!"

Alanna put him in a headlock. Without fanfare or too much struggle, in a way that was so simple it was actually shocking.

James did his best to pretend that wasn't happening, projecting calm and control at the cops who were now *definitely* considering shooting someone again. "One of you tell me what's going on here." He didn't make it a question; JP's lessons kicking into action. "Also, your colleague will be fine. Eventually."

"Um . . ." One of the officers, the one who'd lowered his weapon more fully, kept shooting his gaze between James and where Alanna was choking out a flailing, shouting Madden. "Is that . . . Byrne's kid?" he asked.

"Alanna?" James raised his eyebrows. "Yes. She works for us now. Didn't you know?" It was his favorite kind of statement. Not really a lie, but not exactly useful either. He'd also learned that from JP.

The cop made a choice. Holstered his weapon, and motioned his partner to do the same. "I remember her. Her father . . .?" The other cop, a slightly older man, nodded, and put his own gun back in the holster. "Okay. What do you need?" He still looked like he had reservations about Sergeant Madden, who was now pinned into the grass and losing consciousness, but he wasn't shooting and that was something.

"We need to get into the building," James said. "And we need to know why you're out here, too. What's going on?"

"You wouldn't believe us. Um . . . sir?" the younger cop said. James just stared at him, not bothering to let his annoyance with being treated as an authority get in the way.

Old Cop cut in. "You just watched him block bullets. Don't tell him he won't believe shit." He turned toward James. "We've received multiple dispatch calls from the building over the last hour. Thought they were hoaxes at first, but now it's a suspected active shooter. Backup's on the way. But when we tried to approach the building, whoever's driving the bus struck the approaching officer."

James closed one eye, focusing on the vision enhancement on his good side. "There's no one in the bus." James sighed with resignation. "Fuck."

"They left?" The cop spun around. "If there's no one outside . . ."

"No," James corrected him. "There was never anyone in the bus. Okay. We're wasting time." He ignored the questions and weird looks from the cops. Now that it was established that he was "on their side," they probably wouldn't shoot him. "Handcuff Madden," James ordered, as that thought woke up in the back of his head.

"We're going to move in. You can support, or stay here. But stay out of our way."

"You can't just—" one of them yelled at James as he started walking back to the van.

"Shut up!" James barked. "Don't think I've forgotten that you just shot at me! Sit down and shut up, or start helping! I don't care which, but you're done making decisions here!" He didn't even know he could yell in that harsh of a voice, a dire scowl on his face as he walked past the van toward the back door, slapping a hand on the side with a hollow thud.

"Situation?" Sarah asked as he rounded the back. Several people here had guns out of their own, ready to start shooting on his command.

"It's taken care of. We're going in fast. On foot, though; the buses are hitting cars that get too close."

"Shit. Dungeon?" Nate queried.

"Probably." James nodded. "This is bad. What's it *doing*?"

"Nothing we like. Let's go stop it," Sarah offered, trying and failing to stay cheerful. James could see her hands shaking, but she was still preparing to move with the rest of them.

James nodded and looked around at the people here. "Okay," he said. "This is a public op. Last chance to back out." He mostly directed this at the camracondas. But they were already flowing out the back of the van and onto the pavement.

Behind them, the second van was also unloading as they saw the first group mobilizing. JP hopped out of the driver's seat as Other James and Simon led a mixed group of lifeforms out of the back. They were both plugged in, but not connected yet, since there wasn't any Wi-Fi to piggyback on, and it turned out human souls used kind of a lot of bandwidth. They could use hotspots from their phones, but they were about to go into a dungeon that flung phones out of its breach without their owners attached.

When the first camraconda moved out from behind the van, James was worried one of the cops was going to start shooting again.

He cut them off with a glare that could melt steel, and made eye contact until they broke off and took their hands off their guns. It turned out, no matter how much authority or legal right to shoot people you had, someone you thought had a job description of Federal Wizard was intimidating.

Alanna joined him on the lawn as their group assembled behind him. James was standing with his hand shading his eyes, staring at the two long yellow buses idling in the roundabout. He was trying to project authority and calm, even while inside he was starting to get worried about the increasing number of cars piling up on the street. Mostly police, but a few people who were clearly panicked parents, and also a news van he spotted coming down the road. This was becoming . . . problematic.

"Everyone's ready," Alanna said. "Madden's down for the count."

"Yeah, holy shit. I didn't think he'd just start shooting. I shoulda just had Secret eat his memory." James let out a shuddering breath. "That was so fucked up. One week earlier and we would have just been murdered by the police."

"Yeah . . ." Alanna trailed off. "So, what's the play here?"

"For the police?" James was trying to joke. Trying to use humor to cover the terror of someone trying to murder him. "I vote we steal their guns."

"The school."

"Oh." James turned away from his observation of the hostile vehicles and the overturned police SUV. "Okay. Looks like one of them hit that cop car hard enough to flip it into the flagpole. That's a problem. Also, no one's moving in there, so I hope they got out. Clearly the things can move. Let's see if one of the camracondas can lock them down."

They called up a camraconda wearing hard-formed plastic plate, this one as yet unnamed but adorned with a pair of carved pencils stuck to its head as a fashion statement. It focused on one of the buses in the distance, and then shook its head side to side.

"Large. Pushes back," it said. "Could stop. Hurts. Need less momentum."

"Hm." James glanced back at the vans where the group of about a dozen Order members were milling around, eying both the increasing pile of traffic behind them and also the police who were shooting them an equal number of shifty glares back. "Okay. We've got that paperweight, right? The one that doesn't move in the direction it's pointed, that nearly crashed the van on the way here? Bring me that. And get everyone formed up. We'll make a run for the front door, and sort it out from there."

Alanna saluted him and started moving, while James went back to scowling. The problem, he realized, was that they had no idea what was going on. The police were here already, for *some reason*. The front doors were also shut, but that wasn't a problem. James's mental list of who had what blue power had a couple options for that in their little crew. No, the big issue was they just didn't know what was going on. And for that, they needed to reconnect with Secret and Lua, who were . . . well, inside.

James turned to address the humans and camracondas approaching. His own core group was here, along with Other James and Simon. Nate, Deb, Frequency-of-Sunlight, and the mongausse. Even Virgil had jumped when asked to come along when he heard what was going on. Sarah stood at the back, idly flipping the pencil James had given her in her fingers. Reed and Nikhail from Research were here, too, along with a couple of concerned-looking members of Sarah's support group. It was getting harder for James to keep track of everyone. It was also weird to see everyone in street clothes and not armor, weird to be going into this like it was a huge fight and not just a rescue op, weird that the dungeon had shifted behavior to something categorically *insane*.

"I'm on point. I'll stall the bus pointed to the right, then I need every camera eye on it. Alanna; board and disable. Everyone else, run for the door. Reed, you've got 'remove entrance,' right? Use it."

"That'll just make a wall," the Research member said, confused.

James blinked at him. "What? No. It's . . . there's doors there, but there's something weird about them on the other side that I can't quite see. So remove them."

"Yeah. That just turns it into a wall," Reed argued.

"Your power says 'remove entrance,' not 'remodel building'!" James snapped, one hand in a claw on his forehead. "I am one hundred percent sure it can do this. Remove the doors, leave a hole! You can figure it out." His voice softened. "You can do this. Let's move. And be sharp; something's clearly wrong."

"Um . . ." Anesh raised a hand. "We're not gonna get shot from behind, are we?"

"You, you, and you." James pointed at people wearing bracers as Alanna jogged back and slapped a metal weight into his hand. "Set the bracers for nine-millimeter bullets, and keep to the rear."

"James, that's not an answer." Anesh spoke with high-pitched concern as JP and Nate flicked their eyes to the mental displays of their confiscated Status Quo items, and shifted to the back of the pack.

"It's a solution, though. Just hope these things don't break the dress code. Alright. Follow in five seconds," James announced, then set his feet in the grass and kicked off so hard he left divots of dirt spraying up into the air.

He cleared the lawn going faster than a lot of humans could manage. The acceleration orb didn't make him an Olympian, and he knew there were a ton of people who could outpace him, but the way it took away a lot of the energy cost of actually getting to these sprinting speeds was kind of huge. And despite having to manage carrying an object that wouldn't move in one direction, he still flew across the distance.

James's legs pumped as his shoes slapped down onto asphalt. And as soon as he did, the roar of an old diesel engine flared in his ears. One of the buses, the one facing his direction, jerked forward into motion, lunging toward James like a metal predator.

He planted his feet instead of trying to dodge. The thing was moving fast. Faster than a bus should be able to spring forward. Not that he could judge, given what he'd just done. James whipped his arm out in front of him, rotating the paperweight so that its front face pointed toward the bus, then pulling his fingers as far back as he could around its edge.

The bus hit going maybe twenty miles an hour and trying to accelerate, but it wasn't actually a motor vehicle anymore; it was something the dungeon had brought to life. If it had time to build up speed, James could easily imagine how it could have gone faster, but right now it seemed limited, and that meant it only hit *pretty* fast, as opposed to *deadly* fast.

Not fast enough to fold the whole bus around the object, though, but enough to make a hell of a dent and arrest its forward momentum. It also locked the paperweight into place as metal bent to grip it, and James jerked his hand back as fast as he could. He tried to roll backward, but he wasn't quite fast enough, and the upper half of the bus slammed into his shoulder as it tried to overwhelm the tiny object holding it back.

James went sprawling down to the pavement, just in time to watch the partially stuck bus freeze, its rear wheels a foot off the ground. Feet flashed by him, and a hand reached down. He grabbed it, and was jerked up and running again as the camracondas slithered past; the group of them keeping their eyes locked on the bus, though James could see that their fanged mouths were hanging open as they sucked in air, breathing heavily as they strained to keep the bus in place.

Alanna came next. She swept in from behind the group, planted her hands on the tilted front hood of the bus, swung herself up, and slammed a metal baseball bat at high velocity into the windshield. Not waiting for a second swing, she shoved herself feet-first through the cracked glass, ignoring the sharp edges that would have turned a normal human into a Jackson Pollock painting. The mongausse, trailing her like a rainbow afterimage, just plowed through the closed door of the bus, the living magnetic field slipping through cracks like the door wasn't even there.

James didn't see what Alanna did, but he did see the whole line of the bus shudder, falter, and then fountain out a spray of red sparks that quickly vacuumed back into the cab. A minute later, while the mongausse exploded out the driver's window, Alanna crawled back out of the hole she'd made on the way in, vaulted off the hood of the dead vehicle, and headed to join the others. The other bus, facing away but still somehow aware of them, was already peeling around, driving over the lawn and leaving deep tire furrows as it looped around to close in on the delvers.

"Look!" Sarah panted, pointing up at the school's front façade as they ran. "Look!" James cast his eyes up as he launched himself up the curb toward the front doors. He saw, in multiple windows, students. Teenagers. Rows of them, pressed to the glass. They were watching him, watching the Order closing in. But they didn't look amused or confused or anything he expected. Instead, he saw them banging their fists on the thick glass windows, mouths open like they were screaming. They looked panicked.

They approached the door, Simon and Other James hitting it first, followed by everyone else as they moved in an only barely organized mob; some Order members jumping over the blocky concrete benches to make room for the camracondas to slither up the front path, many people kneeling down to catch their breath. James saw the front doors, but they weren't like he remembered them.

This school had a sort of airlock design to the front entrance. Two big sets of double doors, and then two single doors on the outside; all of them leading into a kind of central room that had a fancy floor emblem and all the school's trophy cases and stuff, before leading to the second set of doors that led into the building proper. There were also doors off to the sides of that interior entryway that led to the office, on the left, or the library, on the right. It was cramped, and inefficient, and James disliked it immensely.

Right now, he disliked it because the doors were *dripping* with some kind of black sludge that ran through the cracks and pooled near their base, and he could see that inside the liquid rose up to about knee height. Also, the handles for the doors on both sides appeared to be organically separating into something that looked like barbed wire: plant-like strands with ferocious metal burrs on them.

"Reed," James said, surprised to realize that he wasn't out of breath. All those morning jogs were paying off. "Remove this entrance," he ordered.

The curly-haired researcher slapped his hands against the side of the building. A grimace crossed his face, but this time, he didn't question James. He'd seen the students inside; everyone had. Also, there was a bus bearing down on them, and they really only had a minute at most before it got around the corpse of its fellow. "Not a wall," he muttered to himself. "Just go . . . away!"

A muffled *whomp* noise sounded. And then, the doors were gone. The vaulted ceiling was gone. The lights were gone. There was just exposed wiring and pipes, rough gravel foundation, and a gaping, cavernous hole in the front of the school.

There was no more entryway. At *all*. Reed's head reeled back, blood flowing from his nose and eyes as he pitched backward. "Nate! Grab him!" James commanded, as everyone rose into motion.

There would absolutely be time to be concerned about that later. Right now, as everyone surrounded Nate while he threw an arm under Reed's shoulder and carried him through the gap, they were mostly concerned with getting away from the bus that roared by the entrance, ramping over the sidewalk and nearly clipping a camraconda's tail before they slithered the last inch forward just in time.

The group burst through the space where the entrance used to be, and into a place that James didn't quite recognize.

The floor was a bowl, indented in the front lobby. The stairs to the second floor had been copied, and placed half-jutting out of the wall of what once was the administration office. The stairs, both the original and the new set, were elongated to inhuman proportions. The area looked like what would happen if someone had fed the school into a machine learning algorithm, told it to generate another school, and then just taken the first distorted result that came out.

"What the hell is this?" Deb's voice summed up the wide-eyed confusion of the group as they stalled to a halt.

"This looks like . . ." James started to say, running a hand along an irrational pipe that jutted out of the ground.

". . . like dungeon geometry," Anesh finished.

The lobby sat silent, but for the distant dripping of what James hoped was only water.

"Doesn't change anything," James decided, voicing what was almost certainly an inaccurate statement. "We still need to get Lua and Secret. Second floor, her office. Let's go."

"Where are all the students?" Alanna asked as they headed to the base of the stairs.

James pivoted around the stairs, laid a hand on the railing, and started motioning people up. The camracondas were startlingly adept at adapting to steps in general, but here, where the stairs started getting to two or three feet in height, they needed a little extra help.

It was as Deb was two ledges up, reaching down to help Frequency-of-Sunlight up to join her, that the sounds of dripping were interrupted by a scream. Deb's yell echoed raggedly against warped stone as a clawed, brown-furred paw, the size of a baseball mitt, jutted out from the gap between the stairs and bit into her leg, ripping through the jeans she was wearing.

Simon and Other James were already moving. Even unconnected, the two of them were easily in sync and rounded the corner under the stairwell in seconds, while Frequency-of-Sunlight panickedly froze Deb in mid-fall before she could be easily dragged backward and through the gap.

The thing let go before anyone got to it. All James saw was a flash of fluid brown fur and molding scales, as a creature the size of a small horse made curving bounds across the small open space and through the door of a dark classroom on the ground level.

"What the shit was that!" he yelled. But no one had an answer for him.

They scrambled up the stairs faster after that, thoughts plaguing James that they'd come completely unprepared. He had been so sure that this group could handle the dungeon, and they probably could. He just hadn't expected the dungeon to be the whole building all of a sudden.

Once they surmounted the top of the overly lengthened staircase, the group settled into a nervous circle. While Nate cut away the leg of Deb's pants, matted with blood, and started performing first aid, Deb checked on Reed, who had been placed next to her in a seated position against what used to be a bench, eyes blank, head rolling.

"He's not dead," Deb said, getting a sigh of relief from James. On the balcony hallway opposite them, overhead, one of the lights *cracked*, black lines suddenly running through the light itself. "Looks like overextension. We've seen this a few times; he'll be okay, but he's going to have a headache that could kill God when he wakes up."

"How about you? Can you move?" James asked. Deb just shook her head, frowning down at the leg she couldn't easily put weight on. "Okay." James rose to a low crouch and nodded to himself. "Anesh, Dave, Nate, um . . . you two . . . and Cold-Wind-Friction. You stay here with them and keep watch. The rest of us, we're moving forward." The designated people nodded and started moving to places where they could keep watch.

"Yeah, how hard could it be to cross two hallways and one office door?" Alanna said, voice oozing sarcasm.

"You know what?" James growled. "Next time I have to go anywhere near a school, I'm bringing an assault rifle. This is insane."

"I'm pretty sure I have to report that to someone," Nate sniped back dryly, and it took James a second to realize the gruff man had made a joke.

He laughed as he pulled the doomsday pen out of his pocket, flipped it over, and offered it hilt-first to Nate. Nate, though, pushed it back. "I've got a gun," he said simply.

"I thought we left the guns in the van?" James asked.

Nate shrugged. "I didn't. Thought it might be useful. Something's wrong though, it's yanking against the holster."

"Mine too," Simon chimed in. "Like it's being pushed out."

James let out a long gust of breath. "Alright. Well, don't drop them. Guess the dungeon is only *trying* to ban some stuff today. Everyone else, let's go. And keep an eye out for survivors. You guys set up here, we'll send anyone back your way. Evac by telepad if you need to, or when you have clusters of six."

"Got it." Dave nodded, saluting without a trace of irony. "Good luck."

The reduced group rose and moved forward. There was a fire door nearby that led back to a cluster of classrooms, and James knew there was another one on the other side of the school. Or he thought he knew; maybe it had warped already.

Either way, this one was shut tight, its handles displaying the same barbed security as the front door, and he suspected it would be locked tight too. He cursed at Reed already having KO'd himself; not that it hadn't been dramatic to carve ten tons of rock and metal out of existence, but it sure was inconvenient that their best lockpick was unconscious.

"We can cut through that classroom," Simon said. "If the building's the same."

"You used to go here, right?" James asked him. "Was it always this dark?"

"No." Simon grimaced. "And look." He pointed up. Some of the lights overhead had those strange black cracks through their luminosity. There were more of them growing on the lights farther away, though the ones overhead seemed still for now.

It was spreading. They didn't have time to check everything; they needed to pick up their allies and get to the heart of this, *now*.

James wordlessly nodded at the door, and watched the dark classroom through the panel of windows as Simon moved up and pulled it open, keeping out of the way behind the wooden surface as he had to pull *hard* to scrape it across the floor.

Almost instantly, there was a sick, wet screaming from inside. James had been worried about students, but this was clearly something inhuman. It was a screech he'd heard once before, though, and when he saw Alanna tense up, he knew she found it familiar too.

When the first ratroach dove out of the liquid darkness and tried to knife Sarah, Alanna was already moving. Her fist struck it like the wrath of a particularly vengeful boxer, and it folded sideways as chitin and bones cracked under the blow. Its shiv, made from the leg of a desk chair, went clattering sideways. Simon rolled out from behind the door, snatched it up, and brought it down through the thing's throat.

"What the fuck was that?!" Virgil barked, falling back on his ass as green blood and red sparks painted the carpet. The blood was hissing and smoking, lightly corrosive for no real reason except that the dungeon liked its creations to be cruel. The three-armed corpse, a mix of insect and mammal parts with too many mismatched eyes staring dead at the ceiling, was one of the main problems the Sewer tended to create.

"Ratroach," James started to say, eyes wide. "They shouldn't be . . ."

But then the next one rushed them. And the next. And the next.

James, Simon, Other James, and Alanna formed a semicircle around the door after they'd killed the next two. The things could only come through so fast, as they jostled with each other to push through the door. A pair of camracondas behind them flickering momentum off of their enemies made the ratroaches easy prey, but they couldn't keep this up forever.

Especially since the bodies were stacking up.

"How many of these fucking things are there?" James asked as he crushed the throat of a ratroach holding a splintered club. This one had half of a rat's muzzle, the rest of its face exposed bone and muscle surrounded by a ring of ichor-dripping chitin. The skeletal feature was repulsive to look at, but it didn't keep it alive any longer, as James flipped the stunned thing to the side to have any extra life crushed out by Sarah's boot. "Could they even fit this many in the classroom?"

"Sure," Simon said. "But listen? There aren't more in there."

James strained his ears over the sound of crunching chitin. Simon was right; there were screaming battle cries starting up just before they plunged forward to their deaths, but before that, nothing.

"We need to get in there," he said.

Alanna nodded. "Okay. After the next one, let's rush it." She barked out a countdown, guessing roughly at when the next ratroach was going to spill forth. On the count of one, just a little bit early, one of their screaming faces started to emerge from the curtain of darkness leading into the classroom. It froze almost right away, and Simon and Other James grabbed it, jerked sideways hard enough to snap its neck, and pulled it back to the growing pile of corpses.

James and Alanna put their shoulders down and rushed forward, James with his keys dug out of his pocket and folded between his fingers, thumb on the button for his mini flashlight.

When they cleared the threshold into the dark interior, Alanna's hand found his shoulder, and he almost instantly rammed his shin into a desk. Flicking the light on, he was mildly surprised that it worked in what he assumed would be unnatural darkness. The sounds of fighting, of bug monsters screaming, cut away to nothing. And all James saw was . . .

"Nothing?"

He swept the light around while Alanna watched his back. Desks, a couple of computers, backpacks on the floor. His heart lurched as he saw not one, but two bodies. One of an older bald man, glasses askew on his face. He was sitting in the chair behind the teacher's desk, a crude wooden spear driven through his chest. Another was a student, just a facedown lump of what used to be a person, in a pool of blood on the tile floor.

There was nothing else here.

"Is it a coincidence that they stopped coming out as soon as we stepped in here?" Alanna muttered.

"Fuck, I hope so," James said. "Actually . . . we need to know." He turned back toward the door and called out "We're coming back!" before sliding out the door.

"Anything?" Sarah asked him, eyes watering from the smell of the corpses and their caustic blood.

A scream answered her, and a second later, another ratroach breached out into the light. James delivered it a quick one-two, letting Alanna catch its arm, rip the knife out of it, stab it, and send it flailing back into the dark. "Back inside!" James ordered, and Alanna followed him without question.

The rest of the rescue team filtered in after them, bumping into each other and some of the desks in the darkness as they left behind the growing barricade of corpses.

"What's going on?" Simon asked in James's direction, as the humans, who had both thumbs and flashlights, started casting light beams around the room, revealing the trashed classroom with its overturned furniture and blood splatters.

"It's spawning new monsters," James said grimly. "Doesn't work if we're in here, or maybe if there's light. I dunno." He groaned. "Shit, if there's more rooms like this . . . We can't move forward if this is behind us pumping out these fucking things. Why is it even *doing this?!*" James shouted, waving an arm outward at the empty room.

He stepped over to the windows. He could see out just fine, though the hallway was starting to darken too, slowly. The classroom's second door still led past the barricaded fire door, though from here he could see there was another pair of student bodies lying in blood puddles. What were their options? Telepad out and come back with guns? Would they even be able to?

Nate had brought a pistol in, so maybe the domain didn't extend this far into what used to be the real world. It *felt* like a dungeon, James realized suddenly, but weaker. Incomplete. The atmosphere, something about it, it prickled at his skin and tugged at the thread in his mind.

He had changed, since that first time he'd set foot in Offici-um Mundi. Not just that his calves had solidified into actual mus-cles, or that he'd learned sixteen ways to punch anything vaguely human-shaped to death. But something inside; something vital. There was a part of James now, perhaps developed in time with his toughen-ing body, that was constantly aware of *where he was*. Whether the bed he woke up in was in reality or a dungeon, whether this door led to somewhere normal or somewhere indescribably elsewhere. He'd only brought it up a few times, mostly to Anesh and Alanna, and both of them confirmed the feeling. Hell, he and Alanna almost had the ability to sense magic items at this point. At the very least, they had a keen eye for when something was just that little bit off from normality.

This space, James decided, was warped. It wasn't all the way a dungeon, but something was going on with it. It was like it was being dragged under the waves. Which further invited the metaphor that the mainland of reality was being flooded with the oceans of the warped spaces beyond.

"It's not spawning while we're in here," Alanna said, cutting the silence like a knife.

"No," James agreed. "Which means that it probably can't dump spawns on us while we're walking. Or on the rooms we saw the other kids in." He turned, holding up one hand to try to gauge direction. "They were upstairs, front of the school. So, there should be at least one around that way, and another on the other side of the building. Minimum. We should focus on evacuation first." He looked around. "Okay. Alanna, Sarah, and Frequency, with me. Everyone else, we'll clear the one across the hall and you can split across to get to the classroom. Wish we weren't in a hurry here, but we are."

"Frequency is not here," one of the camracondas spoke up, and James realized it was Cold-Wind-Friction. "Stayed. I came."

"Wait, what? Why?" James asked, confused.

"With Deb. They two together," the camraconda answered, like that explained anything.

James clapped his palms together in front of his mouth, nodding. "Okay. I have a *lot* of questions about that. Later! Doesn't matter, same plan. Let's get moving."

"What about this one?" Alanna asked. "Maybe it's the dark; do we have lights we can leave here?"

"I've got a lighter," Other James offered, flicking the small flame to life. "We could set it on fire."

"Tempting, but this is our way out," James said. "Maybe we move the wounded up. Yeah, actually. Go get Nate. I'm claiming this room as our forward base."

Something shifted as James spoke. Something he felt rumbling in his ribs like an earthquake, only it was all around him and not under his feet. Like the distorted sensation of the dungeon taking over the place was cracking and rotting away around him.

Overhead, black flakes poured off the light fixtures like coiled vines, hissing smoke and dropping to the floor to burn away. On the walls, small holes that had been dripping black sludge sealed up behind ordered concrete and drywall. And all around, the feeling of *wrongness* snapped off like a switch had been thrown. The darkness banished in an instant as the overhead lights beamed perfectly mundane fluorescent rays through the classroom.

"Noooooo." James held up a finger as he drawled out the word. "Naw. No." He glanced at the shocked faces of Alanna and the others. "Can't be that easy, right? No."

Alanna rapped her knuckles on one of the walls. "It feels like it changed." She cocked her head. "Oh man, do you hear that?" No one else did, so she tapped at an ear. "In the distance. Something screaming. James, I think you pissed it off."

"Alright!" James strode over to the slain teacher, and gave a soft "Sorry, sir" as he pulled the spear out of the man's chest. "Now we're *really* in it." He slammed the butt of the spear—really just a mop handle with a shard of glass hammered into the tip—into the floor. "Get the others up here. It's time to move."

They should have brought more guns. Outside the windows, on the other side of the closed interior door, James could see the scrambling form of some kind of rat-thing. It had six clawed legs, and it scratched furiously at the floor in places before flinging itself forward in bursts of movement to a new spot. It sniffed at the bodies of the dead high schoolers. It took a bite of soft flesh with jagged, infected teeth. James wanted to shoot it. James wanted to shoot it out of a cannon into the fucking sun. But it moved on, and he was left feeling relieved, rather than anxious or vengeful.

He tried dialing Lua's number again, but got no answer, or cell service, unsurprisingly. He tried focusing Secret into existence, but got similar results.

They should have brought an army. But instead, he had seven knights, three of whom were camracondas, one of which was a dog made of magnets. James wanted to scream. But instead, he just turned back to face everyone, fingers tight on the haft of his weapon.

The dungeon was reaching out into reality. James briefly thought back to what JP had said earlier; that things like this must have happened before, so why didn't they make it into the books? And he realized that Status Quo, or someone like them, should have been here already, shooting everything and blowing up the building, calling it a gas leak and a tragedy.

What happened when Officium Mundi did this? What happened if they didn't stop it here? Did it just keep spreading? Taking territory, until the Earth belonged to the rats and the bugs and the dripping black?

James tapped the spear into the ground. Maybe the Order had brought exactly what they needed.

The wounded were moved up. James shot Deb and Frequency-of-Sunlight a look as the camraconda slithered in at full reared-up height so she could support the limping nurse. He'd talk to them later. Or maybe he'd just remain pleasantly confused forever.

"Okay!" James said. "Here's the deal! As long as we hold this room, the sewer can't spawn more rats in it. So when we leave, barricade the doors, and hold it. If we find more problems, we'll come back and check in." He tapped his foot. "We're out of time now. Let's go."

James kicked the door open, jammed the spearpoint into the weird bulbous rat thing that was trying to jolt by, shook the leaking corpse off in a spray of red sparks, and strode forward into the hall. Pipes had started sprouting from the wall in bismuth patterns, and that black mossy stuff hung from the ceiling, darkening the whole interior. He stepped to the side, letting Simon take the lead as they rushed the door on the other side of the hallway.

James and Simon struck down the ratroach that lunged for them rapidly. Something about these newly spawned ones made them weak, or maybe just disoriented. They were naked, carrying only their makeshift weapons, unlike the ones from the Sewer that had been scrounging the scraps from slain students. And they were so, so fragile, James thought as he jammed his knuckles through this one's eye, popping the aqueous humor before ushering the second team through the door.

The team claimed it, just like he had done with the first, and the room snapped back to something resembling bright, ordered reality.

This was where they split up.

"Ready?" James asked Sarah and Cold-Wind-Friction, assuming correctly that asking Alanna would be obvious, especially as she was currently adding another backup ratroach knife to her belt.

"Ready," both of them said together.

He hardened his eyes into a glare as he led the quartet down the hallway toward Lua's office. James liked to think that he was a reasonable person, but right now, well. The dungeon's monstrous creations were about to have some of the shortest lives possible.

CHAPTER 4

James and Alanna pressed their backs against a low wall of lockers, trying desperately to ignore the smell of whatever was leaking out of them, while Sarah and Cold-Wind-Friction did the same on the other side of the hall. It turned out, their camraconda ally was remarkably flexible for their kind, with more of the corded "muscle" in his back than the others had. This came in handy when hiding involved contorting into specific positions for minutes at a time.

They were hiding because, for all of James's bravado, they had rapidly run into something they couldn't easily stab to death.

The thing was a rat-king designed by someone who had *heard* of rats, in theory, but only ever seen close-up pictures of their skulls. Two meters across, it was almost a ball of jutting muzzles and teeth. Near its center, fifty panicked, furious, unthinkingly hungry red rat eyes peered out at the world. Skin and muscle were pulled across it in taut and random sheets; sometimes it was exposed bone, sometimes it was almost a normal rat. Except that each of the "heads" that made up its creation were three feet long, with snapping fangs and crushing jaws and *far* too much flexibility and motor control for what should have just been an unconnected mouth and neck.

They were hiding because so far that had proven effective. The things—there were three of them in the school so far—were nearblind, deafened themselves with their constant rodent screams of fear, and probably couldn't smell anything over the choking scent of sewage any more than the group could.

In addition to probably not being able to see, hear, or smell, the twisted fusions of rat faces were also pretty dumb. So, as soon as this one passed by their little hiding spot, Cold-Wind-Friction froze it, briefly, and everyone slipped around the corners of the locker segments they were on. The squealing picked up at a higher volume a second later, but the team was already moving on, unspotted.

"I hate those," Alanna whispered to James. "Also, I'm really not clear on how this place could grant fuckin' *empathy* as a reward."

James glanced around the next corner ahead of them. The upcoming hall seemed clear; straight shot to the rear stairwell, and Lua's office was right off of that. He replied to Alanna in a low voice as he motioned the other two forward. "Gotta know how people are feeling in order to maximize trauma." He shrugged lightly, regretting the gesture as he felt the soreness still baked into his shoulders.

Cutting off a growl while she crouch-ran across the open hall, Alanna ducked behind the solid central railing of the stairs. "Looks clear," she called back to the others. "I see Lua's door."

Rising up, James walked forward. Not normally; he was still absolutely on guard. But moving in a sneaky position was only so sustainable for someone who had only really been working out for half a year or so.

They were *all* on guard. The team had fought through hell to get here. Ratroaches were one thing, but when the skull-kings started showing up, and the carpets of beetles, and the animate sludge tendrils where the leaks had gone on too long, it turned every step into a potential ambush by something seemingly designed to make them gag. Every one of them was uncomfortably marked by ichor, blood, or sludge in some pattern, to the point that Cold-Wind-Friction had started asking about whether it would be more effective to put him in a shower or a dishwasher to get the scum off. And he wasn't even waterproof, fully.

Their running duel with the dungeon's forces through the halls had also led to them "claiming" two more spawn rooms. Both had been empty of human presence, and they'd had to double back to reclaim one when a squad of ratroaches broke past them in a skirmish. It led to a temporary working understanding of the dungeons that they'd never quite put together before, but which fit for both the Akashic Sewer and Officium Mundi.

The dungeons were perfectly capable of changing things in their territory. And, as it was becoming increasingly clear, "their territory" was not specifically the compressed outside-real-world bubbles that he tended to find them in. There seemed to be an almost physical restriction on the dungeons, though; if they wanted something to be their territory, they had to *take* it, and hold it. And so far, there hadn't been a single change made while anyone was capable of seeing it happen.

Observation, and occupation, were the limiting factors. And it had clicked in James's head fairly quickly that this matched the Office as well; the Order had claimed the tower by the door, and for whatever reason, the Office never claimed it back. It never reset, because it was their territory, not the dungeon's. Here, though, the Sewer felt . . . weak. It was desperately clawing to take more of the school, and twist it into its own. But all it actually took was James telling it to get out, and it had to leave a room. He had the distinct feeling that if he tried that in the Office, *that* dungeon would just laugh at him.

James gripped his pilfered shiv in as comfortable a way as he could. He missed his spear, which had been eaten by one of the skulls in a terrifying display of jaw strength. He also wished the Wi-Fi here was working, so he could connect to Alanna. She'd found one of the makeshift weapons that was a pair of prongs, and it was apparently close enough to a traditional jitte that her long-unused skill had fired up and turned her into even more of a nightmare for the average ratroach. James was stuck with mostly punching them, and while he was getting used to it, the sensation of chitin and flesh crushing under his knuckles was still stomach-turning, and it also bruised his hands.

"Body," Sarah pointed out, a sad pain in her voice as she leveled a finger at the shape on the dimly lit floor. At least there were exterior windows nearby, so they didn't need to rely on the overhead lights.

James approached first, kneeling down to check for a pulse that he knew he wouldn't find. He couldn't see a face, but the person was clearly in a police uniform, and maybe he had a gun on him.

Rolling the body slightly, though, James jerked his hand back and let out an involuntary yell of panic. Alanna was at his side in a flash, while James flailed backward, shaking his hand furiously.

"What, what's going on!?" she demanded, Sarah echoing similar sentiments from behind them.

Not knowing how to explain, James just pointed, trying to distance himself from the body. Or what used to be a body. And he didn't have to explain. Because out from under where there should have been a human face, tragically twisted in death, there was instead a wave of glistening white maggot-things, inching their way across the rug, disturbed by James shaking their home.

They spread out from the officer's body, the hunched police uniform deflating as more and more of the maggots flowed out, following their brethren. Where once there had been a corpse, now there was only a writhing mass of insects, slowly finding a collective direction, climbing the wall.

Climbing the wall. James made a mistake, and looked up.

Overhead, the ceiling was covered in cocoons. Dangling white protrusions, finger-length, hanging from the ceiling like a layer of grass. The maggots climbing the wall seemed intent, now, on joining the others, as the whole swarm shifted directions, slowly inching their way upward.

"Oh, fuck," Alanna bit out, looking behind them. Patches of the ceiling along their current path were likewise covered. Probably everywhere they'd found a corpse. "If one of those got in my hair, I am going to vomit."

"I might just anyway," James tried to say, gagging on the words. "Let's . . . just fucking get Lua and leave." He pushed himself off his ass and dusted off his pants, vigorously.

With silent agreement, and careful steps that kept them out from under the ceiling patches where the pale worm things hung, the group moved up. It should have been easy, but when James reached for the door handle, they got another unwelcome surprise.

Sixteen read the number in red neon, projected just past the handle and sitting as a clear marker that the door was not just locked, but *sealed*.

"That's bad," James said, tilting his head to catch the attention of the three others who were circled around him, watching the halls. "Check it. The dungeon locked the door."

"If they're in there, that contradicts what we just thought we learned," Alanna groused.

Sarah clicked her tongue. "Maybe it's just harder for it? Or maybe the door's only locked on this side. Or . . . they're . . ."

"Yeah, enough of that." James reached out again to pay the sparks out of his growing pool of death points. But again, held off at the last second. "Seventeen. *Eighteen.* It's ticking up," he grimly concluded. "And fast, too."

"Oh, that solves a lot of puzzles." Alanna sighed in relief.

"What?"

It was Cold-Wind-Friction that replied to James's confusion, digital voice the same calm tone it always was. "It telegraphs. We are moving. It is watching. Does not want the outcome; obstacles."

"Yeah, what he said," Alanna agreed. "It locked the door *now*, because it saw us moving for it. It's upgrading it as fast as it can, but it must be hard because we're watching. Open the damn door before it gets out of range."

James didn't argue, just gripped the handle, and felt the heat of thirty-odd red sparks flowing out of his fingertips.

Then he pulled, and the door handle rattled. Locked.

"Okay, *this* I can deal with," he announced, dropping to one knee and pulling out the lockpicks from his inside coat pocket with a practiced move. His hand brushed against where his gun should have sat, and the absence made him feel mildly naked for a moment, before he started selecting tools. It took him about two minutes to get the cheap school-issued lock to crack under his ministrations, and from that point, there was nothing to do except swing the door open.

A blast of sound and light greeted him as he pulled the handle. His brain barely had time to register, even with his enhanced sensory suite, that there was someone kneeling behind a desk with a gun. James just caught a bullet on his bracer shield, lines of light bursting to life and making him glad they hadn't encountered anything to make him switch targets yet.

Another three shots further deafened him, followed by the distant sound of multiple people shouting, before the gunfire ended and he could see again.

The downside of constantly keeping his cognition up was that he saw *everything*, and that meant that when the shield light went off, it was a quite painful form of sensory overload if he wasn't ready.

"Stop! Stop it!" A woman's voice was yelling, alongside another younger voice, still female, adding, "Cut it the fuck out, you shithawk!"

The yelling wasn't required. Cold-Wind-Friction had very neatly locked down the school's police officer, whose finger was halfway down the trigger of their weapon as they were prepared to continue unloading into James. His dress uniform looked torn and rumpled; daily attire that didn't include body armor hadn't stood up well to the horrors that had emerged this afternoon. The officer had an almost crazed look in his eye, like he'd already given up on rescue ever being an option.

James stepped over the threshold, motioning everyone to follow and *very carefully* not breaking the camraconda's line of sight. They piled in, Alanna closing the door behind them after a sweeping glance down the halls outside. "Hey, Lua," he greeted the woman slumped against the filing cabinet to the right of the door, hands over her ears, still crying out softly for the uniformed man to stop shooting. "Hey . . . okay. Everyone else."

There were students here. Lua's office was not that large. It included a desk, a couple of filing cabinets for records, a leafy green potted plant that looked *suspiciously* mobile where it was leaning over toward James as he walked in the door, and no windows. There were three chairs, one clearly Lua's, the others for the kids she saw. One desk, overturned. The desk wasn't quite pressed up to the door, but with the chairs packed to the side as an extra barricade, it did leave a fair amount of floor space behind it for . . . James counted, six, seven, eight, *nine* . . . students to huddle together on the floor.

They didn't look happy; they didn't look comfortable. Most of them were staring at Cold-Wind-Friction as he moved up between the adults, security camera eye never leaving the cop who was protecting them. But they were *alive*.

"Stop that." James casually brushed away a knife-sharp leaf from the broadleaf potted fern that was edging toward his throat. "We're here to help, you jackass plant." He stepped up, keeping a questioning eye on their camraconda for confirmation, and wrapped an arm up, over, and around to the back of the cop's grip to carefully pull the gun away. It went into James's shoulder holster once the safety was on. Then, and only then, did Cold-Wind-Friction let the officer move again, and his finger immediately slammed down like the trigger was still there.

"Freeze!" he shouted at the rescue team, like that would do anything.

"No?" Alanna asked, sharing raised eyebrows with Sarah. The two girls nodded to each other behind James's back. "Yeah, no."

"Is anyone hurt?" Sarah asked, stepping over their barricade and taking a knee next to Lua. "Hey. Hey. It's okay. We're here. We came," she started softly talking.

Half of the cluster of students started to rise to their feet, and another half erupted into questions.

"No, everyone sit down," James ordered. "Yes, we are here to get you out. Yes, this is happening. Yes, I am a wizard, thank you. Yes." The last *yes* was directed with a pointed glare at the officer who was rising to his full height and glaring at James. It also didn't answer any question that had been asked. "Yes, I *am* annoyed that this is the second time today the police have shot at me. You know, I'm starting to think that y'all don't like me much."

"Who are you?" the cop demanded, his loud voice and silencing the students behind him.

"Order of Endless Rooms," Alanna introduced them while James brushed past the cop. He saw the man tense up when he did so, like he was considering striking out. But James calmly ignored him, and moved to start checking on the students instead. "We're here to evacuate the building. Your assistance is appreciated."

"Shouldn't we go with 'FBI,' instead?" Sarah asked from where she held a sobbing Lua, gently stroking the older woman's hand as she let the stress of the day catch up with her.

"Oh, yeah. FBI. We're here to . . ."

James tuned them out, and started talking to the high schoolers.

It had been a while since he was in high school. But he still remembered how it felt, and how no one had ever talked to him like he was an adult. He hadn't *been* an adult, of course, but it wasn't like the dismissive attitude had helped him be less rebellious. So it wasn't an orb skill or JP's lessons on impersonating law enforcement that he brought to the conversation, but his own experience, filtered through a day of hard fighting and stress.

"Hi," he opened with. "We fight monsters. What can you guys tell me about what the fuck is happening here?"

With quiet words and a tone that made it clear he was listening to them, James got a piecemeal account of the day.

It had started off with a fight. A couple of the kids had seen a handful of other students, ones the group more or less agreed were assholes in some way, arguing with a couple of the nerdier denizens of the school. There were mixed reports of if it was an argument, a conversation, or good old-fashioned bullying. But either way, by the end of it, the whole group of them had stormed off together. This was sometime around first period.

When they'd vanished into a shack out by the football field that no one remembered being there before, there'd been some outlandish rumors flying around. When those rumors had hit the school security guards, they'd reacted by calling the police, instantly on guard about another shooting.

At the mention of the last shooting that had happened here, James bit his lip and didn't make eye contact.

That had been just after lunch. There had been some weird noises, strange smells, and fewer kids than normal in each class during third period. Then, the lights started going out. The monsters began roving the hallway. The police showed up, and died. And the only person who seemed to have any idea what was going on was the woman who everyone thought was the counselor, grabbing everyone she could get her hands on, striding through the halls like a demon, and snapping the neck of anything that got too close.

James smirked. Lua had probably burned every charge of her blue for this. 'Rotate sixty degrees,' as it turned out, was one of those subtle verb use cases that was instantly lethal if used properly.

After that, they'd hidden here.

The timeline helped put things together, but it didn't explain why today, of all days, the dungeon had decided to freak the hell out and start trying to eat the building and everyone inside.

"Has anyone seen Secret?" James addressed the room, cutting off both the conversation that Alanna was having with the officer and the bonding moment between the camraconda and the plant. Though that last one might have just been the two pieces of Office Life suspiciously eyeing each other.

"Which secret?" one of the students asked.

"We're changing his name after this, I swear," Alanna said, exasperated. "Every time. Every time, James."

Rolling his eyes, James explained as best he could. "He's blue, kinda snake-esque? Either four feet or ten miles long, depending on how long you look at him? Lots of eyes?" He saw horrified expressions from some of the students. "Friendly?" James added, in a questioning tone. "No?"

"Lua, where's Secret? He was with you," Sarah gently asked.

"He led off one of the skull things," Lua said, composing herself to look up at James. "He said he'd find us, but he hasn't come back. He couldn't hurt them; said he wasn't strong enough." She sniffed, wiping at the corners of her eyes. "I'm so glad you came. Sorry to complicate your day off."

"I haven't had a day off since that time I taught a stapler how to play Magic."

"That *was* you!" one of the students burst out. "No one believed me!"

James snorted a laugh. "Okay. So. What's our goal now?" He turned questioningly to Alanna and Sarah. "Get them out, then . . . the dungeon?"

"Yeah." Alanna nodded. "Whatever happened, it was after the kids went in. So maybe we can stop it today. Otherwise . . . get Research to build us another foundation cracker? Bring the whole place down?"

"I've heard worse ideas," James admitted. "I'm worried about Secret, though. If he can't fight back because the Sewer's out in the open, then that's official Bad News. He's manifested right now. I'm not actually sure he can *die*, but I don't want to find out."

Alanna sucked in a breath through her teeth. "If we cut off its territory up here, it saves everyone. The sooner we do that, the better. Wasting time on evac just means more potential problems, more things we'll get sidetracked on."

"What are you *talking* about?!" the police officer—one J. Clarke, according to his name badge—demanded. He'd been, to his credit, trying to be patient. Especially once Alanna identified them as FBI, however unbelievable her pitch really was. But they were talking about monsters and ghosts and one of them had stolen his gun. "Who *are* you?! Why is there a snake thing?! What is going *on*?! I'm the fucking adult here, and I've got the badge, and I'd like some answers! And my sidearm back, while you're at it!"

"Alright," James said, turning to him with a cold anger in his voice. "Mister adult. You're the resource officer here? Well, you work in a building that has a bubble of extradimensional space 'below' it." He made finger quotes to punctuate his words. "If I were to describe it with human emotions, I'd call it angry, spiteful, and cruel. It's made of bugs and sludge, and it hates you. Possibly personally. Sometimes, it lures students in, and gets them to kill each other for books that don't have words in them. You are unequipped to deal with it, and never noticed it existed. Now it's out of its self-imposed cage, eating people, and taking over a chunk of the real world. And no, I'm keeping the gun, because you shot at me. Give me your extra ammo."

James glared down at the officer, the two of them each trying to project authority over each other. Before any more words could be exchanged though, one of the students raised her hand.

"Um . . . I found a book?"

"What?" James glanced over.

"It just appeared in the corner over here. One of the filing cabinet drawers was open, and this thing just popped out and jammed it? When I took it, the drawer slammed closed and it won't open now." She demonstrated, and the drawer flashed a green *one* at them. "Is it . . . is it important?"

"It could be." James nodded, sighing. "May I have it? It could be useful to us."

"Sure." The girl shrugged and handed over a tome that looked like a legal textbook.

James looked at it in his hands for a minute, turning it over a few times. Sure enough, something about it felt . . . off. Like it didn't quite belong in the real world. It was a feeling he was starting to associate with some of the items from Officium Mundi. Though, interestingly, not the orbs themselves.

"Sarah," James said, handing it to her. "Alanna and I both have one, and I don't wanna find out now that stacking them is a bad idea. You're up."

She nodded, dusting off her knees as she got up, helping Lua up alongside her. "We should fall back to Nate before we move for the breach," she said as she took the book. "Get these kids out of here." Sarah opened the book. The room filled with the sensation of pages turning, and learning occurring. And then, the whole thick tome crumbled to dust in her hand, the specks of crumbled paper and leather vanishing from reality the same way they came in.

[Lesson Begun : Sex Ed 0/100]

"Good?"

"No. The Sewer has a sense of humor." Sarah scowled. "And it would be funny from the Office, but this is just gross."

"Tell us later," Alanna whispered from the door, her ear tilted toward the frosted glass pane. "Something's coming."

"What kind of something?" James whispered back, drawing the cop's gun and checking the magazine. Four bullets left. *Not worth it*, he thought, jamming the gun back into the holster. He could punch his way to a new knife. He scowled at the officer, who still looked like he was planning to chokeslam James to get his gun back. "Students?"

"No." Alanna's huff was a grim acceptance of the incoming fight. "Ratroaches. And . . . crying? Shit, they have prisoners."

"Well, so much for hiding," James said. "Cold, target any holding students. Sarah, left, Alanna, center. Lua? You got anything left in the tank?"

"I used all my charges. I'm sorry." She still sounded on the edge of a breakdown.

"It's fine," James said, while Sarah flipped over one of the chairs and started snapping the legs off with loud stomps. "Stay back, keep everyone else clear. Clarke, you want in on this?"

"Give me my gun back and we'll talk."

"No," James repeated bluntly, watching Sarah drag the pencil he'd given her across the wooden dowels of the chair legs. "Everyone ready?"

"Don't forget Ferndinand!" Lua exclaimed. "Don't leave him here. Please."

"The . . . right. Yeah, of course." The potted plant. It had been up in the air if the things ever could be domesticated, considering they all seemed to be bloodthirsty jerks. But the one here in Lua's office looked content enough, even if it was pushed off into a corner away from where anyone might casually poke at it. James pointed at a couple of the kids. "You two look tough," he buttered them up. "Can you haul this potted plant with us? I know it sounds dumb, but I swear it's a good idea." They nodded. "Okay. *Now* are we ready?"

Voices, digital and human, called assent.

Alanna signaled from the door where the noises were getting louder. They had been noticed, obviously, and their foes were surrounding them.

They didn't give the ratroaches a chance.

Alanna slammed the door open with her shoulder, catching one of the creatures in the jaw and staggering it backward. It didn't break, though; they were getting tougher. Their skin didn't burst open with a single strike, their bones didn't splinter just from being thrown down. But the attack did clear a path for the combatants to plow into the unsuspecting pack that thought itself the ambushers.

The revealed scene was one of about a dozen ratroaches, four of them holding a pair of human teenagers in vice-like grips. They were arrayed around the door, with the kidnappers being near the back and the better-armed ones up front in a loose semicircle around the door. James noticed that their weapons were different now. Some of them still had filed-down shivs or table-leg clubs, but at least a couple had knives made of unpolished bone.

Alanna smashed into the central one with a thrown elbow, bringing her makeshift jitte up to catch an incoming club, twisting it to the side and ignoring the assailant as she rained right hooks down on the staggered ratroach in front of her. Behind Alanna, James kicked off the doorframe and delivered a punch to one of the ratroaches to the right, hitting where a human would have had a kidney. The mangy fur rippled under his knuckles, and he felt something inside the creature rupture. It still lunged for him, smoking blue bile dripping from the sides of its diseased maw as its organs broke. James slapped aside one of its arms, caught the other two on his own raised arm, punched it in the stomach again hard enough to make it bow over, and then planted a foot on its fallen head to leap over and lash out at the next shocked target.

As soon as James and Alanna were out of the way, Sarah started violently picking off any ratroaches that hadn't moved fast enough to get clear of the melee. She moved like a dancer, arms extended, metaphysical muscles straining, as she warped the magnetic field around her. Both arms down, step forward, slide one foot past the other, one arm up, one arm back, pull, and something in the air *snapped.*

The field collapsing was audible to even the unaugmented humans as Sarah turned herself into an organic railgun. One of the wooden chair legs, magnetized by the dungeon tech pencil, cracked forward so fast it basically vanished from view and then reappeared through the skull of one of the ratroaches.

The thing never knew what hit it. One second, it was snarling with dripping green ichor, a claw and a knife lunging for James's back. The next, its brain matter was splattered across the far wall in a whorl pattern, chunks of bone and flesh and eye painted in a horrifyingly violent deconstruction.

The ratroaches faltered. Perhaps . . . perhaps they had miscalculated? Gotten too greedy. After all, they already had two captives. A retreat, then . . .

Another head exploded. Alanna planted a captured knife through first one's heart, then again through its backup heart. James dug his thumb up to the second knuckle into an eye socket, ignoring the screaming until he cut it off by slamming the rat's skull against the floor with a throw and a slam designed to crush the less-durable bone these things had under their patchwork skin.

The survivors tried to run, and found they couldn't. Any time one of them turned to flee, they froze, and were cut down. Methodically, without mercy, though James and Alanna did try to make it as painless as possible. They were *furious,* but they didn't actually hate these things. It wasn't like the ratroaches had any real agency, as far as the Order knew.

Still. For the first, and last, time in their short lives, the hunting pack of ratroaches understood what it meant to be afraid.

"Clear!" James's voice echoed off the hall as he bloodily yanked the edge of the makeshift club he'd stolen out of the shattered chitin of the last one on his side.

Voices came back to him. "Clear!" "Clear!" "Rats no more."

"Lua! Get the prisoners! Let's move, before they send something else!" James ordered, grabbing up the knives around them and sliding them through the belt loops on his pants. He tried to wipe the grime and blood off his hands, and found that there was no longer a clean spot on his pants to do so. "I fucking hate this place," he muttered to himself.

"Welcome back," Anesh greeted him when James stepped through the door to their first "claimed" classroom. "You just missed Simon's crew."

"How're they doing?" James asked, tired. His head hurt, his knees hurt, and his hands could barely grip properly, which made stabbing very challenging. "Also, hey. Brought some friends."

"They got two classrooms evacuated. A lot of students got sorta herded in there? We're getting them out. Also, bad news. Nate's gone." Anesh said it with a calm voice, so James started when his brain caught up to the words that didn't match the tone.

"Dead?!" he demanded.

Anesh blinked, startled. "What? No. Oh! No! No, we decided to try to rearm, after the second wave of rats came through and he ran out of ammo. I made the call to send Nate to get us our weaponry. Telepad out, but no one can teleport *in* to the school. So we can't do repeat trips. Confirmed he's not dead; just that we can't get anything in. Texts, too. Total blackout, one way."

"That's fucked up. So, the Akashic Sewer is trying . . . what? To make a hell for the people inside? It doesn't seem to care about anyone outside."

"Yeah, this feels weird," Anesh agreed. "Oh. Reed got up, then promptly got stabbed by a ratroach because he's never thrown a punch in his life. He went out with Simon's team and the students for first aid. We need some kind of medic orb, won't lie. Other James got hurt, too. He's out of the fight, though he should live."

"So where's Nate?"

"Outside, past the increasingly dangerous police barricade. Signaled him to not try to get in, especially since unlike you, he's not bullet resistant."

James groaned. "We really need to start duplicating bracers. Not this one, though. I'm down to five blocks left." He shook his arm. "Another idiot tried to shoot me."

Anesh gave a sideways glance to the glowering police officer who'd come in with Lua and the other rescued students. "Hm" was all he said. Then, "We should move to Canada."

"Do they have dungeons in Canada?" James retorted with a smirk.

"Almost certainly," Anesh shot back without thinking about it.

The two of them paused as they considered that. Status Quo had been, at the end of the day, *wrong* about the dungeons. They weren't just centered in this part of the world; they were all over. El and her own experiences were proof of that. Why, then, wouldn't there be dungeons in Canada?

"We're gonna need passports," James said, throwing his head back to gaze idly up at the ceiling.

"That's a tomorrow problem," Alanna cut in, stepping up to them. "Hey," she shot at Anesh. "I'd give you a hug, but I'm covered in intestines."

"Gross. Thank you." Anesh offered her a fist bump, which she took with a smile. "So, what's the plan? Where's Secret?"

"No idea." James shook his head sadly. "He can't fight them. I'm wondering, legitimately, if he can only actually deal with stuff that's secret. Or if the secret part is what he needs to . . . I dunno, turn the information into direct action. And now that the school's just exploded out into the spotlight, he's weak to what's going on."

"Weak like fire on water type, or weak like electric on ground type?" Anesh inquired.

"He's not a Pokémon, man." James rolled his eyes.

Anesh gave a half shrug in agreement. "I mean, he's more of a . . . you know what? Anime references later. Do we *have* a plan? Are we retreating? The entryway is still rubble, I don't think the dungeon can recover from that, so we have a path out if we need it."

"Earlier today," James explained, "a group of kids went into the dungeon. Then this shit started. So whatever they did, they set this off. And I fucking wish I knew if it was because they made it mad, or made it *afraid*, or something else. But if they did something to trigger this, then we need to try to put the monster back in the box." James didn't like that it fell to them, but he could see that his partners were on the same page about what they needed to do next. "We're in real trouble if this gets out of hand. I'll be honest, I do believe the military could handle this, easy. But how long would it take to put soldiers here? And how long would they take to contain it? What if it keeps going? We're in a suburban residential area; if the dungeon starts taking over houses, or parts of those parks that are all over the place, it's going to get out of control basically in a day or two."

"So we stop it now. You don't need to convince me," Anesh told him. "Are we going in after it?"

"Yeah," Alanna said. "Though I'm not sure I agree with James. About the military thing. I've been talking to Officer Clarke. You know, without antagonizing him." She poked James in the shoulder. "And he is just fundamentally not ready for this. The police didn't even think of shooting the buses outside that're alive. And we've seen more than a few dead cops inside, too. And teachers, and students. I'm not saying that the students here are wimps, I'm saying that, like, a football player could probably take a ratroach straight up. Maybe two on one. But the students would have outnumbered the monsters massively at first."

"Fear kept them down?" James mused. "No, that doesn't add up quite . . ."

"It's not just fear. *Lua* was afraid. But she got up and fought. James, you've got a cut just about your eye; were you afraid that was gonna blind you?"

"I mean, yeah." He shrugged, then made an *ah* noise. "We're all afraid," he said. "And we're carving through them. So it can't just be fear."

"Other people hesitate. And it's not just that they aren't trying to adapt. It's almost like the reverse. They're forgetting solutions they already have that might work." Alanna cracked her knuckles against themselves. "And I don't know why we're immune."

"Secret?" Anesh suggested. "He *is* active in the building."

"But not here," James said. "And that usually matters when he's physical."

"What if it's . . . Okay, this is kinda weird . . ." Alanna thought about what she'd just said, and shared a slightly bitter snicker with her boyfriends as they all realized the absurdity. "Okay. James, you can feel magic items now, right?"

"Yeah, the book too. Even though it's . . . not the Office. Hm."

"We're changing," Anesh said. "And not just because of the rewards. That's your point?" Alanna nodded at him, and he rubbed at his chin. "I don't think I like that."

James cut through the center of their conversation with a slash of a flat palm. "Okay, I'm putting this scary talk on pause for a bit, to get us back on track. We have a plan."

"We do?" Anesh asked.

"We do," Alanna confirmed with a nod. "What is it?"

James wanted to roll his eyes, but was too tired to do so. "We split the group; enough combatants to get the students out, and the rest of us to the breach. We go in, we stab what needs stabbing, then we run."

"What if we die?" Anesh asked politely, like he was posing a question at a business conference and not asking about their mortality.

With a considering nod, and an appreciative hum, James answered, "Don't do that."

"Okay. Good plan."

"Wanker," James shot at him with a smirk.

"That's my word!" Anesh gave a mock gasp.

"Guys, you're adorable, really. I'd love to watch you be incredibly gay today, instead of doing this. But we're on a clock here. We should get what we need and move," Alanna prompted the two of them.

They agreed, and got to work.

By the time they'd evac'd the other students, and Lua, and Deb, who'd refused to leave everyone behind despite her injury, Simon had returned alone, along with the mongausse and a story about what a pain it was to drop off the rescued students and dodge the police and news crews. And with a little organization, they had their final strike team.

James and Alanna: tired, sore, and still ready to fight, their pockets and belts full of stolen knives. Anesh: much more ready to get into a scrap, despite being the last one of his bodies left. Sarah: currently sharpening table legs into magnetic spikes. Dave: wearing a bomber jacket and fiddling with a pair of laser pointers, both magic but in different ways—hopefully he could remember which was which. Cold-Wind-Friction: bloodied and messy, but still ready to fight, alongside Frequency-of-Sunlight: out for punitive revenge on behalf of her friend. Virgil: fiddling with the laptop and trying to pretend he was calm. And Simon: oddly out of place in his isolation, gently petting the distortion that was the mongausse, and trying to pretend he was okay on his own.

They were all a mess, all needed a change of clothes and a two-hour-long shower. They were hurting, bruised and cut and scraped. And they were *pissed*. Even Virgil seemed to have a quiet ire to his motions as he snapped the laptop shut, placed it in a sling on his side, and clipped a cord from it into his brain. He might be a condescending jackass sometimes, but that didn't mean he was in any way okay with murder, and this place was gonna pay for thinking it could step out of line like that.

James reloaded their one pistol with the magazine Alanna tossed him, pilfered off Officer Clarke during their chat.

"Ready?" he muttered, more to himself than anyone else.

They were.

They moved. Fast as they could. They could see over the railing of the balcony that more of those massive rat things were nosing around down below, on the first floor. They kept to the inside, out of sight, and made a new route. A straight shot toward the back of the school, and the wide windows on the balcony that looked out over the football field. They only had to kill a couple of ratroaches that tested them, and with the camracondas present, it wasn't even a fight.

The plate glass was double-pane, vacuum sealed, and durable enough to handle abuse from rowdy high school students, which was saying something.

Sarah spiked it in three spots with her magnetic spears, planted her feet, and shoved the wooden stakes apart, rending a ten-foot hole in the window and shattering most of it into shards that tumbled to the ground below.

The noise absolutely attracted attention, but they were already moving. Despite being on the second floor, they had an easy way out, in the form of Dave and one of his four slotted blues.

"Raise floor" once, twice, three times, and once the grinding noise ceased, they had a series of reasonably survivable jumps instead of one twenty-foot fall.

James went first, boots scattering broken glass and slipping a little on the uneven surface. Dave had a lot of magic, but he was still working on fine control, and it showed. But it got the job done, as the group made the drop ahead of the skull-ball-thing rapidly closing in on their rear. Sarah was the last one down, covering their retreat and the slower camracondas with a magnetic snap and a launched spear. A lack of red sparks indicated that she hadn't killed the thing she'd already decided to call a skullaton, but it shattered a couple of the leering visages and elicited a pained scream that bought them time.

They hit the ground, and formed a loose line as they started moving to the fenced gate to the field. The revolving metal bars were kept shut for high school sporting events, but otherwise should have been open. Now, though, a glittering red *two hundred and twenty* shone on it. James paid the cost without thinking; he'd killed enough ratroaches today that he'd need a few doors to start to really drain his pool of reminders of his violence.

He still held it open, though, cheating the dungeon of its perverse kill tax as he ushered everyone through, before letting it slam behind them and giving the finger to the pack of ratroaches carefully crawling down the makeshift staircase they'd erected.

It was a straight run across the field, and they took it at a reasonable pace. Nothing was chasing them, so they jogged, or slithered, enough that they were moving quickly but not enough to exhaust themselves before more fighting. Overhead, two helicopters did lazy circles; news or police, it didn't matter, really. James spent the whole time waiting with his nerves on edge for part of the field to unfold into some kind of spiked pipe trap, or a cloaked football monster or something. But it didn't. And they made it to the sheet-metal shed on the other side without incident.

The structure looked like it might have belonged, if you hadn't already been told it didn't. But once you knew, it was clear this thing had been put here as either a prank or a mistake, or by some kind of outside malevolent force that had no design sense. In this case, James knew it was the latter.

The door was locked, but only in a mundane fashion, and even then the lock might have been the most durable part. Alanna tested that by snorting derisively at it, stepping back, and giving it a sideways kick hard enough to break one of the flimsy hinges.

Inside, there was a hole in the blackened dirt floor, surrounded by rotting sports equipment. The breach in the ground looked like a series of thin pipes had punched their way to the surface and were currently trying to claw the gap open even wider, leaving just enough open space for even a reasonably wide human to drop in. The feeling that he was standing on dungeon territory here was, James thought, oddly *subdued* compared to the rest of the school.

"Last chance to back out," James told everyone. No one said anything. "Alright. Let's go kill this thing. See you on the other side."

He went first, with Alanna close behind him, dropping his feet over the edge and seeing how they hung in the inky darkness. James knew that he'd have to fall to get anywhere, if this was like last time; and that no matter how much he clung to the walls, at some point there was going to be a wrenching sense of distortion. Also, it might steal something of his again. Just to be safe, he threw his cell phone out to the side, on the off chance he could get it back later. Then he dropped. And the others followed.

And then, they were gone, and reality had only the sounds of sirens and helicopter rotors to keep the empty field company.

CHAPTER 5

"I'm telling you, I don't know where they went," Nate pointedly told one of the officers manning the cordon around the high school. It was the truth.

There was a sea of flashing lights at this point. Two dozen cop cars and growing, four firetrucks from two separate stations, a handful of ambulances, and, for reasons he wasn't clear on but hadn't questioned, both a parks department patrol vehicle and a transit police van. This mess of wheels and steel was complemented by the backed-up traffic of frantic parents trying to get to their kids, cars left abandoned, and a swarm of concerned citizens and casual observers throwing themselves right up to the line of the police tape. It was then further complicated by the small army of news vans that had descended like locusts.

Nate didn't have a high opinion of the press. Being in the Navy had sort of drilled into him that talking to reporters was often a career-ending maneuver, and his time keeping secrets for the FBI had given him a clear picture of just how wrong about some big things the cameras could be. Not that reporters didn't try their best a lot of the time, or sometimes have a little help getting to the wrong answers, mind you. But they'd always added another unwelcome step to any job he was doing.

His time with the Order, short as it was, had blown a hole in the veil of the world. Magic was real. So were monsters, though he'd always known there was a perfectly human flavor of those walking around. Five months ago, he would have called his new prep cook a *monster*. Now he just called them Knife-in-Fangs, and showed them how to skin potatoes.

The point was, it highlighted to him that his initial suspicions, of the news in general not having the whole truth, had been totally accurate. So when a news van rolled up, Nate kept track of them, but made sure his face was always pointed away from the camera. A challenge, when the cop he was talking to kept trying to get him to move.

And also answer questions. Questions Nate didn't have real answers to, and wouldn't have given real answers to even if he did.

"So you're telling me," the captain, an older, barrel-chested man with a round face and flushed cheeks was saying, pausing for short sharp breaths every few words. "That you. And your 'friends' . . ."

"Fellow agents," Nate corrected firmly, tapping the FBI badge on the table. It wasn't actually his; he'd had to ask JP to make him a forgery of his own badge, which had stung a little. He was leaning into it right now, though.

"Entered the building. Saved a bunch of students. Got in a gunfight. Split up. And you don't know. Where the rest of them are?"

"Yes." Nate, with Herculean effort, avoided rolling his eyes. "Which is why I'm talking to you, asking you to keep me—"

"And the snakes?" the police captain interrupted him.

"Are being *very* polite to you." Nate folded his hands in front of him, pressing his fingertips together. "Look, buddy, I don't know, or want to know, what your problem is. I just need you to follow orders, okay?"

The captain narrowed his eyes. "No," he drawled out in a rough, deliberate voice. "There's been a lot of reports around here lately. Of people impersonating the FBI. And I don't think. You're with the Bureau. At all."

Nate wanted to headbutt the nearest wall until the knot of a headache behind his eyes went away. Or, if he couldn't find a suitable wall, this guy in front of him. Or just *James*, for fucking this all up.

He was the actual FBI—for the next three days until his retirement was official! He was the only one *not* committing felony-level fraud! Why was it all falling back on him?!

"I am being *polite* by informing you of our presence . . ." Nate started with, but he'd seen the look in the captain's eye before. No matter where you were in the world, there was a sort of attitude that was universal when people had decided they were right, and you were screwed. "Oh, fuck it." He turned, grabbing the potted plant that had frustratingly been left in his care. "James is a bad influence on me," he muttered as he stalked away, ignoring the protesting shout from behind him.

He almost worried the captain was going to shoot him. But the man had bigger concerns on his plate than Nate right now, and besides, he'd already adjusted his bracer to match the .45 ACP on the man's hip.

The bracers were so absurdly unfair. He would have killed to have one when he was a more active field agent. He literally *had* killed for less. Getting used to stuff like that was just part of his new world.

"Reed," he called out to the young man who was sitting cross-legged against a cop car. "Get whoever's left, and let's move. See if anyone has a 'feeling' about where we should be; you're all too good at that, right?" Nate paused, then demanded, "Why are you hand-cuffed?"

Reed looked up at him, and Nate noticed a pattern of bruises on his neck that he couldn't be sure had been from dungeon combat. Reed looked like he was going to say something, but the curly-haired young man just got out a wet cough instead, badly spitting a wad of blood to the side before answering. "I am under arrest," he stated.

". . .Why." Nate didn't bother to ask, just expressed annoyance. "Get up," he said instead, reaching a hand down to pull Reed up from under the shoulder. Turned him around, and reached down to the handcuffs.

Nate didn't have a blue absorbed right now; he still couldn't actually do that like the others could. He only had his bracer and a bracelet for magic firepower. And he also didn't have a library of bizarre orb skills to draw on like everyone else.

But he was, and always would be, a smooth operator. And he carried handcuff keys.

"Hey, what are you . . . !"

"I outrank you," Nate snapped at the officer that was coming around the car toward them. "So does he." He nodded at Reed. "Let's go." The words came out hard and angry. "Make sure they didn't arrest anyone who needed a doc, and then go figure out what else we need to shoot."

"Yes, sir." Reed gave him a shaky salute, and Nate resisted the urge to roll his eyes. The salute was far too authentic. Nate would have preferred sarcasm right now.

Then he realized something. "This is how James feels. All the time." He sighed. "Fuck. I bet he doesn't have to deal with this. He's probably having fun right now, while I have to go see if the local LEOs are trying to find the off switch on the camracondas. Goddammit." Nate stalked through the mass of parked cars filling the street like he owned the place, which was usually enough to get people out of his way.

If it weren't for the fact that he knew James actually was probably having a harder time than he was, Nate might have been serious in thinking this was unfair.

James spat onto the ground, trying to clear the burn of bile off of his tongue. The transition to this space, this disgusting underground sewer hellscape, still felt like it was intentionally painful and disorienting. Though it was only his second time here, so what did he know. And this time he'd been bounced against the slimy pipe wall of the chute at least three times before the slope deposited him here.

He wasn't the only one to have thrown up, losing whatever was left of their lunch. "Fortunately," the smell was lost among the overwhelming acrid stench of human waste, black mold, and whatever the hell the probably-toxic wisps of fumes in the air were made of.

They were in a different entry room this time. Similar, but still noticeably different. A shallow bowl of needlessly rough concrete, stained black in patches from blood and bile and probably a million other things James didn't want to know about. The wall around them was studded in points where the joints of pipes escaped the concrete, but most of it was intact except for a few randomly placed faucets that dripped a thick orange sludge down into open grates below.

"Status check!" James called out.

A chorus of affirmatives came back at him, along with a few people still coughing. The camracondas looked out of it, too, and Cold-Wind-Friction had spat up some kind of oily vomit. But everyone was here.

They still had armor on, if they were wearing it, too.

James snaked his hand inside his coat. The gun he'd taken was still there, and no longer pushing against the holster either. "Something's up. Anyone missing anything?"

Alanna looked down at her person, and the two dozen knives she'd confiscated, stuck through her belt and pockets. "No, shockingly," she said, wiping the back of a gloved hand across her mouth. "Fuck, something's changed."

"I think we crossed the bridge of *something changed* about four hours ago," James rebutted. "Alright. Everyone take a minute, but get ready to move. Virgil, get that local network set up. Frequency, keep an eye on the hall please. Everyone else, just stretch, breathe . . . shallowly, and when the network's good to go, we'll link up and move out." Simon raised a hand to ask a question, and James answered without needing to hear it. "I brought the intermediary plugs, you don't need to do a full hive mind with us. Also, I'm sorry James isn't here," he said.

Simon shrugged. "It couldn't be helped," he said. "Thank you, though."

While Virgil flipped open the laptop and started creating a Wi-Fi hotspot that would hopefully encompass their group for the duration of their stay here, James looked around the room. Alanna was handing out knives, Dave was poking a finger through a ragged hole in his jacket and scowling, and Simon and Sarah were both taking the time to clip more hardware into their skulljack braids. James took their lead and plugged his own braid in while he kept scanning.

The walls. There was something weird about them. His instincts knew it, but he hadn't quite figured it out yet in a way he could put into words. They were that same gray concrete as ever. Jagged rocks and pipes, splatters of some dark goop, random graffiti, flickering red emergency lights, jutting faucets and spikes . . .

There was graffiti here.

It was written in pen, in highlighter, and in a couple cases, in blood. But there was a *lot* of it. And it had *names*.

"Guys." James nudged Anesh, who was trying to get some chunk of debris out of his shoe without letting his foot touch the floor. "Look. No name eaters. There aren't any local infomorphs like there should be." He pointed around the room, and everyone's eyes followed.

"You think Secret was here?" Sarah immediately asked.

"Doesn't feel like the corpse of that one we found," Alanna mentioned, like that was a sentence people were allowed to say casually. "But the last time we were here, we could barely make out the words, and especially not the names. So what changed?"

"'What changed?' is the million-dollar question of the day." James sighed, and regretted it as he tried to avoid breathing through his nose as the stench crept in.

From where he was tapping away at the keyboard, Virgil asked, "Is the smell new too? Because it is vile down here."

"No, this is basically the same," James confirmed. "This place sucks."

Dave snorted, spitting out onto the corner of the floor. "I didn't believe you about how bad it was. I was wrong! You were right."

"Much as I love hearing that, are we good to go?" James asked Virgil.

"Network's up," he replied, closing his eyes and probing the Wi-Fi hotspot through his skulljack interface. "Stable enough for light connection. You three, avoid full connectivity. This isn't the best laptop, and if the battery dies somehow or I get thrown off a cliff, you'll be in trouble. Battery shouldn't die, though."

"Are there cliffs here?" Sarah asked quietly. "I'm hoping no."

"Not last time, but it sounds awful enough and that's the theme today, so *probably*." James rolled his eyes. "Alright. Anything else before we move?"

"Can we have a soundtrack?" Alanna asked. "If we've got the Wi-Fi running anyway. I could stream some Linkin Park to everyone. Really set the mood, you know?"

Everyone stared at her. Even the camracondas, who didn't have the same context as everyone else, gazed unblinking eyes at the bloodied woman in the middle of the room. There was a moment of silence.

"No?" Alanna said. "Sum 41, maybe? I'm just thinking that if we want the authentic high school experience . . ."

"Lights on, link up, anyone with good low-light vision to the front. Virgil in the middle of the pack. Frequency, front, Friction, rearguard with the mongausse, Simon, make sure the distortion dog stays away from the laptop in combat if possible, please." James drew his gun. "Sarah, with me. Dave, with Alanna. Alanna . . . I'm not saying I don't love your music taste . . ."

"I've got an Offspring album on my phone too, if you want something a little more contemporary that fits the theme!" she offered. "And I even have my phone this time!"

James wanted to rub at his eyes in exasperation, but his hands were covered in flecks of dried blood and ichor. He couldn't even sigh properly without feeling like he was poisoning himself. But he saw what Alanna was doing, and he appreciated it. He just didn't have the energy left to play along. "Just keep an eye out, please. Let's go kill this thing. Or at least enough of its minions that it thinks twice before trying this again."

The group, feeling just a little less tense, moved into the pitch black of the tunnel.

"Oh yeah, this would definitely get infected. Without treatment, anyway." The woman poking at Deb's ankle wore tangled black hair in a simple ponytail, and a messy white coat with the sleeves rolled up. "I can bandage this up and get you a tetanus shot, but you really ought to go to an actual hospital," the veterinarian told her.

Deb tried to smile, but it turned into a wince and a hiss as the other woman dabbed disinfectant on the claw gashes on her ankle. She'd already accepted that her favorite pair of jeans was either getting transformed into something shorter, or getting thrown away. And Deb wasn't sure she was prepared to be the kind of person who wore jorts.

"Thank you," she told the vet, instead of saying any of her other thoughts out loud. "I do really appreciate it. You were just close by and open, you know?"

"Sure." The vet looked up at Deb sitting on the counter, like she wanted to say something else. "Well, I can't take human health insurance for anything but the cost of the rabies shot, so I may have to charge you a bit. Unless this was done by someone's pet, then they might have insurance for it?"

"Oh, no. Not a pet." Deb clenched her teeth and shuddered. "Not a human's, anyway," she muttered.

"Um, what?"

"Shit, I thought I said that quieter." Deb laughed. "Just a joke. Sorry."

"Uh-huh." The black-haired woman looked over to the duffel bag Deb had carried in with her, complete with hard-shell knee pads sticking out of a corner mesh pocket. She glanced back at the young woman who'd limped into her business and asked for help with a "scratch."

Two in a week. Her dad had always said, "Once is happenstance, twice is coincidence, three times is enemy action." But she'd figured you had to go through times one and two to get to three. And maybe if people asked at the second one, they could dodge a third.

So the vet decided to say something, after she'd wrapped the wound in clean cotton and administered the kind of shot they really only kept on hand because it was required, and not because rabies was a problem anymore.

"Hey," she asked, as Deb was gingerly testing her bandaged ankle and ignoring the throbbing pain in her arm. "I have a question."

Deb looked up with raised eyebrows. "I can pay, I swear," she said. "Um . . . might have to expense account it, I guess. Not sure how that . . . But it's fine! Charge what you need to!"

"No, not that." The vet took a deep breath, prepared to run and lock the door and call the cops if this turned bad. "Are you . . . have you . . ." She stumbled over her words. "Do you like the snakes?" she blurted out suddenly.

"What?" Deb asked in confused surprise.

"I'm sorry! I know I'm not supposed to say anything! I just wanted to ask!" The vet held up her hands defensively, prepared to bolt out to the front lobby and get her receptionist to help her hold the door shut. "I won't tell anyone, I swear!"

"Oh. You mean the camracondas!" Deb realized suddenly. "Holy shit, wait, is this the same place they brought Neil? That's . . . whooooops!" She laughed, relief flooding her at the strange sincerity of the veterinarian. "Sorry, hey, it's okay. No one's mad about anything," she tried to reassure the doc.

"You're not going to be in trouble for this?" the vet asked. "Or me either?"

"Nah, it's fine." Deb waved a hand. "We have a common-sense policy on secrecy. And yes, I like at least one snake. Though not the one you met." She gave a little grin and glanced away. "Um. Anyway. I can pay you and go if you're uncomfortable . . ."

"Are you the good guys?"

The question was blunt and brave and almost caught Deb off-guard. But by the time the words were done, she already knew the answer.

"Yes," she said with a firm nod.

"What did that to your leg? Really? Because it wasn't a dog."

"Giant rat." Deb paused, then widened her eyes as she realized something. "Oh heck, I've become an adventurer cliché, huh? Anyway. I should get going. I need to make sure some other people are okay."

"Right, of course. Um . . . *should* I give you a bill?"

It was a real question. Was it right to bill people who fought monsters? And it did seem pretty apparent that the girl who'd limped in here did that.

Deb nodded simply, though. "Yeah, I can leave a phone number or something. I'm easy to get in touch with. Would you accept gold or magic items as payment? Just . . . in case I want to avoid our accountant. Again. Oh, and would you be open to helping us if we need first aid? Just in case."

"Yes!" The vet cleared her throat. Adopted a more professional tone. "Um . . . I mean, yes, that would be acceptable."

"Great. Here." Deb wrote down a number on a scrap of paper from her wallet and handed it over. "Thanks again for your help. Nice to meet you . . . ?"

"Oh! I'm Dr. Marris!" She paused. "Amy, though. If you want. I don't know how to . . . process most of this."

"That's pretty common," Deb admitted with a bob of her head. "I'll be in touch!"

She limped out of the clinic, shaking her head with a tired smile. *One thing after another*, she thought, as she pulled out her phone and messaged the Order's chat server.

"Possible medical contact. Owe her for some help, seems nice. JP, wire me money for the bill, unless you want me giving her magic glasses or something." Blunt social force seemed to be the easiest way to get JP's attention.

Deb closed the app without waiting for a response. Still no contact from anyone at the school. She tried, and mostly failed, to quell the acidic worry in her stomach. It had been hours. She hoped they were okay, but panicked stress filled her as she imagined the dozens of things that could have killed everyone by now. Hell, even just getting past the police line had been a feat she'd need to thank Nate for next time she saw him.

No matter what, Deb thought as she headed back to the operation zone, no matter how messed up her leg was, she was having an easier time than James.

"This is too easy," James said.

They'd been walking for half an hour, on high alert, and it had started to wear on him. On everyone. Keeping their eyes open, ears tuned to even the smallest sound, muscles ready to spring into action in response to an attack, a trap, even just a slight stumble. All of it added up to an exhausting experience. Human bodies weren't really designed for guard duty, and the energy it took to keep constantly rechecking the surrounding environment really burned through any kind of mental focus. The fact that they were all mentally connected through the skull-jacks partially eased the burden, but also added a new layer of stress to it that was mostly novel and a challenge to deal with.

And worst of all was the fact that *nothing was happening.*

As they stole their way forward with rapid footsteps, moving as fast as a walk could take them without tripping over tails or breaking into a jog, through a maze of pipes and unstable floor and pitch-black concrete, the strike team failed to encounter a single thing.

No tiny chittering bugs that tried to bite chunks out of their flesh. No dripping rat-things, liquid sacs ready to burst and spray caustic fluid across them. No gnashing teeth or screaming beasts. No forgotten corpses.

Nothing.

"Agreed," Alanna said, responding to James. "What do we do?"

"Keep moving," Anesh said, voice firm. "It can't be empty. Not entirely."

"It could be. We don't know the rules," Sarah said, voice tense as she stuck close to Alanna. "We never have. We're playing the game blind."

"We keep moving," James agreed with Anesh. "But I think we go a bit faster. Everyone take a few minutes. Battery and water check," he announced.

They paused, taking a moment to double-check the power levels on the phones they were all using as flashlights. They had actual flashlights, too. Small ones, anyway. The entrance hadn't taken away any of their kit, and James kicked himself for not at least trying to bring one of the rifles in here.

He sipped at one of their bottles of water, stretching the soreness out of his legs while everyone else largely did the same. They didn't know how long they had to go, so they were pacing themselves. But it didn't seem like they were going to get any easy answers. James rubbed his eyes, trying to push back the exhaustion, and gradually felt a second wind settle in his chest as they took a short rest. He wasn't close to getting used to this place enough to actually relax, though.

"Okay. Everyone good?" he asked. They'd taken their break largely in silence, no one wanting to waste breath on words, especially if it meant they'd have to breathe in more of the smell afterward.

Everyone agreed, and they started moving again. Faster, this time.

It was ten minutes of a slow jog later that someone called a halt.

No one was too tired to keep going, though Virgil seemed to be largely putting up a façade of athleticism that everyone else had authentically earned through constantly running away from threats to their lives. And the camracondas didn't ever get tired, as far as anyone knew. Maybe they did, but they weren't saying otherwise. Instead, it was Anesh who brought them all up short.

"Hey. Door," he said, swinging his light around to highlight the rusted red metal door embedded in the side of the network of broken pipes and concrete.

James took a second to look at it, and motioned with a nod of his head. Alanna stepped forward while Anesh held the light, and stuck her hand out to the pitted metal of the handle. A red *twelve* flashed in the air over it, and she looked back at the group.

"No." James shook his head. "These are just side rooms, remember? I don't want us getting distracted by every door we pass."

"Could be an access tunnel or something," Simon suggested. "It's not like we have to go in." He said it with the voice of someone who absolutely did not want to go in.

"We could split u—" Dave started to say, and then stopped, holding up his hands to fend off the array of incredulous glares shot in his direction. "Okay!" he acquiesced. "We can't do that!"

"I'm opening it," Alanna said, letting a stream of sparks flow out of her palm and into the door. She shouldered the rusted hulk open with a few jerking blows, and then once it was loosened, stepped back to deliver a kick to the base of the door that swung it inward the rest of the way. "Lights."

They pivoted some of their lights toward the inside of the room, cutting away the inky black. It was a room, too. A single small box of something that might once have been a classroom. The light didn't do much for the blackness on the walls, because that blackness was a creeping dark mold that was gradually consuming the drywall. Instead, it showed off a few rows of single-piece chair-and-desk setups, cramped so close together that there would be no way to walk between them without rearranging the whole room. The teacher's desk at the front was set against a massive blackboard, with a crack down the middle like a fault line, and words and numbers carved into it with what looked like imprecise claw strikes.

There were skeletons in some of the desks; desiccated strands of both flesh and clothing dangled off of them.

Alanna shut the door.

"Okay. No distractions," James ordered. "Let's get moving. It's a straight line to the arena."

They moved on without complaint.

They took breaks every mile or so. A few minutes to recharge before moving on again. Still nothing attacked them, nothing jumped out. They passed by more doors, and one whole side tunnel. But they kept going in a straight line, aiming for where they at least knew there was an exit.

During one of the longer breaks, James found himself talking to Anesh.

"You know," Anesh was saying to him, "the telepads don't work here right now. Since no one can teleport into the area. But they might work in the Office."

James was too tired to quirk an eyebrow. "We know they work in the Office. We've used them before. And once to *leave*, but that was worse than the drop into here," he said instead. "Why do you bring it up?"

"I mean, for the heart," Anesh told him. "That's what we're all thinking, right? That we can actually find the center of this place and stab it?"

"Okay, yeah. When you say it like that it seems insane," James muttered.

"More or less than . . ." Anesh motioned an arm around limply at their surroundings. "Anyway. We could just use the telepads in the Office. Or any dungeon we happen to find. Once we know what to call the center, anyway. Once we know what to write."

"What if they're also protected? Also, holy shit, we need to learn how to protect from stuff like this ourselves," James groaned. "We're so far behind, and we don't even really have context for it. It just feels impossible."

"James, focus. Telepads." Anesh shook his boyfriend lightly by the shoulders, then grimaced and wiped off whatever drying fluid had been on his coat. "We can protect against a lot of stuff with a moon base."

". . . You lost me. No, wait." James held up his index finger, closing his eyes for a moment while he thought. "Okay, I'm caught up. No. That's pointlessly dangerous," he countered, looking around for anyone else who looked like they had the energy to back him up. "Sarah, do you want a moon base?" he asked his friend.

Sarah and Frequency-of-Sunlight paused the conversation they were having, looked over at James, then back at each other. They did this twice.

"What is a moon?" Frequency asked, her digital voice bouncing loudly off the nearby pipes. It would have alerted every monster nearby, if there'd been anything to alert.

"The bright white light in the sky at night? The big one? That's the moon," Sarah filled her in. "It's actually a rock orbiting the Earth and I just realized you guys probably didn't get taught orbital mechanics. Okay. We'll come back to that. James, are you guys ready to go? We're just gossiping about camraconda sex over here if the break's over."

"Why." Dave and Cold-Wind-Friction asked with a single unified voice.

"This could save our lives, Dave!" Sarah's serious protest was a shattered illusion with the smile she wore on her face. "I now grow stronger by learning about—!"

"Yeah, okay. Let's go," James agreed, cutting off that line of conversation and pushing himself off the cleanest pipe he could find that he'd chosen as a bench. "Anesh, if we survive this, we can work out the limits of the telepads. I swear to you, I will make that happen for you. I love you, and I will give you a research budget or something. Now everyone make sure you've got your grim stolen knives, and let's go."

Another three miles before they got anywhere. James counted himself lucky that he normally dealt with a dungeon that encouraged much longer treks, otherwise his legs would have given out by now. And when they finally did get to that room lit in flickering, sticky orange firelight? When they all flicked off their lights, pulled their weapons, moved into a ready combat position, and prepared to fight for their lives?

They stepped out into an empty arena.

No jeering, snapping crowds of ratroaches in the "stands." No single monster to greet them with a knife and an offer of an easy exit. Just an empty floor, freshly carpeted in crushed gravel from their last visit, with an unguarded rusty iron portcullis and those standing tilted lockers over by the exit hole.

"Anyone got any green sparks?" James asked grimly into the silence, motioning to the lockers as his voice echoed flatly like he was all by himself in a gym.

"Where the hell *is* everything?" Anesh asked, confused, arms falling to his sides, stolen makeshift knives dangling loosely in his grip.

Alanna strode past them as they fanned out to search the room. Dave hopped up into one of the stands with a boost from Sarah, checking around the hewed stone benches with a shrug. James just stood there, trying to work out what the hell was going on while they failed to turn anything up.

"Anyone wanna go home?" Alanna asked, voice weary as she held out a hand to the portcullis. "Exit's still *there*, it's just . . . no one's here."

James tapped at his chin, staring at the ground while everyone turned to look at him for an answer. "No," he eventually said. "There's still something wrong here. Let's keep looking. Virgil, you've been mapping this whole place, right? Not that it isn't mostly just a straight awful line." The other man nodded, tapping at his laptop. "*Why* is it empty?" James demanded.

"We don't . . . know?" Dave asked, wary.

"No, I mean, that's the point," James said. "Why is the dungeon empty, and upstairs the real world is full of monsters? What the fuck changed down here? And, if we're in the clear from name eaters and rabid critters, why the hell haven't we found any corpses? You remember what those kids said. Like, eight students came down here earlier today. *Where are they?* No, we're not leaving. We double back to that turn, and keep checking. Unless anyone has an actual explanation?"

No one did. So, they did what was becoming a strange usual routine. Took a break, then moved out.

Half an hour later, when they found another empty arena, James was starting to get annoyed.

"I can *feel* something," he hissed out. "We were getting closer. But it's not here. What's going on?"

"No, I got it too." Alanna nodded, and a glance at Dave and Anesh showed they had similar reactions.

They were standing in the middle of another one of the exit arenas, though this one had polished wood for its floor. It could have been elegant, or at least a usable basketball court, if it didn't also have intentionally jagged splinters and rusted nails pointing upward every few feet. The gate here was a single slab of granite, also eager to charge them a few hundred red sparks to, presumably, head back to reality.

James idly flipped the knife in his hands. "Okay," he said. "We're getting closer. Let's backtrack to the last intersection, and try again. Virgil, still good on battery?"

"I'm plugged into the Lair's power, so yes."

"Wait, what?"

Virgil shrugged. "I brought the power strip that's connected to itself no matter how far the distance is. The laptop has infinite power."

"Did you . . . and I can't believe I'm saying this ten miles deep into a dungeon . . . did you bring an iPhone charger?" Alanna asked him.

"I don't use an iPhone."

She rapped her knuckles together in amused surprise. "That's not what I asked!"

"I've got one," Sarah cut in, before casualties began to mount. "We can switch off as we go, if it matters. But we should get moving. I feel something too, and it's . . . weird."

"Right, you've got more delve time than all of us, huh?" Alanna nodded.

"Not really," Sarah admitted. "I've spent more time inside a dungeon, but I think there's a difference when you're a prisoner. Like, Frequency and Friction don't have the same sense you guys do, and they literally grew up there."

"Same with Magneto," Simon added from where he was watching the door back to the tunnel, deliberately running his fingers through the magnetic field of the mongausse.

"We see feel more and less," Frequency-of-Sunlight confirmed in her makeshift English. "Nothing special. Cannot hear the interference you can."

James nodded. "Okay. Well. Next time we hit an intersection, we should try to lean into that. Let's go."

More tunnels. More pipes. They skipped over doors in the walls and a hatch in the floor. They passed by a question about bats written in blood on one of the small patches of exposed concrete around them, which Dave answered without thinking, earning him a flaring addition of a few green sparks. They still failed to find anything trying to fight them.

When they hit the next intersection, they waited for the more experienced delvers, the ones who had been inside Officium Mundi long enough that they were starting to develop these strange new instincts, to stand in front and try to feel for where they needed to be. They chose a direction, and started out again.

The next time they took a break, they ran out of water.

"Why didn't anyone bring a bottle that's connected to the faucet back at the lair?" Anesh joked. "Virgil brought infinite power. It just seems reasonable that we have an endless supply of all our basic resources attended to by literal magic."

"It's not infinite, it's . . ." No one listened to Virgil pedantically correct the statement.

Alanna cut him off, mostly unintentionally. "Oh man, we should have brought the lunchbox of holding!" she announced, the humorous realization restoring some of her mental energy for a brief flash.

James laughed. "Oh, hell, that's a really good point. We should test if that thing keeps food fresh, too. If it does, we could have an emergency ration pack for any kind of, you know . . ."

"Thirty-mile hike through a dungeon that smells like shit?" Dave asked.

"Okay, when you say it like that, I don't really want lunch," James admitted.

"How's your feeling, by the way?" Dave asked. "Mine kinda went away."

"Same," James said. "Though it really felt like there was *anything* this way."

"Light shown in far distance," Cold-Wind-Friction chimed in from where he was keeping watch on the upcoming tunnel. "Something is ahead."

"Okay. Well. If this one turns out to be nothing, we can leave," James announced. "Being stuck down here dying of dehydration doesn't seem like a winning move. Everyone ready? One more go."

They were. They started moving again, even Virgil, who was currently lagging behind and using the skulljack Wi-Fi connection to *text everyone complaints*. James put a stop to that pretty quickly by transitioning to using the text overlay system to keep a running tally of things they passed for "statistical analysis," correctly guessing that Virgil's untampered *need* for organization would prevent him from cluttering up a useful source of information.

They approached at a walk, not wanting to rush and be tired for what might be an actual confrontation. And it turned out to be something of a good call, when they made it to the tunnel's mouth.

There were bodies lying here, just on the threshold of whatever lay beyond.

What lay beyond was actually difficult to see. It looked like another arena, but the light was cold, like it was covered in a thick fog that their flashlights weren't enough to overcome. But unlike the others, this one lay on the other side of a *door*.

The door was huge. They'd sort of noticed, on approach, that the corridor around them had been getting wider, but here it opened up to something almost cavernous. Just to support this massive steel blockade. It looked like a hatch, or the door you might see on a bank vault; and unlike everything else in this place, it was *pristine*. Untarnished metal, untouched by anything hostile, sitting down here alone in the tunnels.

It was also sitting open.

The bodies were exactly who James feared they would be. The strike team moved up cautiously, with both camracondas on watch to freeze anything that might even pretend to be a trap, but nothing jumped out. The lack of an ambush just put James more on edge as he knelt down and rolled over one of the limp forms.

"High school kid. Just a teenager," he said, his nose filled with the scent of blood now added to the aroma of the dungeon.

Nearby, Sarah checked on another one, while the rest of the team examined the door. "Looks safe to go through?" Alanna muttered. "What happened here?"

There was a metallic *ping*, a noise that cut through the rest of the dripping, creaking sounds of this sewer. James looked over to where Anesh scuffed his boot against the ground again, getting a repetition of the sound, before bending down and plucking a small object off the floor.

"Bullet casing?" he said, confusion in his voice.

James moved his hands down the prone corpse in front of him. The kid bore wounds that spoke of this place's monsters. Bites, scrapes on the arms under a torn hoodie, bloodied knuckles, and a massive bruise around one unblinking cold eye that looked an awful lot like he'd run into a wall. No phone, no weapons, no anything; when he'd come in, either he'd done so totally unarmed, or the interdiction had still been in effect. And then, James found the lethal strike.

"This kid was shot," James announced. "That's what killed him." He looked over to the next corpse, and saw a similar red starburst stain on the chest of the football jersey that one was wearing. "Him too."

"How did anyone—" Anesh started to say before he was cut off.

A half-gasped scream startled all of them. "I know this guy!" Sarah suddenly said as she composed herself, jerking back like she'd just touched something that shocked her. "This is . . . this is Scott!"

"What?" Dave and James chorused together, both of them moving closer along with Simon to shine an extra light on the student's face.

It was, undoubtedly, one of the two kids they'd saved from Status Quo not even a week ago.

"I never actually met him. What the fuck is he doing here?" James demanded, staring down at the dead kid's face. "*How* did we miss this? Who *shot him?!*"

"Better question," Simon asked in a small whisper of a voice that almost went unnoticed. "Why is he smiling?"

James scowled. "Why weren't we keeping an eye on him? What the hell happened?"

"Lua was watching him at the hospital," Simon said. "When she and Momo came back, they brought the other one, but Scott had his sister there with him."

Alanna snapped her fingers in a rapid staccato, the noise startling half the group. "His what?" she demanded, pointing at Simon.

"His . . . sister?" the man repeated slowly. James was suddenly struck by just how out of his depth Simon looked, and wondered if he had the same expression on his own face. "Graham stayed at the Lair for a while, after Status Quo, but he went to stay with Scott when . . ."

"When he left," James stated. "Because he couldn't stay with his parents anymore. Because?"

"Because Status Quo relocated their families," Sarah murmured, eyes going wide. "And wiped their memories. So they didn't have anyone left."

"So *who the fuck* picked Scott up from the hospital?" James asked. ". . . and where's Graham now?" The other teenaged delver certainly wasn't among the dead here.

A shiver of chilled fear passed around the group, and everyone turned their eyes back to the ajar vault door.

"One way to find out," James said, rising, and gingerly stepped over the fallen bodies. He approached the vault door, rested a hand on it, and applied a little pressure just to make sure he'd have some advance warning if it was going to slam shut on him. Then, with a deep breath and a worried glance back at everyone behind him, he slipped through the gap.

He flicked his light off as he stepped into the room. It was useless in the cold glow of the interior, anyway. Not just because it didn't shine over the ambient light, but also because the room was *huge*, on a scale that James was having trouble comprehending.

It felt like he'd stepped outside. But not onto anywhere on Earth. No, there wasn't a vista on the planet that could make him feel as *small* as this room did, and that counted the time he'd almost fallen into the Grand Canyon on a family vacation.

The floor was smooth, a material something like concrete, tinted slightly blue by the hostile cold of the light that emanated from no-where and everywhere. It stretched off for what felt like hundreds of miles, into the far distance. Maybe thousands. Maybe more. There was no horizon. There was no orienting line where angles of visibility stopped. Overhead, the ceiling was simultaneously too close, and too huge, to feel anything other than a sensation of being crushed. The entire room was filled with a feeling of being all too real. Like the concept of "a very large room" had been dropped here and left to wait for them.

The party fit inside easily.

"What the fuuuuuck . . ."

Dave might have meant to mouth the words more than say them, but they came out anyway. Beside him, Cold-Wind-Friction pressed against Dave's legs, both the camracondas trying to keep themselves as rooted to the ground as possible.

James empathized with that. It did feel like he could just float away at any second here.

"There's something over there." Alanna pointed off in a random direction. James followed the line of her finger, and sure enough, there was . . . well, it was just a spot. It could have been miles away, but it was there. Somewhere out there. He glanced back again at their entry point, and jerked in surprise to see that the room extended around the massive vault door. The door itself was just perched in the middle of the flat plane, like everything else. A portal back to a realm that itself had only one open portal back to reality.

"Virgil," James commanded. "Keep that fucking mapping pro-gram going."

"I'm doing it manually using—"

"Just . . . dude, just don't let us get lost in here. If we lose track of the door and can't telepad out, we're dead. Slowly."

"Right . . ."

"Let's go," Alanna said, taking the lead. "And no one break off. I don't wanna lose anyone here."

They huddled close together as they crossed the open plain, no one wanting to accidentally wander off and lose sight of the group. Not that it would be possible, really; they could see things out to a million miles away. But it *felt* possible. Like they were only one misstep away from getting lost in the enormity of the place.

And it was, lacking any other defining features, enormous.

The walk went on for so long, one of the camracondas got tired.

They stopped to rest a dozen times, and still, the one thing they could see in the distance didn't appear much closer. By the third rest, James was thirsty. By the tenth, no one had said a word for an hour. Even Frequency-of-Sunlight, who would often make small comments or ask little questions about odd things, had lapsed into quiet.

The only noise that broke up the hike was the echoing impacts of their footfalls on the floor. Or, in two cases, just a constant soft scraping from slithering across it.

By the time the object started appearing to grow larger, James's feet hurt so badly, he just wanted to sit down for a week. No one else was in better shape. They'd long ago left everything that wasn't needed for a straight-up fight back at one of their rest sites, lightening their load as far as it would go. But they'd easily hiked, jogged, and sprinted a combined total of twenty or thirty miles today. It was just an estimate, but it sure *felt* accurate. So less carry weight could only go so far.

When they got close, it happened rapidly. All of a sudden, James's eyes resolved on what they were approaching, and then, they were practically *there*. No time to rest, to recoup. Just a sudden arrival, due to a misjudged distance in this bizarre, endless, massive place.

The single difference in the endless floor was a pyramid of stone steps. At its peak, arms stretched up into the air, was the soft figure of a familiar curly-haired pudgy high school student that James had rescued. Graham stood with his back to the group, but James still recognized him almost right away, just based on the context of what was going on. The teenager didn't react to the sounds of footsteps, heavy breathing, magnetic distortion, or tails slithering on concrete.

At the base of the pyramid—which was only maybe six steps tall, and nothing like the monolithic stairs Dave had carved out of the grounds of the school overhead—were two things. The first was a gun. It lay on the ground where it had been dropped, slide racked open to show that the last bullet had been fired. It wasn't like any gun that James had ever seen, though it was undeniably a firearm. A sleek black piece of hardware, with too many low angles in it to ever be comfortable to grip, and a trigger too far forward to be stable. This was a strange creation of a weapon that felt closer to a failed experiment than a gun. And it *did* feel off to him, when he looked at it.

Not as off as he felt when he looked at the other thing, though.

"Oh look, visitors!" the girl spoke, voice outwardly cheerful, but with an undercurrent of promised violence that made James's teeth itch.

She was tall, with long red hair that dropped thick curls down over her shoulders. A round, grinning face with wide eyes looked at the approaching party the way a cat would a mouse. She was also short, with trimmed-back black hair and ears that looked a little too large against the sides of her narrow skull. She was well-muscled, she was rail-thin, she had ivory skin and she had an almost ashen complexion.

James grimaced, tilted his head sideways, slapped himself, and looked at her again.

She was a lot of things. That's what she looked like, really. A lot of things. A human composition, but not a human. Not like they normally came, anyway.

"Oh, interesting." She hummed in five different voices, though James only actually heard one, even if he knew the others were there. "You shouldn't have been able to see that."

"What are you doing here?" James asked.

"Helping!" she replied unhelpfully.

"Wow, yeah, walked into that one," he muttered.

Sarah stepped up next to him. "You're Scott's 'older sister,' aren't you?" she asked. Her voice echoed against the open concrete around them, before muffling itself against the endless expanse.

"For a while, yes!" The girl giggled, bright and oppressive in the cold light. "And you . . . mmmh. Yes. You're a prisoner, aren't you?"

Sarah frowned, but said nothing.

"Such an interesting collection, come to see my—"

"Please, stop talking," James cut her off, and turned slightly to face the rest of his group, purposefully ignoring the thing's mock gasp of indignation. "What do we do here?" he asked them.

"Graham's doing something," Dave pointed out. "That thing isn't . . . normal."

"Grab the kid, run." Alanna shrugged. "Get him away from her, anyway." She inclined her head toward the grinning woman standing between them and the pyramid.

James tilted his head back. "Hey, are you here to fight us?" he asked.

"Not at all!" she happily admitted in a way that made James's spine ache.

"Okay. So, we're—"

"But I'm going to anyway. Alas! We cannot have things the easy way!" Her grin hadn't slipped, but she also now wore a frown, and a thin line of a mouth, and a scowl. "You brought me this delightful opportunity. So I think I'll let you walk away. I can feel the movement tool you have on you; go ahead, get out. I won't stop you. But you're not interrupting."

Movement. She said the word, and James's eyes unconsciously flickered over to Anesh and Dave, who were carrying their group's exit telepads. Anesh caught his eye, and gave an almost imperceptible shake of the head.

"Problem," Cold-Wind-Friction stated as the woman continued to patiently tap her foot and hum to herself while she waited for them to decide.

"What?" James asked, glancing down at the camraconda.

"She moves."

"Yeah, she . . . wait." He narrowed his eyes. "You're freezing her."

"Both of us." Cold-Wind-Friction said, not breaking eye contact with the woman. "She moves."

"Hm. Might be the only reason she isn't trying to kill us right away, though. Keep it up," James muttered. "Alanna." James got her attention, and jerked one thumb out to the left. She nodded and started moving around the woman, while James began circling her from the right.

"Oh, well this hardly seems polite!" she exclaimed, like they were at a tea party and not in the heart of some monstrous sewer network.

James took the blunt approach as he slid a knife out of his belt and tested its weight in his off hand, his right going to the grip of the gun in his coat. "What are you?" he asked her, directly, still trying to look through the mess of *things* she was projecting but only getting the impression that he was supposed to be looking at a woman who was dangerous.

"Beyond you," she said, and it sounded like the first honest words she'd said all night.

"Let's find out." James snapped his hand up, and started shooting.

He and Alanna stood at a wide angle around the woman, so that his partner was kept out of his line of fire when the bullets started. Not that it would have mattered; James didn't miss much these days. His upgraded Aim adjusted his arm automatically, and the shots flew exactly where they—

The woman was *gone*. She just moved, taking a light step forward with casual grace, but at a speed that James could barely track. He adjusted his aim, somehow instinctively compensating for how fast she was, put three shots around where she *could* move, and then had a sudden problem as she turned and rushed him.

One shot hit home, splattering through her arm and spilling something that was almost blood behind her as she flew through the air toward James. But instead of red, it was silver, and smelled like gunpowder. Then she slapped the gun out of his hand, and he felt bones grind against each other with the impact as he was disarmed.

She was right there in front of him, mirage flesh and a massive grin, and James knew instantly that she could hit him fast enough to kill him outright. He didn't even have the energy to try to dodge as he saw her fist ball up.

Which made it good timing that the mongausse chose that moment to hit her from the side, causing the fight to lose all sense of order or planning.

Despite not technically having mass, the magnetic dog bowled her over, ethereal jaws snapping at her face in a way that almost seemed to concern her more than the gun had. But then the two of them skidded to a stop, and the woman had come out on top, in a crouched position with one hand holding the mongausse by the throat. She jerked her arm back, and *flung*. Magneto sailed through the ranks of the strike team that were charging her, hitting the floor two hundred feet away and rolling for another fifty, making distorted pained whines the whole way.

The two camracondas fanned out, doing their best to push her momentum toward zero, but while they seemed able to keep her explosive bursts of motion from being too powerful or frequent, they weren't actually able to stop them from happening. Dave planted his feet before the woman and lashed out with one of their stolen spears, but she just punched through the haft of it, shattering the weapon and nailing him in the ribs. The extra force of the strike sent him staggering backward.

While his companion was gasping and trying to stay upright, Simon ducked around Dave's flailing form and tried to stab at the woman. She laughed with contempt and shifted backward, easily avoiding the strike with footwork alone. But her enemies kept moving forward as a unit. James tapped into the local Wi-Fi network with his skulljack, still operating out of that laptop, and they started coordinating wordlessly, sending Alanna around to keep her hemmed in, even in this massive open space.

Dave recovered and took another swing at her in unison with Simon, their timing perfectly set up to push the woman to use one of her bursts of speed. She did exactly that, twisting to the side like a dancer, laughing in delight as the two men almost hit each other. Her foot lashed out as she moved to catch Simon's own, imparting enough force through the impact to flip him onto his face with just the edge of her toes.

But then she was where Sarah wanted her.

A magnetic snap was all the warning anyone had before a spike of wood splattered through the woman's leg, tearing it out from under her. She sprawled to the ground in a gory liquid metal mess, but managed to catch herself with a single hand, then flipped over and was gone before the second spike scored a line on the concrete.

James rushed to the spot where she reappeared, his teeth clenched and his knives out. They didn't need to kill her, he reminded them through the link. Just keep her away. A silent order sent Sarah moving up to the pyramid to retrieve the kid, while the rest of them kept the fight going.

"Interesting," the woman said, eyes narrowing, then flickering between James, Sarah, and finally settling on Virgil, still in the back rank with one of the camracondas. He had a club, but he was far more useful keeping the network smoothly running and the group organized than actually fighting here. Just being able to know where the camraconda sight lines were was enough; hell, it was the only thing making this a *fight* and not just a mass execution. "You're cheating," she accused mildly.

James wanted to say something witty, but he was basically out of strength at this point, so he saved his breath and just flung a knife at her before pulling another one out of a coat pocket. She slapped it aside without looking, and then, without James really understanding where she got it from, she drew a weapon.

It was a just a rifle. An old bolt-action, clip-fed, from before even semiautomatics were common. But there was something wrong with it. It wasn't really a rifle at all; it was a part of her. Just like she was a pastiche of appearing human, the gun was an amalgamation of what it meant to be a bolt-action rifle. It wasn't just her rifle, it was *her, the rifle*. And underneath the simple exterior aesthetic, it felt very, very similar to the one that was lying nearby on the floor.

When she aimed it, James's eyes went wide. "Virgil!" he screamed out, diving forward to try to intercept, to throw her aim off, to do *anything*.

The shot punched a hole through Virgil just like a normal gun would. There was a brief flicker on their network, and then, the wide-eyed blond-haired man in their back rank toppled to the ground like a puppet with his strings cut. Blood poured out of the wound in his chest, but he was already dead. The laptop at his side clattered to the concrete with him, and the woman sniffed lightly and raised an eyebrow before she put another round through that, too.

The skulljack link cut off. But at this point, James wasn't listening to it anyway. He was too busy rushing the thing that had just shot one of his people.

Alanna came in from the opposite angle. The woman, standing on a single intact leg, slipped the gun back to wherever it had come from as she turned to grin at James. The shots had seemed to exhaust her. For a little while, she was . . . weaker, perhaps.

She seemed almost surprised when James slammed a knife into her throat, even though she had only milliseconds earlier successfully grabbed Alanna's strike and snapped Alanna's forearm in the process. Just casually pinching down with her thumb and two forefingers until muscle ripped and bone snapped and blood sprayed. But the Order wasn't done, and Simon came in, sliding into a tackle that took her leg out from under her and sprawled both of them onto the ground.

James, Dave, and even a wounded Alanna all piled on, pinning the woman down with knees and knives in a furious attempt to contain her.

Doing so was a mistake. The carefully maintained lines of sight for the camracondas, devoid of the backup of the skulljacks for planning and visualization, were broken all too rapidly.

The woman flowed like water, a million pieces of a human pooling backward and reassembling themselves near the base of the pyramid in the blink of an eye. This time, she carefully kept herself flickering with motion to wherever the camracondas couldn't see her; though the two of them began circling too, and soon at least one of them would be able to lock her down.

The strike team formed a crescent around the monster. And behind her, James saw Sarah exhaustedly surmounting the last step of the pyramid. They just needed to keep her attention for a few moments longer.

The woman looked back at them. Her wounds had magically healed, and she still wore that arrogant grin, but all the same she seemed diminished from before. "Children," she scoffed. "Playing my game. Playing with my toys. How very rude of you."

"I didn't see any posted signs," James called back. "Maybe you should have explained the rules first!"

She laughed and laughed, throwing dozens of heads back to let out the sound of bells. "Oh dear, no!" The thing chuckled. "That's the first rule of them all! The only thing that keeps you safe," her voice took on an instant and very dark edge, "is your ignorance."

Then she leapt forward, and the fight renewed in earnest.

Up on the pyramid, Sarah crawled around to Graham's front to face the kid. He was still standing there, arms raised, face looking upward. He didn't acknowledge her approach at all, so she glanced up to look at what he saw, and instantly regretted it.

He was reaching for something wrong. A point where the universe had lost its grip. A crystalized piece of everything and nothing. It was raw, unmitigated potential. Bound only by the imagination.

It was absolutely not something a human was supposed to be touching.

"Graham," Sarah whispered to him, shaking him lightly. "Wake up. We gotta go."

He didn't look at her, but he did answer. "I can't," he said.

"What? No, come on. We need to run before she kills anyone else."

"She won't kill anyone. She's nice. She's Scott's sister." His voice was somewhat monotone.

"I doubt that very much!" Sarah hissed at him, peering down at where the thing that absolutely was *not* the late Scott's sister was slamming Simon into the ground, holding him by the back of his head as she hammered him into the floor before one-handedly tossing him into Frequency-of-Sunlight. "Please! We need to get out of here, and deal with the dungeon before it kills any more people!"

"The dungeon can't kill anyone anymore," Graham informed her. "I'm dealing with it."

She looked at him, shocked. "What?" was all Sarah could think to ask.

"Scott showed me how to get here. And his sister gave me the tool to open the door. Now I own this space. The dungeon can't hurt anyone now." He said it like it was all perfectly logical. His voice was as calm as if he were discussing doing homework or eating ice cream.

Sarah winced as she heard bone breaking and light laughter. "You shot them?" she asked, horrified. "You killed Scott, and the others?"

"We had to open the door." Graham sounded confused, like it was obvious, like it should have been obvious even to himself. "What . . . Scott?"

Below the pyramid, the woman took one of their knives and shoved it through Dave's armor. Only the first inch penetrated his left breast before the shoddy construction of the makeshift weapon broke it apart, but he still screamed, unfamiliar pain causing him to drop and claw at the wound. The gap in the line of people fighting gave the thing an opportunity, and it capitalized upon it by flashing past Anesh, leaving another dropped blade embedded in his upper arm before appearing behind Cold-Wind-Friction.

Frequency-of-Sunlight howled a warning in a digital voice, staring at the woman-shaped monster. James was already staggering into another rush to force her to at least focus on him. But it didn't matter. She'd identified the camraconda as a threat that she could solve now. Cold-Wind-Friction whipped around and caught her in his gaze, slowing her down enough that the blade of her hand just sent him reeling and didn't tear his head off, but as he jerked back, the woman pulled a cavalry pistol out of nothing and shot him through the base of his head. A retort sounded and the bullet punched through cables and camera, and the camraconda flopped backward unmoving.

"Scott's dead!" Sarah said, her voice breaking into a shrill scream. "And the people up on the surface. People are dying! Graham, whatever you're doing, the dungeon isn't *gone*. It just isn't *here*. You're not saving anyone!"

"Oh, dear." The voice from behind Sarah made her eyes go wide, but she didn't turn around.

"Graham," she said as calmly as she could. "I know you can let go. No one's mad at you. But we need you . . ." Her eyes flicked up to that point of nothing and everything, that *thing* that was, blatantly, the point from which this whole dungeon had grown. "We need you to put it back. To let it back in. And then I need you to *run!*"

The last word came out as a strangled noise as the creature picked Sarah up by the throat, stared at her for a second, and then turned and flung her down into the ground at the base of the pyramid.

Sarah had a brief moment of realizing she was in freefall before she hit the concrete headfirst and felt something inside her break. She tried to roll to her feet, but her legs weren't obeying her. Nothing was, actually. Distantly, she heard James screaming something in a hoarse voice. And then, some kind of rushing noise; the sound of dripping pipes and molten mold all flowing back into place. She heard Graham crying, wailing that he was sorry, over and over, heard the thing-that-was-not-a-woman scream in frustration, before that noise was abruptly cut off. She tilted her eyes as far up as she could, and saw Virgil's body on the floor, about thirty feet away. Cold-Wind-Friction, too. There were orbs next to each of them, hovering lightly over the different forms of blood.

Her heart ached. People were dying again. Just like last time. Sarah didn't even remember the last time, she just knew it had happened, and it was all coming to pass again. She'd known this would be a mistake, but she'd trusted James. She could just barely see James's legs as he sprinted toward her.

Oh, poor James. He was going to hate himself for this, Sarah thought as she closed her eyes. The rushing noise pooled in to fill her ears, until there was nothing else. Just the feeling of a hand on her shoulder, and a small spark of something forced into her. And then, everything went black.

For both of them.

The most interesting thing about waking up at all was that James hadn't expected to do it. But now that consciousness was returning, he felt like he'd forgotten something important. That wakefulness, though, was just enough to let his body properly react to the sinking terror that was plaguing him in his dreams.

Heart racing, James jerked upright in bed, sucking in a massive, gasping breath of air. The remnants of a nightmare clung to him like spiderwebs, but he'd already forgotten the details. He held a hand to his chest, panting, and felt something tug on his fingers.

Then he realized that he felt like he'd been hit by a truck.

Repeatedly.

James looked around. He was in one of the Lair's bedrooms; the lights were on, which was weird. He must have been unconscious and just recently dumped here. But then his eyes landed on the IV drip next to the bed, and the tubes going into his arm and one of those monitor things on his finger. He . . . didn't have an explanation for that one. He looked down at himself, throwing the sheet back, and saw a cast on his left leg, and another on his right hand. They'd both been signed. A lot. And they *itched*.

What the hell?

He rolled sideways, kicking his feet off the edge of the bed. He had underwear on, and also a coat of bandages, so he wasn't technically naked. That was good enough. James gingerly settled his feet onto the floor and, using the IV stand as a cane, started walking himself to the door.

The hallway was certainly familiar. He really was in the Lair's basement. Either that, or having a massive trauma-induced hallucination. But James figured a hallucination would hurt a hell of a lot less than this. It felt like a metal spike was being driven into his leg, constantly.

He'd almost made it to the elevator when he got caught. To be fair, he got caught when the doors opened, and Anesh and Alanna had stepped out. "Oh, *hell* no," Alanna instantly said, and in short order he was half-ushered, half-carried back to his room and bed.

"What happened?" James demanded as soon as he was able to get words to form properly.

"Okay. Well. What's the last thing you remember?" Alanna asked him. She'd pulled up a chair next to his bed, and from the way she and Anesh moved, James got the distinct impression that they had *favorite chairs* here in this room.

"Sarah dying," James said, without thinking about it. "I remember . . . trying to do something. And the dungeon coming back? And then I blacked out."

Anesh nodded. "Almost right. Sarah's not dead, let's get that out of the way. *You* nearly were, though."

"You fucking dumbass," Alanna added, for flavor.

A wave of relief made it much easier for James to focus. "What?" he said limply, still not really focusing that *much*. It was easier, not easy.

"Sarah broke her neck, and a lot of other things. You, in an effort to stabilize her, dumped about three months' worth of whatever 'rest' is into her," Anesh explained. "Now, we know that 'rest' isn't exactly sleep, because that *would* have outright killed you. But you either dipped too deep, or you wrote a check that should have bounced, because *you* have been unconscious for two months, and unhealing for the first one."

"Oh." James leaned back into his pillow with a sigh of relief. "Okay. Good. Is Sarah . . . okay?"

"She can walk, if that's what you're asking," Alanna said. "Whatever you did kept her alive, and Frequency stabilized her until we got to a hospital. It was close, but you really did save her life."

"What happened after that?" James probed.

"You should rest."

He snorted. "Come on. I've been asleep for months. Let's do this."

"Graham restored the dungeon. Whatever he'd been tricked into doing, he was pushing the native dungeon out of its space, which is why it was in the real world. Sarah got him to undo it, and all the monsters and weird shit dragged back in, mostly. Some of the stuff like the mold or broken furniture or . . . um . . . monster corpses . . . are still out and about."

"Uh-oh," James groaned.

Alanna nodded. "Yeah. That's probably bad."

"It's not that bad," Anesh countered. "No one knows what to do with them. The FBI was onsite—the *actual* FBI—and Nate made contact with them. They're now sort of aware of us in a more official capacity, and we're classified as a special consultant group, just so you know. Someone will absolutely be wanting to be talking to you now that you're awake."

"Why?"

"You're our leader, asshole," Alanna informed him. "Even if we did make the call to work for the feds without you. But in our defense, you were dead."

Anesh nodded. "Yes, that. All of that." He kept going, though, rattling off points rapid-fire. "We've only done three Office runs since you've been down. Mostly to hold up the bargain with the doctor to provide more hearts, and to replenish our telepad supply and a few other orbs. Momo thinks she can maybe make a teleport defense thing, but I think she's having a laugh. Graham's been locked up here since the incident, by the way. He's not our prisoner, he just won't leave. Blames himself for everything."

"I should talk to him," James said quietly.

"No, you should nap," Alanna reminded him. "You can talk when you're a hundred percent again."

"That's never going to happen." James smiled ruefully. "This is my fault. I should have been better. People died because I didn't pay more attention to . . . everything."

Alanna slapped him on the top of the head. Hard. James yelped while she lectured him. "It's not your fault when other people make choices!" she announced with fire in her voice. "You can do your best, but ultimately, other humans get to have a say in things too! And sometimes they fuck up!" Her face twisted into a sad snarl. "Sometimes we fuck up," she said, quieter.

"Virgil and Cold-Wind-Friction had funerals," Anesh told him. "They . . . we said goodbye."

"They shouldn't have . . ." James stopped. Of course they shouldn't have died. But they did. They had. He could sit here and bemoan it, or he could pick himself up and try to do right by them. "Okay." He breathed out. "Sorry. What else is going on? Is the world panicking over the dungeon thing? What did the news see?"

"It got talked about as a school shooting gone horribly wrong. Everyone forgot about it in a month." Anesh clenched a fist in front of his face before looking up at James. "Your country sucks," he said. "You know, if we link up, we technically all have Canadian citizenship, and we can just *leave*."

"No way I'm explaining that to the border guard," Alanna ribbed at him.

"Oh. We opened our link." Anesh snapped his fingers as he remembered. "We can share awareness, and at a pretty high range too."

Alanna shrugged. "As long as we can hear each other. Which makes cell phones kinda powerful. As has ever been the case." Now she snapped her fingers. "Someone retrieved your phone, so you know."

"Attic's doing okay, too," Anesh added. "I dunno if Sarah ever told you, but she calls it Clutter Ascent, which is kinda cool."

Alanna gave a short *heh*. "Yeah, it's nice. Deb and Alex mostly took over managing that one for now. It's very . . . kind. Comforting.

They're trying to encourage it. I guess that's something we can actually do, huh? Weird to think about." She looked at James. "Um . . . what else. The pandemic got worse?"

"Oh, *good*," James drawled out. "That makes everything so much better!"

"Well, it does mean no one's at the building you used to work in. So getting in has been a lot easier."

"Wait, so like . . . is everyone dead? Is this the end of the world?" James tensed up. "I'll be honest, I assumed it'd be something dungeon-related. Is the plague magic?"

Anesh corrected him. "No, it's just that everyone has to stay home." He shrugged. "It's not like it's too bad. Though it does suck not being able to go out to eat anymore." He looked over at Alanna. "Is there anything else? What am I forgetting."

Alanna stared at James, her eyes worried. "Are *you* okay?" she asked her boyfriend.

James thought about it for a while.

People had died because he'd led them to a fight they weren't prepared for. They'd learned more in that time about the dungeon than they had in the last year, though. They'd also saved who-knew-how-many lives. He thought back to interviewing Virgil, and how he'd said that he wasn't ready to die to make the world better, but he'd still be up for the small stuff. That smug jackass had helped to put a living nightmare back in its bottle and kept an unknown number of people from their own grim fates. It was . . . well, it wasn't fair. But it probably never would be.

"I'm not okay," he settled on. "But I will be. What happened to the woman?" James asked.

"Gone," Alanna told him. "Soon as Graham came to his senses and the dungeon came back, she was fucking out of there."

"So, what was she?"

"As near as anyone can tell?" Anesh laughed. "Nothing. She was a ghost."

"Ghosts aren't that well-armed," James protested. "She had a gun that . . . I think she seriously overestimated our defenses, because

I could *feel* the thing from fifty feet away. And she pulled it out of nowhere. I think she also supplied the gun that Graham . . . used."

Anesh hummed. "Graham said that Scott's sister gave him the gun. And she and Scott had learned how to kill the dungeon, but they needed his help." He cleared his throat, looking away for a second while he composed himself. "I think he was hypnotized, or something like it. Or maybe Scott was, and spread it to him, like a memetic hazard. He sure as hell spread it to the other six kids they took down with them into the dungeon. And then Graham just . . . shot them all. To open the last door."

"Why?"

"He doesn't remember. All he knows is that it had something to do with a secret door."

"Oh shit! Secret!" James exclaimed. "What happened to him?"

"Oh. He, and you'll love this, he got *lost*." Alanna cracked a grin, dispelling the dark mood for a minute while she looked at James's disbelieving face. "Yeah! Turns out, when all the maps are public and everyone knows how to get places, Secret can't take directions for shit! He ended up in the gym, cloaked a whole bunch of kids from one of the skullballs, and then hid until Nate found him. Oh, Nate wants hazard pay because he fought the skullball with his bare hands, and *I* think we should pay someone to draw art of that. Like a cover for one of those old adventure magazines where a manly man has to fight Nazi crabs or something."

"So we're still here," James said, feeling his energy start to drain and largely failing to process most of what Alanna had said. Maybe he was just tired, but he was pretty sure after a certain point he'd just been hearing random words. Either that, or his girlfriend had actually just said 'Nazi crabs' on purpose.

"Yeah. We're still here," Alanna told him, taking his free hand.

A second later, Anesh added his own hand to the pile. "Not going anywhere," he said in his soft accented voice.

"Okay," James said. "Alright," he muttered, feeling his eyes droop. "I gotta get . . . caught up on . . . paperwork. And we . . . we need to find . . . that chick." He closed his eyes for a second. Just a blink, really. "Find her and shoot her," he clarified. "And then . . ."

Anesh and Alanna held his hand while he fell back asleep.

"Okay," Alanna said after a minute. "Back to work?"

"Back to work," Anesh agreed. "Gotta make sure this place doesn't burn down until he wakes up."

"Yeah," she agreed.

The two of them left, silently closing the door behind themselves, and leaving James snoring. They didn't begrudge him the rest, though. After all, he'd had a *really* long day.

CHAPTER 6

"It occurs to me," James said as he leveraged his way down the hall to the elevator, a crutch under one arm to help with the cast still wrapped around his foot and ankle, "that I am probably never going to have time in my life for video games again."

It was a sad thought. James was the kind of person who really loved relaxing and digging into a good game, or at least he liked to think of himself that way. For a long part of James's life, his identity had been focused around that culture, for better or worse. Often worse, if he was being honest. But the thought that this half-day-job, half-higher-calling thing was now taking up so much of his time that he wasn't going to be able to keep that part of himself? Well, it was a weird feeling. Like he'd slowly given something up without noticing.

That thought made him realize that, not counting the mild coma, it had been weeks, or even months, since he'd even gotten to sit down and play D&D with his friends.

They'd traded the time they spent bonding over dice and jokes for time spent nearly dying in sewers. And for the first time, James wasn't sure he actually *liked* this shift.

He also didn't like being in charge. He really needed, James decided for the fifth time, to find someone to take his place. A successor of sorts. And it wouldn't be *that* hard, either; while he'd been down, the Order had organized itself into a much more well-oiled structure.

The logistics slack had been picked up by Karen, who was actually far, far more competent at it than anyone had expected. Once the issue of available funds had been temporarily solved through value extracted from the Office, and those the Order was sheltering were more or less resettled into normal-esque lives, Karen had turned out to be a lot easier to work with, too. James hadn't had a chance to talk with her in the two days since waking up—he actually hadn't talked to anyone except Anesh, Alanna, Deb, and Dave—but he'd sort of come to understand that a large part of her hostility had been on the basis of the early assumption that he was just *kind of an irresponsible jackass*. And while he wanted to take offense to that, and actually did take offense to the *irresponsible* part, James could all too easily see how his constant joking could come across as rude or disrespectful. Especially with the generation gap in play between the two of them. The fact that he'd followed through on his oath to help everyone was worth a lot to someone like Karen, and once she'd stopped seeing him as . . . well, as a standard D&D adventurer, wandering around and causing two problems for every one he solved . . . she'd lightened up considerably.

In a similar way, Harvey had been doing more for their security side than ever before. Not alone, though; Nate had offered a lot of tips of the trade, until the Order's FBI contact had shown up and sort of tried to wedge his way into everything. He was a guy named Randall, and while, according to Harvey, he was *helpful*, he was also kind of a twit. He had trouble with concepts like the camracondas, or using powers for security things.

Hesitation. James winced as he remembered the school. So many people could have fought back, could have saved themselves. But the average person wasn't tempered for combat, and of the people who were exceptional in that regard, most of *them* weren't prepared for dungeon combat. He thought back further, to the first time he'd been in Officium Mundi, the very first time he'd fought a strider.

Two puncture wounds, mild blood loss, panic, and a visceral re-sistance to using the amount of force needed to rip a living thing in half. He'd hesitated, too. If it'd been a shellaxy that'd tried to gnaw on his leg, he'd be dead. So he couldn't blame anyone, really. It was just sad.

But also, he hadn't hesitated because it was *weird*. He'd hesitated for perfectly normal human reasons. There were a lot of people for whom the hesitation had seemed almost reinforced into them; like the very idea of something as fantastical as a ratroach made it impossible to even consider fighting back.

Security, though. Their building now had cameras. The buildings around them *also* had cameras, and James had been assured by his partners that the absolutely illegal hidden cameras were very well hidden. The building itself also had a couple of new armaments and security tricks in case they ever came under direct assault, and the whole Order had been drilling emergency response plans while he'd been down. James would need to catch up on those over the next few days; he didn't want to be the one in the way if they had to deploy to a new dungeon, or handle some other crisis.

They'd also apparently acquired some new office space, too. Actual office space, with room for expanding their support staff. Though when James asked how they were supposed to keep that secure, Alanna just told him that it was "a surprise."

When he'd limped his way into the elevator, *finally* cleared to start moving around and having woken up to no one left to stop him, James got something akin to an answer.

"Goddammit, we need to start labeling these things," he'd spoken to himself, glaring at the elevator panel where a new button was sitting like it belonged there. It was marked, which was new, though the fact that it sat well above the button for the basements and the ground floor was pretty telling all on its own. Floor thirty-two. "Also, come on, Alanna. This isn't a surprise, this is just a normal Wednesday around here. The biggest surprise is that I didn't wake up to learn that we've got an underground bunker and a new radio tower now," James said to the empty elevator as he elbowed the button for the first floor and waited for the doors to close.

He sighed and closed his eyes, leaning back against the wall. Two months asleep, and he was still exhausted. The short walk down the hall had left his limbs feeling like jelly, and the only thing keeping him from going back to bed was the feeling that he really didn't want anyone *telling* him he had to be in bed.

James was fueled by whatever was in that IV bag, and also by an internal reactor that ran on spite. But a friendly kind of spite. Whatever the joke version of spite was. Spite that told him that he should show off to his friends just how undefeatable he was.

He was still trying to come up with a better emotion when the elevator door dinged open, and confetti exploded in a wave of color into the cab.

James had spent a whole heck of a lot of time over the last year getting into life-or-death fights. More time still getting into life-or-casual-maiming fights, too. Through the forge of battle, and also through actual intentional training, and maybe a little bit of magic, he had turned his reflexes into something that kept him alive, and more importantly, something he had under control.

So when the crowd of people yelled "Surprise!" and fired a confetti cannon into the elevator, James managed to keep his shock to something approximating a loud squawk.

As he stumbled forward on his crutch while the shredded paper fluttered to the ground, unused to having a broken limb holding him back, he was greeted by a small crowd, colorful streamers, and a hanging sign positioned perfectly to be seen by someone stepping out of the elevator. Anesh and Alanna grinned at him from where they headed the group of delvers, smiles of both amusement at their own antics and relief that James was finally up.

"How the hell did you set this up so fast?" James asked with barely contained amusement of his own. He motioned a hand at the garbage-can setup that had exploded confetti at him, and mostly at the sign overhead. "Also, why does that sign say *Happy Birthday?*" Then he glanced behind him at the elevator floor. "One last question; who's gonna clean that up? 'Cause . . ." He looked down at his leg, then back up, with a raised eyebrow.

"First of all, don't dampen our fun with things like *keeping the office not a mess*," Alanna rolled her eyes at him.

Anesh stepped forward and gave James an awkward hug, trying in vain to find a way around the crutch and arm cast. "We've had this set up for a week. And the sign is because it was the only one we could find; all the party stores are closed."

"And also because you missed a birthday," Anesh reminded her.

"Oh shit, I did, didn't I?" James realized. "Shit, I'm old now. Old and broken!"

"You're not even thirty, you baby." A voice came to James's ears through the amused rumblings of the assembled group. People were starting to filter away, the surprise part over, but more than a few were sticking around to say hi. And one of those was Sarah. The people left, including Alanna and Anesh, parted around her as she walked stiffly forward to greet James. She was still wearing a neck brace, still obviously hurting, but she was also still smiling happily at him. "Also, I'll clean up the confetti. It was mostly my idea, even if I did get Tyrone and Daniel to set up the cannon for me."

"You absolutely will not!" Anesh protested. "I'm gonna go find a broom." He stalked off with purpose.

"See, the great thing about being broken," Sarah said, smile not even slipping a little bit, "is that I can *make people do chores*, just by suggesting that I might try!"

"I'm gonna have to remember that trick," James said, smiling back at her, holding back small tears in the corners of his eyes. "I'm glad you're okay," he said feebly.

"Thanks to you." Sarah elbowed him. "Alright, I'm gonna go sit down. Go, talk to people, catch up. You've been asleep a long time." She shooed him away.

"Talk to—*whump!*" James let out a gasp of air as something settled onto his shoulders.

Secret had never really been heavy, exactly, no matter what his actual size was. And that size was still kinda up for debate. It was weird to have a companion who was literally open to interpretation,

James thought. But he wouldn't have Secret any other way. And as the very young ancient sea serpent form coiled up around his torso and rested his head on James's shoulder, James reached up to pet the infomorph that was his close friend.

"I have missed you," Secret bluntly stated, several of the eyes along his form pivoting up to look at James with concern. "There have been a number of new people, but none of them could replace you."

"Damn!" James exclaimed. "There goes my plan of retirement!" He grinned at Secret. "I'm glad to see you too. I hear you were all heroic and shit back at the school?"

Secret *snorted*, a noise James had never heard him make before rippling out through vents in his scales all across his body. "I was helpless. I did what I could, and only wish it were enough."

"Pretty sure we call that *life*, my dude," James admonished him. "But I get it. I don't feel like I did enough either."

"You saved everyone," Secret whispered.

"I saved Sarah. Barely. She did the hard work," James replied, equally quiet. "And I didn't . . . save everyone." He swallowed the lump in his throat. "Alright, alright!" James tried to wave down the conversations that were popping up around him. "Everyone calm down! I need to sit down, and I'm absolutely *positive* you all have things you need to tell me!" That got laughs, even from Nate, who seemed to find it hilarious. James didn't wait for him to recover from his belly laugh, instead just moving through the crowd. "So I'm gonna hit up my office, and y'all can just drop in over the course of the day, okay?"

"It's six p.m.," Deb called over to him. She was half leaning on the wall, half leaning on Frequency-of-Sunlight, who was braced against the wall next to her. James glanced at them, gaze lingering for just a second as his brain processed the fact that they totally *did* look like they were dating, and then he glanced back out the front windows.

"Okay, well, the night then. And probably tomorrow, so . . ."

"Also, that's not your office," Momo chimed in unhelpfully. The grin on her face was, James realized, probably how he looked when he was having fun with people in this same way.

He sighed. "Alright," he said. Then he turned, still wearing Secret like a cloak, and hobbled back into the elevator. With only brief hesitation at the thought that this might be a trap, he leaned forward and jabbed the new button for a floor that hadn't existed when he'd gone into his long nap. "I assume you all know where to find me!" he called smugly through the closing doors. "Which is good," he confessed to Secret when the elevator sealed and it was just the two of them, "because I have no idea where they put my office."

"It is a *secret!*" Secret said sagely, bobbing his head. "I will show you."

"Thanks, buddy." James leaned against the wall and sighed as they started ascending.

James hobbled out of the elevator and blinked against the evening sunlight. The sun hung low in the sky over the horizon, and was in the perfect position to turn the exterior plate-glass windows into gleaming panes of light, casting warmth and shadows in equal measure over the floor he'd stepped out onto.

Which was good, because without that, he may well have thought that he'd somehow stepped into Officium Mundi. Or woken up from a dream to find that he was living in a nightmare.

Fortunately, his brain caught up to reality pretty quickly. There were a few cubicles here, but only two rows of them, in a nice, normal configuration. Six desks with comfy-looking padded chairs, topped with normal laptops that weren't trying to kill anyone. There was a wide open space over to the right that probably took up most of the floor space, with a couple of big smooth tables in the middle of it, and more comfortable chairs lining them. A few people had left backpacks or water bottles around it, and the whole thing reminded James more of a study group than an office space. The clock on the wall wasn't a memetic threat, the water cooler wasn't going to explode, the vending machine . . .

Okay, the vending machine looked *incredibly* suspicious. The bucket of fictional-denomination dollar bills taped to the side also confirmed James's deduction that it'd been wheeled in from outside. And by outside, he meant outside of reality itself. Same with the potted plant that felt like it was eying him with suspicion.

"Hey, Ferndinand," James greeted it. "Good to see you got out of that. How's it shaking?" The potted plant didn't reply except to rustle a little at him. "Good, good." James turned away and walked over to the window, lifting a hand up to shade against the glare so he could look out.

A city greeted him down below. Human, but still something he'd never seen from this angle before. Purple and gold sunset light on the horizon held sway over a skyline of towers and skyscrapers. The light glittered off a thousand windows, showing off the cityscape below from a height James hadn't been expecting. Networks of roads and stretches of highway overpasses stared up at him, strangely empty of cars during what should have been rush hour.

"What the hell?" he muttered. "Where is this?"

"Los Angeles," Secret told him from his shoulder, enjoying the sight of the city himself.

"Where *is* everyone? Why's it look so . . . quiet?"

Secret rippled. "I am given to understand that most people are staying home, in an effort to curb a disease," he said.

"Ah. Fuck. Wow, that looks surreal," James said, lingering for a second to watch the sunset. When he turned back to the office, he sighed. "So, which cubicle did I end up with?"

"That one." Secret gestured with his snout down to the end of the floor. There was a short hallway at the end, with signs up that pointed toward the emergency exit stairs and the bathrooms, but before that there were a few more doors. Around the perimeter of the floor were a handful of actual offices. James wandered over and took a look at the first one, and was only mildly surprised to see it had a nameplate for Karen by the door. *Logistics and Accounting.*

James moved on, passing Harvey's office and a couple of other empty ones before coming to the end of the hall.

"You guys gave me a literal corner office?" he asked, bemused.

"It has a lovely view," Secret told him, confident.

James shook his head with a grin as he pushed the door open and walked in. His desk was here, the Goodwill-salvaged one he'd been using in the cramped front office of the Lair. In fact, all his furniture was here. Except for that one beaten-up IKEA bookcase; that'd been replaced by something that looked a lot more elegant and a lot less like something that he'd ever actually pony up the cash to buy. Of course, money just kind of . . . wasn't much of a problem anymore. Between their skills and casual looting of cash and valuables from the dungeon, they had a real actual goddamn pile of cash on their hands that James had never really anticipated. He still wasn't quite used to being free from the specter of poverty.

His office *also* had a potted plant, though this one was some kind of standing vine thing in the corner where the two windows met, and it was either not sentient or doing a great job of faking it. It made the whole place feel a lot more comfortable and alive. Same with someone having upgraded his chair, and he gave that person a thankful mental nod as he sank into the seat.

There was a cup of coffee on his desk, and it looked like it was still hot. There was also a bottle of ibuprofen, which he looked at suspiciously. This seemed like the kind of loving support that his partners were fans of, which James still didn't actually know how to react to. He wasn't used to being taken care of. He loved what they had growing between them, he really did, but it was all so new and he just wasn't familiar with being loved.

Behind him, the elevator dinged, and he spun around awkwardly, expecting . . . well, nothing. He didn't know what to expect. But he sure as hell probably wasn't supposed to be here, if someone from whatever building he was in happened to stumble onto this floor. But wait, maybe he was supposed to be here? This was *their office*. This was clearly a tower building; the Order didn't *buy* the whole thing, unless JP had gotten a lot bolder with his cons and finance crimes. What exactly did the building's guide have them listed as? Monster hunters? Meme . . . people?

James felt a headache coming on as even his thoughts got away from him.

Fortunately, when the elevator did open, it was Anesh who came walking out of it. He took a glance out the window, but moved past it like someone who'd already taken the time to stare out at that particular sight.

"What do you think?" he asked.

James looked around again. At the smooth lines and fresh paint, the space of a modern business doing modern business things.

"I kinda hate it? But also my office looks neat."

Anesh made a fart noise with his mouth, and rolled his eyes at James. "We'll get rid of the cubicle walls. They're just there to pin stuff on anyway." He looked over James's shoulder. "You like the office?"

"I like the office," he said, and noted the pleased look on Anesh's face. "How the hell did we get this place, anyway?" James asked, turning to lead Anesh back to the . . . back to *his* . . . desk, and the chair waiting for him there.

"Ah, so," Anesh started the sentence in a way that made James sure this was going to be amusing. "We had, briefly, a blue power for 'remove entrance.'"

"I remember that. Reed demolished half of a building. It was metal as fuck."

Anesh rolled his eyes. "Exaggeration, but sure. Anyway. So, a lot of businesses are having a hard time right now, and a lot of smaller startups have just outright closed. JP got this place off a group that was making an app for dog play groups . . ."

"That sounds suspicious," James interrupted. "But also like exactly the kind of thing someone would do. Sorry, carry on."

"Shut up and let me finish. We bought their lease off them cheap to help them recoup their losses, and then set it up the way we liked it." Anesh cocked his arms out, hands on his hips as he gave a satisfied look at the workspace around them. "Nice and millennial!" he declared.

James waited a second, but then felt like he had to prompt the next part. "Anesh . . . why does the elevator go here?"

"Oh! Right! So, Momo's kinda been burning through blues lately, looking for something of long-term value and mostly getting stuff like 'condense hydrogen.' But at one point, she got one labeled 'transfer control,' which she promptly rolled her eyes at and started trying to clear out so she could slot a new one." Anesh sighed as James gave him an open-palmed *why* expression. "I know. I know. Anyway, we caught her with the last dozen charges, and started experimenting. Turns out, you can transfer not just the controls, but the entire apparatus of something, from one physical point to another. And then we had someone else with a 'connect door' ability that we were mostly using for remodeling, but you *know* how the wording on these things gets." Anesh took a nostalgic moment to look out the window again. "There were a couple others, too. I'm certain we'll be able to recreate the effect sometime in the future, but for now, we used the last of the important ones just on this."

"Holy shit, that's a long range," was what James took away from all that.

Anesh grinned. "Actually, no!" he said cheerfully. "We had to fly her down here, and then back up while holding focus on it the whole way. Twice! Because she lost focus the first time and it snapped back! Momo hated the experience and refuses to use the elevator now because, as she claims, 'it knows what it did.'" Anesh laughed. "That's also where a couple of the other orbs came in, for getting the flights and also helping her stay focused during it. Momo might have had some kind of seizure afterward, actually, but says she's fine, and no one really believes her."

"'Kay. Terrifying. So, what about the stairs?" James asked.

"The stairs are stairs, James. Do you want us to remove the door there, too? We can. Though we're mostly just keeping it locked."

James glanced at the door to the stairwell. "I'll be honest, I was expecting it to magically be an extra Office dungeon entrance. Also, I kind of assumed that we were going for security through lack of doors? Fuck, I have so many things that should be questions about the elevator, but I kinda feel like I inexplicably understand exactly how it works and it's very frustrating."

"Fire escape paths are important, James," Anesh scolded him. "Anyway. Hi. Welcome back. How do you like it?"

Looking around, James felt a little left out. Like he hadn't been involved in putting this place together at all. But then . . . he also hadn't had to move furniture. And this was proof of concept that the Order could operate without him around all the time. Also, the view was *amazing.* So when he spoke, instead of voicing any of his concerns, he just said, "I love it." And really, he wasn't lying. It was quite tempting to just go watch the city and the sunset for a while. But it was *also* tempting to plod into his new office, slump into his chair, and open the bottle of painkillers.

Which he did.

Anesh followed him in and settled into the chair on the other side of the desk with a satisfied noise. Whoever had been put in charge of furniture had used the budget pretty damn well.

"So, I've got a few things I want to get you caught up on, and then I'm positive there's other people who want to talk to you," Anesh said as James settled in and started poking at some of the papers sorted neatly on his desk's surface. "Don't bother with those, they're mostly gonna be lists of things. I can get you up to speed faster."

"Alright, hit me." James nodded at his boyfriend.

"Okay." Anesh took a deep breath and checked his own notes. "So, first off, orbs. Still not sure what the trigger is, whether it's time in the Office or candy bars eaten or whatever, but long-term delvers are all consistently manifesting the ability to absorb more orbs of different colors. There's also absolutely something about mindset in there, too, because Dave's growth in that regard has stalled, even though he started out with more 'slots,' and some people, like Alex, now have four goddamn blues at a time."

James hummed appreciatively. "That's kinda awesome. The powers from those are always the most unbalanced bullshit."

"No kidding," Anesh agreed with a nod. "And sometimes they combo. The biggest limiters are the fact that they *really* do take a toll on the person using them, in some abstract way, and also their limited charges."

"It's too bad we don't get to see our mana pool. Assuming that exists, and they aren't just using our blood as a fuel source or something." Wistfully, James propped his chin on the back of his hand, elbow leaned on the desk. "If we had a way to recharge . . ."

"Well, we do. We have a way to recharge something, at least," Anesh cut in. "And that ties into the next thing I need to brief you on. We've sorted the loot from Status Quo, and we've got a list." James didn't even say anything, just perked up and raised his eyebrows, a clear motion for Anesh to continue. "Okay. Bracelet. You know this one; binds to a gun, burst fire, reload." Anesh rapidly rattled off the abilities of the item. "Here's the thing; we found about two dozen of them in the . . . basement . . . trove, that didn't have the reload ability. And from what we can decode of their notes . . ." He took a deep breath. "You'll hate this. From what we can figure out, the items were made from life force. And the more 'powerful' the life, the better the item. So, the bracelets that we've found are . . . eh. They're not great? The abilities are all at lower levels, the cooldown on binding is almost *a year*, and the lack of the reload is pretty big."

"I am thoroughly disgusted," James flatly stated.

"Yeah," Anesh agreed. "Anyway. All the agents' bracelets had the reload, which means . . . well, the sad obvious truth. They were using delvers to make stuff, and the stuff that was from baseline humans they just piled up in the basement like scrap."

"Ugggggh." James headbutted his desk. "I now regret not shooting more people."

"Really?"

"No. Not really. I regret having to shoot anyone at all. But for fuck's sake, that's monstrous." He sighed. "What other blood magic did we get off them?"

"Okay. Bracers. Mostly what we know; change what it shields against, and shield against the thing. The shield cooldown drops as it gets to a higher level, by the way, which means that as the levels go up, it becomes . . . well, theoretically, at a certain point it would have no cooldown at all. But we did get one off the director that has a third mode, which doesn't have a cooldown at all. It actually charges off of the shield itself, and then breaks weapons that were used to charge it. That one's kinda cool, and also horrifying, because we don't know if it counts things like fists as a weapon? Oh, and as with all dungeon magic, it's a real Scrooge about information."

"Please tell me you didn't vaporize anyone's fists."

"No, not yet," Anesh said, like *yet* wasn't the most worrying word so far. "Anyway. Greave, which is *not a boot*, you should know!" He looked like he'd had a non-zero number of arguments about this so far. "First power is pseudo-passive, and enables very precise foot-work. Again, like with the others, the only thing that seems to scale with its level is how fast the charge cooldown goes. Second power is an active kick. It's the same kick every time, but while you're execut-ing it, your leg can't break, and it hits with a specific amount of force. That force, by the way, doesn't come from anywhere. These things really hate physics."

"I'm with them there. Physics was never my strong subject." James snorted. "It's all just math, but without round numbers."

Anesh hid a smile from his partner. "That's . . . *objectively* untrue, but I'm not going to fight you on it. Moving on! Earring. Invisibility on massive cooldown, something that makes an attack hit exactly on a slightly lower one. Glove, left-handed, we've found them with up to four modes, and this is where we learned that *some* things will un-lock new powers when you level up the previous ones enough. Each power is just a strike that's strengthened against a certain material type. And I mean strengthened in the *your fists* can *melt steel beams* kind of way."

James held out his good hand. "Give me the glove."

"Wrong hand, love," Anesh stumbled over the last word slightly, but it was clear he still meant it.

"Dammit!" James snapped his fingers in mock frustration. "Okay, soon! What else do we have?"

"A handful of one-power things, none of which really stand out, though they have powers that are . . . more utilitarian? There's a hair clip that has a 'complete paperwork' ability that Karen is in the process of powerleveling. Not that you actually can with these; the cooldown time is the bottleneck. Also, a brooch with 'purify food' that Knife-in-Fangs is doing the same with. Status Quo clearly didn't focus on those as much as the combat ones, which is . . . expected, and also awful."

"I feel like we made a mistake not killing all of them," James reiterated.

Anesh bit his lip as he replied. "Yeah, Randall—the FBI contact—said largely the same thing. He's going to want some time from you today to berate you for not taking prisoners as 'intelligence assets.'"

"Where in the hell would we put prisoners? The basement? The closest thing we have to a prison is currently housing a giant invisible cat that thinks it's a god and is prepared to fight anyone that wants to argue that point. Like all cats." James almost, *almost*, slapped his desk in annoyance, stopping at the last second before his still-damaged hand impacted the surface. "Wait, we still have the cat, right?"

Anesh nodded. "We do," he said. "Oh! Right! One of those one-ability, low-level items has something that is, for real, labeled as Inner Spirit Reignition. And it works on blue orbs! In fact, it works almost exclusively on blue orbs—in addition to providing what feels like a very energetic mental boost, kind of like drinking eight shots of espresso at once. Anyway, it ticks up slotted blue orbs by one charge every time it's used. It's not . . . a lot? And the cooldown is monstrous. But it's there."

"I've had that much espresso before. The coffee shop calls that drink the Black Hole."

"Ugh. Americans." Anesh rolled his eyes.

"Oh, come on! That can't just be us! I'm sure plenty of places have gross coffee drinks too!" James protested. "What's the spirit thing?"

"It's a really ornate crown that doesn't fit in the projector copier before you ask, and we only have one of them. I'm not sure what Status Quo was doing with the thing in the first place."

"Alright. So, magic items are good. What else do I need to know?"

"Um . . . we found three more books in the aftermath of the school showdown. Still didn't want to double up on anyone, just in case, so Alex, Simon, and Tyrone now have lessons for algebra, writing, and social studies, which they're working through. Sarah leveled her lesson up—Deb and Frequency-of-Sunlight are *absolutely* dating by the way—and chose Health as her reward. Uh . . . what else . . ." Anesh looked down at his notes. "We're building a language pack of orbs, since we might need to operate globally at some point. Oh, the duplication ritual doesn't work without the projector, by the way. Momo wanted me to tell you we tested that; the projector is the 'focus.' She hasn't been able to make any, though."

"She . . . hasn't?" James muttered, looking blankly off to the side. "I feel like that's not right but I can't remember why. Still, if she can, that'd be cool. I'd love to have someone who could make our own magic items around. Anything else?"

"Honestly, that's pretty much it," Anesh said with a shrug. He looked up at James and gave a sad little frown. "We're . . . still looking for our families. Alanna and I have been using that iLipede that maps social networks, and it's just . . . it's like a whole swath has just been carved out. You can see the edges pretty easily, if you look. I think those people would remember us, honestly, it's just something more abstract. Like the connection itself is what was attacked." He sighed, shrugged again. "I wish I had better news. It's been . . . it's been almost three months and I don't even know if my parents are alive. Or yours. And I'm sorry," he finished, feeling lame for not having a good answer.

James met his boyfriend's eyes, leaning across the desk with his good hand extended in a beckoning gesture. Anesh took his hand, holding tightly while still not quite fully meeting James's gaze. "Hey," James told him. "It's okay. I mean, it's obviously not. But you only need to worry about you; I can live without my family, okay? Don't pile everything on yourself."

"Like you do?"

"Like I do." James nodded sagely. "It's stupid and awful, don't do it."

"Not to . . . be an overbearing partner, but . . ."

"No, I don't plan to take that advice myself, thank you though!"

Anesh nodded. "Gotchya," he said. "Okay. Secret? Bite him every time he says anything like that."

"I shall be effective operant conditioning." Secret crept up the back of the chair from where he'd been lurking to pointedly stare at James with a dozen eyes, his voice somehow more menacing than normal for something that didn't actually fit into the space it occupied.

James raised his arms over his head in a gesture of surrender. "I'll be good!" he lied.

"Sounds like I walked in on bullshit." Alanna's voice came into the room as she strolled through the door. She'd cut her hair short, and despite her energy, had tired dark circles under reddened eyes. "Catching him up?" She pointed the question at Anesh, who flashed her a thumbs-up. "Well, I brought you a friend." Alanna stepped in, leaning up against the doorframe to let someone past.

"Jaaaaaames!" Sarah clearly wanted to burst into the room like some kind of human-shaped whirlwind. She did not get to do that. Instead, her entrance was much slower and more deliberate. Mostly because of the brace wrapped around her neck. "James! You're alive! I knew it!"

James raised his eyebrows at her as she came in, taking the seat that Alanna had left vacant with an almost delicate motion. "You literally saw me fifteen minutes ago. Also, I refuse to believe you didn't visit me at least once while I was down," he said. "You must have known I was alive. Or is that what you meant?"

"Yep! Once I got sent home from the hospital, I used the extra sleep hours at the apartment to recharge, and dumped those into you. Also, Alanna told me you weren't dead pretty quickly because she's cool like that," Sarah confirmed.

"*Anyone* would be cool like that. Who just forgets to tell someone that their friend is alive?" Anesh demanded, shocked. Then a thoughtful look crossed his face. "Wait, no, I just realized how our lives are. Nevermind."

"Yeah, actually, about that," James interjected. "You're telling me a lot about the stuff we've gotten—"

"Oh! The program emeralds! We've been using those too!" Anesh cut him off, before shutting up with a guilty look. "Sorry, right. You just reminded me"

". . . but not about what's *going on*. We're working with the FBI now? And have there been any other crises?" he asked, mildly worried to hear the answers. "For the last month . . . subjective time . . . there were nonstop problems. Police, school dungeon, Status Quo, probably something else I'm forgetting? Don't tell me that it just went . . . quiet . . . while I slept."

Alanna winced, and looked away. "Well, we had a few . . . um . . . small things?"

"Secret," James said in a dry voice. "I'm gonna need you to bite Alanna's toes every time she lies."

His long companion made an amused sound. "I shall endeavor—"

Alanna sputtered and shushed Secret, waving her hands wildly at the serpent. "Shaddup! And look, they weren't that important, or dungeon-y, at all! There was a small building fire that we teleported a person out of. There was a bar fight that got out of hand that we may have intervened in. And there was a secretive plot for someone to make a couple hundred grand off an investment fraud thing where we stopped an assassination attempt and may have brought ourselves to the attention of the—"

"No, stop!" James held up his good hand. "Was that last one JP? Was JP the *villain* in that one?"

"Surprisingly, no! Though he did turn us onto it. Did you know he got two more ranks in different finance-related skills? He's . . . becoming a problem." Alanna gave a wide, wary smile, full of teeth and guilt.

"Becoming?" Anesh muttered into his hand.

Secret spoke up. "He trades hidden information like it is currency. He didn't need to orbs to become a problem."

"Be nice," Sarah admonished him. "Yes, we've had some adventures while you've been sleeping. Well, they have. I'm still . . ." She trailed off, motioning to her own obvious injuries. "*And,* yes, we're working with the FBI for now. Or more like, they acknowledge we exist, make legal troubles go away, and somehow can't wrap their heads around magic? I don't really understand. Research is running experiments on Randall, and it's *hilarious.*"

Anesh cut in. "Also, Alanna keeps fighting the police, even though they aren't interested in us!" he burst out.

"Anesh!" Alanna scowled at him from her spot on the wall.

"What?! He asked about problems, and you left out the big one!"

James took a deep breath. "What," he asked, politely, "is the big problem? Wait, no. Is this some kind of revenge thing because those cops shot at us? We can let that go. I'm still mad, but we don't need to fight all of the police yet." He gave Alanna a desperate look. "Do we? Please don't tell me we're starting another war. Especially not with the abstract concept of law enforcement."

"We are not starting another war," she comforted him.

"Don't think I didn't hear the secret emphasis in that sentence." James pointed at her with a frown.

Anesh tried to explain. "After the school, there was a short break where things settled down. But there were . . . James, there were a lot of bodies. There were a lot of parents who wanted their kids back. And there were a lot of people angry at how the situation got handled."

"It didn't get handled," Alanna interjected, arms folded. "The police should have . . . I don't even know what they should have done." She sighed. "But they shouldn't have tried to stop us from helping, at *least.* Shouldn't have been shooting random people."

"I mean, I agree," James said. "But also we were a bunch of random people with guns rocking up to what they thought was a school shooting. I'm annoyed, but I can only be *so* annoyed before it becomes unrealistic. So . . . what happened?"

Alanna gave a derisive snort. "Well, the parents organized a local protest to demand cop accountability and a revision of the budget."

"Okay . . ."

"And the police shot at them." Sarah spoke with her usual gentle tone, which made the words coming out disturbingly abrupt and jarring.

"O . . . kaaaaaa . . . what?" James stared at her, then back to Alanna. "*What?*"

"Rubber bullets, tear gas, there was a march to the park by that one library you like, and about halfway there, there was a police line with riot gear and stuff, and they just . . ." Alanna shrugged like it was normal. Somehow. "Anyway, the next protest, I was there."

Anesh stopped gnawing at his own lip. "Yes, she was there, wearing shield bracers and flinging tear gas canisters back at the cops. And possibly breaking someone's arm?"

"They can't prove it was me," Alanna defended herself, poorly. "And it was at *least* two arms." She continued to fail to defend herself.

James waved his good hand between himself and his friends. "Sorry, so, the local police, the guys who have one of the *best* images for cops in the entire country, reacted to a call for accountability by . . . doing a brutality?"

"Yes," Alanna said, nodding along with Anesh as he added his own "Correct."

"And we're working with the FBI, even while this is happening?" James demanded an answer. "Whose side are we on, anyway?" He was getting angry now, and feeling the limited energy he'd woken up with starting to rapidly drain away. "Also, what the fuck happened to Madden?" he demanded. "I can understand the other cops being twitchy. I don't like it, but I get it. But he was *insane.*"

"I think he just couldn't handle it." Anesh sighed. "You told me you were flippant with him?"

"I was a little cryptic," James admitted. "Because when I tried to tell him stuff, he . . . well, he was weird. He kinda acknowledged that Secret was there, but he wouldn't *accept* it. So I tried to nudge him toward answers on his own. Hoped that would actually help him with processing what was happening. And I may have been a bit of an ass about it."

"Yeah, well." Alanna looked a little annoyed. "Normally your wiseass routine is cute, but this time, it may have been a bad idea."

Anesh nodded, glancing at Secret as he spoke. "To be clear, I don't think you're the bad guy here. He . . . well, he looked into the abyss, and he flinched."

"And then chose to shoot at me," James pointedly clarified.

Sarah clicked her tongue. "Well, he was a bit of a dingus, yes."

"And then, yes, that," Alanna agreed. "He *chose*. He's wrong. But there's a degree of responsibility to take, too. You didn't exactly make a strong case for him to join our side, did you?"

James didn't have much of an argument there. "I suppose not," he admitted. "That said. What . . . what is our side?"

The others in the room looked at each other, and back to him. There was a heavy moment of quiet. The truth was, none of them really felt like they knew what side they were on. Other than each other's, that was.

James took some time to think, while his friends did the same.

The Order didn't have a stated goal. Not really. Not yet. They had ethics guidelines, operational procedures, and a mission statement, but it was all in the abstract right now. They didn't actually have actionable objectives. Things that they could point to and say, "Alright, let's tackle this problem." They responded to disasters that they saw, both mystical and mundane, and they saved people. The saving people was how they'd gotten into this organizational mess in the first place, really. But it wasn't exactly a *goal*, was it?

What, after all, was the point of saving someone's life, if you were just going to drop them back into the normal world where they couldn't pay rent, couldn't give their kids a good life, and might die at the hands of a random plague or also *apparently* the police?

No, they needed something to reach for. And again, his thoughts wandered back to his vague fantasy. An arcology. A designed society, a proof of concept for something bigger, maybe. Or, alternately, just a refuge for the people who needed it. But increasingly, it was looking like *the people who needed* it was the entire population of Earth. And systemic change wasn't really something that they, a group of about thirty people who were at most level two wizards, were capable of on a large scale.

So what? Work with a world power? Sell their services as unorthodox agents to global intelligence agencies? Buy a small island and start their own nation?

Actually, that last one was basically just the arcology plan, but smaller and dumber.

And none of it actually answered the question of whose side they were on.

Were they pulling for the country? Not just the American government, but the culture, the nation itself? James sure as hell didn't feel like it. And Anesh certainly didn't have any motivation for patriotism; for this country or his own home. Technically, they could all become Canadian citizens at the drop of a hat, but that didn't *solve* anything. If Canada was a perfect utopia, James probably would have heard about that by now.

Most of all, he didn't want to side with the FBI. He didn't want the Order of Endless Rooms to ever be anything like Status Quo.

"Is it," James asked into the quiet office while the last rays of sunset dipped away through the corner window behind him, "too cliché to say that we're on our own side?"

"How much do you like Neil Gaiman?" Sarah asked quietly, staring out the window, the words coming a little too casually.

That one didn't take much thought from James. "Oh, like, a lot," he replied easy.

"Little cliché, then," Sarah informed him. "Is this gonna be about the arcology thing again?"

"I think it might get there," James said. "We need . . . we need to do something different. We need to be thinking bigger, *doing* bigger. We went from explorers, to survivors, to . . . protectors? And we're still down at ground level, staring up at blades of grass and thinking that someday maybe we can climb them. No, we should be more. We should be bold, and stupid. Nothing is ever going to get done with us sitting on our asses." He glanced at Alanna. "You told me once, when we started, that the only true evil was to have power and refuse to *try*."

"I did," she mumbled. "I did," Alanna repeated louder. "And I still believe that." She straightened her shoulders, nodding at him with a sharp motion.

James bobbed his head back. "Okay," he said. "We, not just us, but the whole Order, need three things." Everyone, even Secret, focused their attention on him. James ticked off on his fingers. "We need a goal to reach for, even if it's an insane one. We need the power to achieve that goal. And we need to stop waiting around to have that power, and start actively seeking it out when we need to fix specific problems. We need to stop being *afraid* of what we can, or will be able, to do."

"Are we afraid?" Sarah asked.

"I am," James admitted frankly. "Sarah, I . . . I can kill people with my hands. Or with magic. Or with a gun. Hell, even without having some kind of absurdly dangerous blue orb slotted, I'm already an action movie protagonist. *Lots of us are.* Did no one else notice that the primary foot soldiers of an entire dungeon were *cannon fodder* to us? Maybe they were designed to kill teenagers and not a pack of roving millennials, but still." No one had an answer to that. They'd noticed. They knew. "So let's build something. Fuck secrecy, and fuck nations. Fuck sides. Let's build a goddamn world, on our values, our ethics. And let's build it sideways enough that no one can bomb us out of existence for challenging them."

Alanna ran a hand through her hair. "Man, I . . . I wanna be with you. But that's . . . big. Where do we even start?"

"We start by declaring it," James said. "Then we allocate resources to it. Take Research and let them start fucking around with orange orbs like they want to. Do it safely, but don't be afraid to do it. Step up our dungeon explorations. Step up our search for new dungeons. New magic, too. Recruit. Find the people that *want* this, and bring them in. Then find the people that need this, and give them the support they need to survive until they can join us and help build a utopia." He took a deep breath. But he didn't falter. Didn't slow down. "It's time we stopped pretending that we're not here to make an impact," he told them.

"What about the woman from the Akashic Sewer? Or other groups like Status Quo? You know there *have* to be more. Status Quo thought that there were only a handful of dungeons, all up here," Alanna pointed out to him. "And we know that's bullshit."

"Yeah," Sarah confirmed. "They had bad intel. Or were just lying. What happens when these other groups notice us?"

"They get out of the way," James said quietly. "I don't want to be a monster. But if they're like Status Quo . . ." He trailed off and let the implication do the talking.

No one said anything, but they all nodded. They knew. It wasn't a preemptive strike if your opponent threw the first punch fifty years ago, and hadn't stopped punching since.

"And the . . . woman thing?" Anesh asked.

James pushed himself to his feet, and turned to face the darkened windows and the glimmering lights of the LA city skyline. "I think she's like us," he said. "I think she's a delver, who's been doing this for a long, *long* time." James glanced over his shoulder. "And I think that, no matter what, she's our enemy. Not just an obstacle, or an opponent. She is . . . fuck, man. I'm friends with a stapler, Dave's now some kind of life-partner thing with a dragon, and my adopted son is ten miles long and fits in my office somehow. But *her*?" He shook his head, an angry frown on his lips. "She's a monster. And we go in with that in mind."

Sarah's soft tone contradicted him. "Even if she was just a very *very* old delver, she still should have died. We practically ripped her in half and she walked it off and killed two people, and that was while she looked tired." She met James's eyes. "I don't think it was just dungeon magic. I don't think she's human, I think she's something different."

"That could also be true," James admitted. "Which means it'll be hard to figure out how to match her. But as long as she doesn't kick down our front door and start shooting, I believe we can get there."

They stood up, then, with nothing left to say. Anesh helped Sarah to her feet, and Alanna stepped forward. All of them looked at him, at each other. There was something in their eyes that hadn't been there before.

"You know?" Sarah asked him. "There's a reason people think you're the leader. There's a reason you're good at it."

There wasn't much more to say, even though there were more words that would be needed in the near future. His friends and lovers left, after extracting a promise from James to go home and go to bed before too long. In his *actual bed* this time, too. And he did intend to follow through on that, after he'd gone through some of the reports that had been left for him. And after one more thing.

James waited for the elevator doors to shut in front of them, as they rode it down twenty floors and north about a thousand miles. He really did spend some time reading up on what had been going on. The infomorph project was being redrawn, that was nice. And their supply of blues was low. No surprise there. He made notes on short-term tactical objectives. Sent a couple emails. Set up a notice with his bank that he'd sometimes be using his debit card from LA so he didn't get dinged by the anti-fraud software.

After half an hour, he got up and went to the elevator himself, and hit the button for one of the basements.

The ride down didn't seem to be as long as he would have liked, to have time to compose his thoughts. And before he knew it, he was limping out into the hallway that led past Research and then toward the vault.

He passed through the lit domed space in front of the elevator where a pair of camracondas and one human kept watch. There was supposed to be a security check here, but no one stopped him. They just saluted when he walked by. James did his best to move with purpose, no matter how the knotted feeling in his heart got worse as he walked.

There were a couple of people in the Research area, too, though it was quieter than it should have been. The pen of shellaxies was quieter than James remembered; a couple of them were standing at the edge of the pet fence near where Virgil's desk had been, like they were waiting for him to come back. James tore his eyes away and moved toward the vault itself, trying to ignore the hidden gazes from the couple of programmers down here working on skulljack modifications.

The vault door was locked, as it should be. James punched in his code and fingerprint, and was relieved to see it was still valid.

The door hissed as it opened, and he stepped inside. The camraconda priestess had moved her temple to a more suitable space at some point while he'd been out, but there was still something of spiritual significance to him here. Something he needed to see.

Against the right hand wall was a secure cabinet. The kind that stores used to keep electronics locked away, but still visible. It wasn't actually locked, but that didn't make the two objects contained on its shelves any less valuable. Any less devastating.

Two things. Two orbs. One a flickering emerald green, the other a blazing red.

"Cold-Wind-Friction" read the small engraved metal plate under the first. "Virgil Thomasi" read the other.

James couldn't stop the burst of sobs from somewhere in his chest. Somehow, it hadn't really felt real until right now.

He'd failed them. He'd let them down. Let them *die.* They'd fought for him, because he'd asked. Because they'd trusted him. And he hadn't been fast enough, or smart enough, or good enough, to save them.

It wasn't clear how long he stood there, one arm leaned against the cabinet, slumped forward onto the glass. But eventually, the tears dried. The pain retreated, even if it didn't fade away forever. James straightened up, wiped his eyes, and steadied himself.

"I'm sorry," he whispered. It wasn't enough. He knew that. It never would be enough. But standing here forever wasn't going to change anything either. "Responsibility, yeah?" he said to himself, and to what remained of his people in front of him. "Okay. I can handle that." James sighed. Maybe that was a lie too. Maybe he was just setting himself up to be crushed by the weight.

But he was going to try.

Two and a half months of sleep. *Time to get back to work,* he decided.

CHAPTER 7

James was currently sitting in what used to be his office, half his fingers steepled in front of his face still in a cast as he leaned his elbows on the new desk that now occupied the room. He was sitting on the other side of the desk from where he normally would, facing a middle-aged man in a gray suit.

The man's name was Randall, no last name given, and he was a bit of a twit. In James's opinion, at least. Big nose, crew cut, and the kind of narrow eyes that made him look almost perfectly neutral all the time. He wasn't exactly the kind of person James thought of when he thought "FBI field consultant." But then, that was probably the point, wasn't it?

The bigger problem was that Randall was skeptical to an unhealthy degree. Actually, the bigger problem was that he was probably reporting back to an agency that it *might* not have been a good idea for the Order of Endless Rooms to tether themselves to, but James had been experiencing a mild case of being in a magical coma at the time and hadn't been on hand to argue. It was just a constant irritation to have this guy interrupting conversations to ask people to *prove* that there was magic at play.

He never called it magic, either. And while the ongoing shifting battle lines of who used the term 'magic' and who said things like 'dungeon tech' were a running joke to most members of the Order, it got a lot less funny when this stuffy jerk started criticizing them for improper terminology.

As if James wasn't the one *writing* the terminology in the first place.

It wasn't that Randall didn't accept the weird stuff. He had met Secret, was aware of the Akashic Sewer, and had apparently been taken on a brief non-combat tour of Officium Mundi. He'd witnessed blue powers in action, and at least one instant of matter spawning from nowhere due to the power of an absorbed orange orb. Not specifically Anesh duplicating himself, though; they were keeping that much more dramatic magic a little under wraps.

They weren't quite prepared to tell him about the Anesh thing. Or about lot of things.

They were serious about taking advice from him, where it mattered. Harvey, specifically, was basically taking full-time classes on security and counterintelligence, even if they didn't quite have the resources to apply the majority of them at the moment. And right now, James was even trying his best to listen to the guy with an impartial ear.

Which was hard, because, as mentioned, he could be a bit of a twit.

"You made several mistakes in your handling of the terrorist organization OA-1," Randall was saying. He kept his eyes tilted to the side, reading a sheaf of papers and not even bothering to glance at James. "To begin with, your handling of—"

"Sorry, OA-1?" James interrupted him. "You must mean Status Quo, why the name change?"

"It's how their internal documentation refers to themselves," Randall blandly offered. "Now, your strike against the—"

James cut him off again. "Why are we using their name for themselves? That seems like an amount of casual respect that I do not possess toward their corpse." He got in some practice speaking like he had fallen out of a high fantasy novel; Secret was being a good influence on him.

His comment went entirely ignored, in a way that almost amused James. There was a tendency he knew he had to bias himself toward people who appreciated dry wit the same way he did; Randall here clearly did not. To the point that he just didn't acknowledge it. James wasn't sure if it was because the man was purposefully needling him, or because he was an idiot, but either way, it was funny and annoying in equal measure.

"Your strike against OA-1," Randall was saying, as if James hadn't spoken, "was effective, but failed to maximize use of force multipliers that you have access to. Despite a preemptive attack against an unaware enemy, you still sustained casualties that weren't needed." He pulled a piece of paper to the front of his sheaf and started reading. "The things you call camracondas should have been deployed in greater numbers. Also, any other autonomous units you can create should be made use of at every opportunity where they can replace human operators. You lack useful long-range support, specifically sniper cover. Your organization also clearly requires training in small-unit tactics; I've reviewed the footage and—"

"Uh . . . how?" James cut in. "The footage thing. We leveled the building."

"From your own body cameras." Randall eyed him like he was an idiot, and James cleared his throat quickly, holding up an apologetic hand and hoping the FBI consultant didn't question too hard about why he had never seen a single one of those cameras in the building. "Now . . ."

"No, no. Not done yet," James jumped in again. "The camracondas are people, not weapons. Ditto for any Life we create; that's not an efficient weapon. If for no other reason than that using living things as weapons always, *inevitably* backfires. Case in point; my secret base has several dozen expatriate camracondas in it." He paused for a heartbeat, tapping his fingers in a pattern on the desk as he leaned back. "Also, it's super unethical."

"Ethics isn't a part of the math of an efficient operation," Randall informed him, looking exasperated.

James nodded. "That's nice," he said, instead of what he was actually thinking.

"This also ties into your handling of prisoners," the fed continued.

"We didn't take prisoners." James tried really hard to not sigh deeply. In this moment, he wanted to be doing literally anything else aside from having his actions second-guessed by this asshole. "So, that kinda covers that whole section."

Randall glanced up, hard eyes meeting James's own. And suddenly, James realized, he knew that this man wasn't some inexperienced idiot who spent his days moving paperwork around. There was a feeling, laser-targeted on his soul, that the guy in front of him was a *killer*, in a cold, calculated way that had nothing to do with either ethics or emotions. The feeling passed in a flash, so quickly that it left James wondering if his imagination was just getting out of hand.

"Yes," Randall said blandly. "You failed to apprehend any of the surviving members of OA-1. Instead, you chose to release those that you had in custody, creating the window of opportunity for the reformation of their organizational structure, the creation of new hostile groups, and the resurgence of the same threat you set out to eliminate. Except now, every hostile agent knows of your existence and an outline of your capabilities. Furthermore, you forfeited the potential intelligence that could be gained through long-term interrogation of the membership of OA-1, especially any leadership that went unidentified."

James scowled. "I have a number of counterpoints," he said, and got a brisk *go ahead* hand motion from Randall. "First of all, we have nowhere to house prisoners, long- or short-term. I know I keep calling this place a secret base, but it's not like I'm a Bond villain, with underground holding cells and a shark tank. We don't have anywhere to hold people."

"That is a valid point." Randall nodded. "Though space could have been acquired."

"Maybe," James conceded. "Second point, though; taking prisoners wasn't our objective. Our goal was to remove their ability to effectively function as an organization. As far as we know, that was their headquarters, and roughly half their staff is gone. As well as their ability to produce more of the ma . . . of the specialized gear that they use for their murderous field operations. We weren't interested in wiping them out, just in taking away their ability to keep doing what they were doing."

"Also valid," Randall admitted. "Though you forget something important. Or perhaps haven't learned it yet."

"What's that?" James leaned forward a bit, actually curious. This was starting to feel more like a conversation and less like a rundown of his faults.

Randall tapped his papers into an orderly stack against the desktop. "The people you fight are under no obligation to tell you the truth." He gave the smallest of shrugs, barely a twitch of the shoulders. "You have no way of knowing, without proper intelligence, if this *was* their headquarters, or their only point of operation. Because people *lie*." He hissed out the last word. "You didn't even track their remaining agents to potential safehouses after the combat concluded. Amateur."

"And instead, we should have, what? Locked them up and tortured them?" James's face set in a hard frown. "I'm not really interested."

"Torture doesn't work," Randall told him, his gaze going back to a flat neutral. "You should be aware of that already. Long-term interrogations rely on human rapport and ideological conversion. Short-term on appealing to self-interest. Torture is for the vengeful, the inefficient, or the stupid. That's why the CIA makes use of it heavily."

James turned a yawn into a strangled cough to hide something that was trying to be a laugh. "Okay!" he said, after he'd caught his breath. "Wasn't expecting that," James muttered in a low tone. "So, cheat more in a fight, take prisoners, got it. Anything else I did wrong?"

"It's not about what you did wrong. It's about fixing flaws before they get you killed." Randall spoke in his neutral voice, but James got the distinct impression that he was being talked down to like he was a child. Though, from Randall's perspective, he probably was; and once he noticed that, James decided that maybe pulling his head out of his ass and actually taking objective advice wasn't the worst idea. "The only other problem is that you failed to capture the more valuable assets available during the operation."

"We took most of their stuff." James raised his eyebrows. "What . . . Oh."

"The . . . *ahem* . . . items . . . aside, you failed to acquire the means to produce *more*." Randall's comment was the closest he ever really got to an overt acknowledgment that magic was real, and that it could be applied to practical matters.

"Yeah, no." James shook his head. "From their own documentation, it looks like those things take not just blood, but something on par with the abstraction of life itself to run. You literally cannot use them without killing people. So, no. Blew 'em up, and I'll do it again if I need to."

Randall tapped a pencil on the desk in a slow rhythm. "You didn't know that at the time," he flatly accused.

"Had a feeling." James bit the words off. Then he collected himself and tried to answer more calmly. "Actually, I *did* have a feeling, and those instincts tend to be good about this variety of thing. Not only that, but there's a case to be made that it would be a very bad habit to get into, to use blood as a resource for something non-medical."

"Hm." The agent made a note. "Well. That's all for now. I wanted to make you aware of my assessment. A more comprehensive report will be completed soon, now that I have your input."

"Thanks." James put forth a massive effort to not roll his eyes as he stood up. Then he realized what he was doing, and corrected himself. "Actually thanks. I know this has probably been a lot for you, over the last couple months. And I do appreciate the advice, even if I decide to not follow it."

Randall actually looked up, and this time, his gaze didn't feel quite so dangerous. "Good," he said. "Now leave. I have work to do."

Ah, and they had been so close to a bonding moment, James thought as he closed the door behind him.

Overhead, the sun blazed. It was a beautiful June day; hot, but not sweltering, clear blue skies, and a slight breeze to make being outside just perfectly comfortable. Around them, the hum of insects and the light rustling of trees filled the air, along with the smell of earth and pollen.

It was marvelous, and James was covered in mosquito bites.

"We couldn't have done this anywhere else?" he griped. "I feel like we've been walking for an hour."

"It's been fifteen minutes, you giant baby," Alanna chided him from the front of the line.

"My leg is broken!" James called back to her, propping his crutch under his arm and using his good hand to swat at whatever was trying to drain all the blood out of his neck. "And while I am aware that I could fully use my acceleration boost on limping, that seems like an *awful* idea! I should have stayed back at the Lair. JP was teaching me how to fight with a sword."

"One-legged?" Anesh cocked an eyebrow. He was behind James in their three-person hiking line, carrying a heavy cooler braced against his thighs in an awkward walking position, and a heavier duffel bag over his shoulders. "That doesn't seem . . . easy?"

James let out a flippantly dismissive noise. "I needed something to do. And JP's the only person who didn't care that I'm injured. Honestly, I kinda felt like I didn't have a whole lot to do, especially since some nerds keep trying to get me to nap all day."

"You need your rest, you ass!" Alanna yelled back over her shoulder as she shoved a tree branch out of her way. "You nearly died! We *all* nearly died!"

"And yet, here we are." James waved his crutch at the woods around them while he tried to figure out how to maneuver over the log in front of him.

The three partners were out for the day, nominally because Anesh wanted to do some closer experiments with one of the bracelets liberated from Status Quo's agents, but mostly just because they wanted to spend a little time together. Originally, Anesh was just going to take one of them to a local shooting range, but everything being closed for the lockdown, mixed with the fact that they probably didn't want to show off any gun magic in public, had led them here. To a spot that Alanna had known about, and had a fondness for.

It was a little clearing in the trees; maybe sixty feet wide, with a few large and mostly flat rocks poking up out of the ground on one side. The remains of a fire pit stuck out next to one of the rocks, evidence that they weren't the only people to know about this place, but overall it was a nice little spot to stop and enjoy the beauty of nature.

It was also far enough away from any other human that they could do some target practice and not worry about being interrupted.

"Nice place." James grinned appreciatively as he settled his butt onto one of the rocks, propping the crutch up next to himself and slapping another bug off his leg. He'd worn shorts out of necessity, the cast on his leg and also the heat making any longer pants a pain. But he'd almost begun to regret that choice. "You sure it's okay for us to just hang out here and shoot off guns?"

"Oh yeah, it's fine." Alanna nodded. "My dad used to bring me camping here. I mean, you were in the car; you know how far off any main road we are."

"I admit, I started to get nervous when your directions took us driving down dirt and grass." Anesh grimaced as he dropped the cooler into the soft earth.

Alanna threw her arms up. "It's totally legal! They're technically park roads anyway!"

"I more meant that I was worried James's car was going to fall apart."

"Hey!"

"James, the most durable part of your car is the passenger window, and that's only because we got a new one installed for you while you were in a coma."

"My car is a noble beast!" James protested. "It has survived twenty-four years of—"

"Yes, that's largely the problem," Anesh interrupted him. "Get a new car! We have the money for it!"

Alanna sat back on one of the rocks opposite James, and cracked open a can of soda with a snap and a hiss. She didn't say anything, choosing instead to just enjoy the sunshine as it filtered through the tall trees above, and listen to her boyfriends bicker good-naturedly.

It really was a great day for this.

The three of them spent some time throwing jokes around, and getting comfortable, before Alanna finally stood and stretched languidly like some kind of woman-shaped lion in the sun. "Alright," she said, unzipping one of the bags they'd brought and pulling out a small black case. "We got you a gift," she said to James.

"Is it," he asked, "something dangerous?"

"Everything's dangerous in its own way . . . Okay, okay! Yes!" She laughed and used one hand to bat away the crutch that James was trying to poke her with. "Here, take a look," Alanna said as she placed the hard plastic case on the rock in front of him.

He snapped open the latches and pulled the lid up to reveal a very specific model of handgun set into the foam insert of the case. A Walther P38, exactly the right one for the skill orb he'd picked up on some long-ago dungeon delve.

Next to it, there were three loaded magazines of nine-millimeter ammo, and also a small bracelet in its own little pocket. James looked down at the gun for a minute before reaching out to pick it up, turning the heavy metal weapon over to peer through the open slide. "These things are always heavier than I think they'll be," he commented quietly as he set the gun back in the box and wriggled his fingers through the loop of the bracelet. It was a loose silver chain with a small clasp that could tighten if needed. James was prepared to let it dangle from his wrist until Alanna fussed with it for him. For a magic item, it looked almost plain. Just a chain with a few small fingernail-sized ovals of similar silver material hanging off it like charms. There was a single thin crescent of something that might have been bone that came to rest against the back of James's wrist, and that was it. No fancy decorations, no glowing runes, it was almost a disappointment but it really couldn't be, because it was actual magic.

"The bracelet's already bound to the gun," Anesh told him. "Though it's a different one than you originally had. That one still has about sixty days left until it can bind to something new, since you got your last gun vaporized."

"You say that like it's my fault!" James protested, mouth hanging open slightly.

Alanna laughed to herself as she sipped at her canned drink, then latched onto the tab with her teeth to hold the can up while she rummaged around in the bag again. She came back up with a couple of long poles, sharpened on the end, one—not alive—stapler, and a cardboard tube. Realizing she'd made a mistake thinking she could carry five things, one of them spillable, all at the same time, she took the time to abandon the can on top of a rock before walking to the other side of the shaded clearing, and driving one of the poles into the dirt under the carpet of dead leaves and pine needles. Once both poles were secure, and she'd safely ignored whatever James's comment about spears had been, she popped the tube open, pulled out a sheaf of paper target sheets, and stapled a silhouette to each pole.

"Alright!" she announced, walking back over. "Range line! If we're fucking around with guns, we're doing it safely!" Alanna walked a straight line past the boys, carving a furrow in the ground with her heel.

"Headphones?" Anesh offered James a pair of muffled ear protectors as they stepped up to the line.

James looked at them for a second, then down at his hand. He'd set the crutch against the rock, figuring he could stand for a bit without help; his leg wasn't *that* badly shattered or anything. But he still only had use of one hand's fingers. "Um . . . do you mind . . . ?"

Without waiting for him to finish, Anesh smoothly leaned over and slid them into place on James's head, following it up with a light kiss on the cheek. It felt comfortable; not just the headset—James would correct him at some strategic point in the future about the headphones really being earmuffs—but just the whole action. It occurred to James suddenly just how comfortable they'd gotten with each other, how completely their lives had fully blended together over the last year-and-change of adventure.

Standing behind them, having affixed a pair of earplugs, Alanna started giving range safety orders. "Alright!" she barked out loudly to be heard over the ear protection. "Safeties off!" She paused while the two did so, mostly Anesh, who had to look at his gun sideways to make sure he was doing it right. James just flicked the safety like he'd been holding a gun his whole life. "Fire when ready!" Alanna told them, when they were both in shooting positions.

James adopted a bladed stance, one leg forward, left arm almost straight out. It was, a weird part of his brain informed him, the shooter's stance they trained officers on back in the days of trench warfare. It was also weird because his skill had him automatically adopting a very clean form of the stance, but with the wrong leg extended for a left-handed shot. He corrected. Tilted his head at just the right angle to look down the pistol's sights, and then reached out to file a mental request with the bracelet on his wrist, and triggered the "cluster shot" ability.

The air filled with the cracking of firearms as James and Anesh took careful shots at the targets downrange. James went slower, letting Alanna keep a close eye on his form from the side as he let the bracelet's power take over and do something fucky with the space inside his gun, but even so, his magazine ran out before Anesh's did. There was a pause in the noise while James tried to reload with only one-and-a-half functioning hands, and Alanna corrected Anesh's posture a bit.

"Elbow *up*," she was telling him, hands correcting his form. "Remember, we're not going to be target shooting; you need to get used to keeping your feet so you can rotate your torso to focus on actual things trying to murder you. Try it like this."

They practiced their aim for a bit, half honing their skills for what James had resigned himself to being the inevitability of a fight in the future, half just goofing off together. Anesh took a break after a couple magazines of shots to also stare at James and his use of the bracelet, idly drinking some off-brand soda and making commentary on how it didn't actually seem physically possible for the magic to be doing its magic. He was looking *closely*, too, with Alanna using their bond to dump hours and hours of perception into him while Anesh also recorded the process as closely as he could get without being unsafe.

"Of course it's not possible!" James's voice was louder than he intended as Alanna helped him take the ear protection off. "It's literal magic, my dude!"

"Bah," Anesh gave the best possible rebuttal he could muster as the friends stowed their weapons and took seats on the rocks. "It's just . . . well, the Office stuff all kind of manipulates matter, in some way. It moves things around. I don't think we've ever seen anything from it that *makes* stuff. Unless you count line items on a schedule, but I count that as moving around information and memory. But this looks more like it's layering physical actions on top of each other in the same moment. It's time nonsense again." He looked down at the can in his hand. "Also, you know what's weird?"

James leaned back and reached out a foot to tap at the prone form of Alanna, who had doubled over with laughter as Anesh asked what was weird *on top of the gun magic*. "Is it the bracelet's reload thing? Actually, quick question on that. Would it be a good idea to have one bound to one of the heavier rifles that we can rechamber, so that we can just . . . manufacture bullets? I feel like that would save us a lot of money, depending on if we can take the created bullets out of the guns."

"Uh . . . yes? Probably? I'm honestly not sure what the value of a single charge is. Maybe text JP when we have cell service again?" Anesh shrugged. "But no, I was going to say it was weird drinking normal human soda. Can you tell me the last time you had a soda that wasn't from Officium Mundi? Like, something . . . and I hate to say it . . . normal?"

They thought about it for a second. Eventually, Alanna raised a hand. "I have coffee basically every day?"

"Wizard coffee?"

She lowered her hand, tossing her head back and forth in a comically dramatic fashion that James and Anesh both found cute. "No, coffee from the place down behind our apartment. Though they could change their name to Wizard Coffee and probably do okay by it."

James nodded. "I would drink at a place called Wizard Coffee."

"Of course you would," Anesh gave him some friendly mockery. "You're trying to set yourself up as a wizard king or something. You've gotta be on brand."

"Fuck that. Wizard king is a coward's title. It implies you have some kind of idiotically tall tower, and never actually do anything useful." He snorted derisively. "You know," James said, turning slightly serious, "I honestly think that's what the FBI thinks I'm up to?" He shrugged, tilting his head back to look up at the sunny sky overhead. "Honestly, I cannot believe that they're dealing with us because they think we're 'experts' in the unknown. Randall has been in our Lair for more than five minutes, he should know the closest thing we have to expertise is the uncanny ability to fall ass-backward into new dungeons."

Alanna let out a grunt as she rose and dusted the dirt off her shirt. "Yeah, it feels bad. Even Nate hates it. Or he's a better actor than we gave him credit for. I don't get why we don't just wipe Randall's memory and kick him out."

There were a number of reasons to not do that, which James and Anesh took it in turn to list off. Secret wasn't some kind of *Men in Black* memory-wiping device, for one thing. Also, the man's supervisors would be instantly alerted that something was up. Not to mention that he might have bugged the Lair anyway. Also, it was probably unethical. And there was, of course, still the off chance that he was operating exactly as he claimed; just a liaison between the FBI and the mysterious group of people who somehow had an in behind the curtain of reality.

The most telling thing about why that last one was concerning was that it had been months, and somehow, in all that time, their FBI liaison had failed to provide them with concrete information, leads on any weird happenings, or even go so far as to ask for advice.

"I don't think I like him much," James commented, regarding Randall. "He's just kind of an asshole. Useful, sure, but I absolutely don't trust him, and he's a dick, and I wish to end our arrangement with the government."

Alanna nodded. "I'm getting increasingly more onboard with team 'down with the man' these days," she said. "But there's a bit of a problem."

"Getting rid of him?" Anesh asked.

"You make it sound like we're gonna do a murder," James commented from his position on the sunny rock as he tried to gently flick a beetle off his knee. "No, the problem is that they're not going to want to let us go. They want us to be an asset, or a resource. So this has the potential to get ugly. I'm not saying it was the wrong choice to go to them when it mattered, but . . . well, it's not simple now that we're here."

Anesh nodded, tossing his can into the trash bag they'd brought to keep bullet casings and wrappers in. "No joke," he confirmed. "And it's getting exhausting having to pretend some things aren't real," he added.

"Oh yeah. I wanted to ask about that," James said. "Before I fuck up; I know we're keeping your duplication thing secret, but what else? Skulljacks, I'm assuming?"

"We're keeping the duplication secret *because* of the skulljacks," Alanna said. "They are, hands down, the most cataclysmic tool in our arsenal." She sighed as she wandered over to pull down the shooting targets. "Look, James, the cluster shot thing is so fucking ridiculous, it literally puts all three bullets in the same hole. And that's maybe one percent as horrifying as the idea of the US government having people on payroll that can dig through the secrets of anyone they want." She rolled up the paper and offered it to Anesh, who started packing it back up in the cardboard tube. "It's the most potent intelligence-gathering tool in the universe, short of actual astral projection, *maybe*."

"Or some other bloody bullshit we haven't encountered yet," Anesh added.

"Yes, or some other . . . yes," Alanna admitted. "That thing our boyfriend said."

James found himself unable, and also unwilling, to disagree. There were several things that he wanted in life, and several things he wanted to see from the world. *Any current government having mind powers* was probably one of the last things that would ever show up on either of those lists. Unless it was just an emergent property of the whole world having mind powers, and the government being made up of normal people.

Normal people with skulljacks. Or their future-iteration equivalent.

It was weird to think about. But they weren't really aiming for personal growth and small-scale change anymore, were they? At some point, they were absolutely going to unleash the skulljack on the world, and they needed to be ready for it.

He was going to have to hire a new programmer, James realized. Honestly, he should probably hire an entire division. Stumbling on Virgil had been . . . a minor miracle. The guy had been a genius, and while he'd sorta known it, he'd never gotten a big head about the whole thing. Replacing him . . . wasn't going to happen. But replacing his role would be doable. Five or six compsci students might have enough concentrated ego to create a black hole in the basement, but James was willing to take that risk.

"Today was nice. We should get ice cream! That'd make today perfect," James stated, breaking himself out of his morose thoughts while still staring at the clouds. He waited for the other two to finish laughing—and agreeing with him—before asking, "So, what's the rest of the week look like? I'm getting the leg cast off tomorrow, and the hand one sometime next week. But aside from that . . . delves?"

"Not sure it's safe . . ." Anesh started, but Alanna caught his eye and gave a little shake of her head. He quirked a nervous smile at her, and corrected himself. "Ah, yeah. Officium Mundi tomorrow. Whatever goofy thing Sarah's calling the attic on Friday . . ."

"Clutter Ascent," James added cheerfully.

"Why." Anesh half-questioned, rubbing at his forehead. "Why not a normal name, like . . . Attic . . . something . . ."

Alanna, wide grin on her face, snapped her fingers at him. "That's why," she gleefully pointed out. "Also, it's just . . . don't you think it's cool? The whole world has sterilized titles and names down to professional business things only, and it's boring. We *should* name things new stuff. Cool stuff! Let's live in the *fun* world!"

After a moment of groaning and eventually relenting when he found he agreed with his girlfriend, Anesh continued. "Alright, fine. A few people are going into Clutter Ascent on Friday; we're doing a lot of research on its development, by the way. And then that's mostly it. No major events, no planned crisis . . . oh! Crisis response training on Sunday, for anyone who can make it. Small-unit tactics, same day, at night. Am I forgetting anything?" He looked over at Alanna.

"We're keeping an eye on the school, obviously," she said. "And we will go in if we can. We need to actually get a book and keep it for replication. Oh, and we're aiming for purples this time in the office; gotta put that kit for any new people together!"

"Wait, no classes?" James glanced at Anesh. "What about that one thing that was only available during the summer?"

Anesh looked askew and mouthed out *what* . . . before blinking himself back to reality. "Wait, what? No. That . . . I took that class. I don't need to take it *every year*. Also, I'm basically done with everything school-related, except tutoring."

"I wanna meet your math girlfriend!" Alanna demanded from the sidelines.

The guys ignored her, James politely, Anesh with a flushed face. "Well," James started to ask, "if you've got time, wanna start doing basketball practice again? I missed too much during the fight with the Old Gun, and I want to . . ."

"James, I know I just had a whole thing about cool titles, you can't just name things like that. You have to ask us first!" Alanna interrupted. "What if one of us had a better name already, huh? Then you'd look pretty dumb!"

"Do you?"

"No!"

"So . . ."

Anesh stopped them. "I'd love to do some basketball. Alanna, you want in on this? Oh! We should put a hoop up in the back parking lot! We could get the whole Order in on this!"

"I'm kinda surprised you're this into it. I thought that it'd be a betrayal of cricket or something."

Anesh shrugged. "You know, I feel like it's kind of like the art thing."

"Art thing?" Alanna and James asked in unison, Alanna offering James a fist bump afterward, which he awkwardly returned with his off hand.

"You know, where people say they'd love to be able to draw, but never practice drawing?" Anesh clarified, and got a pair of *ooooohs* back in instant recognition. "Well, I suddenly know how to do this thing. I'm not going through the early slog of getting good; I'm already good, and now I can get better, but we're right in the meat of the thing. It's fun."

"And you're not squandering basketball," Alanna reminded him.

Anesh rolled his eyes. "JP overreacts to things," he muttered with good humor. "Anyway. We about ready to head back?"

"Yuuuup." James hauled himself up with Alanna's help, and they set about packing up their little spot, making sure there was no garbage, policing their brass, and stowing the guns. The walk back to the car was a lot easier for Anesh with the cooler lightened, and easier for Alanna with all the bullets fired, and the trio were just happily relaxed as they pulled back onto the dirt road to head toward home.

They spent the drive discussing what kind of litmus test they should use to make sure they didn't hire assholes. Which turned into an hour-long conversation on what it meant to be an asshole, and how people could change, and then turned into James talking about this one anime he once saw and half remembered the details of. Overall, it was a great use of a beautiful June afternoon. The only issue was when James wrested control of the car radio away from Anesh, and the escalating argument about what qualified as 'country' music, which Alanna put a stop to by threatening to make them listen to political news podcasts.

Then they got ice cream. And it really was perfect.

CHAPTER 8

The Lair, a place that had become important enough to everyone to get its own half-joking capital-letter name, was the sort of place that contained multitudes.

Sometimes people said that and they meant it as a metaphorical sort of thing. Something to indicate that there was a hidden complexity to a person or group. And to be fair, they *did* have deeper layers to them. But when the people who hung out or lived in the building said that the Lair contained multitudes, they were usually talking about basements.

At least three different attempts had been made to label the basements, and all of them failed when someone would get B1-A and B1-B mixed up in the elevator, or when a sign would get knocked down and go a few days without being replaced. Or just when someone would think it was funny to joke about not knowing, and then realize they'd actually gotten it mixed up by failing to properly drill the information into their heads.

So Reed called his basement the Research basement, because that was where the lion's share of Research did their work. The other basement was . . . he didn't know. The living basement?

He discarded that name pretty quickly. If dungeons really were alive, a conclusion that they'd sort of arrived at with a little help from the world's largest experimental accident, then that meant one of his friends had died in a living basement. So Reed was kind of averse to the title, even if the other side *was* the basement people lived in.

People including himself, as of recently. So really, he couldn't even say that *this* was his basement and *that* was for other people. Currently, he was roommates with three camracondas and an iLipede, though that last one was mostly because the thing kept creeping in when they weren't looking and trying to eat their lamp. Possibly because it looked too much like an orb. Or maybe it just liked their company. It didn't matter; living with people was awkward, but Reed didn't exactly have anywhere else to go unless he wanted to drain their thinly stretched funds to get an apartment somewhere.

Today, carrying on his new tradition of distracting himself with work, Reed was looking at a pile of documents with a blank stare and wondering how he'd ever gotten from the guy who just liked figuring out what magic items did, to the guy who people trusted to look at classified documents.

The papers stolen from Status Quo weren't exactly stacked up on the desk he was using, but he did have a cardboard banker's box full of what he planned to check today sitting next to him, and another box on the other side that was filling up very slowly as he read over the documents and scanned the files into a digital form.

A *lot* of it was getting sent to Karen and a few people working with her to try to track down where the enigmatic enemy had managed to dump certain families on short notice. Reed was pretty sure he recognized the document type on first glance at this point, though there was the ever-present issue of the black bars covering up keywords and names. Status Quo probably hadn't thought much of the problem of relocating people within a few days, because they had a *lot* of experience doing it.

In many cases, it wasn't even done to other unknown delvers. Just to people who had witnessed something or *might* have had a connection to someone relevant. Status Quo had the power to uproot lives, fog memories, and shred a *lot* of records, and they used that combination of magic and mundane force liberally as a solution to almost every person they ever ran into.

Reed didn't like them much. Not that anyone down here really did, but he felt like he got to dislike them in a special way, since he was the one combing through their paperwork for any mention of other magic items they might have stockpiled or any dungeons they'd left alive.

His work was cut short by a shadow partially blocking the white light from the overhead tube as Nik slid up to the other side of where he was working. Nikhail's look had been steadily changing ever since he'd been broken out of Officium Mundi, but even though he was decidedly more masculine these days, Reed still got exactly the same vibe every time his friend and fellow explorer of the unknown sidled up to wherever he was working.

"So, I'm looking at these magic headphones," Nik said, holding up the thin white cord with a pair of archetypical earbuds on the end. "And I've got a question."

Letting the manilla folder full of redacted documents he was holding drop to the desk, and seizing the opportunity to do literally anything else, Reed looked up at his fellow Researcher. "You can't take them, I'm giving them to Momo later."

Nikhail tilted his head, headphones still dangling from his outstretched fist. ". . . Are you trying to woo her with gifts?" he asked.

"Don't . . . don't say it like that. Also, *no*. Those ones teach you how to break whatever they're plugged into, and she wants to use them to make a totem to see . . . well, that." Reed waved a hand idly. "It's part of our endless plan to stumble into identifying stuff and finding ways to make our own magic."

"Wait, really? These aren't the ones that translate jazz into spoken poetry?"

"You're thinking of the black ones with the fuzzy ear things." Reed looked around as if the magic item might be easily in sight, but it wasn't, because they'd *sort of* learned to keep the objects of power contained in labeled cardboard boxes.

Nik was undeterred. "I thought those were the ones that remind you about appointments."

"No, that's your phone." Reed laughed at his own joke. "Was there . . . something about those?"

Raising his eyebrows and holding his closed fist back up, Nik dropped the tangent and remembered what he was going to ask. "Right! The headphones! So, these are . . . obviously an Apple product, right? Even though they're from the dungeon?"

That, at least, Reed knew how to answer. "Legally, no. Also, as a piece of hardware, no." Despite the signature shape and all-white design, the headphones were *technically* not the same as the kind you could buy off store shelves. But only barely. "Why do you ask?"

"Oh, I was thinking—mostly as a joke—about how it's kind of impressive they haven't broken yet. And then I was wondering about what the threshold for 'broken' is for stuff like this that's more delicate electronic equipment." Nik dangled the earbuds from pinched fingers. "Look, this one already has a knot in it, *somehow*. I've actually screwed up a pair like these—well, the non-magic Apple ones—by tugging on something like that too hard, so would doing that just . . . vaporize this?"

"Possibly." Reed leaned forward, looking at where the headphone cord had bunched up. "Don't do that, I guess? Maybe listen to them, so they can tell you what would break them? That's the whole point, right? Momo won't care if you use them."

Nik nodded and started trying to carefully untangle the headphones with one hand while pulling out a phone to plug them into from his pocket with the other. Setting his phone on the desk as he failed to make headway with the cord, he carefully undid the knot, strung it out, and tugged on it slightly to straighten it out of its default coil.

And then the whole thing broke down.

Watching a magic item made from a blue orb break was honestly a really cool thing if you played it back in slow motion, which Reed had done for a bunch of different tests with the various pens that wrote in specific fonts that they tended to find a lot of. There was a threshold of damage that any given dungeon tech item could sustain, and once that was crossed, the whole thing fell apart *fast*. Lines would appear across it as the weaker parts were pushed away from each other. Then the smallest pieces would begin to dissolve, turning from solid matter into a lightly glowing blue glitter that would fade from existence shortly after showing up. Oftentimes, the small pieces falling off would mean that larger pieces were no longer connected, but the dissolving effect propagated from the edges of where things had fallen away, and would consume the rest of the object within about a quarter of a second.

That last part was kind of important, because it meant that if you broke an item by accident when no one was looking, you might never know what happened to it unless you found the orb it dropped and deduced what was missing.

The orb itself was also kind of weird. Lots of things, like those aforementioned pens, weren't actually large enough to fully contain even the smallest of the Office's orbs. But that didn't stop them from showing up when the items broke, and on camera, it looked like the item itself had been *covering* the orb, with a tiny bit revealed as the thing broke away, and then an optical illusion slid more of the orb into sight.

Neither Reed nor Nik had magic eyes yet, so they didn't really have to worry about seeing anything mind-bending without recording the accidental destruction of the dungeon tech. But Nik did fumble the orb onto Reed's desk, sending the small glowing blue ball rolling across the folder he was working with. On reflex, Reed slapped a hand down on it before it reached him, sending another puff of that vanishing glitter out as it broke.

[+1 *Skill Rank : Bureaucracy—Corporate—Shipping—Footwear*]

[*Problem Solved : Lunch Acquired*]

"Aah!" Nik jerked back as a plate with a sandwich and chips on it appeared next to his head where he had tried to lunge for the orb before Reed broke it.

Reed felt like he could do a little yelling too. But there was a weird satisfaction that he got from pretending to be calm and collected in the face of the nonsense that was his daily life. "Don't yell at my lunch," he told Nik with a steady voice. "Also, Momo's going to want to have words with you. Also, that was *great* timing."

"Aw, fuck." Nik sighed. "Will she accept an apology, 'cause I'm really sorry?"

"I mean, probably. She's not some unhinged lunatic, she's just weird and frantic," Reed said with a sigh. "And un . . . rested? Unslept? Tired all the time. Sorry, I've been talking to James a lot lately and I'm starting to believe that the way he talks is normal."

Nik looked almost like he was actually upset. "I seriously didn't mean to—"

"Why are you freaking out over this?" Reed cut him off.

"Because I . . . broke a magic item? Why *aren't* you freaking out!" Nik demanded, voice cracking.

Reed shrugged and ate one of the chips that had appeared on his desk. Ketchup flavor, which was out of the ordinary but not too bad. "Two weeks ago, Anesh and Alanna brought me a prescription bottle that *seemed* to turn anything in it into ibuprofen, including just . . . uh . . . dirt. Alanna said I should look into 'increasing throughput' so we could . . . do something with that. She said a lot about it, it was hard to follow."

". . . And?"

"And I ran over it with one of the rolling chairs a half hour later." Reed admitted. "And then one of the camracondas used the blue orb and got a skill rank in breakdancing, and solved a problem that was so small I don't remember it. And no one cared." He ran a hand through his curly hair, soft fingers tugging at the unruly mop as he stared across the open room full of cluttered acquisitions both magical and mundane. "Most stuff probably isn't irreplaceable. I mean, don't break the Status Quo crown on purpose, but also . . . it's fine. We'll find something else, and adapt."

"You're weirdly chill about this." Nik gave him a suspicious stare.

"I've been going to therapy," Reed said, comfortably using the almost-tangent as an answer. "Trying to deal with losing my brother."

Nik jerked back. "Ryan died?! When?! He hasn't even been on any delves, and I'd know, 'cause *I've* been on every delve!"

That information was new to Reed, who thought that Nik had just been enjoying the relative freedom that working here brought. Freedom which he kind of didn't take advantage of himself; no one was *making* him stay in a basement and read classified documents about war crimes, after all. He got paid regardless; he could have gone out and done fun stuff every day or something.

But the basement had magic in it. And Reed just kind of internally shrugged to himself as he realized that Nik was probably going into Officium Mundi every week for exactly the same reason. That was where the magic came from.

The delving approach was a lot more hands-on than Reed wanted for himself. He liked the process of poking and prodding, taking meticulous notes, thinking up tests that were as useful as possible in a broad context, that sort of thing. Every time someone brought in a *thing* and said "This might be magic?" he got a burst of energy unlike anything else.

He did *not* get that feeling with the dungeon. Reed wasn't really interested in *ever* going back into a dungeon. For one thing, he couldn't run fast enough to outpace even a mildly interested strider, much less something like a tumblefeed. And having a body that was best described as 'like a marshmallow' also made him unsuited for fighting back, which was fine, because he didn't want to fight anyway.

It wasn't really relevant to what Nik had asked him, but the perspective sort of helped Reed understand his friend a bit better in that moment. "Oh, right," he said, answering the *actual* question, and not his own thoughts. "No, Ryan's not dead. He just left."

"Again, when?!" Nik said in that tone that was like a shout but at half the volume so he didn't bother the handful of other people working down here this afternoon. "What do you mean *left*?"

"Uh . . . it's . . . a little personal," Reed admitted. "And I don't want to talk about it?"

"Yeah, but *I* do." Nik ignored the polite attempt to establish boundaries. "I thought we were friends!"

"Us?"

"No, me and Ryan!"

Well, that was a jarring thing to hear. "Okay, ow." Reed started laughing. It was too dumb to take personally, and suddenly it was all just hilarious to him. "Fine. He . . . found out our family remembers him." Reed pretended to go back to studying the papers he had dropped. "Not me, though. So he asked that I don't 'ruin it for him,' and he moved back home. Fun fact, our grandpa is *stupidly* rich, so he gets to . . . eh." Reed trailed off, not knowing where he was even going with that.

Letting the awkward silence take over, he flipped through four pages of relocation forms, made a note on what part was probably a zip code, and then dumped the folder into the 'out' box before grabbing a fresh piece of nightmares.

". . . Seriously?" Nik said eventually, after staring open-mouthed at his friend and technically boss. "He said that?"

"Yeah, apparently he doesn't want them to think he's weird, so he's just kind of pretending I'm not real, and going along with it." Reed was surprised how easy it was to say. The whole thing had been eating at him for a while, and it felt exactly as cathartic to tell someone else as his therapist had told him it would. Which was a bit annoying, honestly, but only because of his own stubborn and cowardly refusal to open up. "Anyway. I've been thinking about—"

"No! No, not *anyway*!"

Nik's yell was loud enough that it attracted attention from some of the others nearby. John and Taste-of-Air, especially, were doing that thing where they silently agreed to drop their own conversation and pretend to still be working as they listened in on the juicy workplace gossip. It was, if anything, a powerful interspecies bonding moment to learn that both humans and camracondas were dying to know about the small secrets going on in other people's lives.

Reed continued, ignoring Nik. ". . . Anyway, now that I'm thinking of people who are gone," he said with a morose little smile, "maybe we should clear out Virgil's desk."

"No, no, I think I'd rather talk about your asshole brother," Nik declared. "Hey, let's get Plan to eat his brain."

"Please don't be a bad influence on the *single* stable new infomorph we have here." Reed groaned. "No one can figure out how to make new ones, we can *barely* manage to feed Plan, and James has made it pretty clear that if we create an unstable infomorph again he's going to . . . uh . . ."

Nik raised his bushy eyebrows. "Murder us?"

"No, he didn't actually say what he'd do," Reed mumbled. "I don't think he knows how to threaten people. But also I feel a strange compulsion to not disappoint him."

"Magic?"

"Either mind control or respect, and I'm not sure which is less likely."

Nik scoffed. "Hey, I *like* James. He's cool."

"See, that right there? That sounds like mind control." Reed chuckled to himself. "I'm serious though. We should go through Virgil's files and things. We can't just keep leaving his desk there like we're expecting him back."

The words made Nik turn his head and stare across the cold concrete of the open room. "I'm serious too," he said bitterly. "I'd rather find a way to mind-wipe Ryan than to . . . what's even the term? Go through someone's effects?"

Reed snorted a surprised laugh. "That term might mean something different for us in the future."

"Yeah, let's talk about that," Nik said with a rapid jerking nod. "Not . . . anything else."

"Virgil's gone," Reed said tersely, suddenly finding a heat in his voice that he wasn't expecting. "We can't just . . . leave his shit there. If nothing else, think of how irritated *he'd* be that we're wasting floor space."

Nik's mouth twitched in a small approximation of a snarl as he paced back and forth on the other side of the desk. "I just . . ." He stopped and stared up at the ceiling. Tried that deep breath thing that he'd seen James do a lot, and found it kind of helped. "Virgil was a jackass and he was never not a prick to me and *even then* I don't think I have the energy to deal with him being dead yet. Can we just do it later?"

That seemed reasonable enough to Reed. "Sure," he said, and then named his price. "But you're going to have to listen to me monologue for a bit."

"Oh." Nik realized he may have made a tactical error. "It's not gonna be about something dumb, is it? The last time you cared about something enough to monologue, it was *Star Wars* and I had to gnaw my own arm off to escape the trap."

"What is it with everyone and not wanting to talk about Star Wars, anyway?" Reed seemed genuinely confused. "I *like* the movies! That's *why* I want to talk about them! I'm not gonna be weird about it."

Nik stole a few of Reed's chips as he answered. "I think we're all too used to the internet, where everything is worse."

"Well it's not my surprisingly deep and philosophical analysis of the cultural stability of the Sith. *This time.*" Reed threatened his friend with a pointed finger that was far less menacing than he thought it was. "I just want to rubber duck about the telepad tests."

Nik wasn't sure if that was better or worse.

The term *rubber duck* had been in use for about as long as humanity had possessed both computers and rubber ducks in the same place at the same time. The idea went that if you were stuck with a technical problem, and you explained your code to a rubber duck, the solution would come to you a lot easier. In reality, the duck probably wasn't required, and it was just that expressing ideas out loud meant a person had to actually think through how to explain something, which led to identifying obvious points that could be worked on. But the duck was a powerful symbol, and symbols like that tended to stick around in some form. Programmers were a lot like dungeons in how they latched onto metaphors, really.

And really, it did work. Nik did it a lot when he was working with people to figure out how to determine if a coffee mug was magical, and how to do it without breaking anything. He just wasn't sure how much energy he had to *be the duck* today.

But Reed was already talking and Nik definitely didn't have the social battery to escape the conversation now.

"It's the line of sight thing," Reed started with, and Nik groaned inside. And outside. "Yeah, I know. It's just . . . okay. Between how Secret and Planner eat things, and how the Office tends to be all . . . bureaucratic, I guess . . . I think we can safely say that the dungeon tech objects like to do their work on structured information."

Nik threw Reed a bone. "You can't prove that, but sure, let's say so."

Reed grimaced as he realized that even accepting *that* meant that this whole thing could be undermined by one weird test. "Addresses always work. Any address, anywhere. Well, I mean, not *any* address, we can't prove that and no one is willing to teleport into the Kremlin just to try. But every address we've tested."

Nik nodded along. "Yup. I helped with those."

"And if something that has a legal distinction is written down but not a specific address, the telepad defaults to a 'central' area of it. Like, if you put a city, it will put you on Main Street."

"Yeah, and *not* the geographic center." Nik had been there for those tests too, and had needed to sprint around a corner and teleport away when a bunch of people saw him and wanted to ask if he'd just appeared from nowhere. James said they weren't a conspiracy, but *being super awkward* was a much more powerful motivator.

Reed kept going. "I even understand how the telepads are . . . uh . . . is it okay to call them *sassy?*" he asked, and Nik just shrugged at him as he moved out of the way to let a woman wheeling a table on a little handcart walk past. Three camracondas followed in her wake, either hissing excitedly or out of breath. Reed ignored the normal part of his day. "If you write down something abstract, the telepads will interpret it as literally as possible, and find a city or building with that name to drop you in."

"I was thinking about that, actually," Nik interrupted. "That's *mostly* put us in English-speaking countries, so far. And of those, mostly not literal England, because their place names are odd. Do the telepads have a language barrier?"

The headache their most important tool gave Reed intensified. "Thanks," he whined, trying to sound good-natured and mostly failing. "Great. Thanks. Love that. What *really* bothers me though isn't that we keep teleporting to the middle of Arkansas for a bunch of tests, it's that all those rules, all those careful little lines with clean definitions, just *vanish* if you're looking at something."

"Mmh." Nik's noncommittal noise around a mouthful of Reed's manifested lunch was followed by a quick swallow as he wiped the corner of his mouth. "So, it's not about the weird rules, it's about the rule that breaks the rules?"

"Yes. Also, stop eating my sandwich." Reed tried to shift the plate away from Nik, but his friend just went back to pacing in front of the desk, intent on eventually ending up next to the food. It wasn't like anyone here went hungry, and going upstairs for lunch would be good for Reed anyway, but it was a personal affront for Nik to keep stealing *his* food. "Everything is *structured*. Addresses in a government system takes top priority, followed by ad hoc addresses including paired symbols, then broader place names by tiered geographic size and alphabetically within that. Addresses that don't exist default to taking names first, then numbers. You can't teleport to the moon."

"*That* experiment was fuckin' dumb." Nik voiced the opinion everyone had shared instantly upon hearing about it.

Reed felt like he wasn't getting to *monologue* so much with all the interruptions. "And every one of those restrictions is . . . every one of those restrictions *except the moon one* vanishes if you're looking at where you want to go. *Then* you go exactly where you wrote!"

"Wait, actually?" Nik asked. "So, if you write *home* while looking at your home, you don't end up in Arkansas again?"

"No, which is good, because I think we're in danger of having our 'oops' budget cut." Reed went back to subconsciously tugging at his hair. Not hard enough to rip it out yet, but he was building to that.

"I just . . . we're supposed to be making sure the telepads are safe, and useful, and finding every corner case so that the whole Order can use them, you know?" Reed's voice was strained, almost pitiable. "And I'm just . . . feeling like an idiot. And tired."

Nik stopped where he was reaching to steal another bite of sandwich, letting out a breath as he dropped his antics and patted Reed on the shoulder. "Two things," he said. "One, don't be so hard on yourself. Basically everyone is working on that. Two, why not just say that the line of sight rule takes priority over the others? It's still a *rule*, right?"

". . . Oh." Reed dropped his hand and straightened up. "Oh. Yeah, that makes sense. Also, we should see if it works with other senses, like hearing. Thanks, Nik. You're a good rubber duck."

Nik stopped patting him on the shoulder. "I know what you mean, but that *sounds* like it's an insult." He laughed. "So, should we go find a stack of telepads and start adding to the list of rules?"

"No. I need lunch. And you need to go apologize to Momo."

And Reed needed to put the Status Quo documents away. And also read over a couple of people's reports on magical coffee mugs. And send James a request to try to make a yellow totem. And figure out how many people they had space for down here, since the Order was going to be hiring new people soon, he'd heard. Oh, and also talk to a couple of camracondas about the orb splitting thing that some of them could do. Plus there was a whole new headache in the form of the Status Quo magic items they had piled up down here.

"You have lunch," Nik tried to lie to him.

"I'm not eating six surviving ketchup chips and a sandwich you already ate half of," Reed told him, standing up and wishing he hadn't broken the refilling ibuprofen bottle as his tired body protested the motion. "I'll meet up with you here in an hour."

"Yeah, okay. Also, one of the camracondas stole the chips, so you don't even have those."

Reed actually was impressed. "Wow, they're pretty sneaky when they want to be." He nodded appreciatively as he headed for the stairs.

It was a normal Wednesday in the Research basement. Half his job was reading paperwork from murderers. And he was tired, and had a headache, and felt overwhelmed. But also there was nowhere Reed would rather be.

CHAPTER 9

**Order of Endless Rooms, Operations Manual
Section 1, Part 8: Chain of Command**

As the Order grows, the flow of authority and responsibility becomes less clear and requires more written and explicit guidelines. This has the benefit of making it easier for individuals to understand where the lines are, but it also has the downside of making those lines seem inviolable. So, this is the mandate of the Order that you should follow above all else.

Embrace responsibility, and share authority. If you are needed, and feel competent enough to act, then step forward and act. If you need help, ask. If a decision seems too big for you, collaborate. We are all in this together.

That is the spirit of our organization. And while you may report to someone for a project, or have a clean spot on the chart of authority somewhere, the real world gets messy sometimes. So remember that: we're all in this together.

The Order doesn't have common tiers of management or authority. Instead, what we have are positions that reflect our membership. We are a collection of specialists, and though what we specialize in may change day to day, the things we choose to focus on have leadership roles attached.

For example, someone who considers themselves a part of Research may also work with the support group, and participate in delves. When they want to run an experiment to see if a blue orb can be used to create a sentient motorcycle, there's someone with authority in the Research division who they draft a request to. On a delve, they answer to their team leader, and if a combat situation arises, they follow orders through the delver's chain of command. When checking up on survivors, a leader from the support group will provide them with a schedule and the phone numbers to call. Or, if they've taken on more responsibility, maybe they'll be the one drawing the schedule and dividing the checkups.

There is no one clear chain of command. There is no one who is in charge—even the person you might think should be—and *no one* who has ultimate authority. We all have responsibilities to certain facets of our operation, and fundamentally, we have to trust each other.

In the event that trust breaks down, or you believe authority is being abused, the following list contains the positions to contact, in order from first to last . . .

James ducked under the attempt by the stuffed shirt to grab him. The dungeon employee lurched off-balance in stumbling steps past him as James landed rapid stabs into its side. Blunt force trauma wasn't especially effective against these things, seeing as they were still fundamentally made of paper stuffed with dust, but hitting them always had the opportunity to open rips in their skin. James wasn't hitting it with his fist, though; he was using a short blade, which had a *very* high chance to open holes.

The first time he'd faced off against one of these things, James had only barely made it out alive, and that was mostly because Anesh had bailed him out. He'd been powered by dexterity coffee, freshly equipped with martial arts skills, and fighting for something important, and he'd still gotten the *crap* kicked out of him.

It was amazing what changed when you had actual combat experience.

The main lesson James had learned was that you had to get over your body's desire to *not* put your full strength into strikes. Even when you were actively trying to hurt something, the human brain would still subconsciously pull punches, and getting past that was the work of a hundred small fights and hours of training. That, and knowing the patterns and motions of different dungeon Life; the tricks they could pull, the amount of damage they could do if you weren't careful. And knowing how to keep moving, to use momentum and speed as defensive forces, and keeping a constant situational awareness of where you were standing relative to the thing trying to eat you.

It wasn't just the combat experience, obviously, though that was important. There was also just . . . more to the delvers than there was back then. More teammates, more tactics, more powers snapped up from various orbs or books, more old secrets, more new Secrets. And, in James's case in particular, a new sword.

The stuffed shirts weren't all uniform, either. Which complicated things, to say the least. Some of them were strong enough to crush bones and fling humans through the thin cubicle walls. Some of them were *strong*, but the kind of strong that just surprised you a bit, instead of surprising you to death. Some of them wore masks made of sticky notes that camouflaged their inhuman nature with a more lifelike face, and it was basically impossible to tell which until they pulled their faces off and threw the suddenly brightly colored flailing thing at you. Some of them carried purple orbs, and would use them to create infomorphic Life as a form of "cursing" delvers.

That last one was happening now, behind James. Which was a shame, because they were trying to get the orb before it could be used. But also because he wasn't watching as the third stuffed shirt transformed the orb into a living idea, which Anesh dodged, and which James was caught in the crossfire of.

All of a sudden, there was an almost manic compulsion running through James's mind. An idea that was insidious, because it was his own mind thinking it. It wasn't some alien invader that he could have some epic mental duel with; he simply now had an idea in his head, that had its own agenda, and that he'd be thinking about, because it thought itself with his brain cells.

It was a schedule. A strict timeline of when he was to be at work, at the gym, in bed, even how long to take brushing his teeth. And it made James falter for a brief second.

In that second, Alanna and Anesh, with support from Ganesh and Secret, fell on and finished off the damaged paper pusher they were fighting. And also in that second, the monster that James had taken his eyes off, the one that was leaking dust and shredded paper from a pair of nasty gashes, hit him in the side hard enough that it knocked him back over one of the desks that were just standing out in this field of carpet like wooden boulders.

James sprawled on the ground, staring up at the strange pattern of fluorescent lights overhead. The bars of white light were positioned at strange angles to each other; almost, but never quite, a perfect right angle. They chased each other in strange lines across the false ceiling, jagged scars of light that were at the same time haphazard and mesmerizing.

It wasn't a memetic effect; James had just thunked his head onto the floor as he'd fallen, and between that and having the wind knocked out of him, part of his brain felt like just staring at the ceiling was a good plan.

When the paper pusher tried to follow up the strike by lashing a kick toward James's prone head, he processed that information about two seconds too late.

Fortunately, the fake dress shoe never made it to him. Alanna lunged forward in a rushed motion, and managed to smash her war hammer into the thing's knee just before it made it to James's face; at the same time, Ganesh strafed it with his mounted laser, setting a line of fire down its back. The paper pusher howled in its fake human voice as it toppled over, overcommitted to its attack. As it hit the ground, crushing the long carpet under it, Anesh caught up to his partners, and neatly stabbed down at the thing's head with the long spear he was carrying. He missed the first one, but after Alanna kicked it back out of its roll, Anesh's spear found the thing's vital bits, and the remainder of the shredded paper that stuffed the creature's insides spilled out onto the ground.

"Ow," James said as Alanna offered him a gloved hand and hauled him up. He'd meant to say *thank you* but instead, he just kind of managed a grunt of sore pain.

"You've gotta be more—Anesh, put out that fire—careful next time!" Alanna chided him. "What happened?"

James rolled his eyes, and his shoulder, trying to somehow magically fix the bruised muscle under the hard armor. "New infomorph." He sighed. "This one has me scheduled to be 'at work' right now, which is good, because . . ." James swept an arm around them at the "office" they were inside. "But yeah. Secret, do you mind . . .?" He left the question unspoken.

Secret, in his half-ethereal form, coiled around James's legs as he raised himself up to speak. "Hmm. Yes. I do not mind," the infomorphic serpent said. "Be careful while I am elsewhere," he spoke, before lunging forward and tunneling his ghostly body through James's chest. He didn't emerge out the other side, and James sighed again as he resigned himself to some weird dreams later tonight.

"I've got a question," Anesh asked, kneeling down by the dead paper pusher and ripping away a hole so he could stick his hand inside it and pull out the yellow orb within.

Alanna and James spoke at the same time. "Shoot." They shot each other smirks.

Rising back to his feet, and dusting off his free hand, Anesh held up the orb. "Why the hell do some of these require amateur butchery to get to?" He turned it over in his hand, noting that it was quite a bit smaller than some of the orbs they'd gotten from paper pushers before. It wasn't a surprise, though; the only reason they'd tried to ambush this group was because the trio all had a feeling about the relative strength of the Life they were facing. If any of these paper pushers had been Puppets, they would have run, no question.

"It's actually professional butchery," James said, slipping the bottle of water he'd cleared his throat with back into his bag. "Since we get paid for this."

"*Do* we get paid for this?" Alanna asked, her eyebrows brought down in concentration, mouth a straight line in thought. "I mean, there's a reward, certainly, but are we salaried?"

"Yes," James said. "JP and Karen set up actual pay rates. It's direct deposit, off of our loot here and also the investments from said loot."

"Are we . . . James, did we turn into capitalism at some point?" Alanna demanded. "This can't be right. You're a communist."

James patted her on an armored shoulder, leaving behind a dusty handprint. "I promise it's temporary until the revolution." He didn't bother to correct her. To a casual observer, a lot of his ideas might line up with communism, but it wasn't actually his thing. He just didn't say anything, because then he might have to admit that he didn't know what the name for his ideology actually was.

"Guys, focus. The orbs," Anesh cut into their banter, as Ganesh settled on his shoulder with a buzz.

"Honestly, I think it's just because they're sorta hollow." James shrugged. "So there's a space inside. Unlike with, like, striders or whatever, where the orb doesn't have a place to go, so it just pops out on the surface."

"Good enough theory for me." Anesh nodded. "Anyone want an orb?" He offered the mid-grade yellow to his partners.

James quirked an eyebrow at him. "What, no copying it for abusable powers?" he asked.

Ever since they'd gained the repeatable—and absolutely abusable—ability to duplicate things, even magical things, the rate at which people actually used orbs had gone way down. Small yellows, sure. And ones they'd already copied, either because they had extras or because they weren't worth saving, since they only gave ranks in adding headers to a Microsoft Office document or something. Or just blues that had been absorbed to fill slots. But for stuff like more important and unique specimens, especially purples or greens? The delver ranks of the Order had kind of stalled out; everyone was waiting for an iLipede analysis or a copy-test, just to make *totally sure* that they weren't going to regret it later.

It actually made James draw a connection between how they were behaving, and the actions of someone playing a particularly long JRPG, holding onto those max-heal potions until *well after* the final boss, *just in case* you needed them eventually. Developing strategies to play without potions at all, because the player never used them anyway.

Which, when he shared that thought, had led to a discussion about whether or not the copy-paste ritual was actually some kind of insidious psychological weapon that Officium Mundi had deployed against them, instead of a reward of sorts.

"No, we're not copying the mixed orbs," Anesh told him. "It's just . . . Okay, first off, it's a pain in the ass to actually get the optimum space use for each ritual, and I've already got the box with the foam insert for smaller orbs. So that's me being lazy. And, in further laziness, it complicates our upgrade kit build. But also? Between testing on greens, keeping our telepad supply up, and also trying to develop a stockpile of Status Quo gear? We just don't have the time or coffee to fuck around that much."

"Wait, we're short on coffee?" James asked.

"Always. We will never have enough," Anesh informed him. "But also, the ritual takes *time*, and until we start leaving people posted in here while the door is sealed to harvest coffee and run the ritual, we're starting to hit a wall in terms of how many goes of it we get per week."

James clicked his tongue. "Huh. Well. Good to know, I guess." He felt that anxiety in the back of his skull again, like he should be solving this problem in some way, but he didn't know where to find a foothold. "Anyway, I'll take an orb, if the guy with zero percent contribution to this fight is included."

"You stabbed a guy," Alanna told him reassuringly, tossing him one of the yellows. "And you have a new brain friend!"

James rolled his eyes as he cracked the orb, hoping that Secret ate his new brain friend before it became too much of a problem.

[+2 Skill Ranks : Acrobatics—Flips]

[+.7 Skill Rank : Knife—Carving]

[+1 Skill Rank : Math—Probability]
[+1 Emotional Resonance Rank : Relaxation]
[Problem Solved : Snack Acquired]
[Certification Added : FSSAI Central License]

"Does anyone know what the FSSAI is?" James asked the others as he sorted through the information that he'd just acquired.

"Aren't they the people who made *Shadowrun?*" Alanna asked idly as she looked through her own orb effects. "Also, score. Three ranks in fishing."

"Score?" James questioned her sanity.

"You're thinking of FASA," Anesh corrected. "And what kind of fishing? Maybe we could arm you with a fishing rod and really lean into James's anime fantasies."

"Is that an anime thing?" Alanna shot back. "It seems . . . hm . . . No, now I can see it. Fishing rod with some kinda weighted end, just absolutely destroying a bunch of idiot teenagers trying to mug me. Yeah, okay, that's anime. Okay! I've decided, James, I will be your fishing waifu." She made the statement a dramatized declaration.

Anesh slowly turned away from Alanna and the mental path he'd set her on. "Sooooo annnnyway . . ." he said to James. "We'll look that up when we get back. And I got a point in astrometrics! So that's pretty cool."

"Oh yeah, I got math points too!" James high-fived his boyfriend. "You know, eventually, you'll need to find something to do with all this math knowledge."

"I'm thinking of getting into space travel," Anesh replied, earnest excitement on his face.

"Shotgun the first dungeon on Mars," Alanna cut in.

"Dammit!" James snapped his fingers. "She beat me to it," he told a confused Anesh, shaking his head wistfully. "Alright. We all good here? We've still got a ton of this place to comb over."

His partners nodded, ready to go.

They were out far from the door today. Miles out, farther than most delvers went, *way* beyond the safe limits for new members.

Maybe beyond their own safe limits too. Out in the wild places, where the geometry twisted into a surreal blend of the natural and the artificial, where they had to adopt safety protocols in case of hypnotic screensavers or camracondas. Where there weren't even the rudimentary sketched maps, or already-written guides to the Life and landscape. It was a frontier where dangers that could one-shot an entire party could be lurking under any random patch of carpet, right alongside new rewards, new treasures, and brand-new sights to see.

It was *perfect*.

Right now, the three of them were in a great grassland. The walls of the cubicles had fallen away, bit by bit, as they'd approached the prairie. And when the last one had dwindled to nothing more than a small lip to step over, they'd arrived.

The carpet here was no flat, hard, corporate-approved thing. It was waist-high, swaying in the breeze of the air conditioning units. The hum of the machines, normally muffled to the point of being inaudible in the expanse of the dungeon, was loudly present, along with the swishing of the long grasslike carpet strands. There were no walls nearby, though every now and then they'd come across a line where the carpet had been packed down, like there'd been something sitting on it for months or years. Like a cubicle had once stood here but been removed long ago. Those lines formed game trails through the grassland, and sometimes made for opportune biking paths. There was still furniture, though. Desks stood at strange angles, jutting out of the ground like boulders. Sometimes they had perfectly flat surfaces, but other times their hard wooden or metal corners poked up into the air as half of the object was buried in the floor. And the wildlife of Officium Mundi, always there in ones and twos or small clusters or nests, was much more exposed out here in the open.

The paper pushers prowled the plains in packs of two or three. They roamed both on their feet and on all fours, their limbs always morphed into inhuman configurations to help them clamber forward over desks or pluck things off the ground. The purely human construction of suits and ties clashed with how they moved like feral beasts to surmount desks and watch for prey with paper eyes. Ironically, despite being in groups, the delve team was finding the monsters remarkably easy to ambush; the false employees spent most of their time facing each other, not watching their surroundings.

Striders here made burrows in the carpet, finding shelter under the overhang of the desks alongside other small Lifeforms. The team hadn't seen any iLipedes yet, but there were a handful of other creatures that shared the little nests. Small collections of unlikely allies, waiting to scavenge off whatever came their way, or perhaps to ambush a larger creation.

There was one other type of larger creation they'd seen. It looked like someone had taken a full bushel of pens and pencils, and turned them into a porcupine. Dozens of layers of *very* sharp-looking implements fanning over its back like a series of coats, rattling and rustling as it waddled across the carpetgrass. They'd not tried to engage the things—which James wanted to call pencupines and which Anesh said lacked originality—mostly because at one point they'd seen one of them rear up and lunge forward to snap a strider out of a burrow with alarming speed. The motion had revealed a sinuous body, a bare skeletal structure made up of flexible desk lamps, with the coats of quills looking more like manes as it rose up. One big plastic cone and the light bulb inside served as the face. But it didn't emit much light; instead the bulb had just cracked open along a zigzag line, and glowing teeth had scythed through the shell of the unwary stapler.

"You know how the pencils in here are always, like, unfairly sharp?" James asked his partners as they stood on a ridge fifty feet away, watching the thing compress itself back down to a dome shape and waddle back into the taller carpet.

Alanna lowered the pair of binoculars she'd brought. From outside, this time. "We've been through the same traps, yes."

"I vote for not touching those," Anesh chimed in. "Even if we find a friendly one. We just feed it from a distance, and then run before it tries to hug us."

"Good plan," James and Alanna agreed quietly.

Their exploration of the grassland continued.

Despite the fact that the entire area was very open, with no walls to hide anything, the prairie held more secrets than they were expecting. The desks, visible when they cut away or rose up over the carpet around them, were troves of curiosities—assuming they could avoid pissing off the residents. It was here, with their bikes parked in one of those small clearings, that Alanna finally found what she'd wanted from day one.

"It's a wallet of holding!" she announced dramatically, holding the folded leather out like a badge to show off to James and Anesh as she yanked a four-inch stack of dollar bills out of it, the paper appearing from seemingly nowhere. "Behold! Finally! The *one thing* this stupid place never helps us with, within our grasp!"

James bit his lip and shot a nervous glance at Anesh. His boyfriend stepped back, hands held up. "Oh *hell* no," Anesh told him. "You crush her dreams. I'm just over here on lookout."

"What? Heresy!" Alanna declared, pulling out twenty clearly fake driver's licenses and scattering them across the desk. "This is exactly what I've wanted! I'm so happy, James."

Ah, hell. She looked so happy, with a big goofy smile on her normally serious face. It killed James a bit to ask the question that Alanna hadn't gotten to yet. "Um . . . so, not to rain on your parade of holding. But did you actually check that it can store things that aren't . . . wallet things?" He spread his hands in a peacemaking gesture. "I'm not saying it's not cool! If nothing else, it'll make it easy to deal with the briefcases, assuming we can even find . . . but yeah, can it store a gun, for example? Or just money and IDs?"

Alanna looked at him, the expression of glee freezing on her face before crumbling away. She muttered something, flipping the wallet back over as she plucked the P-09 out of her holster. Alanna took the time to unload the weapon before trying anything dumb. Then, holding the wallet open with a couple of fingers and still grumbling, she settled the butt of the pistol into the bill slot.

And with a triumphant, wide-eyed look, she watched as the gun slid neatly into the leather rectangle.

"I am so fucking happy right now, I could cry," Alanna announced, closing the wallet and shoving the entire thing into her pocket.

"Well, bugger me," Anesh commented. "That's pretty cool."

James, meanwhile, let out a strangled *hurk* noise, a riotously worried expression on his face. "Alanna!" he gasped out, clawing at his hair in panic. "No!"

"What? What's wrong?"

"You just fucking folded a gun in half!" he shouted. "Why! What?! How! *What?!*"

Anesh glanced around them. "Quieter, mates," he hissed in a hushed voice, catching his partners' attention. "Something's moving." He turned, sweeping his gaze across the landscape, as Alanna and James ceased bickering in an instant. It was all fun and games until they actually needed to be serious; and in those moments, they snapped away from childish behavior in an instant.

Their heads were on swivels, scanning across the grass around them. James could hear it too, now. It was something like a low humming, a whirr that rose above the noise of the unseen fans in the distance. Mechanical, surely. He wiped sweat off his forehead as he tried to spot it; the armor was hot enough already, but the lights here felt like the beating sun.

James looked across the carpetgrass, to where he could see the cubicle city far in the distance. His eyes swept the landscape. There were a few more desks nearby, something probably a half mile away in the direction they were heading that looked like a tree, and the carpetgrass swaying in the fake wind. He could *hear* the sound around them, but he couldn't see anything.

"There," Alanna hissed, pointing. The others followed her finger, and with a slight mental nudge from Anesh, Ganesh and their one dummy drone launched into the air to get eyes on it.

James noted where she was pointing. There was something bowing the grass as it moved, a tunnel being carved through the thick carpet. But whatever it was, the thing was low enough to the ground that it was practically invisible to them. It was making a wavy line as it plowed ahead, but weirdly, the carpet wasn't staying trampled behind it. Instead the material was springing back to full height almost as soon as the thing was past.

"Oh, shit," Anesh murmured, his eyes closed as he watched through the drone's camera via skulljack link. "Um . . . it's turning this way. Probably a hundred feet away." He stepped backward, opening his eyes as he turned, and started climbing up onto the desk.

"What the hell is it?" James asked him, following without questioning why they were kicking paperweights and pens down onto the floor.

"You'll hate this," Anesh told him. "It's a carpet cleaner. Like a Roomba."

Alanna snorted and instantly relaxed. "Okay, that's not nearly as bad as I was think—wait, why are you guys on the desk?" Her eyes narrowed again as she looked back over the waves of carpet.

"Because it just sheared through the back half of one of those quill dogs!" Anesh hissed. "Get on the damn desk and hope they can't climb!"

"Quill dogs. Of course." James patted Anesh on the shoulder. "That's perfect. 'Cause they're porcupine quills, and writing quills. Genius." Anesh didn't bother to correct his boyfriend on the unintentional nature of the pun. He just took the compliment, and focused on their new mortal peril.

With slightly more forethought than the boys, Alanna also started dragging their bikes over to near the desk with rapid movements, plucking the metal frames and their stock of extra gear off the ground and repositioning them like it took her almost no effort to quickly move a couple hundred pounds of stuff. With the bikes near their desk rock, they could drag them up if they really needed to, assuming the thing got near.

The whirring noise intensified as the unseen creature closed in on them. Anesh kept his shared vision with Ganesh on it, but even from overhead, it was heavily cloaked by the density of the carpet-grass. The three humans on the desk just watched, and held their breath, as the thing got closer and closer.

When it came near them, it didn't breach through the tall wall of carpet strands and into their little clearing. Instead, it skirted the outside. James caught a glimpse of a glittering silver body, like a beetle's shell. Thin gossamer wings, just barely cocked up over its back, caught the hot light from above. It was flat, keeping itself *very* low to the ground, but even from here they could see the way the grinding roller of teeth and bristles on its front brought down the carpet strands in its wake as it passed by. And it was *big*. James placed it at five, maybe six feet across. It might have been flat, but it had a lot of mass, and it had this feeling of something heavy. Tough. The whirring from it sounded far less mechanical when it was this close, more like the singing of crickets than the engine of a vacuum, but as it passed by, and got farther into the distance, the noise went back to sounding more and more like the distant attentions of janitorial staff.

They waited another few minutes until Anesh confirmed that it was gone.

"Well, dang. That was weird," James offered. He took in the rolled eyes and derisive snorts the others gave him, and brushed them off. "I mean, yeah, even compared to what we normally see here. Look, even the little guys around here all curled up under the desk again." He motioned to the cluster of striders, now huddled in their burrow. They'd been getting more familiar with the delvers, and as they hadn't tried to staple anyone, the group had let them be. Now, though, they cowered in a terrified cluster. "Do you think those things just roam around here?" he asked, deciding not to try to poke at the scared staplers.

"They must," Anesh mused, speaking as he thought through it. "They clearly do something to the carpet. Maybe it's a kind of hunting ground maintenance thing."

"They keep the carpet tall and clean so things live in it so they can eat those things?"

Anesh shuddered as Ganesh landed back on his shoulder and they retrieved their secondary drone. "Yeah, I mean . . . it really just chewed through the quill-thing. Like its mouth was too big. I do *not* want to fight one of these."

James let out a hum while Alanna took a minute to pick up the scattered stack of bills that she'd flippantly thrown out of the wallet earlier. "Do we want to head back?" he asked. "We're getting to the point where I'm having trouble keeping track of which part of the walls we came from. Might not hurt to call it here, and just see if we can find a decision tree to trade with on the way back."

"Ugggh," Alanna tilted her head back as she groaned. "I was really hoping we could find out where the paper pushers get their purple orbs from." She stopped, then shook her head. "What a weird sentence. James, this place is making us weird."

"We know," James and Anesh said together.

Alanna continued, unabated. "Also, we haven't even gotten to the other side yet! Just think what could be over there!"

"More quillbeasts?" James asked. "For real, though. We've been in three fights so far, I don't wanna deal with a carpet cleaner, this armor is *stiflingly* hot, and also it turns out broken bones stay sore for a long time? Did no one want to tell me that?"

Anesh gave James a blank look. "You bloody *insisted* on—"

"So yeah, I can get behind heading back. Especially since we've already kind of got a nice trail we can follow on the bikes, and not have to walk them through the tall grass." James shrugged. "And we've still got time. So while I sit and mope about not being able to keep going, you guys can head back out with one of the other teams."

"Don't be so hard on yourself," Alanna said as they started to head back. "Like you said, we're miles in. It's been a long day, and you're still hurt." Her voice softened rapidly as she spoke, realizing that James was doing that thing where he pushed himself well beyond what was a good idea.

Not one to be left out, Anesh added his own thoughts. "Also, you've been riding a bike with a broken hand. And fighting with a broken hand. And *not taking painkillers with a broken hand*. Don't think I've forgotten that!"

It had been a mild argument the other day. James didn't like painkillers in general. Anesh didn't like James martyring himself. They'd agreed to disagree.

They quieted down as they biked, not wanting to yell over the wind and risk attracting anything with too many teeth or spikes. The threads of the carpet around their little trail slapped at the armored shells on their legs as they pedaled past, the grassy stuff whipping around their bikes and dragging at the handlebars and the milk crates full of stuff mounted on the rear parts of their vehicles.

As they crested one of the small sloping bumps like dunes that dotted this massive field, they looked down to see a pair of the strange porcupine creatures loping parallel to them, the creatures occasionally looking up toward the delvers with their strange lamp faces, but not approaching as they followed their own game trail.

They passed a couple more desks, too. One they'd looted on the way in, one they hadn't gone near just because of the number of desk lamps that were almost certainly explosive that were attached to it. It would have been possible to disarm the flashbulbs of course, but that tended to require coffee, and they'd been saving that. Rightly so, too, as they'd needed it for the fight with the paper pushers shortly after.

By the time they'd made their way all the way back to the door, they'd gotten lost once, been ambushed twice, marked off a half dozen spots on their growing map that were traps, windows, or potted plant hunting grounds, and were almost set on fire more than a few times by a particularly vicious 2.0 that James would have sworn was stalking them.

He'd pocketed the green from that one, once they'd hunted it down, for use back at the Lair. Anesh glumly kept the blue from the presumably magical button-up shirt that the laser had carved in half. And James and Alanna split a few yellows from the small swarm that had converged on their fight as they were trying to catch and murder the shellaxy.

[+1 Skill Rank : History—Baseball]
[+1 Skill Rank : Music—Contemporary—Theremin]
[+1 Skill Rank : Kung Fu]
[+1 Skill Rank : Manufacturing—Bottling—Drinks]

"You know, I'm wondering if maybe I should be holding off on these while Secret is still hunting rogue thoughts in my head," James mused as they walked their bikes back through the outer wall around the home base tower. "Like, do you think that'll cause problems for him?"

"Can you," Anesh asked slowly, "imagine Secret *not* taking the opportunity to be snarky about you causing problems?"

James paused, thought about it for a good ten seconds. "Nnnn-nno. No," he settled on.

"Exactly. You're fine," Anesh said. "Do you guys mind restocking my gear for me? I need to go meet up with myself and see how the rituals are going tonight."

"Go for it." Alanna sent him on his way with a small kiss. "Have fun with the stairs!" she called after their retreating boyfriend.

The two of them fell into an easy routine of unpacking the bikes, unclipping armor, filling the now-neatly-labeled boxes on the ground floor of their occupied tower with orbs and potentially magic items, and helping each other sort through backpacks filled with leftover equipment and the spoils of a few hours in this bizarre realm. It didn't take long for other people to notice that James was back, though, and the trio were far from the only delvers here tonight.

Daniel was just getting back with his team. They'd been out pillaging the lower floors of another tower for more of the magical coffee needed to fuel the duplication ritual. He stopped for a bit to exchange some words with James, mostly complaining that the other towers always seemed either empty, or were *very* heavily guarded halfway up, and tended to force caution from the explorers. He'd found them a good seven of the spires so far, if you counted the time that he and his companion infomorph Pathfinder independently re-discovered the bathroom somehow. They were a lot like James, honestly; they wanted to be finding new things, seeing new sights. He got that.

The next person who approached him was Karen, who was basically the opposite. It wasn't that she hated scenic vistas, it was just that she highly valued reliability. The woman, looking strangely out of place in the half-set of armor that she had been equipped in, was in charge of exactly the thing that Daniel hated: combing over known respawn sites for the ritual coffee, and, for lack of a better term, harvesting them. Her group, which included several of the survivors who hadn't initially had any interest in delving, were becoming experts at knowing patterns and tactics for each specific tower on their route, as the dungeon repeated patterns in its creations. Right now, Karen just wanted to check in with James, and inform him that she was developing a better system for sorting collected orbs. He nodded politely, and earnestly thanked her for her help. He'd had a rocky start with Karen, but she *did* genuinely do a lot for them.

Nate was way easier to deal with. He was just here to keep an eye on Randall. And also to serve lunch. As near as they could tell, their FBI liaison legitimately did not know that Nate had previously been part of the FBI. Randall knew that someone from the Order had contacted them, and his superiors would probably have that information, but for now, it didn't make sense to let him know more than was absolutely needed. Which was why Nate was here sorting through the Lunch Box of Holding Lunch, handing out packaged containers of still-hot curry to people. Nate had discovered the container preserved food, and his chef instincts had kicked in. Not enough to override his job, which was watching Randall and also guarding the base. But enough that he took two minutes to gush about it to James when he handed over lunch. It was the most emotion the bald chef had ever displayed.

Randall caught James before he could find a seat, and demanded to know why the Order didn't make use of camracondas in this hostile environment. James told him pretty bluntly that it was because the Office might still be able to puppet them, and then ignored the honestly creepy way the man started talking about efficient hunting strategies in urban environments to wander off and eat. It wasn't the only unsettling thing about Randall today; there was definitely a sense that he didn't quite understand exactly where he *was*, and James was legitimately worried that there was something dangerous messing with his thoughts. He'd check in with Secret later to make sure.

By the time he made it to one of the makeshift lunch tables, which was really just a desk being used for lunch, two other people had stopped him to say hi and one other delver had mistaken him for the other James, as they were wearing glasses that let them see names at a distance.

When James finally sat down, and felt the tension ease out of his legs, it was the best feeling in the world.

A forkful of rice and curry was halfway to his mouth when JP sat down across from him and started talking about distribution of yellow orbs, and James wondered where he'd gone wrong in life.

Order of Endless Rooms, Operations Manual
    Section 1, Part 10: Response Protocols

At present, there are three confirmed and two suspected dungeons. At minimum, one of them is hostile to human life in a way that actively seeks to harm or kill humans. Dungeons are also now known to breach their own borders and begin to interfere with the mundane world directly. And additionally, there is a constant possibility of action from a hostile, or ideologically incompatible, human organization.

This requires a planned response pattern in the event of emergencies.

While every member of the Order is a potential hero during any given crisis, we currently maintain two "on-call" teams to respond to emergencies in any circumstance.

During an event, the team leader of the active response team has command. Any available member of the Order that is both willing and cleared for action is considered to be folded into that command structure.

In the case of an event that poses a direct risk to human life that the Order is positioned to prevent, the following actions will be taken:

First, the leader of the scheduled on-call response team will make a judgment call about the threat level and scale of the emergency. This determines if they will respond immediately with the team on hand, or wait for reinforcements from the rest of the Order.

Second, if a rapid response is chosen, the on-call team is to equip themselves and head to the event site. Unless there is a reason to bring vehicles (cargo, evacuees, etc.), the response teams are cleared to use telepads for transport, even into public spaces. Equipment is to prioritize effectiveness over subtlety. Equipment should also follow guidelines for any dungeons involved (see example in Part 1, Section 4-2: Akashic Sewer Restricted Items).

Third, the response team will prioritize the evacuation and medical aid of civilians on site, followed by the elimination of the threat.

This is kept vague not out of a desire to confuse people, but because the breadth of threats that we may face, combined with our constantly shifting capabilities, makes structured training and planning very difficult. While teams train together, and are encouraged to make use of our expanding sources of magic to grow, it's basically impossible to cover all the possible situations we may find ourselves in.

The most important guideline to stick to is to remember that we aren't a conspiracy (See Section 1, Part 2: We Are Not a Conspiracy). We have several incredibly powerful tools to bring to bear against most situations, including the camracondas, skulljacks, the ability to teleport, and possibly the backing of the government. Use every one of them as needed to secure the safety of anyone in need.

The second-most important guideline is tied to the fact that, as our intelligence network grows, we are going to learn about more and more mundane situations where our intervention would be useful. Response to these is at the discretion of the team leader. We are, as far as we know, the only group operational in the area that can respond to another situation like the recent events involving the Akashic Sewer. And if we take casualties during a risky operation, that's less of a safety net from the weird and threatening that exists for everyone else. Be especially careful evaluating risk on these situations.

Response team compositions are to include at least one camraconda, one drone operator, two members with improved weapon skills, and two members with medical skills. Every member is required to have at least one blue slotted.

The response team kit is partially standardized. Team leaders have a budget for personalized gear.

There are designated times for response team tactical training. Non-members are welcome to participate, so long as the training remains focused on the response team and their ability to react to novel situations.

"So, tell me about this plan of yours," James said to Sarah as she held the door of the house they were walking into open for him.

The house was pretty nice. Robin's-egg-blue paint, creaking wooded steps up to a well-used front porch. The door was old, but well oiled, and the key Sarah opened it with worked without complaint.

It used to belong to a guy named Fredrick. Then his attic got haunted, he'd asked them for help, and before they could really figure out what to do about the situation properly, he'd cut his losses and moved.

James had initially thought Frederick had been eaten by the attic, a newborn dungeon that these days Sarah referred to as Clutter Ascent. But then Harvey, who actually somehow managed to keep in touch with old friends from his college fraternity days, had corrected James. Fredrick had moved to a new house, and, as far as he knew, was still both alive and incredibly eager to forget that time when his attic was also alive.

It was bizarrely comforting. Both because it was a case where no one had died, but also because it was familiar to the ongoing situation with Randall. Frederick simply had not *wanted* to believe in magic, had refused to cope with it beyond getting away from it, and had, as far as Harvey could tell, mostly forgotten that he'd done anything except impulse-buy an unfortunately large house from an estate sale in Sherwood. And maybe that was Randall, too; not haunted or cursed or being mind-controlled, just a human that wasn't ready for it all yet.

The two of them ascended the creaking, slightly-too-narrow stairs up to the second floor. Sarah, after she'd told James to take his shoes off at the door, told him of her plan.

"So, the thing is, we've only seen dungeons that are already kind of tainted," she said. "Like, the Office? The . . . um . . . the weird one. The *first* weird one." She rolled her eyes at James, reading too far into his small grin. "Anyway. It's full of people who hate their jobs, and things that aren't fun to be around. It's clearly not evil, but it doesn't have an interest in anything more than . . . well, a business relationship."

"I'll buy that, sure," James said with a nod. "So, the school is . . . what, the literal toxic behavior of the school system, buried underneath the peaceful façade? Does it get to be that metaphorical?"

Sarah's shoulders drooped a bit. "I . . . I dunno, buddy," she said. "But the history of schools isn't a pretty one. And there's still a lot of abuse that happens, in high schools especially. It's possible the Sewer is just eating all that packed-down hatred and resentment, and giving back what it's getting. Or it's a *sewer* and not a *school*."

That made a kind of sense to James, though obviously it wasn't something they could easily confirm. "So, your theory, and the reason we're here . . ."

"Is to tell the Attic a bedtime story, and give it some happier memories to work with," she confirmed with a toothy grin, giving James a twirl and a stiff bow at the top of the stairs.

He smiled back, feeling an ancient tug in his heart as the new memories of the person that was his oldest friend triggered a reaction. James wasn't sure if Sarah's idea would actually work, but if she'd smile like that more, he'd read bedtime stories to tumblefeeds.

"And you've been doing this for a while, huh?" he asked as they turned down the upstairs hallway toward the attic's entrance.

"Since . . . Well, since I could walk again," she said, her casual voice barely stumbling on the words. "Alex, Deb, and Frequency were doing it before that. It's only partly my theory, and it's their plan. But yeah, you've got the outline of it. We just want to encourage it to grow into a friendlier place."

"Is it working?" James asked, legitimately very curious.

Sarah just shot him another smile in reply as she led him toward the stairs.

Halfway down the hallway, James slowed down. The staircase to the attic was already lowered in front of them, standing out even more than normal in the otherwise totally empty house. He didn't really want to get near it; even though he knew the emotional field it put off wasn't 'real,' it was still terrifying, and his heart remembered that sensation.

But Sarah just tugged him forward by his good hand, pulling him into what should have been an aura of overwhelming terror.

Except it wasn't.

Instead, there was something new. The feeling of fear was still there, yes. But it was less overwhelming. More cautious. And there was something else underneath it all. A little excitement, an undercurrent of expectation. Nothing powerful, but James could feel it, and the little hints of something else echoed off the pillars left by the red orbs he'd cracked over the last year.

Then Sarah pulled him through, socked feet taking the stairs slowly, but confidently.

The attic was warmer than he remembered. Though maybe that was just because it was summer outside, and this place seemed to constantly be time-locked at sunset.

Rays of golden orange sunshine beamed in through three identical circular windows, giving a comforting and peaceful light to the floorspace. And what was up here had changed, too.

Someone had cleaned up. Furniture and boxes and clutter had been moved around, the floor swept and cleared of the dust and loose screws and nails, the windows cleaned of cobwebs. James realized suddenly that he'd seen the cobwebs, and never acknowledged them, until they were suddenly absent.

And off to the side, propped up between two dressers and an armoire, someone had taken what looked like every one of the mothballed blankets and bedsheets, combined them with four couches worth of pillow cushions, and built a fort.

James was twenty-eight. Or maybe twenty-nine now. He wasn't keeping track anymore. He was well into that age of being "an adult" when people were discouraged from trick-or-treating or having water balloon fights in the park. As a result, he hadn't actually seen a blanket fort in over a decade. But there was something about this one that seemed . . . perfect . . . to him. It looked cozy, inviting, but also almost iconic in how it stood out. Sheets propped up at angles caught the filtered rays of evening sunlight and lit up with an inner glow. Pillows were arranged in almost hypnotic mandala patterns. It was like he was seeing every pillow fort he'd ever made as a kid, all rolled together, and stuck here in this attic.

"Who . . . made this?" he asked Sarah, hushed reverence in his voice.

"Deb and Frequency did, at first," Sarah said, stiffly dropping down to her knees to crawl under the overhanging blanket in the front. "Come on in!" she called back, sticking one hand out through the gap to motion at James. He followed, trying to minimize weight put on his leg as he crawled after her, and minding that he didn't knock anything down by carelessly headbutting it. From ahead, Sarah's voice came to him. "Alex helped them, after they'd had some time up here. And then I started adding stuff to it too!"

"Adding . . . ?" James pushed aside a hanging blanket with the cast on his right hand, and inched forward. And there, he got an answer. Seated on a throne of thick green-and-white striped couch cushions, Sarah spread an arm at her little kingdom from where she reclined.

The inside of the fort was almost as wide as his living room, though the "ceiling" was much lower. Electric camp lanterns and flashlights lit up the area, and a floor of heavy blankets and quilts made the entire place seem soft and comforting.

"Adding!" Sarah cheerfully stated.

"What the hell . . ." James looked around, craning his neck to see where they'd used yardsticks and gardening tools to brace blankets up, and clipped hanging trinkets into the overhead blankets. "Is this place a spatial warp?" he asked.

Sarah stuck her tongue out slightly. "Nah," she told him. "It just goes back a ways, and it's hard to see how big it is from the front, 'cause we've got that big cabinet thing up there. Nice, right?" She twisted a bit and pulled back a cushion next to her, revealing a hidden space with a cardboard box in it. "Want a snack?"

"Yes," James answered instantly. "How does all of this *stay up*? I could never get my blanket forts to do this." He settled back onto a pillow, not leaning back too hard in case he could topple the whole thing with his weight. Before he was fully settled, he had to snatch a bag of cookies out of the air that Sarah lobbed his way.

Opening her own snack with an ancient sound of crumpling packaging, Sarah popped a tiny cookie into her mouth and answered around the food. "Magic," she said, voice garbled until she finished her treat. "Ahem. Yeah, magic. And also Alex has four or five skill orbs for structural engineering. But also, we're pretty sure the attic helps hold it up."

"Why?" James asked softly.

"I mean, I like to think it's because it likes us," Sarah answered him. "We've been keeping it clean. And giving it stories!"

"Okay, yeah, so, you said that. What does that mean?"

Sarah reached into the bag she'd brought and pulled out a worn paperback. "Well, we come here every day or two. Either alone, or together, and we just . . . spend time here. Do a little cleanup, explore a bit, and then sit and relax together. Share time. And spend some time reading a book out loud." She tilted her eyes upward, though didn't bend her neck back. "And it's just felt *better* lately. This whole place. So I think it likes it!"

There was a pause while James thought about it, rolling over the concept in his head. "So we're treating it like . . . hm. Not a kid, exactly, but someone who needs care?"

"Yeah. And doesn't it feel like someone who needs a friend?" Sarah asked, her eyes sad as she looked at James. "I don't know if the dungeons really map to human thoughts and feelings, but if they did, then they're all hurting. That fear zone at the stairs? People don't . . . James, you can't make something like that to keep people away unless you've *very* scared yourself."

"But we don't know if the dungeons are people," he countered, however weakly. "I'm not saying you're wrong. I'm just saying we don't know what kind of life they are. Like, a fungus is alive, but it doesn't experience the world the same way as a human, or a dog, or even a fish."

Sarah nodded. "I do get that. But so far, we're seeing results, yeah? Like, smell the air." James gave her a concerned look. "Smellll iiiit!" Sarah urged him, grinning madly.

With more trepidation than he was prepared to admit to, James took an intentional sniff of the attic's air. He paused for a second, consciously thinking about the scents in this place for the first time since he'd climbed the stairs. Then he took a much longer breath.

"Cinnamon. And . . . fresh-cut grass?" He lost himself in thought for a second, eyes cast down to the blanketed floor. Memories of a thousand childhood moments compressed down into those faint scents hanging in the still air. "Why?" he asked.

"We don't know," Sarah admitted with a sympathetic tone. "We only know that it's changing. It's a little better lit, a little less likely to spawn rusted metal. And I can't tell you if it's because it likes us, or because we're poisoning it with kindness and cookies. But it's happening either way." She sighed. "I worry that we're hurting it. We can't really talk, you know? Either because there's no easy way for it to communicate to us, or because we're operating on different wavelengths like you said, or just because it doesn't talk to its food. I'm invested in helping because, you know, you've met me." Sarah laughed as she reclined on her throne. "But I do worry that our version of help isn't what it needs. So it's just a lot of guesses, and keeping an eye on it all."

James watched her for a second as she made herself comfortable on the pillows, his reclaimed childhood friend trying very hard to look like she was confident and in control, all while slowly burying herself in a comforter that was probably larger than James's whole bed by itself.

"And it's a great secret fort," he finally said, smiling at her.

"Oh dang, it is *such* a secret fort!" she announced. "Secret would love this place, wouldn't he? Or would he love it if we . . . kept it secret? He's confusing."

James laughed. "Honestly, I don't know half the time. I think he feeds off the concept of organized information, not specifically secrets. But, like, he can also just straight up eat information, and I *think* there's a difference in kind when information is kept hidden, then made public. All infomorphs can do that one. He's just . . . named Secret."

"Creepy! But also cool?" Sarah held her hands out like she was balancing the two options.

"I'll invite him sometime, when he's not busy dealing with *other* hostile infomorphs in my brain." James flopped back against the edge of a structural support couch on the other side of the blanket wall. "So, storytime?" he asked, tossing his coat into the corner and reaching for the cookies that Sarah had thrown him earlier.

"Storytime!" she announced, holding up the battered paperback she'd brought with her. "And also apologize to the nice dungeon for being rude to it. And then, after storytime, we can go find some mysterious furniture and do mind art at it until we get more connection sticks."

"God, I love our lives." James chuckled to himself as he settled into a comfortable position. He felt positively gleeful that he'd understood that sentence in its entirety. "And I'm sorry, sentient attic. I didn't mean to imply you didn't have a right to exist. I love the blanket fort. Now, what're you reading today?"

"*The Lies of Locke Lamora.*"

"Uh . . . really?" James blinked, looking over at Sarah. "I'll be honest, I kind of assumed you had a collection of fairy tales or something."

"Did that! I think the dungeon liked it, since there's sometimes coins arranged in fairy rings around her now. But also I like this book and that's what we're on now." Sarah stated it like she was daring James to argue.

He didn't really have to consider it long. "Alright," he said. "I mean, I love this book too. Let's go."

"Of course you do. This is your copy!" Sarah said it like a joke, but a second later, she looked away from James, training her eyes anywhere but where he could see. There was still a lot of hidden sadness there; little memories or moments that James had forgotten. Had been made to forget.

James didn't fail to notice. He didn't really know what to say; he wanted to tell Sarah it'd be okay, that they were getting better. But those words didn't feel quite enough for that all the time. So instead, he just reached across the blanket fort with his healing foot, and poked her in the ankle.

"I've probably been looking for that book!" he said instead. "You bandit!"

"What?!" Sarah snapped out of her sorrow. "You said you had three copies!"

"I must have!" James protested. "Now I have two! This is a crime of the highest order."

Sarah smiled, wiping away the corners of her eyes. "Alright," she agreed. "What if I read part of it? Would that make it up to you?"

"I accept your offer." James let his head drop back onto the pillow. "The secret fort really does help, too."

And after they finished laughing together, Sarah cracked the book open, plucked the bookmark out, and began to read.

Order of Endless Rooms, Operations Manual
    Section 6, Part 7: High-Powered Individual Threats

No known dungeon has a known upper boundary on the rewards they offer. It is a known fact that there are other delvers out there. Statistically, many of them will have had far more time than we have with the ability to harvest power from one or more dungeons. Also, there is an entire potential space for non-human entities of worrying levels of threat.

The conclusion to draw from this is that there are entities out there, possibly human, possibly not, that are more than capable of killing every member of the Order in a stand-up all-of-us-against-them fight. Assuming they can actually think, it gets way worse for us.

To date, the only fatalities we have sustained have been from such an entity.

If you suspect you are up against such an entity, your first objective is survival. The second is information security, and the third is information gathering. By nature of the problem, victory is not considered an option.

It is possible that our best defense against things like this is simply not being known. This might directly contradict with our policy of not being a conspiracy (See Section 1, Part 2: We Are Not a Conspiracy), but there is a difference between operating openly and leading an existential threat to our home.

In the one encounter with something like this, the threat *might* have made an action that could be called a retreat when the area returned to dungeon control. One potential option for escape, then, is to attempt to enter a dungeon, if available. If not, fleeing to a remote site via telepad and waiting to see if you have been followed is the next best possible option.

If you have an instinct that something is too dangerous, do not attempt to be a hero. Run. Get help. Ensure the safety of yourself and the Order as best you can. Even if it doesn't seem like it's a fight, and it just has something that sounds reasonable that it wants to ask you to do, you cannot trust it without verification. Use distance, or heavy ordnance, to slow it down, and get as far away as possible.

James pivoted his feet on the blacktop, shifting his weight a little more than he was comfortable on his bad leg. Pushing suddenly off the ground, he looped around Anesh before his boyfriend could respond, and took off at an angle toward the basketball hoop at the end of the parking lot.

James heard Anesh's footsteps catching up fast behind him. So he turned, got a good grip on the basketball he was bouncing as he ran, and passed to Simon.

Other James caught it instead, intercepting it right before it got to Simon. He started to break away toward the other hoop, but then paused, turned, and passed *back* to Simon. Then, with an annoyed expression on his face, he dashed back after the ball he'd just thrown.

Simon caught it, approached the hoop, got surrounded by his James and Anesh, bounced the ball around Anesh to James who scooped it up, and lobbed it in a lay-up into the hoop.

"Points!" he announced, throwing his arms into the air as Anesh and the others panted for breath.

"Goddammit!" Other James gasped out. "Using the link is cheating!" he accused Simon.

Simon dusted himself off, and tried to compose himself to look as impervious to criticism as possible. "There is no rule in basketball that says—"

With a bellowing laugh, James cut him off. "Okay, okay, no! I know you scored us points, but you can't use the *Air Bud* clause to justify mind control. Also, why are you guys linked up for this anyway?"

"Practice," the two of them said in unison.

"Alright." James sighed. "Anyone wanna keep going?" He looked around in the Friday night twilight at the makeshift basketball court they'd made. Alanna and Sarah were sitting on the sidelines along with a handful of camracondas, eating popcorn and watching the boys play basketball. The wind lightly swayed the trees between them and the parking lot next door, and the smell of barkdust and hot car fumes from the road nearby filled the air. "Alanna? Frequency? Want in on this?"

"How am I to play?" Frequency-of-Sunlight asked, the most recent version of the voice modulation program letting the light sarcasm come across perfectly. "I am of a snake."

"Good point." James tilted his head back and yelled up at the roof. "Dave! You want in on this?!" he bellowed.

A second later, Dave's head poked over the ledge. "I'm busy. Ask Daniel."

"We did. He was busy too," Anesh called back, before turning back to James. "Why am I getting involved in this? I'm out anyway. You lot are exhausting."

"Oh sure, blame us." James ribbed him as they all headed over to where a pile of water bottles sat waiting. "Well, thanks for that anyway. It was fun."

Anesh nodded. "Yeah! We should do this more often. How's your lesson going, anyway?"

"I need to check my syllabus." James intoned the last word with the mental stomp needed to bring up the information he was looking for.

[Lesson—Basketball : 48/200]

Not bad progress, all things considered. At this rate, it'd be a month or so before he earned another upgrade. And they really were upgrades; James had come to appreciate what was probably the most straightforward reward of any dungeon. The lessons basically just handed out stat points, and while they were often for stats that you wouldn't find in your average RPG, they were still incredibly powerful in what they let a baseline human do.

It was a good way to end the week. And while for James, there wasn't really a set weekend, he felt like he'd started to get back to a position where he was comfortable with the Order, and himself, after his injury and coma.

His casts were off, his body was healing. He was mostly caught up on what was going on around here. There'd been discussions and plans about the future, about how they wanted to grow, and why. And for once, James felt like he was ready to take action on his own agency, rather than just respond to the newest crisis.

To be fair, he was aware that merely thinking that was often enough to summon a crisis on its own. But that wasn't his fault; he was incapable of *not* taunting fate.

And yeah, there were problems. There was still a lingering feeling of anxiety around the Lair from the loss of Virgil and Cold-Wind-Friction. Even when everyone was having fun together, it was hard to totally shake the knowledge of something so much bigger than all of them, looming out there somewhere.

Also, Randall was still working here. And while the FBI hadn't actually asked anything of them, or interfered in their operations, James still wanted to preemptively end their relationship before it got out of hand. Or played into the FBI's hands.

There was also the endless search for other dungeons. Anesh had gotten back into that, in a big way, and a few other people had joined him. They *knew*, now, that more were out there. Hidden, hiding, locked off, or just obscure. But they were *real*. Officium Mundi wasn't a fluke, and the Order wanted to meet the next one on *their* terms.

It was part of a change that was happening lately. And James liked how it was going, even if it did leave him feeling uncertain sometimes. They weren't just scrambling to catch up anymore. They were the ones hunting. Or building new things. Planning and being proactive. It wasn't his style. But maybe it would have to be, if he ever wanted to save the world.

And that was the goal, wasn't it? Saving the world? Because holy shit, the world needed it. And every bit of good that the Order of

Endless Rooms could put out into it was worth something. And these days, more and more, they had the ability and the *power* to output a lot more good than you'd expect from a group of about a hundred random people, some of whom were snakes.

James snapped his fingers as they walked toward the Lair's back door. He needed to look into hiring some new people.

He made a mental note. That was for tomorrow. Tonight, they were gonna watch a movie, not get in any fights, and take a very deserved rest. He was looking forward to seeing if he could get a camraconda to argue with a member of Research about Star Wars.

CHAPTER 10

Spire-Cast-Behind was having a lazy day.

There was likely a context in which you could call it a *strange* day, but subjectively, it was no stranger than any other day she had experienced so far. Though there was a foundational confusion that was always there, so maybe it would be better to say every day was somewhat strange. For one thing, that there were days at all.

As a camraconda, she had been created with an amount of distant academic knowledge that had slowly unpacked as it became relevant. Days as governed by nature had never really come up, though she could have told you how long the standard workday was, and what overtime happened to be. Which mostly meant that to her and to most of her species, days were eight and a half hours long.

Usually her people would sleep every third day or so, but there weren't many functional clocks in the tower she'd awoken to true life in, so actually knowing if she was correct was impossible by now. With no way to record it or actually keep time, it would just be a rough estimate, the truth of the matter fading into history.

Here, "outside" of the biomes of cubicles and hard carpet, a day was twenty-four hours. So most people were expected to sleep and then also be active within a single day. Despite Spire-Cast-Behind's chosen name, this seemed *far* less of a good idea than simply having a dedicated sleep day, even if the math on how many hours you slept was the same.

But then, the humans and cats that ran this other world had apparently been required to contend with a *very* insistent overhead light source. So she didn't blame them too much. The sun made the days, the days were what they'd built their society around, and so the sun was really the one in charge.

So, she was having a day.

Some camracondas had begun a habit of watching the sun rise and set, taking the considerable effort to climb the drop-down ladder to hang out on the roof of the building. They would silently observe as the sky would change colors from brilliant oranges and reds to softer purples and pale blues before the sun stabilized overhead and the day really began. Different groups for the morning and evening, but still a sizable chunk of their population wordlessly basking in the simple joy of a world that worked without something puppeting it.

Silence was sort of the default state for a camraconda. They could hiss, and whine, and even scream a little bit. But they had never really known how far the protection of their tower of cramped boxes had stretched, so loud noises weren't something they'd ever gotten used to making. And forming a language out of just the hiss was . . . perhaps possible. Spire-Cast-Behind didn't actually know. She knew things like statistics about auto manufacturing and what species of owl lived in an *Asia*, whatever that was. She didn't know about linguistics, which would have actually been useful.

And now many of her species had another option to speak. One of the invasive weapons of Officium Mundi, the name the humans gave her home, repurposed and turned to a boon and not a curse. She herself wore a small tight harness with a pair of speakers connected to her mind through a long cord that didn't match her own exterior color. Not that fashion was something she cared for, it was just amusing.

Virgil had made it for her himself. And now he was gone, along with her brother. Spire-Cast-Behind didn't know how to feel about it. Angry seemed like a good selection, but anger didn't come to her freely anymore, after the first day or two. Instead she felt hollow when she thought of them. Two more people lost to her. And Cold-Wind-Friction had come *all this way*, only to die now. It was . . . it hurt. She thought she had been done hurting.

For so, so long she hadn't let herself feel anything, to keep that hurt staved off. And then when the Order had ripped away the chains of the old world and brought her here to a new one, she had felt *gratitude*. Relief in a flood that threatened to overwhelm her entirely. But they weren't even done there; they also gave gifts. Speech was one, and she was meant to meet with someone later this week to discuss that further. But there were more treasures shared.

Food. Water. *Privacy*, even in a limited form where you might need to share a room with a few other corded serpents. But what rooms they were. No edges that threatened to topple away from the whole of the structure, no hard corners that dug into the body when slithering across. Instead they had blankets, bedding, and mattresses.

While she had previously been aware intellectually of what a bath was, and now was familiar with a bed, Spire-Cast-Behind was still a little fuzzy on what could possibly be *beyond* those two, or how it tied into her shared room. Shelves, maybe? Whatever it was, it wasn't really important, despite what James insisted. What was important was that the camracondas had a king's ransom worth of soft things that they could sleep in to their biomechanical heart's content.

This was how she was spending the start of her day. Not sleeping, exactly, but curled up with the end of her mouth resting on her own tail. Camracondas, unlike "real" snakes, didn't really have what she'd heard some humans calling a *snoot*, since most of her head was centered around the rectangular living metal structure of the camera through which she saw the world. But that didn't stop her from finding a comfortable position after having slithered loops to wind underneath two different soft fuzzy blankets, and laying her head down to rest.

She'd already slept. And now she could lounge here, warm and free, and do nothing but think and feel. Even if that thinking was painful sometimes, it was still worthwhile.

It was also a good time to practice her speaking, since the several others that she shared this room with were either on the roof, or wandering the hallways of the Lair, or trying to find ways to make themselves useful. Many camracondas would understand reveling in the newfound power of speech, but if they were trying to sleep, it could become irritating, so Spire-Cast-Behind enjoyed the time alone.

"Hello." The voice didn't sound right. It did exactly what it was supposed to, but it wasn't right. "Hello." Same tone, identical. But still off. "Hello, I am . . ."

She didn't finish the sentence, and it didn't so much trail off as it stopped dead. Spire-Cast-Behind wasn't simply forcing her thoughts into the speakers as voice, like they'd had to do at the start. Instead, there was a program of some kind made with something from her home. Again, it was from Virgil, in a way. And it was so much easier.

Spire-Cast-Behind *knew* English. Just like she knew about what hurricanes were and how to groom a dog. The information had been in her head from her creation, just with no outlet. And camracondas learned fast, so those with her that didn't know the vernacular already were able to quickly pick it up. But there was a difference between technically knowing the words, and having experience speaking them. And what she was doing was still one step removed from speaking.

Even now, she wasn't sure she could practice sentence structure on her own. Where the pronouns were supposed to go was hard to remember. But that wasn't what she was trying. Instead, she was trying to get the rather confusing user interface of the program that was running on a small computer plugged into the back of her head to change a setting.

"Hello." The word was so simple. Spire-Cast-Behind liked it quite a lot. You only needed to say hello to new people, and for the first time in her several-years-long life, there were new people aplenty. "Hello," she repeated out loud into the blankets covering her body.

Ah, there it was. Whatever she had changed had worked.

"Hello." A third time, and she trembled with barely contained joy, closing her eye and simply letting herself sink back into her bed. "Hello hello hello hello." Over and over, repeating the word. And each time, hearing something *different*.

That little program Virgil had grown and modified, which let them streamline turning thoughts into words so well that it might be reflexive one day and not a mentally taxing task, allowed her something that no camraconda in any world had ever had before. Each time she spoke that one word, it was *different*. Contained within a range of resonance, articulation, tone, and volume. Not uncontrolled, but with tiny variances inside her parameters that made her sound . . .

Not human. But she wasn't human. Instead, it simply sounded like a voice. Like *her* voice, now.

"Hello," Spire-Cast-Behind murmured, dialing down the volume as she writhed under the tangled mass of bedding. "Yes. Hello. Yes, good. Is good. *This* is good." The new program let her put emphasis on things, even casually.

Years ago, when the camracondas had first realized that they couldn't leave the place that was both shelter and prison all at once, they hadn't really understood at first. They *knew* things, but they didn't know what to do with that knowledge now that they weren't being given orders. Early on, they had realized that the things that were with them in the stacked cubicles they now resided in were all they were ever going to have.

That hadn't stopped them from trying to make use of those things, though. If anything, it meant they found meaning and expression in even small acts of artistic creation. While she didn't really feel like an artist at the time, Spire-Cast-Behind had, after a week of practicing the motions, taken a single piece of paper. And with a line of her own venom and a fang, had drawn a simple, slightly warped circle on it.

She wasn't sure why she'd done it. She'd been bored, maybe. Searching for purpose, probably. But something about the action had made her feel free in a way that she never had before. She still had that piece of paper; the knights of the Order of Endless Rooms had *brought it with them* when they'd fled the Office. It was sitting on a shelf in this very room.

While she hadn't made art again, instead leaving the materials to the others who seemed more taken to it, the sensation hadn't ever really faded. It was the first thing she'd ever really done for herself, without a command she wasn't allowed to disobey. It was a kind of magic.

And now, that feeling of freedom, of an imprisoning force cracking and sloughing off of her like sliced cables, was bolstered by a twin moment of pure expression. The sensation of having her own voice. *Her* voice.

The camraconda didn't know how long she spent there, nestled up in her bed alone, repeating simple words and phrases that vibrated a more natural, semi-random cadence, reveling in how life changed.

For so, so long, life hadn't changed. And now she was in a place where changes came fast and light, like rain.

Oh, there was rain. It was different from what Spire-Cast-Behind had thought it was going to be. The concept of an ecosystem where water cycled through the environment made perfect sense to her, but she'd never actually touched water before coming here, so the way being wet *felt* was novel. It was also a bizarre experience to feel differently about being wet in different contexts. Rain, for example, felt annoying, while showers felt comforting, which didn't make sense, since they were just big rain all at once.

Spire-Cast-Behind didn't really know why she even felt those things, but it was interesting to explore them.

Speaking of exploring, there was some of that to be done today. Somewhere in Spire-Cast-Behind's thoughts, a small piece of a living idea resonated with its other pieces, and nudged her in a reminder that she couldn't actually spend the whole day in bed. The nudge was polite enough to let her ignore it if she wanted, but she decided to follow the impulse anyway.

She *could* just stay here all day. Spire-Cast-Behind was no stranger to spending hours at a time listlessly staring at a blank wall, lying motionless to conserve energy and wondering what the difference was between surviving and waiting for death. But this was different. She wasn't hungry, the need for more orbs to keep operating replaced by a diet of food and water. She wasn't trapped; the door was rigged up to be easy for her to open and she could go anywhere she wanted. And maybe that was the thing. She *could* stay here. It was a choice that she could make, and that made it appealing.

But the nudging part of her thoughts was becoming rather insistent, so she slithered herself upright, casting off the fuzzy blankets and toppling the arrangement of round stuffed animals that Taste-of-Air enjoyed setting up. Her day would probably still count as lazy, since she'd spent at least a few hours of it lounging, but she shouldn't avoid speaking to the others forever.

Spire-Cast-Behind dropped down off the mattress to the area rug that dominated the floor. The humans had been *apologetic* that the best they could do for the concrete room was to cover it with soft comfort, which . . . well, Spire-Cast-Behind did technically understand. So much of her imprinted knowledge was about corporate etiquette, and how the display of wealth equated to status and soft power. This room would never pass for a place to meet someone for a negotiation. But it wasn't really supposed to, and she'd pieced together on her own that she shouldn't accept apologies for things that were not slights.

She liked her shared room. Liked the shelves with all their art they'd brought along, liked the little low Japanese-style table for making *more* art or having breakfast, liked the row of low hooks on the wall by the door that they could use to assist with getting dressed.

It wasn't exactly a place made for her, and it might never be, but it was home.

Spire-Cast-Behind slithered herself up to one of those pairs of hooks, grabbed her favorite modified coat in her fangs, and used deft movements of her head to drape it in the space. Twisting lithely once it was in place, she maneuvered her body to let the garment curl around her side, and then with a second twist connected the pieces of velcro so it would stay on. And then she was ready to leave.

Not, the camraconda admitted as she used the lever to push her door open and make her way into the basement hall, that she actually had a problem being unclothed. It was simply that she liked how it felt to have something of her own with her.

Elevators were a problem for a camraconda, but not as much of a problem as stairs. Technically, this was true for humans as well, so Spire-Cast-Behind didn't really have that much of an issue with using her face to awkwardly press a button. And eventually, she did get to the basement that was "sideways" from the one she lived in.

Slithering into the open room that the people who studied her home used, it wasn't too hard to find the person that she had promised to talk to today. Mostly because she was in the process of arguing with Reed, and seemed to be adeptly wearing her opponent down.

". . . absolutely, under no circumstances, ever, am I going to let you do that!" Reed's voice was a higher pitch than many other humans, but Spire-Cast-Behind found it comforting. It sounded a lot like how she imagined many of her own people would sound if they had their own natural voices; constantly anxious about the state of flux their world was in. Just a little overwhelmed at all times. She empathized with him.

In contrast, Momo's voice was enthusiastic and ready for anything, which was a deception of the highest order. But it was also aware of that, and so, funny. Or at least, Spire-Cast-Behind thought so. "What ifffff . . . I bribed you?" Momo was saying as she sat on the edge of someone's desk, feet clad in long black boots kicking in the air.

"Do you have any idea what James pays us?" Reed asked rhetorically as he dismissed the offer.

"Not really," Momo admitted, taking it seriously. "I figured I'd offer orbs or something. Oh! Or we could get one of the relation-sticks from the Attic dungeon—"

"I thought we weren't calling them that."

"—and then I'll owe you from whatever we end up sharing." Momo's offer ignored Reed's protest on naming conventions. Spire-Cast-Behind wasn't sure why the humans seemed so hung up on titles and monikers sometimes. As long as the point got across, information wasn't lost, so what was the problem? Momo continued as the camraconda approached closer. "Bit of a gamble for a bribe, *sure*, but what if we end up sharing cuteness? You could get *all this* for the low price of just . . . letting me . . . you know, have a cat."

Reed pressed his face into his hands. "That *cannot* be how they work." He groaned. "Also, that's a terrible bribe."

"Yes." Spire-Cast-Behind interjected herself into the conversation. She was reasonably sure that this was okay, since she was supposed to be here, but she often struggled to find windows to start talking to people. Most of the camracondas here did. "Unneeded resource. Cute." She inclined her head toward Reed.

He pulled his head out of his hands and looked at her with a tired confusion, while Momo started laughing, and Spire-Cast-Behind rapidly began to worry that she'd said something wrong. "Uh . . ." Reed titled his head to look at her.

"I think Spire's flirting with you!" Momo said between laughs.

Spire-Cast-Behind was not doing that. Romance and sex were more of those things that were academic to her, but not yet experienced. Some of the others of her nest had begun to let themselves feel and live both sides of that coin, but not her. "Inaccurate," Spire-Cast-Behind settled on telling Momo. "To be cute. Not line up with job. For Reed."

"Oh!" Momo gave a delighted gasp of laughter. "I get it! He's not flirting, he's delivering a burn powerful enough to barbecue your soul!"

"Souls aren't real," Reed said, like it was a reflex. "If they were, it would ruin a lot of theories, so they can't be."

Spire-Cast-Behind was reasonably certain that wasn't how science worked. She was also becoming increasingly frustrated with trying to convey her thoughts when she didn't know how to put sentences together all the way, even if she fully understood the replies. But she couldn't fix that instantly. What she could fix was Momo's error. "She," she told the girl sitting on the desk.

"Whu?"

"For myself," the camraconda reiterated. "She."

"Oh! Sorry!" Momo's instant transition from a form of humor that Spire-Cast-Behind read as ironic, to a sincere apology, was jarring. But it was also welcome; it signaled a form of empathy that wasn't new to the camracondas, but hadn't ever had a chance to be spoken aloud. Momo leaned forward to look at Spire-Cast-Behind with what was probably curiosity. "How do you tell?" she asked.

Reed shook his head, curly hair bobbing in the still air of the brightly cluttered concrete environment. "Coloration, right?"

"Incorrect." Spire-Cast-Behind hoped the word didn't sound too harsh in her new voice. "As for humans. Aesthetic decision," she reminded them.

Momo stopped swinging her boots and cocked her head. "Wait, what?"

"Spire, do you think . . . wait, what do you think pronouns are for?" Reed asked with a growing confusion. "No, hang on, Momo, *are* pronouns an aesthetic thing? You'd tell me if I needed to know this, right?"

"Sure wouldn't," Momo lied to the Researcher as she tried to clarify for the camraconda. "So, a lot of people use pronouns for, like . . . biological differences? Actually, are camracondas dimorphic?" She had to know. It hadn't come up, but Deb and Frequency-of-Sunlight were dating or something, and Momo *needed* to know.

That was an easy question, one that Spire-Cast-Behind could answer without confusion. "Yes." She nodded, and saw the humans start to nod. "Sexual dimorphism," she added. "And optional gender quadmorphism." That was probably a word. Language played with words like that all the time anyway.

". . . What?" Reed looked so lost. Maybe it wasn't a word after all. Or perhaps he hadn't had his coffee yet. Humans needed coffee for certain higher-order brain functions.

Momo was back to laughing. "Wait, so, you guys use pronouns for *style*? How do you tell what sex a camraconda is then?" she said as she caught her breath.

"Examination. How tell, humans?" Now Spire-Cast-Behind was curious. This wasn't even remotely what she was here for, but this conversation was revealing in its own way.

". . . I mean, I was gonna say pronouns, but that's not even really always true, is it?" Reed muttered. "Also, Nikhail would get real mad at me if I said that."

"So, can you have kids?" Momo asked suddenly.

The question confused Spire-Cast-Behind, until the imprinted knowledge in her lit up and began forming connections with the real world and the words she'd heard. Meiosis, gestation, variances in how species gave birth, statistical and theoretical knowledge that had lingered untouched for years. The broad strokes of the biology of an ecosystem.

And it was something that wasn't for her. Wasn't for her people. It was natural, in a way they would never be. A whole method of existence, locked off from them, for a reason she couldn't fathom and didn't care to know.

It had been happening less recently, but every now and then Spire-Cast-Behind ran into something that made her want to slither back into bed and force herself asleep until the distress went away. And now it happened again.

"Are you okay?" Momo asked, and Spire-Cast-Behind realized she was silently staring at the floor, her posture drooping like a wilting vine. "Spire?"

"Hello." Spire-Cast-Behind said on reflex as she snapped back to attention. "Yes. Will be. Future okay." She hated the broken language that came out when she rushed. And she was always rushing. But it sounded more like her, at least.

Reed stood slowly, like he didn't want to startle her. "Okay, I'm gonna . . . go do a thing," he said. "Do either of you need anything while I'm still here?"

"Yes! Let me pet the weird cat!" Momo demanded, remembering why she'd stopped Reed in the first place.

Ah, there was a misunderstanding happening. Spire-Cast-Behind could clear this up, and she was fairly certain she could pattern out the right words too. "No," she admonished Momo. "Cat is very large. *Would* kill you." Ooh, she even pronounced the emphasis correctly. Speaking was becoming even easier. Spire-Cast-Behind was quite proud of that.

For some reason, Reed started chuckling as he backed away. "Allright, have fun. I need to go read more proposals for trying dumb things with orbs."

Momo waved at him, and Spire-Cast-Behind tried to emulate the motion by bobbing her body. After he was around a corner, Momo sighed and shook her head. "You know I know the cat is huge, right?" she asked. "Like, I know you're looking out for me, and I appreciate it, but I know the cat is huge."

Spire-Cast-Behind hadn't known that. She tilted back, looking past Momo's head and thinking as she watched a pair of humans walked by carrying an oversized microwave. She decided they were supposed to be here, as Momo didn't react, and refocused on the human woman. "But it would kill you," she decided.

"It might not." Momo shrugged. "I mean, like, why would it? We feed it pretty well. Maybe it'll be grateful."

"Puppet," Spire-Cast-Behind reminded her. "Dangerous. Violent to you."

Momo frowned. "Because it's a green orb kinda life?" she asked, and the camraconda nodded with a bob in reply. "But so are you, right? I mean, some of the paper people have different colors of orb. Do you?"

That question hadn't occurred to her. "No," Spire-Cast-Behind said, her conviction in her knowledge cracking. "I was puppet. Previously," she mused out loud, letting her stray thoughts filter through the language program. "Is that odd?"

". . . Girl, you cannot ask me what's odd and what's not," Momo told her with a stare that probably meant something to the human, but the camraconda couldn't make out the nuance of. "Like, I wanted to talk to you today 'cause a million billion years ago, you said something about the totems I make, and I had a bunch of questions about turning glowing red golf balls into witchy devices that tell me how many boats there are in the city. *Odd* was wayyyyyy back behind us at this point."

"Because boats are odd." Spire-Cast-Behind looped her head around. That, at least, made sense. "Understand."

Momo's expression was readable enough that even the camraconda, new to the experience of reading humans, could figure out that she was having some kind of baffled thoughts. "Boats are fine! I'm talking about the magic! Magic is new to me and I'm confused by it now tell me how to make totems! *Ahhhgh!*" The last thing wasn't so much a word as a strangled noise that seemed to indicate distress.

Spire-Cast-Behind didn't think that Momo had a healthy way to deal with her own emotions. Not that she had any place to criticize, since her own method was to shut down and feel nothing. But Momo seemed easily rattled.

"Connectors," Spire-Cast-Behind offered as helpfully as she could.

"Buh?" Momo made another confused noise as she shoved her hair out of her face.

Spire-Cast-Behind tried to figure out how to word it. "Small, many sharp legs. They glow. Connectors. What makes them."

"Oh, the iLipedes? Yeah, that's where I got the idea in the first place. But they don't really get creative with them! And it's really hard to get enough red orbs to get the ones we have down here to stop eating them and start making their webs. Or connections, or whatever you said. That thing you said, but pretend I got it right the first time. I swear I'm paying attention, I'm just . . . I'm just tired." Momo's voice broke slightly as she sagged down on her makeshift seat.

It seemed like many of the humans around here were often tired. Spire-Cast-Behind could understand. She felt tired a lot too. But something Momo had said stood out to her. "Are there connectors here? Down here?"

"Eh? Oh. Yeah, sure. A couple. They sometimes want to come back with people. We don't kidnap them or anything." Momo shrugged as both of them watched someone awkwardly walk through the open space carrying a covered birdcage. ". . . Okay, weird," Momo commented before shifting her focus back to the conversation. "So, you can't help me build a totem that'll force everyone within ten miles to know detailed statistics on stuff?"

"No. Maybe. Why?" Spire-Cast-Behind had a lot of questions beyond *why*, but she would need time to put them together. "What statistics?"

"I dunno, whatever I feel like. Maybe something about carbon emissions or something, just to mess with people." Momo sighed. "Thing is, I just don't have enough red orbs to play with. People bring some back, and *I* get some when I tag along on the delves, but it's not like we copy them, you know?"

Spire-Cast-Behind felt like she was overusing a single word, but it was coming in really useful for this conversation. "No," she stated. "Copy?"

Momo perked up. "Oh yeah! We've got a magic thing that duplicates stuff! My vote was for bricks of gold, but we're just using it for fancy magic items and teleporters instead, which is probably fair. It doesn't have a lot of room, though. Only, like . . . what, a foot on each side I think? And a little less than that tall. So no one wants to waste it on my bullshit yet." She shrugged, scratching at the backs of her hands and clearly upset by it but not saying so.

That wasn't large enough to copy many things. Her own orb wouldn't fit inside it, if she were to be harvested. That had actually been a concern in the first few days, but it had faded with time and shared interactions within the Order. It also certainly couldn't have enough room to duplicate a camraconda, or a human. But it might fit a connector—an iLipede, as Momo had called it.

Almost as soon as she'd had that thought, Spire-Cast-Behind dismissed it. That wouldn't help at all with the human's investigation. If the bottleneck was orbs, then having more creatures that fed on them wouldn't solve anything.

Maybe they didn't need to feed on orbs at all, though. She hadn't actually taken in what she'd thought was the only possible source of energy for . . . weeks? Lots of days. And she hadn't died. Was it possible iLipedes had a similar opportunity? Spire-Cast-Behind hissed to get Momo's attention away from the caged bird she was watching on the other side of the room, and asked her question. "Could feed connectors?" She felt a fire of embarrassment light up as she failed to properly articulate. "Feed them food. Not orbs. Save orbs for project." Each word was painstakingly placed, but Spire-Cast-Behind managed to express herself.

"Can the lil' guys eat things?" Momo mused as she took in the suggestion. "That *would* help cut down on how many orbs we go through. And that would mean more for me! Which, if I don't scramble my own brain, I could probably do something cool with!"

"Worrying." The word slipped out, which was delightful.

Momo flapped a hand, not understanding how emotionally important an accidental piece of speech was. "I'll be fine. No one can actually prove it's brain damage. What do you think iLipedes eat anyway?"

Spire-Cast-Behind wasn't sure. "Start small?" she asked. "An granola. Or an cereal. Small things."

"Mmmh. Yeah, that makes sense. Maybe see if one of them wants one of those oatmeal cookies Nate foolishly left within my range of scavenging." Momo licked her lips, a clumsy tongue making an alien motion. Placing a hand around her stomach, she looked down, then over at Spire-Cast-Behind. "I'm hungry. Wanna get lunch?"

At no point in her time here had Spire-Cast-Behind felt like her needs were neglected. But she didn't actually know what the appropriate meal times were, and asking for food could often feel awkward. So whenever a lunch was offered, she was eager to take anyone up on it. "I accept," she declared as Momo hopped off the desk, and then spent a few seconds trying to reposition everything she'd shifted around while she'd been up there messing with someone else's workstation. "Lead please," she instructed Momo.

The erratic girl might not have been someone Spire-Cast-Behind fully understood, and she *certainly* didn't know half of what Momo was talking about as they waited for the elevator and the human started monologuing about sympathetic material uses and the frequency of triangles in totem design. *But,* she was excellent at pushing elevator buttons, and carrying plates of food from the kitchen.

She also complimented Spire-Cast-Behind's jacket as they ate, which placed her at the top of the list of humans that Spire-Cast-Behind would kill for if it ever came up again.

Lunch was something Momo called vegetarian stir fry. Spire-Cast-Behind used her tongue and fangs to pick each individual piece out of her bowl, savoring the mix of sweet and salty that she'd spent her whole life not even knowing was an option. Momo continued talking about her totem project while they ate, and Spire-Cast-Behind did her best to reply when she knew the answer or had something to offer. She almost felt like they were on level ground for the conversation, since she was capable of speaking while eating, and Momo was . . .

Well, humans weren't actually capable of articulating around mouthfuls of food. But that didn't stop her lunch companion from trying.

It was a lazy afternoon, and Spire-Cast-Behind was content with it.

Later that night, Spire-Cast-Behind caught up with a group of others. Her own people. Or maybe that was the wrong term to use now. She'd had a lot of time to think throughout the long days, and every time it came up in her musings, she wasn't quite sure what her people were.

Were her people camracondas? Or only *these* camracondas, who had survived their trial and been brought to an unpromised home? Only her strain of camraconda, with this specific model of camera head, and the same rounded shape of the tail?

Or was it even closer and more personal than that, and her people were the three others she shared a room with? Or *bigger*, in the other direction, and her people were the people who had been there for her when she needed them; everyone from the other cabled serpents who were slowly picking names and finding voices, to the humans and their mixed allies who had liberated them.

Spire-Cast-Behind liked that version. She liked the idea that her people could include Momo, and James, and all the others that brought her here.

It did make it confusing to sort her own thoughts out though, when she wanted to mark a memory of having met with a group of camracondas that were part of her surviving family. To share new knowledge and experiences, to revel in being able to *communicate* at all.

Outline-of-Green had picked a name for himself, fascinated by the shapes and scents of the supposedly natural growth around them. Color-of-Dawn was still avoiding everyone, but had been coaxed out to make sure it knew about the update to the speaking programs.

Scent-of-Rain and an unnamed sibling had been to the meeting the humans called a support group. The idea was still a bit unfamiliar, but the point was to talk about their feelings, to make sure that everyone had an opportunity to self-express, and to validate the existence of emotions. And even with their more limited communication option, both camracondas reported that they felt . . . not better. But more whole. Or like they could keep going forward more easily than before.

For her own part, Spire-Cast-Behind demonstrated what she'd found the speech facilitation program capable of, and took her time to explain the process of making "her" voice. Not all of the others wanted to try that route, with some insisting on learning to do it with no interface at all, which was a serious challenge. It might take them days, or weeks, to figure it out on their own, and in that time the others would be growing more practiced with their voices. But, the counterargument went, if they could do it with no help, the voice would *actually* be their own.

There was no right answer, only feelings on the matter, and a shared sense of exploration. And so what if it took time? The humans talked about things like *next year* in real, concrete terms, and not as an abstract dream that they might die before it happened. And now Spire-Cast-Behind could dare to think that way too. To consider that she would be alive in a month, a year, a *decade*.

She was going to grow old here. Better yet, she was going to learn if camracondas even grew old at all. What was a month learning a language compared to *that much time?*

One of her siblings, filled with the long-ago-imprinted knowledge of what a fish was, wanted to learn more about that. Another one wanted to learn what a spreadsheet was. One wanted to know how to actually make the things that they used as bedding. There was so much of this fantastic and bizarre world to know about, so many things that seemed alien and new and desirable.

They had so much time now. To choose names and learn who they were, to open up to each other without wondering who would be the next to run out of life or be claimed by heat rot. To be *alive*.

Spire-Cast-Behind would forever cherish the first pieces of art her people had made, those early expressions of freedom in a world that would rip away their very thoughts if they strayed outside their prison. But while some of her siblings looked for ways to enshrine and honor their past, she saw something different. She saw what was *ahead* of them.

She saw some of her kin with smaller knowledge imprints filling that gap with curiosity and fumbling creativity. Making *new* art, with help from human hands, out of materials they'd never had before. And in those little moments, there was the potential for an endless future alongside the people who had fought for them.

Communicating this was impossible. She didn't know the right way to pattern the words yet. But Spire-Cast-Behind was nothing if not determined, and so she worked on the phrasing and syntax silently as the gathering ended and the variously colored camracondas split apart to return to their rooms or the common areas or the roof to watch the sky and the cars and the trees.

She was still working on it as she got back to her own room, using the hooks to doff her coat with a rip of velcro as she slithered to the bed. Wriggling into the blankets, and finding a warm spot where Taste-of-Air was already sleeping, Spire-Cast-Behind twisted her cable muscles to roll herself up against her companion, pressing into the other camraconda's back and curling up together as she felt exhaustion closing in.

Composing an explanation would have to wait until tomorrow. But she tried to sink her fangs into the memory of where certain words should go, and used that little mental nudge that was excellent for studying to remind herself what a definite article was.

Humans had long days. And so, too, had she.

When she woke up, she might even remember some of it.

CHAPTER 11

"Alright, I've got a proposition," Alanna was saying.

She was sitting with Anesh in James's fancy new office, a whole state away from home. The three of them were eating lunch together, supposedly taking a break from their responsibilities but actually just brainstorming ways they could impact the world. Ways within their actual real capabilities, not just pipe dreams.

"Is it going to be duplicating the wallet you found?" James asked. "Because I'm still *super* concerned about the fact that you folded a pistol in half."

"Yeah, in retrospect, that was a really bad idea," Alanna agreed readily. "Especially since it came out creased, and I *absolutely fucking will not* try to fire it now."

"What're you gonna do with it?" Anesh asked around a mouthful of gyro. He'd opted to break basically every reasonable security suggestion to take the stairs down to the ground floor and visit a food truck that he'd "heard good things about." How he'd heard of a random food truck in another city several hundred miles away was anyone's guess, but with Anesh, there was always a near-constant possibility that he had in his head a given piece of information.

Alanna shrugged, turning away from watching the traffic out the window. "I'm thinking I maybe mount it on my wall with a fancy engraved plaque that just reads *hubris*."

"Good plan. So, what's your proposition?" James prompted her.

"What?"

He sighed and leaned back in his padded chair, dropping his fork into the takeout tray on his desk. "You said you had a proposition, and then we derailed you."

"Oh! We should end crime!" Alanna stated bluntly, before taking another mouthful of salad and failing to clarify, like that had been a normal statement.

"Alanna, you can't just say stuff like that. I love you, but your addiction to dramatic pauses is tearing this family apart," James snarked at her, smiling behind the lunch held up to his mouth.

She made a fart noise at him, but did start speaking to clarify. "Okay, so, I've been doing some digging in FBI statistical databases, which our good friend Randall is weirdly willing to provide us with. Did you know roughly ninety percent of crime in this country is motivated by financial pressure?"

"Is financial pressure coded language for poverty?" Anesh asked politely.

"Yes!" Alanna jolted to her feet, pointing at her boyfriend in an overenthusiastic acknowledgment at Anesh's words. "It is!" She started pacing back and forth on the pleasant carpet of their skyscraper office. "And that figure includes violent crimes, too, by the way. Even though violent crimes are actually only a small fraction of total crimes committed. These numbers are for estimates of actual crimes, by the way, not net total arrests."

James tapped a finger to his cheek, processing her words. "So, what you're proposing . . . can I skip ahead here?"

"Please." Alanna spread her arms magnanimously in his direction.

"You're proposing that we address the root cause, and end poverty."

"Yes!" Alanna exclaimed again.

James and Anesh traded a look.

"Okay . . ." Anesh said, slowly building up steam in the conversation. "Now, I'll admit, I think we're leagues closer to being superheroes than I ever really expected to get. We can do a lot with what we have, and we have more and more each week. But that seems . . . like a big ask? Especially since a lot of our power is *not* soft power. We're better at raw action than we should be, but we don't actually have social influence outside of a hundred people, and half of them can't vote in the US. Or anywhere."

James had to agree. "Alanna, you are both beautiful and terrifying, but I don't think that we have the capacity to kill the abstract concept of poverty."

"The average human . . ." Anesh paused, trailing off and starting over. "So, this would be a massive undertaking, yes? And the average member of western civilization is . . . I don't want to be a knobend about it, but people have been content to let poverty keep going when the means to end it exist already. A few people profit from it, and everyone else is just trying to get by and doesn't know how to change anything."

James glanced out the window to the sprawling cityscape below them. "We really could just start assassinating people who stabilize problems," he said. "Like, people who keep problems going just to benefit from them, not . . . you know." Looking back at his partners, he shrugged. "It's an option. And it's kinda sad that it seems like the easiest way to influence a large scale. I don't think we *should*, and I have a whole list of reasons why it's a bad choice for long-term stability, but someone's gonna bring it up if we start this conversation openly."

"I knew you'd say that," she said. "Which is why I planned ahead, and have prepared some suggestions for other footholds." Alanna flipped open a binder that had been on James's desk the whole time, which he hadn't even noticed. "Now, we don't need to launch directly into getting in a fight with capitalism. We just need to address the roots of what people *need*."

"Water, food, shelter, security, community, entertainment, purpose," James rattled off rapid-fire. "What?" he asked of the surprised looks the other two gave him. "You think I'm fucking around with the whole building a better world thing? That's *happening*, sooner or later. We gotta know this stuff off the top of our heads if we're supposed to make decisions on any kind of real scale. Maslow! Hernton! Do the supplemental reading! We're allowed to learn outside of orbs!" He turned back to Alanna, propping his elbows on his desk and dropping his voice back instantly to a conversational level. "Anyway. You have ideas for addressing these things?"

"Somewhat," she said, a wry grin on her face. "The problem with a lot of them is the issue of *there are eight billion humans.* We can, locally, solve any problem at this point. Or we can assume we will shortly have the ability to cause magic or some bullshit. The dungeon provides shelter and food, if not security. Or we can use greens, or assume that we will have the ability to manipulate oranges soon to create safe spaces of our own. Similarly, with oranges, we can solve basically any scarcity problem. Now—"

"Wait, hang on," Anesh cut her off. "How does spatial contortion solve scarcity? I, too, am looking forward to fitting an entire neighborhood inside our supposedly-one-story leased commercial flex space, but that doesn't actually give us any manufacturing or production capability." He paused for a second. "Though I guess stacking greens might? Have we considered buying farm acreage and stacking orbs there? That could get . . . weird . . ." He trailed off.

"*Now,*" Alanna picked up where she left off. "Using orange orbs to *warp time like we know they can do to speed-grow crops* is a *little ways off . . .*"

Anesh shrunk into his seat a little bit, a sheepish copper flush on his cheeks. "Sorry!" he exclaimed, hiding behind the lamb wrap he was eating like it would protect him from too much scorn.

"But what we do have," Alanna continued like nothing had happened, "is a way to subvert the entire thing. To alter what the core needs are, and basically change the complex list of food-water-shelter-communications-transportation-and-sex-toys from *that,* into a much more compact *electricity.*" She looked James dead in the eye. "If we're stupid enough to try."

His brain spun for a second, trying to catch what she meant, until the thinnest thread of his enhanced memory caught on a conversation from a month ago. One that he'd had with Virgil, and that he'd quietly filed away under the increasingly cluttered header of *oh dear, that will be a problem later.*

"You're talking about mind uploads," James quietly spoke, not breaking Alanna's eye contact. "You want to turn people into digital life."

"What." Anesh quirked a single eyebrow.

"Yes." Alanna raised both of her own, expectation written on her face.

"You guys finished *Ghost In The Shell* at anime night without me," James accused.

"*Yes,*" she drawled out, waggling those same eyebrows.

"Okay," James said, shrugging.

The other two both tilted their heads a little bit. "You're just gonna let that . . . go without comment?" Anesh asked, concerned. "Are you feeling okay? What was in your curry?"

"Curry, mostly. Also chicken." James quirked a smile. "But yeah. Okay."

Alanna crossed her arms in challenge. "Just okay," she stated.

"I mean, I'm not gonna let you turn into a supervillain, wandering around with a horde of autonomous drones, installing skulljacks into people and sucking their brains out through a straw to dump into some data vault in the Arctic," James exclaimed, throwing his hands into the air with a dramatic flourish. "But somehow I *doubt* that's what you meant!" He calmed down a bit. Not too much, but a little. "We've got the skulljacks, we should use them. If that kind of thing works, if there *is* a way to transfer a mind from a human body into a machine, it's . . . I mean, it's on par with a cure for death, right? We don't even have to use it for everyone. I think the biggest problem is that we're going to need to actually create some kind of society that functions while disembodied with a meaningful quality of life." James looked back and forth between his two partners. "Any suggestions?"

There was a fairly long pause while they stared at him without saying anything, before Alanna cleared her throat. "I kinda figured that we'd have a little more of a disagreement about this," she said, clearly uncomfortable.

"Psh." James waved it off. "It's an idea, isn't it? And like with the assassination thing, it's worth discussing early to figure out what's wrong with it and how we can workshop it into something healthier. But . . . a person is a person, right? We don't—shouldn't, anyway—think people are less human if they've lost a leg or an eye. So why not just go all the way, and lose the body?" He tapped the desk with his fork, his enthusiasm and lack of attention spraying curry onto some papers that he hoped he wouldn't need later. "There have to be physical people for maintenance, obviously. We need to generate power, keep the machinery running, that sorta thing. But this is actually something where putting some massive server architecture inside the Office might be a good idea?"

"I would worry that the thing hosting an untold number of minds would, itself, develop a mind, get up, and walk away," Anesh pointed out. "Taking the untold number with it. Or eating them. Whichever is more ghoulish."

"Valid point! Somewhere else, then. An asteroid?"

"Asteroids are not safe just because they're hard to get to," Anesh chided him. "They are, in fact, empty of most of the defenses that our planet has, and void of such elegant luxuries as *an atmosphere* and *the moon*." He swept his hand across the space between them like he was a salesman presenting a planetary shield for consideration.

"But you're on board with us trying this?" Alanna pressed again.

James nodded at her, putting aside the joking with Anesh for a second. "I'm on board with us looking into it. Talking it through, at least," he said, honestly. "It's a potential step. And it's something that we can scale up a lot easier than most of our current small solutions. Assuming we can build the digital space with mundane stuff." James sighed as he realized this was going to require a certain level of logistics outside of what they normally did. "Okay," he said. "Anesh!"

"Yes, sir!" Anesh snapped to attention.

"No, no." James waved him off, clearing his throat awkwardly. "Nope. Don't like that title one bit."

"Yeah, we should save you calling him sir for later tonigh—" Alanna started to say before Anesh shut her up by cramming what was left of his gyro in her mouth.

"Anesh," James tried again, struggling not to giggle as Alanna processed the mouthful of pita bread and lamb.

"James," Anesh said, calm and composed, like nothing strange had happened at all.

"Find us some office space. *Normal* office space. Doesn't have to be fancy or big, but the kind of place that we could host ten or twenty programmers and engineers. People we're willing to *show* the skulljack to, but not specifically people we're looking to recruit into the Order just yet."

Anesh nodded. "Got it," he said. "You need me for anything else? If I go now, I can probably catch people coming back from lunch and get this started today." He stood up as James nodded at him. "Oh. Here, or in Oregon?" he asked.

"I mean . . . anywhere, right?" James shrugged. "It . . . Hm. I guess it does matter for who we're hiring. Let's say Oregon. It's easier to keep things central to us that way, and there's already a couple of tech companies there." He groaned. "Ugh, this is gonna be expensive, isn't it? I just realized that."

"We can get more briefcases," Alanna offered. "Our map of Officium Mundi is getting more detailed. We actually might be able to open those reliably in the near future." She thought about it for a second. "Or we could just start stealing from people who deserve it? Or you could go abuse your card-counting powers again."

"The first one, despite being a ton of money for one person, isn't really enough to consistently keep a highly paid specialist staff around. And that last one doesn't work for long before people get mad," James said. "Although it *is* now kinda mixed in with the boosted short-term memory. Also, we'll put the literal crime on the back burner for now. But I'm not saying no." He snorted a laugh. "Fuck, we used to joke about having plans to rob banks. Now the joke is that we don't have the time. Anyway. Can you do a quick skill pass on everyone who's around today, see if we have any opportunities to bring in some wealth that we can use? I'm gonna go talk to Research and see if we have a toehold for this one."

Alanna stood up, and both she and James grabbed Anesh in a hug before he headed out. "So, we're just doing this now?" she asked James. "I give you one small suggestion, and we pivot toward it? That's hardly fair."

"Again, we're *talking*. I'm not gonna dump a few hundred brains into a hard drive just to test it. We don't have anywhere to put the bodies, for one thing." He grinned at her. "Also, it's a long-term thing. May as well start when we can. Now let's see if we can catch up to Anesh before the elevator arrives, and make him feel awkward for leaving first."

James had been in the basement for six and a half minutes before someone from Research gave him a headache.

At this point, the Research division consisted of a score of dedicated human students of the arcane, a half-dozen other people who regularly dropped in to offer outside opinions, three camracondas who'd gotten really into the study of their own biology and kind of kept going from there, and one infomorph.

The infomorph was named Plan, or maybe Planner, and until yesterday, it had been contained in James's dreams by Secret's attentions.

The idea of converting things that tried to kill them into friends and allies was, in addition to being one of James's more fondly remembered anime tropes, kind of just the way the Order operated. But for some reason, it made James nervous that a weaponized schedule had been quarantined in his mind, plucked out, and then intentionally spread to a small network of other members. Right now, Plan couldn't manifest physically. They couldn't even really communicate with everyone. It was something of an experiment, to see if a group could host the same infomorph in a way that would mutually aid its growth and development.

Secret was keeping an eye on it, like a watchful and vaguely suspicious older brother. But so far, Plan hadn't eaten anyone's memories, and seemed more or less to be accepting of having to acclimate to living in the heads of ten people who were all the kind of people who would hang out in a basement and try to figure out what magic pens did.

James had a headache because these people were exactly that kind of people.

By this point, everyone had become aware of the fact that Alanna had found a wallet of holding. And while, yes, it was problematic that it folded things in half, that could also be a good thing! For example, it could easily replace a metal press with a tiny piece of leather. Somehow. The precision problem was something that was still being worked on.

"I know we have a limited resource budget for duplication," Reed was telling James. "And I'm not saying that we should go overboard or anything. But seriously, I would like to have a giant pile of these to experiment with." He handed James a few pieces of paper stapled into a stack. "Here's the reasons. Mostly, we want to see if we can reverse the effect somehow."

"Reverse the . . . so make a wallet of . . . unholding?" James worked his way through the comment. "I am super confused. I came down here to ask about a computer thing."

"Exactly!" Reed said, ignoring the back half of James's comment. "Now that we know that warped spaces can be made mobile without being part of a sentient creature, we can start to look into using them for applied practical purposes. And a container that's smaller on the inside would be the best logical first step."

James slowly ran both his palms up and over his forehead, dragging them through his long hair in an attempt to buy time for his brain to figure out what was happening. "Why," he asked, eventually. "Why not just a container *of holding*. The classic."

"Well, the wallet maintains mass," Reed said with a sad shrug. "So it's too heavy to do too much with it. It's not compressing stuff, it's just extra space. But if we could make one that has *less* space, we can use it to make lightweight armor!"

"Oh god, this is physics, isn't it?" James let out a long, quiet groan. He glanced around to see if he had any escape routes; but unfortunately, his only options were the vault, which was locked and would take him too long as well as being a dead end, or back toward the elevator. And being trapped in an elevator with someone trying to tell him about physics seemed worse than just listening.

Reed didn't notice, or at least didn't acknowledge his leader's distress. "Logically, smaller-on-the-inside spaces should make things take up more space and keep the same mass. Make a specially shaped un-space, shape it like body armor. Not like where you would go inside the smaller space, but where there's a layer of compressed space between you and the world. Then fill it with steel, or titanium, or whatever. The bag won't fit much because of its compressed insides, which makes it light. But if a bullet or something pierces the bag, then it will always hit the metal because the entire bag is filled with it." Reed looked absurdly smug about the entire idea. "*And*, bonus, because it'd be cloth, and compactable, we could cram a lot of them into a duplication ritual! I checked with Momo, and she says it's probably possible to make, though . . . I'm pretty sure she's never . . . made anything yet. And is just guessing . . ." Reed's eyes drifted away as he nervously trailed off.

"Momo is smart," James acknowledged with a nod, even as he ignored the last part of Reed's speech. "And I appreciate having someone who is arcanely minded, and also has field experience. But I think the two of you forgot something."

"Ah, fuck." Reed didn't wait for clarification, he just dejectedly took back the papers that were still hanging loosely in James's hand.

"Did you want to know what it was?" James called after him as he turned to walk away.

Reed stopped, like he hadn't thought of that. "Oh. Um . . . yeah?"

"Dang, man. You're allowed to know why I say no to things!" James told him. "There's a reason I make so many notes on your proposals." He raised his eyebrows at the younger man who was currently running a hand through his own curly hair. "You do read those, right?"

"Uh . . . yes?" Reed lied. "Sometimes. Eventually."

"Oh my god, read the notes." James rolled his eyes. "The reason this doesn't work is because, assuming Momo could even make it, it'd be an object like all the other magic items. Which means if it's damaged to the point that it's broken, then it *dissolves*, and that's not a feature you want in armor. At least, not without knowing exactly how many bullets it can take before it decides it's done. But damn, man. It's okay to accept feedback."

"Yeah, yeah. Of course." Reed nodded. "Um . . . I need to go feed the shellaxies now. Did you need anything else?"

"Yeah, what would it take to upload a full mind into a digital environment, and keep it running at baseline capacity or more?" James asked fluidly. He hadn't really rehearsed the question, but the words came out easily now that he had a goal in mind.

"Like . . . an AI?" Reed paused. "Or like a simulation of a human mind?"

"Which one's easier?"

"I'll ask around and get back to you. I was reading a study on this the other day, and I have a couple new physics yellows that could help out with the theory, but I'll need to check some stuff. Maybe? I dunno. We could just ask some of the emeralds to do it and come back to it in a decade." The young man shrugged. He had an almost self-mocking tone to his voice, until James realized that it was a little closer to exhausted sadness. "There's still a bunch of those in . . . Virgil's desk." He looked away again. "But yeah. I'll look into it. After I feed the little guys."

"Sure." James nodded at him. "I'll check in later."

Reed waved over his shoulder as he walked off toward the shellaxy pen, leaving James standing in the entry hall of Research.

He stood there for a second, taking in the moment. There were, James realized, a lot of small secret feelings here. Not here in the basement, but here in the Order of Endless Rooms. There were so many people here now that he wouldn't have time to be close with all of them. And while he could be kind, supportive, enthusiastic, and guiding, he couldn't ever get close enough like he could with Anesh, or Alanna, or even Dave and JP. To know their secret hurts and small worries and big losses.

The Research section felt subdued, James realized. It was a little too organized, a little too quiet. And not just because he was down here. Virgil had quickly become its beating heart for only slightly longer than the concept of a research team had existed for them. He'd gone from being a skeptical jackass to . . . well, still a jackass. But one that churned out wonders and miracles on the circuit side the same way Momo did with her totems. And he'd dragged the rest of them along in his wake. To their delight, James imagined. Though he didn't know, because he hadn't asked.

He didn't have enough time. Didn't have the space in the days to check in with everyone. He read *reports* now. That wasn't right. But James felt a level of responsibility for these people under his banner, and he didn't know exactly how to manage the disconnect.

"Oh shit," he muttered to himself. "I need to hire an assistant. Why didn't I think of that earlier?"

The follow-up thought was because it was probably hard to find a professional assistant that would be into the whole dungeon thing. But then again, they'd found an engineer, a chef, and a therapist. Though that last one hadn't really asked. And the chef was an FBI plant.

Pinching the bridge of his nose, James shook his head and turned back down the hall, reconsidering the line in the operations manual where he told everyone they weren't a conspiracy. Maybe just a *little* conspiracy would be okay?

"I may have a small conspiracy," James mumbled to himself. "As a treat."

James paused at one of the doors on the way back down the hallway toward the mezzanine space that the elevator's landing had become. There were a *ton* of doors on this side of the basement, many of them partitioned off to be bedrooms of sorts, but several still served as storage spaces or whatever else was needed. Usually these rooms were simple ten-foot-by-ten-foot concrete boxes, but there were enough cramped closets that you never really knew what was behind a door unless you were familiar with the layout.

He'd paused at this door because he *had* been pretty sure it was a closet with a water heater, a single exposed lightbulb overhead, and about one square yard of actual space. The kind of room that humans didn't ever actually go into and close the door behind them. But his memory, enhanced as it was, was put to the test when he saw there was a sign hanging on the wall next to it. A little image of a stapler drawn onto a hanging piece of cardboard.

Knocking lightly on the door, James waited a moment, and then quietly cracked it open, pulling it out into the hallway and peeking inside.

He'd been mostly right about the contents of the room. Water heater, harsh lighting, piping—did those pipes go to the rest of the building?—and very little room to move around. What he hadn't expected was that a number of steel shelves had been bracketed into the concrete brick walls, and that around the room there were ten or twenty little plants growing. Plants in only the loosest sense of the word; they were thin bronze stems, producing bulbs of neatly aligned staples. And on one of the shelves, tending them, was an old friend.

"Oh, hey Rufus!" James greeted the stapler-spider-crab-friend creature. "I haven't seen you in a while!"

Rufus, his red and black hull glistening in the damp air, was watching the door with his one main eye. He raised a pen leg in greeting to James, and then tapped it impatiently on the shelf in front of him, eliciting both a metal ticking sound and the sense that he would appreciate an explanation for James's absence.

"I was mostly dead for a bit. Sorry I haven't been around. You've been busy!" James looked around the room, before doing a small double-take. "You have more than one plant in here," he commented, idly, reaching out slowly to poke at the carbon-paper leaves of what looked like a fern made of perfect squares. Rufus practically leapt from the shelf he was on to one just below where James was reaching, reaching up with his forelegs to catch James's wrist before he could touch the Office plant. "Wh . . . Don't touch that one?" Rufus nodded. "Got it." James pulled back, and Rufus sighed in relief.

There was a minute or two of James just looking at the stuff growing in the room, before he spoke again. "You've been doing a lot here. I'm sorry I haven't been home much to hang out, even being not dead anymore. Or, I guess, you were here. Shit, I lost track of you a bit. I'm sorry, I guess. That's all. I'm sorry, and your staple plants are *really* cool to look at."

Rufus nodded. James wasn't wrong; his plants were excellent examples of pseudo-organic geometry, carefully tended so as not to run amok. He'd only had a few seeds, carefully carried out of some of the wilder, deeper regions of Officium Mundi, and it had taken him a lot of time and communication tricks to acquire this space and some resources from the Order to start to grow them in a controlled way. The little stapler took pride in his work, even if sometimes he had a fleeting thought that he didn't fully know what his work was . . . for.

"Do you need anything? Like, we could probably rig up a sprinkler system or something. Some grow lights?" James asked, cutting Rufus's thoughts off. The strider's mind changed tracks rapidly, forgetting his self-doubt in that moment. Did he need anything else? The little creature looked around at his growing domain. If he were human, he would have shrugged. What else would he need? He had everything he wanted to work with here.

"I could get you a cactus?" James offered offhandedly.

Rufus's wants and priorities changed rapidly.

"Yo." James poked his head into the kitchen, catching the attention of the pair of people currently being taught how to properly cut a sandwich, and the ex-agent-now-chef teaching them.

For someone who'd lied about the big thing, a surprising majority of Nate's backstory was legit. He *had* been in the Navy, he *had* worked as a galley cook on a naval vessel for a long time, and he *had* held a chef's position at more than one restaurant. The fact that his cooking helped his spying—and Nate did not appreciate it being called spying, though James had intentionally forgotten the technical term he'd used—was just convenient.

Right now, the big man was explaining to the human who'd been roped into helping with lunch today how a knife was used, while also trying to adapt knife techniques to the camraconda who had . . . difficulty . . . without the whole *thumbs* thing.

"A sharp edge isn't magic," Nate was saying. "And I can *say* that now, and mean it. Look. Hold it here, keep one finger on top, and you sliiiiide. Got it?" He walked the person through the motion once, then prompted them to do it themselves. "Good enough. See, this way, you're not just smashing stuff all over the place and making a mess." Nate looked up as soon as he was done, having largely ignored James's interruption midway through. "Boss," he said solidly.

"I thought we agreed we weren't calling me that," James said, slipping through the swinging door and into the kitchen proper.

"You agreed to that, and everyone else kept doing it," Nate told him. "You know, for someone who's in charge, you don't have a lot of discipline around here."

"Yeah, we play it kinda casual," James admitted. "Except for the big stuff," he said, in the same lighthearted voice, but with a serious implication as he met Nate's eyes.

The chef nodded once at him approvingly. "Yeah," he agreed, the two of them sharing a mutual understanding that sometimes, when the stakes were high, this was a group of people that didn't cut and run just because they hadn't had a proper chain of command. "So, what's up? Here for lunch?"

"I had lunch with Anesh and Alanna, actually," James said, feeling mildly guilty. It was weird to employ a professional chef and still eat from food carts instead of your own kitchen. Then again, Nate typically fed thirty to sixty people a day, so James could think of it as just not giving him more work. "I'm actually just here because I'm going out to the store to get a cactus, and I wanted to know if you needed anything for the kitchen."

"Why a . . ." The other human in the room, who James recognized as a member of Sarah's support group, but couldn't quite remember the name of, started to ask.

"Fish oil," Nate said, ignoring everything to do with the cactus comment. A few months here in this bizarre place had largely taught him that questioning things like that would just get him sent down a rabbit hole of conversation, and he didn't have time for it. So, for a different reason than James did, he just rolled with it. "The Sysco order showed up with it broken, and I need it for later."

"How much?" James asked, making a mental note. "And what . . . kind of fish? Is that a thing? I feel like I should know this."

"It'll be in the Asian foods section, and it's probably going to be herring, but it really doesn't matter," Nate told him. "A quart of it," he added.

"Does it oil fish, or oil of fish?" the camraconda, Knife-in-Fangs, asked.

"Of fish," Nate and James said idly at the same time. "Alright, got it," James continued. "I'll be back in an hour or so. Don't burn the building down while I'm gone."

"You're the one going out to buy a cactus for some weird magic thing," Nate told him, circling around the kitchen's central island to start turning knobs on their grill.

James held a hand to his heart in mock offense. "It's not 'some weird magic thing,' it's . . ." He stopped. Thinking about it, James realized, Rufus's weird little garden totally was some weird magic thing. But he wasn't really ready to admit that right away. "Look," he said, deflecting, "there's much more dangerous things in this building than an innocent cactus. Somewhere around here is a Nerf gun that shoots fireballs."

"What?!" Nate barked out the word like a gunshot of his own. "Where?!"

"I actually don't know," James admitted with a guilty smile. "We used up all the darts for it, and it doesn't work with mundane stuff.

If we'd been able to keep one in reserve, we could copy it, but we had to use them all on . . . some stuff." James tilted his head toward the support group member. "Ask him if you're curious sometime."

"A Nerf gun," Nate repeated.

"Yes?"

He slowed his words down and emphasized them. Hard. "A Nerf. Gun."

"I'm so confused." James glanced at the other two in the room, but they gave him a shrug and a hiss respectively. "Yes, a Nerf gun?" He looked back at Nate. "Why is this a . . . big . . . deal." James trailed off as the chef held up his left arm. The sleeve on his chef's jacket was rolled back, exposing a burly mass of tattooed muscle, but also, the one singular piece of adornment that Nate was never without these days.

A small copper-and-bone bracelet. The kind that, if time had been given to it for the cooldowns to tick over, could bind to and reload *guns*.

"Oh," James said. There was a long pause, as Nate just stared at him with a kind of expectant incredulity. "Oh!" he repeated. "We should figure out where that thing went to!" James exclaimed, turning to slide back out the door.

"Yeah, no shit?" Nate called after him, shaking his head as James retreated. "Ugh. Either I'm gonna have to go buy my own fish oil, or he's gonna forget about the gun," Nate grumbled, glancing up at the two prep cooks who were watching with badly concealed amusement. "Back to work," he gruffly chuckled at them.

Outside the door, James grinned to himself. He planned to forget neither the gun, nor the food. Both of those were important.

"Hey, Momo." He caught the girl as he was passing down the hallway back to the front room of the Lair, just next to where a small alcove with a couch in it lay indented into the wall of what should have been the kitchen. "Do you have a minute?"

Momo had a faraway look in her eyes, which was actually pretty normal for her these days. There was a pervasive sense of concern from basically everyone in the Order about how Momo handled her own emotional needs; she was brilliant, frequently saw connections in the arcane nature of the Office's orbs that no one else did, and she threw herself into working with that with a frenetic vigor. But she was also trying desperately to ignore the fact that her family didn't remember her, that she'd traded all her friends for a bunch of adventurers and snakes, and that she lived in a basement. It was a *nice* basement, relatively. And the last time James had seen her room, she'd had something like twenty lava lamps in there, which was great. She'd also been forced to get a real bed at some point. But it was still . . . hard.

So, when she walked by like she was staring at something a million miles away, it tended to be because she had in her pockets a few different handcrafted red orb totems broadcasting information in a very short range, all of it being soaked up by her adapting mind. This was part of how she coped.

"Oh. Hey," she greeted James cheerfully, the silver charms clipped into her hair chiming lightly as she bobbed her head at him. "What's up?"

"I've gotta go pick up a thing, and I just had a favor to ask if you had some time today. Can you try to find where that Nerf gun went to?" James asked her.

"The one that shoots fireballs, or the one that spawns spiders?" Momo asked instantly.

James was already answering by the time his brain caught up. "The one that shoots . . . sorry, *fucking what?*"

"Spiders?" Momo asked, grinning.

"Yeah, what . . . we have that?" James rubbed his nose. "Okay, that's awful. Why did we keep that?"

"In case we need to make spiders. Duh." Momo rolled her eyes, putting on a perfect impression of a sarcastic teenager. "But yeah, I can probably find it. I've been working on a tracking totem, this should be a good test for it."

"Yeah . . . how's that going, by the way?"

Momo gave a side-to-side motion that was half shrug, half excited ripple. "Eh! I've had some good luck using dungeon materials in totems lately. So I'll probably explore that more. A lot of it is trial and error until I can come up with something that works, and then I hand it off to Anesh or Nikhail to do the math on how to replicate it. I hear that we can start fucking around with space and time now? So I'll probably do that tomorrow, after I finish what I'm working on now." She leaned in conspiratorially and whispered, "It's a totem that tells you how likely you are to successfully flirt with people." Momo leaned back, glancing off down the hallway with a sad look. "It's not going well. I don't know how to measure flirting."

James looked at her for a minute before clearing his throat. "Is magic real, and are you a wizard?" he asked. "You have to tell me if you're a wizard."

Momo cackled out a laugh. "I'm pretty sure my official title is 'war witch,' which is cool!" she said. "But yeah, I'll find your wand of fireball for you," she told James.

"Seriously, though. Are you doing okay? Your eyes look . . . not good." James's own eyes softened into concern as he looked down at the short goth girl. She looked, as always, frayed and tired. She *always* looked tired, and James understood that feeling all too well.

"I mean, no," Momo admitted. "Can't go outside, can't go to a restaurant, don't really have anyone I can talk to. I'm . . . man, I'm tired."

"Me too," James said. "Hey, you wanna just hang out and play card games tonight?" he offered. "I've got nothing going on."

"You literally cannot help but cheat at poker," she accused him.

James snorted. "I meant *fun* card games. Like, the kind where you do math as a form of metaphorical combat with your opponent."

"I don't know how to play Magic," Momo countered.

"You're a witch. You'll learn. See you in a few hours!" James called cheerfully, walking backward out toward the main room and waving goodbye at her.

JP rapped his knuckles on the wood paneling of the ajar door. "You wanted a meeting?" he asked, pushing the door open without waiting for an answer.

The office used to be James's office, before JP had claimed—by right of conquest—a floor of a skyscraper for them to use, and then the Order had collectively figured out how to abuse their poor elevator into bridging space and time. He'd not had a lot of time to talk to James lately, what with his friend being mostly dead for the last couple months. So it felt weird to come back to this office, now occupied by someone new, and vaguely unwelcome.

"I've been told you're the financial director for this company," Randall, the FBI liaison on the other side of the shiny new desk said.

The desk, JP decided, had *zero* personality. James's old desk had been something like a thousand years old, bought from an estate sale for a bargain price because no one wanted to haul five million pounds of wood away from the remote hilltop manor where he'd found the damn thing. It had intricate hand-carved details, marred by decades of dents, scrapes, and missed pen strokes. It had real character, a sense of a warm, inviting den where an old man wrote letters to his grandchildren. *This* desk was a modern, lightweight metal and plastic box that looked like exactly what you'd expect the FBI to assign to a junior agent who wasn't worth a real desk.

"I deal with a lot of our financial stuff, sure," JP said in a neutral voice, unwilling to admit how much of that may or may not be crime.

"Your organization, I've been instructed, has reasonable rates for government consulting when it comes to outside context problems," Randall stated in a similar tone that said *I will not be volunteering information.* He finally looked up from his laptop at JP, who was leaning against his doorframe with casual arrogance. "Does that include white collar crimes?"

JP kept his face blank. Unlike James, who had what seemed like a compulsive need to emote and ham up every tiny bit of confusion, JP played his secrets a bit closer. So no quirked eyebrow, no confused grunt. Just a simple statement of, "It depends on the crime."

"We don't know what the crime was," Randall responded.

"As in, you want us to . . . what, scry a potential crime scene for you?" *Now* JP was willing to show some confusion. A calculated amount, just enough to more quickly draw out a straight answer and some details.

"As in," Randall said, "we have reason to suspect there is evidence in an insider trading investigation that has been removed."

"But not *we lost evidence*. Interesting," JP noted, tapping one extended finger on his lips. "You mean, you think there should be evidence, otherwise you wouldn't be where you are, but that evidence isn't there, and you're lost."

"Yes," Randall confirmed. "I can tell you more, but we'd like your official cooperation on this. The agents assigned to the case aren't read in on . . . you. So you'll need to operate with a strict NDA. My superior has instructed me to extend an offer for a contract here."

It was strange, JP thought, that the man could say all that with a perfectly normal tone, and no sign of any distress, and yet the *feeling* in the room was akin to when someone swallowed an entire lemon and was really trying to hide it.

JP wasn't one to torment people, though. Not when those people were swallowing their pride, and their citrus, to offer him money. "I can agree to that," he said. "I'll need to check in with someone else first, but I'm reasonably sure that we can help you here."

"Good," Randall said, a sliver of relief in his otherwise flat voice. "I want you on a plane in two hours."

"I . . . What?" *Now* JP lost his hold on his confusion. "Me personally? And a plane to where?"

"You're the abnormal finance expert," the fed said, like that explained anything. "And New York. We're on a timeline here."

"I . . . um." JP drew himself up. "Yeah, okay. Yeah, that makes sense. Sure." He pulled his phone out of his pocket, already texting Alanna just to make sure he wasn't about to cause any major problems. He figured that out of the trio in charge of all this, she was the one most likely to give him the green light. "I'm gonna go see if I can get Secret in on this. I'll meet you in the parking lot in fifteen minutes."

"Did you want to talk about the contract rate?" Randall asked, and JP could swear he heard a hint of humor in there. James was already corrupting the guy, it seemed.

"Oh, don't worry." JP said as his phone buzzed with a reply. "It's going to be extortionate."

Never miss an opportunity. That was JP's personal motto. And the government asking him to solve magic stock-market crimes was a massive window of opportunity. You could fit a lot of consulting fees through that window. And JP intended to bill them for every single one of them.

It was just another day.

It was strange, to everyone, how quickly it had become normal. Most of them never really thought about it, but some did.

There was a pair of mind-linked partners rapidly approaching total unity, who would sometimes wonder if maybe they were making a mistake. But they wondered it together.

There was a therapist, still working with young students, though now over a digital medium. She'd saved a lot of lives, and taken more than a few in doing so. There were rumors about her, even without the physical classes to help them spread. Students traded private texts and whispers about the woman who could talk to you about your problems, help you figure out what you wanted from your future, and could also kill monsters by staring at them too hard. She wondered if she was doing enough with all her new power.

There were a half-dozen camracondas who spent every morning on the roof, watching the sunrise that didn't seem *real* to them just yet, wondering how much of this world they'd ever get to see. Just watching the endless sky overhead turn colors, being free. None of them paid a single thought to going back to the old prison.

There were so many members of the Order who wondered if they were losing more than they could handle. Who worried about when they'd break. And sometimes they shared that with each other, and found that when they put their worries together, it didn't seem so world-ending.

There was a copy of a copy of a copy of a young Indian-English man, who alternately worried about his own *realness*, and whether or not he could successfully track down the identity of a mysterious dead woman who was a savior figure to the fifty-ish snakes made of cameras and cables in the building he leased for their secret organization.

It was a Thursday.

There was so much that was strange in their lives now. Some of them hadn't even had lives until the Order had bulldozed through and opened up the path ahead of them. And now there were choices. Agency. Power and ability, balanced with responsibility, and the desire to do good recklessly.

It was almost overwhelming.

But every single one of them knew, more than anything, that they weren't in this alone. That they had each other, and they had a fighting chance. Whether that was against an unjust society or a murderous building didn't matter.

They weren't alone. And they were in it, for real now.

CHAPTER 12

Alex felt deeply out of place sitting on the floor in the shadow of the massive stack of cubicles just inside the door to Officium Mundi.

Partly it was the dungeon itself. It was a *dungeon*. Like from a video game. That was . . . stupid. Deeply, intrinsically stupid, in a way that she hadn't said out loud to anyone yet. And even that was something she was divided on; she didn't want to make any of the people who'd saved her life feel weird about it, but *also* it was still really cool. In a stupid way, though.

Who in their right mind would look at a place full of monsters and start thinking about how far into it they could go without dying? Well. Her, maybe. Assuming she was still sane. Alex couldn't discount the possibility that she was in a coma somewhere and this was all just an intense hallucination. But even under the (large) assumption that it was real, at least the first time she'd been here it had been because she'd been technically kidnapped.

The first group, people like James and Alanna and Dave, they'd come in here on purpose. Because it could be profitable, or empowering, or *fun*. The way they sometimes talked about it was so hard for Alex to grasp. Like, she knew people did stupid shit for a good time; skydiving was on her own list of things to try eventually. But she didn't have *bare-knuckle boxing match with a coffee machine* on there, and it seemed like some people here *did*, and that left her feeling a little too sane for this gathering.

So she was in a building that wasn't really a building, inhuman architecture stretching off to a faraway horizon that wasn't even a real horizon and made it look like they were on some kind of miniature ringworld. She wasn't sure if she even wanted to be part of this kind of action, but felt like it was one of the only real ways she could prove that she was meant to be here. And to top all of that off, she'd joined up with a group that she didn't have a single *clue* how to talk to.

"Oh good, you're ready already. Maybe?" Simon's voice made her look up from where she was staring out at a distant part of the landscape, where it looked almost like there was static hanging over some of the cubicles. She was pretty sure it was a flock of printer paper, though, which was a thought that just didn't work in normal life. Normal life that she'd left behind. "Are you okay?"

Alex held a hand up and let her teammate for today pull her to her feet. She felt doubly out of place going delving with Simon and Other James, both because one of them was a half decade older than her, and also because she couldn't tell if she was supposed to address them as one person or two.

She didn't bring that up right now. "Yeah, I'm fine," she said, dusting off the back of the fencing jacket someone had loaned her. Not that there was any dust in here. For a place that went untouched by anyone for months at a time, this dungeon was surprisingly fastidious. "Being slowly choked out by my armor, but I'll live."

They hadn't had an extra of the Kevlar and hard plastic riot armor sets that fit her, since some damage had "occurred," according to Nate's suspicious explanation. So Alex was wearing that dull white fencing jacket and matching gloves, which did a decent job of ensuring that no stapler was ever going to get close to biting into most of her body. She also had her old soccer shin guards on over a pair of jeans, which was . . . not *perfect*, in a place where sometimes things spat lasers at you. But they weren't going anywhere today that should murder her outright.

It *was* a crime against fashion, though. Not much of an issue here, as much as she normally did try to make a statement with what she wore that went beyond saying *I really didn't want to get stabbed.* Her look was completed by a shoulder bag with their medical supplies in it, a baseball bat tucked across the top of the pack's loops, and Alanna's shotgun in a long holster that sat across her back.

Alex felt like she was cosplaying a character from a post-apocalypse movie, except one without a budget.

Simon just nodded at her, his own equipment equally weird. Neither of them were actually that used to being armed, or outfitted like this at all, or around others that were doing the same. But Simon and Other James had done it a *lot* more than she had. This was only technically Alex's third or fourth delve, while they'd been in here a dozen times each.

She followed Simon out to where Other James was waiting. "Okay, I gotta know," Alex said as the trio did one last check of their stuff, preparing to head through the line of cubicles and vanish into the gray jungle of Officium Mundi.

"Yeah?" The two boys looked at her in unison.

Alex pointed at one of them. "Do I stop calling you Other James when you're the only James in this dimension?"

Other James thought about it for a good thirty seconds. "Nah," The broad-shouldered man eventually settled on. "I'll get used to it, and then it'll be weird when we're back."

"You're way too understanding," Simon said with a snort, one tanned arm sticking out of the backpack he was quickly reorganizing.

"There's always too many Jameses." Other James shrugged easily. "We ready?"

Alex had one more question. "You two sure you're okay with me being here? I mean, shouldn't this be Momo's spot?"

Simon and Other James sighed in a single shared huff. "Momo's busy with . . . Momo stuff," Simon explained as he zipped up the pack and slung his arms through the straps, settling it onto his armored frame with a series of shifts. "We mostly just go on our own now anyway. You're not gonna be in the way, just back us up and it'll be fine."

Alex wasn't too close with Momo, but she *did* spend a lot of time around the Lair, so the description of *Momo stuff* plucked a string of knowledge she'd absorbed over the last few months. Small conversations overheard about weird Research requests, glimpses of someone who'd merged goth fashion with legitimately never sleeping, and occasional flashes of random information as a new red totem was put together and quickly broken again. Alex knew what *Momo stuff* meant. *Everyone* did at this point.

"Cool," she said out loud, though without any enthusiasm. And then there wasn't much else to say that wouldn't cause an overt delay. They *were* sort of on the clock; six hours to explore and accomplish the goals that Simon and Other James aimed for every week, and to pick up a few extra orbs for themselves on the way. So Alex followed them toward where the forest of cubicles really started to grow from the floor.

She paused only briefly to turn back and look at the tower near the door. Not to look up at its pinnacle; that was a *headache*, because it was way too tall to fit here under the ceiling and she didn't need to be worrying about that right now. Instead, she caught sight of Deb getting ready for her own exploration into this place, and waved a goodbye at her friend.

Deb waved back, and Alex smiled. A little extra spark buoyed her as she turned and headed after the other delvers, stepping past the invisible line where the outer ring of carpet and drywall that looked like just a large office ended, and the infinite expanse of cubicles began.

Twenty steps in, and she may as well have vanished.

Being back here was still kind of terrifying. But Alex swallowed that fear, and did her best to keep up.

Exploring on the way to their destination had been kind of fun. The trio had quickly worked out where they liked to be as they walked, and how they liked to fight. Which was, respectively, with Alex bringing up the rear, and not much.

The thing that Alex hadn't really realized about the dungeon was just how much combat *didn't need to happen.* The times she'd been in here before, especially while being rescued, it felt like something was always trying to kill her. And to be fair, that did happen at least once, when something that looked like a computer mouse had darted out from under a desk to take a shot at electrocuting her foot. But what also happened were a dozen different passive interactions. Their group passed quietly by hermit crab computer towers and nests of living staplers without a problem.

Especially when they weren't looking in every single cubicle, but following a map instead. It was almost peaceful, except for all the tension.

But they still paused sometimes to look at interesting things. A vending machine with the row of buttons stretching on for what felt like forever, a perfectly normal three-thousand-dollar laptop left sitting out before it went into someone's bag, a hallway where printer paper grew like vines across their path and some sneaky staplers had woven strands of paperclip web across the path, a cubicle that was totally empty except for a single briefcase sitting on the floor.

Small moments of amusement or wonder or profit. All of which, slowly, made Alex feel even more like the odd one out, as it became more and more clear that Other James and Simon were reacting to each other way too fast, without ever speaking.

"This says we need to deliver three designated packages to cubicle Z-Z-1900-22-A," Simon said as he stared at the work order on the briefcase that simply would not open. "I don't think we can do that. I don't even see any packages."

He said it without looking up, but Other James was sweeping his eyes across the empty cubicle and all the ones around while Alex kept watch down the hall. She still noticed though. "Okay, I've gotta ask," Alex said as she tried to not fidget with the baseball bat she had been told to stop tapping on the floor in case it attracted anything.

Other James and Simon sighed at exactly the same time. "Go ahead," Simon told her. *Maybe.* Maybe it wasn't really Simon.

Alex had been aware that the two of them were connected a lot more than anyone else. Most of the survivors of their time being prisoners in this dungeon, herself included, kind of . . . didn't like the skulljacks. They couldn't get rid of them, but they *could* ignore them forever. Or only use them in controlled ways. Alex wouldn't lie and say she didn't think it was cool as fuck that she could kinda sorta use her phone with her brain. But she also wouldn't ever think of going *back* to being plugged into someone else.

Yet these two did. And she really wanted to know why, but as soon as she started to say anything, she realized they probably got bothered about it a lot. And so far, both Simon and Other James had been nothing but friendly and helpful, with the bigger of the two even going so far as to tackle a computer that was trying to eat her about half an hour ago.

So Alex abandoned her dumb question of asking them why, and instead went with something a little more irreverent. She didn't really put *too* much thought into it, either, just grabbing the first stray thought and pivoting to it. "Is one of you, like, the top in this situation?" she said.

The two guys both stopped what they were doing and pivoted their heads at the same time to stare at her with their mouths half open for a reply that had been totally derailed.

Simon recovered first. "It's . . . not like that," he said.

"*I'm* straight," Other James informed her. "So, you know."

"It's true, he literally never stops thinking about asses," Simon told her with a confidential shake of his head. "He's disappointed, *right now*, that camracondas don't have an ass."

The other man nodded. "It's a waste," he declared, his deep voice making the comment even funnier.

Alex did find it funny, and did want to laugh, but she was busy being utterly embarrassed. "No, not like that! I *mean*, if you're . . . you know . . ." She waved her bat around in their direction.

"Plugged in?" Simon offered her patiently.

"Sure. So, is one of you in charge?"

"It's not like that," Other James said defensively. They were back on the common ground for questions he'd been asked a bunch before. "We don't . . . do that."

"Well, we kinda do that," Simon countered. "Hey, do you remember . . ." He waved a hand toward the deeper part of the dungeon, the place where the cubicles formed chasms and hills, and where a simple conference room had held them hostage for months. "That?" Alex didn't really have anything to say, finding a lump in her throat, so she just nodded. "Remember how it didn't matter when you got plugged in? There's no battle of wills or resistance or anything, you're just . . . there, right?"

Alex did remember. She thunked the end of the baseball bat into the cubicle wall next to her, turning away from Simon to pretend she was keeping watch again. "Yeah," she tried to say without her voice breaking.

"Okay, well, it's always like that," Other James said, picking up the conversation, but using words that sounded off coming from him.

Simon spoke like there was no pause between the two of them. "We're both here." Both boys tapped their skulls.

"And it doesn't matter who's talking—" Other James's tone suddenly shifted midsentence, "from whose face." Then back again. "Though I like my own face. I know where all my teeth are."

Despite the existential fear of having her individuality stripped away by a Wi-Fi connection, Alex had to admit, that was a pretty cool party trick. "Okay, I was *trying* to say something that you hadn't heard before, but seriously, *why?*"

They both paused for a moment before answering. "It's just kinda nice," Simon said eventually with a shrug. "And we're used to it now. And we can do *this*." He tossed the briefcase, and Other James caught it with one hand without turning around. "Anyway. Should we get going? The tower's still a half mile away."

They stood four cubicles and one open gap away from a beige ramp that led up into the dark interior of a dark structure. Alex crouched between her two delving teammates as they pointed things out and gave advice for her first time tackling one of these.

It was shorter than the tower at the entrance, but not by much. Too tall to actually fit in here, its walls a mess of angles as each layer of cubicles stacked atop another jutted out in odd ways. One, maybe six or more layers up, was *much* wider than the others, and it created a kind of awning that blocked Alex's view of the higher levels. The way the harsh white lights overhead shone down on it, it felt like half the thing was in almost complete shadow.

The inside she could see from here was going to be only just tall enough for her, and Other James was definitely going to have to crouch-walk everywhere. Nothing moved on the circle of linoleum flooring around the base.

"The thing is," Simon told her, "we don't actually know if the dead zone is for anything in particular. Last week we were taking a break, and we saw a few of the shellaxies wandering by, and they refused to set . . . foot? . . . cable? . . . whatever, they wouldn't walk on it."

"Is it dangerous?" Alex felt like it probably was. Everything in this place was dangerous. She saw Other James shake his head, but she didn't believe him. "I think it's dangerous," Alex muttered to herself.

"Keeps the cubes from growing too close," Other James half explained, half guessed. They had no idea if the endless rows of cubicles actually *grew*. But something certainly seemed to repair and restore them in between delves. "We going?"

"Yeah, yeah, we going." Simon's spoken reply felt like it was almost a performance for Alex's sake, but she appreciated the two of them still speaking out loud when they clearly didn't have to. "Remember," he told her directly, "the stuff in there is going to be a *lot* more aggressive."

Alex nodded, the nerves she was feeling making her come across as irritable. "I know, I know. Shoot anything big." She was their backup plan for if bats and swords didn't cover it. The plan was a *bit* more involved than that, but not much.

She followed the others across the open expanse, half expecting a pit trap to open up and dump her into a giant living paper shredder or something. But her steps landed on the material of the ramp without incident, the rough fuzz of the sloped cubicle wall bending lightly as she followed the guys up into the dark interior, feeling the closest she had so far on this trip to being an *actual dungeon delver.*

Then a stapler dropped on her head, pen legs scrambling wildly as it tried to get leverage to punch a disposable metal fang into her skull, and any feeling Alex had of being a cool professional or smooth operator went right out the window as she accidentally flung the baseball bat away and flailed her hands at her own head to grab the thing trying to bite her.

The tower was *way* worse than the rest of the dungeon. *Everything* here wanted to fight them, and wouldn't listen or hold back like the other things out there would. Within a few minutes of being inside, they'd been attacked by five striders and a potted plant that had almost choked one of the guys to death, and they were barely past the door.

But they needed to be here. These places were the only spots where they could find the bags of magical coffee grounds that powered the duplication ritual. A sentence that Alex's brain rebelled against, but was still *true.* And so she held her ground behind the other two, taking downward swings at stalking staplers that skittered across the walls around them and threatened to leap onto unprotected heads.

She wasn't new to fighting, but she still didn't really think about how *hard* she had to swing to actually hurt something. The first few striders she swatted down were certainly disrupted, but they were on their pen tips and scurrying across the floor to bite at her feet almost as soon as she knocked them down.

Stomping on one of them had felt *really* unpleasant, as its form popped open and a kind of inky blood spilled out. After that one, Alex tried to commit more to her swings, using the bat to really smash into the things that crawled around them in the gloom. In the light of the camp lamp that Simon had tossed into the middle of the cubicles of this first floor, she wore her arms out rapidly as she learned exactly how hard she had to swing to *crush* a living stapler.

The first floor fell quiet abruptly after the sound of ceramic smashing. Alex, panting from exertion and feeling a tingling in her fingers from the repeated heavy impacts of the bat she was holding, jerked her head around sharply as she looked for anything else approaching. But that was it; they had taken out a dozen staplers and one potted plant, and maybe a few other things that Other James might have dealt with out of her line of sight. And it had felt like a *war*.

Her heart wouldn't slow down. And she was pretty sure she was hyperventilating, which Deb had warned her could happen in stressful situations like this. This was *much* worse than the fights they'd gotten into on the way here; this felt like when she'd participated in the attack on the Status Quo building.

A gloved hand brushed her shoulder, and Alex nearly nailed Simon in the face with the bat as she whipped around. "Hey," he said calmly as he stepped back, holding his hands up. "Breathe." She was breathing, that was sort of the problem. "I know this has never actually helped, in all of human history, but try to calm down."

Alex stared at him. The utter audacity of telling her to be calm in a situation like this somehow cracked through the shell of panic that had been closing in around her thoughts. She straightened up, letting the bat pivot around to tap its ichor-stained tip against the floor. "Really?" she asked him, still catching her breath.

"Yeah, not once," Other James confirmed as he rejoined them. "I should know, it never worked on my wife either."

It was a casual joke, but it put a sudden bitter damper on the proceedings, beyond just the stress of the fight. This place, this *dungeon*, had taken a lot from all of them. Not just their agency and freedom for a period of time, but their families, their homes, sometimes their whole lives. Other James had been *married*, and the small sudden reminder that he was one of the people who *no one* outside ever remembered was jarring.

Simon came to their rescue. "Let's grab the orbs and find any coffee down here. There's usually not much on the first floor, but we can stack it by the door for later."

They needed the coffee. It was quickly becoming one of the most important things the Order had access to, especially since apparently today Anesh was going to be making copies of some of the stuff they'd looted off of the Status Quo agents. Alex wasn't sure if it was going to work, but she looked forward to a world where she never had to take off a shield bracer. Where maybe she could feel safe all the time again.

"Here," Simon said before they ascended the ramp, holding out a pair of small yellow orbs to her. "Use 'em. You earned it and they're cool sometimes."

"You fucking liar," Alex accused him, even as she crushed them into glowing dust.

[+1 Skill Rank : Manufacture—Wrought Iron—Lamppost—Norwegian Style]

[+1 Skill Rank : Cooking—Ingredient—Tofu]

"Well?" Simon asked.

"I stand by what I said," Alex said as she walked next to him up the ramp that sagged slightly underfoot, leading the way to the second floor.

It was when they were in the middle of a fight on that second floor, and a 2.0 was drawing wobbly black scorch lines on her jacket while Alex tried to break open its friend with her bat while elegantly shouting obscenities, that she had a fun thought. They didn't have enough shield bracers right now, because they were all sitting in the basement and recharging. But if they made copies, then anyone could have one all the time. This was basic math, and it was only the start of her thought.

Other James interrupted her briefly by being kicked out into the hallway that Alex was fighting in, crashing through one of the cubicle walls and making the ceiling overhead that it was holding up bow downward in a *very* scary way. But he was rolling sideways and throwing the magical returning paperweight that they'd found at his paper humanoid opponent, so Alex focused on her own fight.

She managed to finish off the 2.0 that she was crushing. Simon came to her rescue with the second before it could laser her, and Alex had that strange sensation of her thoughts making connections mid-battle again. Yeah, it would be nice to have a shield, but so far in this single assault, she'd been lasered, choked by a cable tentacle, stapled, and headbutted. A single shield bracer wasn't going to keep her safe if she planned to be the kind of moron that made this part of her routine.

No, Alex decided as she brought the baseball bat around in an uppercut into the brittle plastic of the 2.0 that Simon was holding away from his body as it fired its front lasers in a trio of frantic sweeps. What she needed would be *several* shield bracers.

"I'm gonna trade every share of whatever loot we get for eight shield bracers," she told Simon as he tried to hand her a green orb.

He looked at her blankly for a second, then started to say something before realizing his mouth was full of blood. Spitting a glob into a napkin and throwing it away in a trash can, in a move that was strangely polite for being mid-dungeon, he coughed and turned back to Alex. "I don't think you can do that?" he told her. "Also, you still have to carry your own orbs."

"Why not?" she asked as she double-checked to make sure her fencing jacket wasn't on fire, before moving to help the boys search in drawers and under desks for more bags of the ground coffee that they craved. "We use magic items all the time. Your . . . uh . . . not boyfriend, other half? Partner?"

"Sure, partner sounds good," Other James yelled from the other side of the floor.

Alex rolled her eyes. "He's abusing the magic paperweight he can't lose. You've got that pen that liquifies stuff . . ."

"I think it turns it into ink," Simon said idly as he ratcheted open a filing cabinet drawer.

"*Sure.* So why can't I use a bunch of shield bracers?"

He shrugged at her, hitting his shoulders on the desk that he was crawling underneath. "I mean, you're welcome to try. I just don't know if magic items stack. They never stack in games, anyway."

Alex stopped, standing in the two-foot-wide gap that was pretending to be a hallway, and turned to stare at Simon with a growing sense of worried disbelief. "Someone's tried, though, right? Like . . . no one's dumb enough to think that because a video game did it, real life works the same way, *right?*"

". . . We'll borrow a few when we get back."

"Holy shit, *I* cannot be the one who's most qualified for this," Alex muttered. "That's . . . not allowed. That's gross. No." She stopped her quiet complaining as they moved up to the third, and then fourth floor, but was still having an internal crisis as she started to feel like maybe *none of them* knew what they were doing. Like maybe everyone was just making it up as they went along.

That has been true in life outside of the dungeon. In the normal world, before all this crap had started piling onto her, before her kidnapping and erasure from school and medical records, before her boyfriend forgot she was real, before all that, Alex had gone through the same process as everyone else. Slowly realizing that no one knew what they were doing, that every adult was just stumbling along and doing their best most of the time. That being an expert in a field just made someone an expert in that field, and didn't exactly mean they had the answers to things like how to deal with the trials and tribulations of life in general.

But she'd sort of started to hope that maybe the people who had saved her life, that wanted to be some kind of wizard superheroes and change the world into something better, *might* have had a better handle on things.

"Hey," Alex told the other two as they finished clearing the fourth floor and stacked up twenty pounds of ready-to-brew coffee by the ramp. "I don't wanna be the smart one here. So I'm gonna need you two to step up your game."

"On it," Other James said instantly, giving her a supportive thumbs-up. He paused only briefly before a shadow of doubt crossed his face. "How do I do that?" he asked, turning to look at Simon.

Simon didn't even glance back, just meeting Alex's eyes. "Sorry, you're screwed," he said. "And I guess if we're sharing the one brain cell today, so am I. Next floor? I think we can go one or two more before it becomes too dangerous."

The rest of the tower they handled without incident. It was scary, and intense, and Alex was pretty sure she was never going to be good at *fighting*, even if she learned the proper moves and tactics and stuff. But they were successful invaders and looters, getting out with a bunch of coffee grounds without taking any injuries beyond scrapes and nicks.

"We are so good at our jobs," Other James said smugly, muscled arms folded in front of him as he nodded at the pile of loot that Alex and Simon were sorting into their backpacks. The two glanced at him before Simon shook his head and went back to smushing bags of coffee grounds into pockets that wouldn't zip up all the way. "What?" the bigger man asked. "We are! And Slugger here did a great job!"

"Please, I'm begging you, do not make that my nickname." Alex's voice jumped an octave as she squeaked out a sudden plea. "Come on, you *know* how bad nicknames can get."

"Oh, Other James is the best James-based nickname he's ever had," Simon told her as he stood and hoisted the hiking backpack onto his shoulders with a grunt. "He *likes* it. I can feel it."

"Impossible," Alex said.

Other James nodded sadly. "When I actually worked at the techie wage slave side of the office, I got either Football James, or Boring James," he told her with a look like he was reminiscing as far from fondly as possible. "I don't play football." He spread his hands out.

"You play basketball," Simon said, and then his connected partner turned a flat expression his way, clearly thinking something uncharitable before Simon added, "Fine, you play basketball *now*. I could make you like football," he muttered the last bit under his breath.

"You already did that. I have to enjoy football every time you watch a game," Other James complained as the trio did a quick check of the linoleum dead zone around the base of the cubicle tower, and then started carefully making their way back to where they'd left a trail marking. They did have a map, but the map relied on them going the right direction.

Alex stretched her arms out as she followed them. Her shoulders and arms burning from exertion and the weight of her cargo, but she still felt oddly relaxed compared to when they'd come in. "Are you *sure* you two aren't dating?" she asked casually. "You make it sound like you're dating."

They declined to answer her, and the group lapsed into a partly grumpy and partly amused silence as they walked, keeping an eye on the refreshingly passive strider pack that was crawling along the upper edge of the towering cubicles a row over from them.

Endless beige and gray surrounded them as they headed back. As the cubicles rose around them and blocked out the view of the ceiling, the only splotches of color became speckles of green in the otherwise dark gray hard carpet, or the occasional glimpse of red or dark blue from a desk lamp or stack of binders sitting on a desk as they passed. It wasn't quite monochrome, but it *was* disorienting. Like a fundamental part of the world had been sucked away and replaced with the distilled essence of a sterile corporate environment.

When Alex had gotten a holdover job doing tech support, she had kind of figured that she'd never have to actually get used to the cubicles and little partitioned workstations. She was there for a few months, then back to college. If she'd known that it was going to somewhat literally grow to consume her world, she might have spent more time hating it before it got this out of control.

At least the dungeon was a lot more creative with its walls than any human corporate overlord would be. Like when their path back had to diverge a little bit, and they ended up with a curved hall that wrapped around a support pillar. Or rather, they could see the support pillar, white speckled drywall in the middle of the path rising up into the ceiling. But there were more cubicle walls wrapped around it; long sheets of the beige barriers forming a kind of octagon that surrounded it entirely.

"How are we supposed to get into *that* one?" Alex asked out loud.

Simon and Other James both jolted slightly in a synchronized twitch of surprise when she spoke for the first time in half an hour. And she realized she actually felt legitimately kind of offended that they'd been talking to each other the whole time and leaving her out of it. "Uh . . ." Simon said, clearing his throat. "I don't think there *is* a way in. I don't even know if it's a cubicle." He looked up at the tall walls, ten feet of tan obstacle that didn't have a single entrance anywhere in the shell it was forming. Other James shoulder twitched up in a shrug, but it was Simon who kept talking. "No, she's right. All the cubes have doors."

"I . . ." Alex stopped, cutting off the slightly bitter words. She had been about to reflexively say she wished they wouldn't do that. But . . . why? Because it was weird? Yeah, that was *totally* a valid reason these days. "Alright, maybe it's just a wall so we don't break the big pillar or something," she said instead.

"Could be," Simon said, circling around to the right and giving the water cooler there a bit of space. The things were probably safe, which really just meant none of them had exploded *yet*. Instead of trying to yell back to them as he got a different angle of vision, he switched to speaking through Other James. Or maybe it wasn't a switch at all, and this was just both of them acting for Alex's benefit. "It's weird though, right?"

She shrugged, looking away from the weird construction to instead keep an eye on where a sleepy-looking shellaxy was wandering across the hallway behind them. The computer that could bite her arm off looked kind of cute as it wobbled from one cubicle to the other without noticing her. "We don't have to go into it!" she told Other James. "I just thought it looked different."

"Yeah. Okay, let's keep going. We should be able to take the path on the left up here and get back to where we started." He shrugged easily, and let Alex take the lead as he hung back to meet up with Simon when they wrapped around the octagon.

Which made it weird when that didn't happen.

"Uh . . ." Alex looked back at her delver buddy with raised eyebrows. "Where's Simon?"

"He should be right here," Other James said, tilting his head in the way a lot of people unconsciously did when using their skulljack. "He circled around. He's . . . literally here?" The two of them looked around the space, but there was nothing more threatening than an immobile fax machine, and certainly no Simon. "Well, shit." Other James turned and started jogging back around the side of the circular hall, Alex in tow.

They met up with Simon in a few seconds, but he looked just as confused as them. "What the hell?" he asked as they all came to a stop facing each other.

It didn't take long to figure out what the hell. If they followed the path the way Simon had, to the right, then they never passed the fax machine, and instead ran into a vending machine and a suspiciously still potted tree, before another path opened out of the circle into the cubicles. If they kept going, they'd eventually find themselves back at the start after wrapping around the whole thing again.

If they instead went left, they'd get the fax machine, two offshoot paths, and then a bulletin board with a bunch of work safety notices on it, along with a big motivational poster that instructed them to "Submit to Unity." Simon stole that one.

"Are you *sure* that you two—" Alex started to jokingly rib them, tension fading now that they knew how the space worked.

"Shaddup," two playful voices told her in the same tone.

The real problem the warped space caused was that they didn't actually know what direction the different overlapping hallways that led out of it went. And they also didn't know if one of them went somewhere totally new, so they didn't want to just start smashing until they found the source and broke it. Especially because if they were *already* somewhere else, it could strand them deep in the dungeon.

So they backtracked, again, and chose a totally different route around, eventually making it back onto their map and heading home. Everything easy and clean and smooth.

Which was when the camraconda ambushed them. A couple hundred pounds of tightly bunched cables lunged out and slammed into Simon, eliciting a shout of surprise from both him and Other James as he went down. Half of the shout cut off as the camraconda locked its security camera eye onto Other James, freezing him in place with his fist balled up and halfway into a weak jab. The rest of the snake's body thrashed to find purchase, trying to pin Simon down on the floor as the man tried to wrestle the heavy creature off him, or at least divert its gaze.

Alex was pretty sure it hadn't even seen her before it lunged. Well, she would have been, if she could think. For a moment that stretched on for a long time, she was frozen, staring as Simon tried to get one of his arms free while the other one got gnawed on by a snake that couldn't quite break through his armor with the way Simon was grabbing at its jaw.

Alex snapped out of her paralysis for no real reason. Just that her brain finally caught up to the fact that she needed to *do something*. Her hands were shaking like tiny earthquakes as she shoved her bag away and fumbled for the borrowed shotgun. She drew the long-barreled weapon out of its case and took a stumbling step forward that led into a more confident charge as she ran toward the fight.

Alex might have shouted something, because the camraconda started to look her way. Not enough to let Other James go though, before she jammed the barrel of the shotgun up against the base of its throat. Or . . . was it a throat? Whatever snakes had that was where their jaw ended. Alex didn't know why her brain was focused on *that* and not the vibrating grip she had on the gun.

It would have been so easy to just squeeze the trigger and end the fight. But she didn't. And as soon as she hesitated, Alex knew that she *couldn't*. But she wasn't just going to let the serpentine creature hurt her partners for the delve. "Get off of him," she ordered the camraconda with a high pitched squeak of a voice.

The camraconda didn't move, either to look toward her or to get off of Simon. It was perched, tail half-wrapped around the man on the floor, head tilted upward, feeling the metal of the shotgun shoved against it. Almost like it was considering the situation calmly.

"Off!" Alex shouted, her voice suddenly explosive. "Get off!" She punctuated it by kicking at the tail, making the poor choice to have the worst footing possible as she threatened the creature.

But it did start, slowly, to slide backward. Simon helped as soon as he had both arms free, shoving it aside and then getting bopped in the side of the head by Other James's jab in progress as the big man was freed. The two of them froze again for a moment as the camraconda swept its eye over them, but Alex shifted to circle around it.

"Fuck off!" she told the camraconda. "Stop it! Stop! Get away!" Like she was yelling at a stray dog to shoo it away. It almost got its head around to look at her, but she jabbed the end of the shotgun into the flat surface of its camera face, pushing it away and using the weapon as leverage. "Leave, you asshole!" Alex ordered the snake.

It hissed at her with a kind of unconcerned ire. But then, surprising both of the guys who were in the process of picking themselves up off the floor, it *did* turn and start to slither away, only giving a short glance behind itself as Alex stood in the shadow of one of the cubicle doors with the shotgun braced to her shoulder, aimed down at it.

The camraconda turned the corner, and Alex gasped out the breath she'd been holding for what felt like the last hour of her life, letting the gun sag to face the floor. "Holy shit," she whispered. "Are you two okay?!" Her voice rose as she scrambled wide-eyed to check on Simon and Other James.

"Disoriented," Simon muttered.

"Ugh," Other James added poetically. "Their freeze tag thing doesn't stop thinking, but it does stop Wi-Fi, so . . . headache." He grabbed a heavy hand at the back of his neck, like he could massage the skulljack connection open again faster. "*You* okay? You didn't shoot it."

Alex's shoulders slumped, and she ducked her head, not looking at either of them. "It . . . I couldn't," she muttered.

Simon looked at her, eyes narrowing in concern. "Did you get cursed?" he asked. "We can get Secret to eat it. I think that's a thing he does."

"N-no!" Alex sighed as she realized she was going to actually have to explain herself. "It was . . . it was the colors." She looked down the hall after where the camraconda had fled. "I just kinda couldn't not notice. It's the same colors as my friend's girlfriend."

Simon let Other James haul him to his feet, the two of them dusting each other off and checking the backpacks for how much loose coffee was going to be in every pocket for the rest of time. "Oh," he said simply. And then, when it caught up to him that humans didn't normally have skin in *that* color pattern, "Oh!"

"Yeah," Alex said, not sure if he really understood why she hadn't just taken the enemy's head off. "It's . . . I dunno. I guess I shoulda actually paid attention in history class, because it turns out, it really is hard to fight something when you see it as a *person*."

"That *is* why we're trying to kidnap more of them out of the dungeon," Other James pointed out. "Kidnap in a nice way," he added in a way he probably thought was reassuring and was in reality the exact opposite. "Politely kidnap." He continued digging himself deeper into the hole.

Simon shook his head at his friend's failing social skills as their skulljack link reestablished and their minds brushed against each other again. "Well. It worked out. And good thing, too." He pointed to the shotgun hanging limply in Alex's hands. "Safety."

"I know gun safety!" she protested. "Look, it's pointed at the ground even! I know how to not shoot you guys!"

". . . No, you . . . you left the safety on," Simon told her awkwardly. "Anyway. Let's keep moving. If we go quick, we can get this stuff back in time for them to make a copy of the blue orb I have now, since my magic pen snapped under the weight of my magnificent ass when I got tackled."

Alex snorted a laugh as she slung the shotgun's sheath off her back so she could carefully replace the weapon. "That's a weird way to talk about yourself."

"Don't blame me. Blame him for getting into my head." Simon jerked a thumb at Other James, who made a similar hand gesture, also at himself. "You good to go?"

Alex wanted to laugh, or maybe cry. But they were in the middle of a dungeon made out of hostile cubicles and angry office supplies, so she figured she could hold off on both until she was safely back in her bedroom. "Yeah," she said with a huff of air. "Let's go."

CHAPTER 13

For James, it felt like it had been a week of setbacks and minor irritations that piled up until they weren't minor things anymore, but one amorphous blob of frustration.

Setback number one was that they'd learned that duplicating the blood objects didn't really . . . work. You could do it, sure. And then you ended up with an object at level one, of a single ability. And sure, that wasn't the worst thing ever, for most of them. But the really dangerous magic powers all started to acquire that useful level of danger when you looked at the second or third ability on their lists. James didn't have all of the ability lists memorized yet, but even he knew that a bracer that could record incoming attacks wasn't actually useful without the shield that stopped those attacks. A bracelet that bound to a gun was *interesting* in a certain abstract and philosophical way, but it didn't make the gun sing without the reload or burst fire powers.

It seemed likely, and Anesh and Momo were in agreement on this one, that it was part of the objects' expression of power. From both their own discoveries, and also Status Quo's notes, they knew that the objects were made from the life force of people. And the stronger that life, the better the starting grade of the object.

So when they duplicated the things, they were copying the object, but missing something critical that came with it. And that meant no starting powers. No good ones, anyway.

Technically, they could still use the powers. And over time, they'd level up; their cooldowns would drop, and new abilities would unlock. But when a bracelet had nothing but Bind Weapon at level 1, and it demanded an almost year-long cooldown, and *ten uses* to advance, it didn't actually seem likely that these things would be useful for anyone except future generations.

They had offset that setback by raiding the other two towers within easy range in the Office dungeon, going far enough up that they could supply Anesh with the coffee for six or seven activations of the duplication ritual. No one had made it to the top of either of those towers before the pressure from the overly hostile creatures lurking in them got to be too much. But that was fine, because they still got what they really cared about: more coffee grounds that powered the ritual. All of those had been put to use restocking their tele-pad supply, and also deploying a basic orb survival package across the entire Order.

James had found it satisfying to have their hours of testing and wasted duplications refined down to a package of skills that would make all of them marginally harder to kill. And he took his share of it alongside his partners without a second thought.

[+1 Skill Rank : Melee—Quarterstaff]

[+.3 Skill Ranks : Athletics—Running]

[+1 Skill Rank : Medical—First Aid—CPR]

[Shell Upgraded : Immune System Infection Adaptation Time, -44 Hours]

[+2 Skill Ranks : Botany—South African]

[Local Area Shift : Intrusion Cost—+$129.50]

That last one had been applied to everyone's homes, apartments, rooms, and cars. As well as being layered a dozen times on the Lair itself, to diminishing returns. It was . . . silly. The words all independently made sense, but put together, it was madness. And yet, it did exactly what it said on the tin. Breaking into a place so defended by the magic of the green orb seemed to carry a material cost to anyone trying.

The unfortunate thing was that, while the effect tended to break physical objects on their person first, it *would* switch over to bodily damage if you weren't carrying anything to lose. And in a country where an ER visit could run you a bill of a few thousand bucks, hitting the threshold was not hard. Theoretically, a broken toe would let someone smash their way into their headquarters without any other problems, because even a basic consultation from a doctor afterward would cover the "bill" that the green effect imposed.

It was the kind of weird magic that James *wasn't* as fond of. He liked it when the green orbs were sort of mystical and silly, and this one was *pedantic* and silly. Close, but categorically very different. Still, it was a speed bump for any potential attackers. And James would take what was offered in that regard.

Setback one-and-a-half was that Anesh wasn't letting James actually try to drink the ritual coffee. James wanted to see what happened when used with one of the magic brewers, but it was just too valuable for that right now, so he'd been shot down. Maybe later, when it was worth relatively less to them.

Setback number two was that James had woefully overestimated how much money they had. Or, perhaps more accurately, they'd all kind of undershot at the costs of what it took to keep an organization running.

The Lair had a lease, and so far, none of the green orbs they'd found had lowered that. Though that hadn't stopped them from pouring more and more greens into the place; it was rapidly acquiring that magic that James loved.

But on top of that lease, they were paying their members. Oftentimes, they paid them in loot from the dungeon. There was now a reasonably effective workflow of harvesting viable computer parts, making sure they were mundane, and then selling them off. Same thing with coats and suits. There was small but consistent income to be made, and as they streamlined the operation, that income could be handled with less time and effort, and then put to use.

They paid their people as well as they possibly could, after all. But even after considering that about once a month, they found a way to crack an enchanted briefcase open and add about a hundred grand to their war chest, the cost of keeping people going was *high* when you weren't actually running a business, but instead a magical community organization.

And there were always more expenses. Food, utilities, ammo, drone replacements, armor parts, new equipment to test out, old equipment to replace or repair, furniture for the Lair, random devices Research asked for, extra spending money or bribes or whatever they needed for the real-world nonsense they were up to this week. It all added up.

And when they wanted to pursue a specific project, they were finding that the budget just wasn't there for it.

James had assumed that looking into hiring a score of programmers would be the work of an afternoon. And in a way, it was. But after actually figuring out what the wages would be on people like that, especially if they were kept separate from the Order's more surreal operations and he couldn't pay them in orbs, it had become clear that they just didn't have enough money for it.

The counterweight to that one was that JP had vanished for several days, taking Secret's bemused manifested form with him and promising that he could get the government to pay through the nose for something. He hadn't elaborated, and while James was overwhelmingly curious and planned to have words with JP when he got back, he knew when his friend had his *I've got a plan* face on, which meant he should stand back and let things play out.

Still, the thought of a government paycheck rolling in didn't offset the fact that they were burning through thousands and thousands of dollars a month. And JP could commit all the thinly-veiled finance crimes he wanted; they just weren't in a position to keep that expenditure rate up forever. Especially not if they added a million-dollars-a-year expense for a project that might not work.

So certain ideas were tabled. Set aside, until such time as they could drown the issue in resources. Resources they weren't sure how to get yet, exactly.

Especially the idea of mind uploading; a project that Alanna was still optimistic about even as more and more problems were quickly brought up. It didn't help that the more they talked about it with various people, the faster and faster problems were unveiled. Yes, the skulljacks made it comically easy to get started compared to where human technology was in the mundane world right now, but that was literally just the first step.

They'd need to build, hardware and soft, a place for people to live. But just building a place that could run a human brain didn't solve the problem either. They'd need to actually have some form of quality of life, and for that . . . well, they were more looking at copyright infringement for stealing ideas from the *Matrix* movies than they were pure mind uploads and untethering from the mortal coil.

Also, there'd been a conversation about the fundamental ethics of offering people an "escape" from poverty that cost them their bodies. That thought had nagged at James for a while, and as soon as he'd heard it said out loud by another member of the Order, he instantly understood and agreed with them. If digitizing people couldn't offer them a healthy, fulfilling life on the other side, then they were just building another low-income housing project, except this one literally cost arms and legs.

Having a body shouldn't be a luxury for the rich.

So yeah, that project was on hold.

Still. That had freed up a lot of time to be disappointed with other, unrelated things.

Like how fewer people were frequenting the Lair these days. The Order was taking the quarantine . . . well, it was hard to say it was as seriously as some places, but they were still taking precautions. With their newest collective upgrade, it seemed likely that mundane viral infections wouldn't have the time to seriously hurt them. But they weren't isolated, and they weren't the only people they interacted with. And not just that, but no one knew what would happen to a camraconda if they got infected, and it simply wasn't worth the risk.

So, while they weren't in full lockdown like a lot of the world, they weren't doing as many meetings, weren't letting everyone come in every day, were trying to limit non-essential personnel on delves, and were certainly trying to cut out just "hanging out" around the Lair. For now. Just for a little bit.

It wasn't like the place was empty. But James still felt like it was very lonely there, especially for the people who lived in the building.

Which brought them around to another problem.

Graham was still being kept prisoner in their basement. One of the basements, anyway.

It had been three months since the incident at the school. And nothing they had done had actually convinced the kid to leave that room.

"Kept prisoner" was also the wrong way to phrase it. He was keeping himself a prisoner. Prisoner to guilt, to grief, to anger. The teenage ex-student barely ate the food they left him, had dropped twenty pounds since waking up, and didn't talk to anyone who came to see him. Didn't want to interact with anyone who offered him help, or therapy, whether it was Lua or someone else. They'd actually invested real effort to convince an unaffiliated therapist who specialized in dealing with trauma and survivor's guilt to come try to have a conversation with him. And that hadn't worked, anyway.

Graham hated himself. And if James was being honest, he could understand why. The young victim currently partaking of their hospitality had lost his parents, lost one of his best friends, had his free will compromised by something incredibly dangerous and evil, killed his other best friend himself, and been pushed into an action that had gotten hundreds of people killed. Almost everything that mattered to him had been taken away, and the closest thing he had to a sense of stability was the self-imposed prison of the concrete walls of his basement room.

James dropped in once a day to let him know that he was available. So far, it hadn't changed anything. But he was going to keep doing it.

Graham wasn't the only high school kid who'd been around the Lair lately, either. With the coming of summer vacation, the darn kids these days had a lot more free time. And while there was something like four high schools within five miles of the Lair, only one of them had recently been transformed into a battlefield.

And *those* students, the ones who'd survived, had not all forgotten the Order.

James had, very early on in their life as an organization, made it clear to everyone that they were not a conspiracy. It was something he liked to say to people a lot, partially to drive home the point, but also partially because it was funny. Lately, he'd kinda regretted that, as they weren't really capable of staving off attention from the superpowers of the world, and being hidden might have helped with that. But by this point, it was kind of a part of their culture that magic and the fantastical was something that was okay to share. That they weren't shadowy agents; they were people, trying to do as much good as they could.

This made it almost comically easy for several students to find them, mostly by just looking for the place where camracondas sometimes hung out on the roof or in the parking lot. Once one of them found the Lair, the rumor spread rapidly, school closure doing nothing to slow the spread of intel between teens with phones.

Some of them came in twos or threes, some independently. Over the course of the last couple of months while James had been recovering, twenty-three different teenagers had walked through their doors and started asking questions. Everyone had just . . . told them to come back when James was awake. And that they didn't know when that would be.

James had learned this when the first junior had wandered in, said hi to the camraconda door guard who he'd apparently become familiar with in the four or five times he'd dropped by so far, and asked if the "manager" was in.

He had asked this to James.

A nearby Sarah, naturally, had doubled over laughing so hard that James had a momentary flash of panic that even with her health stat upgraded she would strain her neck again. After assuring him that she was physically fine, James had switched from concern to confusion until the situation was explained to him.

The teenager, and so many others like him, wanted to say thank you. For a few horrifying hours, they'd been closer to death than any child should have ever been allowed to come. And it had been James who had saved them. Not *just* James, obviously, James himself had been quick to point out. And this kid knew that. But he'd already said thank you to everyone else, and he knew that James was the reason the Order existed, and besides that, he had a specific question for "the person in charge."

Were there, he asked, any entry level job openings?

Because—and here James had to struggle not to start giggling—his parents wanted him to get a summer job. But also because he wanted to do what they did. They were heroes. Not just his heroes, but actual heroes. And he wanted to know if they'd take him.

James had looked the kid up and down. He was a lanky teen with no muscle, no poise, and a sort of twitchy nervousness that felt like an itch in the conversation. He'd also phrased his request not as "protect people" but as "fight monsters." None of this was particularly surprising, because he was a high school student. James wasn't so far removed from his own high school experience that he didn't remember how everything had seemed so much simpler then, and how *punch the bad guys* had seemed like a solution to everything.

But he still didn't know what to say. So he told the kid that he'd think about it, and to bring back an application. The kid had asked if they had any, and James told him that the application was a twelve-hundred-word essay on ethics. He had honestly expected that to drive the dude off, but instead, he'd just nodded seriously and said he'd be back tomorrow. And then he left, waving a friendly farewell to Sarah, who was still wiping tears of laughter out of her eyes.

This process repeated itself about ten times throughout the next week or so. James kept telling them the same thing, and kept forgetting to bring up the problem with anyone else when he had time for conversation. He'd kind of given up on being surprised when they started bringing him the essays, and in an effort to buy more time, he just kept sending them out to bring him a write-up on a new topic. He really needed to bring that up with Alanna, because against his expectations, they kept doing it.

Another thing James kept doing was experimenting with the telepads. Though in a much safer way than some people, and arguably with less of a headache than dealing with teenagers.

Basically ever since learning that Pendragon could eat blue-aligned objects and incorporate their powers into herself, James had been trying to get her to eat one of the telepads. But the dragon was a really dramatically picky eater, and while her uncooperative nature was frustrating, it wasn't like it was something that they could change. For one thing, it was super unethical to force a physical change onto a being that didn't want it. But more importantly, Pendragon was, as her name implied, a dragon. And it was one of those situations of "We can't really *make* her do anything."

Pendragon had gotten far too large for James to make her eat anything, unless he happened to have an industrial winch to pry her mouth open with. And really, if the choice was to have a friendly dragon made out of laminated paper with a skeleton of gooseneck lamp bars and claws of rolling office chairs, or that same dragon who could teleport but *didn't like him much*, James was going to pick the former.

He just felt like *he* would eat a telepad if it gave him telepad powers. James knew this about himself for the same reason he knew that it didn't work that way, and that the telepads tasted bad.

However, what had been an amusing source of pseudo-frustration for James had been seen as a challenge by Research. His mild attempts to try to find creative ways to use the telepad had always been just that—mild. He didn't actually *need* to get too clever to abuse the things; they were really, *really* powerful. On their own, they were probably in the top five of powerful Order assets.

Research took this as an invitation.

The majority of their attempts failed, which was good, because some of them were comically dangerous. The telepads would not, it seemed, send you to the moon. They also couldn't time travel; if you tried to make them, they just did nothing. James learned a lot about what the telepads couldn't do, and also a lot about why their tests had required several last-minute plane ticket purchases to bring people home from various parts of the globe.

James instructed them to stop testing that way. It was cutting into the budget.

Research had also finished, more or less, going over the notes that Status Quo had. Their hard drives were encrypted, which was only natural, so they had a couple of programming emeralds working on that problem. Which was less natural. And almost certainly a bad idea for the future of cybersecurity. But the printed and written documentation they had was more or less accessible.

A lot of it was redacted, which was frustrating. A lot of it also used code words, or alphanumeric designations, which weren't explained anywhere. Or if they were explained, the explanation had been redacted. Which was more frustrating. But despite the fact that they seemed to have purged their own records at least twice and there were wide swaths of context missing, progress was getting made.

They'd discovered that the dungeons that Status Quo had actually found were only a slim fraction of the ones the Order knew existed. Status Quo had captured or killed dozens of delver teams with powers and magic that didn't line up to any of the dungeons that the group had in their archives. And while James knew that dungeons could spawn anywhere, Status Quo thought they were limited to this part of the world, so they'd never looked elsewhere.

It was absurd. It had taken James less than a year of knowing magic was real to start looking all over for it. These guys had decades, and while they clearly paid agents all over the planet, it seemed like their operation was more about sniping suspected delvers than actually looking for dungeons. Such a fucking *waste*. It left James feeling sour and angry to learn about, and that was only really the start.

The first dungeon Status Quo had actual access to had been the blood magic one, formed in an abandoned playground near the Oregon coast. If there were notes on how they'd found it, they'd been wiped away, but they had found it all the same. And, through the use of military hardware and heavy construction equipment, removed the object spawners from it, and transplanted them to their own basement. So as to streamline their sacrifices of life force.

On the one hand, this was monstrous. On the other hand, and ignoring all the infinite problems with the first hand, this did speak to the possibility of moving "reward sources" out of dungeons. Like the copier from the Office. Still not worth the risk at the time, but maybe someday.

The second dungeon had been in a church. The Order didn't know which one, but the notes talked about it being Lutheran, and having undergone a schism in the late eighties, which narrowed it down less than James might have expected. That one was apparently why some of the agents shrugged off bullets, and also where the entity their leader had called Authority, or maybe Vested Authority, came from.

It was still unclear, even with the notes, if Authority was a name or a classification of being. Either way, it was a big problem, and Secret had been clear on the fact that he hadn't actually *killed* it, just rendered its attacks broken. Whatever that meant.

What *was* clear from the notes was yet another frustration: both of those dungeons were dead zones.

There was no indication if Status Quo itself had been the ones to destroy them, but either way, there were end dates to the acquisition of resources from both sites. Both dungeons were gone. And while their records didn't actually state why, it lent support to a leading theory of how the dungeons subsisted.

Status Quo had found these places through delve teams. They'd eliminated the teams, posted guards on the sites, and then removed what useful assets from the sites they wanted for themselves. No delves were authorized; the members of Status Quo weren't explorers or adventurers, they were a quarantine crew. So they didn't go in, and they killed anyone else who tried.

And so the dungeons *starved*, eventually withering to nothing, until the only things left were some strange artifacts recovered from the sites after the breaches no longer opened.

Those artifacts were, incidentally, nowhere to be found. Various records had physical testing statistics on them, and there were sign-ins for a chain of custody, but no one could figure out what they *were*, either in the Order or in Status Quo. And they weren't anywhere in the Lair, so far as anyone knew. Unless they were in one of the many banker's boxes, hidden under a sheaf of manila folders full of atrocities done to others, they had vanished at some point. So where they'd ended up was anyone's guess. What was clear, though, was that they didn't fit the patterns of the dungeon rewards. Or the patterns of reality at all, just going by how Status Quo's own records described them.

There was one other thing that the notes had been used for. And it was actually the focus of an entire new part of the Order that had cohered while James had been asleep, and been officially recognized by him after he'd awoken.

They were called Recovery. And their mission statement was to help put lives back together after crises.

It was a job the Order, even before it had a name and a roster, had been doing already. But they weren't, honestly, very organized about it. Sarah's support group was part of the process for the original dungeon victims, and they'd poured a lot of resources into getting people back on their feet and reintegrated with the families or friends that half-remembered them. But it had all been haphazard.

It wasn't much of a surprise to find that Karen had taken charge of the efforts. It had mildly surprised *her* when James had held an official ceremony to name her head of the division that had started to come together under that banner.

He recognized what she was doing, though. She had drive and ambition, but she wasn't hostile. She was doing her absolute best;

and sometimes, the best required spreadsheets and rules to help everyone participating make it work.

Recovery had a budget now, and daily operational tasks. And it really was stuff they'd already been doing; but now, with less likelihood that anyone slipped through the cracks. Less chance the people who needed them would be forgotten, even *if* something like Secret was lurking around with less-noble intentions than the friendly infomorph usually had.

They also had, in terms of Status Quo's documentation, one massive self-assigned objective. James, Alanna, and Anesh still had missing loved ones. Their parents and siblings and even extended family. Swaths of people just removed from their lives.

The man in charge of Status Quo had admitted that some of them had probably been killed, for expedience or because of a lack of another option, it didn't matter in the end. But that the majority had simply been *moved*. And the documentation bore that out. Transplanted to a new city, dosed with both drugs and some effect from Authority to make the transition feel like a blur, installed into new jobs and schools. And all the while, the memory of the delver that had been their family was wiped out of their minds.

James's parents weren't ever going to call and ask if he was doing okay, because they didn't know they had a son. Alanna's sisters weren't going to be able to rely on her to support them anymore. Anesh had lost not just several lives, but also his connection to his past and his heritage.

And Recovery had looked at that state of affairs and decided that they were going to fix that bullshit.

So far, they'd come up empty. But they were nothing if not tenacious. And Karen, as much as she could be downright petty when she'd disagreed with James in the past, was fundamentally a woman of principles. She would be damned if she let *anyone* suffer when the Order could repair their lives.

So they applied their not-insignificant resources to the task. They pored over Status Quo's notes, they found likely sites. Dispatched knights as investigators when it was possible and time and money allowed. Made use of multiple iLipedes that had social and divinatory apps. Repeatedly consulted with Secret. Trawled Facebook.

Nothing. *Yet.* But still nothing.

The real problem with this crime being perpetrated by an organization of monstrous humans, instead of a single alien intelligence that organized monsters, was that humans were really good at being detailed in their attacks. The dungeon's memetic effect that gradually eroded the identity of those trapped within it long-term was dangerous, absolutely. But it left giant information craters. Holes in the physical nature of things, where anyone looking could start poking around the edges pretty easily. At least enough to know there *were* edges. You could eventually find the extra room in your apartment, notice your missed call log, *see that the time was off.*

Humans—these humans, anyway—didn't leave craters. They were professionals, and the pride they took in this caliber would have been commendable if it had been for something less vile. They smoothed over the problems, made the edges fuzzier. Complicated the signs of infomorphic attack with modern subterfuge, bureaucracy, and common old lies. And that was making it hard to sort out where the organization had even bothered to do anything supernatural in the first place.

For not the first time in the last couple weeks, James was internally agreeing with Randall that they maybe should have taken prisoners.

Randall, incidentally, was one of the few things that hadn't been some kind of disappointment in the last ten days. James had been prepared to be surprised by that information, but it wasn't actually that he was being useful, ethical, or good in any way. It was more just that he wasn't in the way, that he'd gotten JP out of the Lair to go solve crimes, and that he was still comically blind to magic in a lot of forms.

Research had been wanting to experiment with Randall, but James vetoed that hard. Although for all that he didn't want them poking the bear, there was actually something very weird going on with the man.

He had *gone into Officium Mundi*. He had seen people throw around spells, do physically impossible things, and spawn things out of thin air. He had met Secret.

The federal agent would nod and acknowledge all of this. And it didn't change his behavior at all. He was aware that magic was real, he was aware that he was here on a job to liaise between the Order and the government when magic solutions were needed. But there was some kind of mental block there, either natural or hostile or even just self-imposed, where he literally did not change his world view one bit in response to the existence of magic.

They'd even tried to get him to use magic items. And he couldn't process their functions; couldn't come up with ideas on how to use them. Again, he knew this was happening. But he didn't, or couldn't, care.

It was spooky. It was even spookier because no one knew *why*. Every infomorph they had available was keeping an eye on him, when possible. They all confirmed that it wasn't being caused by anything like them. But still. No one wanted to risk that kind of problem being contagious somehow.

Even as they were keeping an eye on him, James was pretty sure that it wasn't something that could spread. Unless it was a long-term thing. After all, basically everyone in the entire Lair had advanced in some way in the last week.

For him, personally, it had been after a basketball game.

The thing about the pandemic and the lockdown was that people were rapidly going mad with boredom. And while the Order had a measure of resistance to the disease, many of them *did* have family, and were intentionally avoiding group gatherings.

But a lot of them didn't have those things. Some of them lived at the Lair, and some of them were all alone. Some of them were people like James, Anesh, and Alanna, who had a pretty closed social circle. And while they took the usual precautions, and sometimes griped about wearing masks all the time, they still did use the Lair as a meeting point for a lot of things.

Like basketball training.

Which was why, sometime Friday evening, James found himself thinking a message that read:

[Basketball : 33/400

Aim I, Agility I]

Team games were far more potent for his learning than one-on-one with Anesh had gotten. Anesh was still *good* at basketball, in a way that was kind of hilarious. Like he'd mentioned, the skill put him at the level of *good enough* with basically zero effort. But that hadn't stopped him from continuing to get *better*. In a team game, though, there were so many things to focus on, and James found his magical syllabus rocketing upward a lot faster than before.

He chose agility this time, on the grounds that he wanted to stop getting hit so much. And wasn't sure just how much the improvement changed him.

While he was doing that, the rest of the Order was making progress too. Alex and Neil independently figured out how to internalize orange orbs. And while it wasn't really combat-applicable, being able to break bricks to get a mountain bike, or read a few books to spawn six kilograms of steel, were both practical in different ways. Though the book-based task had instantly drawn a crowd of people debating what, exactly, counted as a "book," before Neil had pointed out that there *was* a stated requirement that the book be at least fifty-two pages long, and everyone got mad at him for not just saying that before the hour-long philosophical discussion.

In between that whole mess, James still found time to take the haul of magically enhanced human hearts to the director of the surgery department that was currently responsible for covering up a lot of awkward questions for them. There had been, pleasantly, absolutely no complaints from anyone that they had used roughly half a week's replication supply to make a care package of almost a hundred stable and usable human organs.

Doctor Nikita was almost exactly the opposite of Agent Randall when it came to magic bullshit, in a way that had made James cackle a hyena's laugh in his car when he'd realized it.

The man had independently derived the existence of something weird going on, had processed the facts, had struck a deal that would save hundreds of lives, putting decades of human life back into circulation, and somehow, didn't seem to acknowledge that it was magic. He knew something weird was going on. And he adapted to it, like a seasoned professional. And he absolutely did not *care* that it was magic. He cared about *results*, not petty things like "the nature of reality" or other childish concepts.

After the weird case study that was Randall's psychological intolerance to the magical? It was refreshing, and easy, even if James got scolded by a wizened old doctor for putting too much weight on his still-technically-healing leg.

He also got kind of scolded by his partners, after one too many nights spent working instead of coming home.

At some point in his life, without realizing it, James had built up momentum. And he hadn't actually stopped to ask if it was a good thing. He worked hard, he spent more and more time keeping up with members of the Order, keeping apprised of the things going on in the group that he really did think of as his. And without even realizing he was doing it, he'd started to prioritize that over his own life, his own friends.

James hadn't actually talked to Dave in a while, even though he knew what was going on with Pendragon. His only contact with JP was a text exchange about their accounting. And in a move that was really starting to annoy Anesh and Alanna, he'd been trading rest with Sarah to spend late nights plugging away at tasks instead of going *home*.

They'd had a long talk about it. No one was really mad, it was just that they were starting to feel like they were losing touch. And also, as Anesh pointed out, it was weird to be sleeping in James's room, in *James's* bed, without actually having James there. Because for all that they shared their lives now, it still kinda was James's room in their collective apartment. James and Alanna's at the most.

James hadn't even realized he'd been doing it. But while they talked, he resolved to fix that shit. The more he thought about it, the more it came to him that he *missed his friends.* They'd all kind of let the constant crisis mill of the weirdness they dealt with overtake their lives, and now James was essentially trying to replace the small connections of D&D games, anime night, and sleeping with his partners, with the wider-scale connections of knowing everyone in the Order, running training exercises, and troubleshooting every small thing.

He'd even missed the gang's movie night because he'd been trying to track down the camracondas' messiah figure's family. Which he could have assigned to anyone, really. It was literally what Recovery was for. Though in this case, it had felt a bit more personal. He'd found them, too, which wasn't really a justification for missing things, but it did feel satisfying. She had one surviving next of kin. James didn't find an address, but sent the guy an email, and left him a message, but hadn't heard back yet.

Even having resolved to do better at spending time with his partners and friends, though, it was still hard to actually do. He'd missed a couple of months, and the current vibe of humanity was already starting to wear him down. For everyone else, daily life had become exhausting, and social events were sometimes more cost than benefit. Anesh especially had lost a lot, no longer doing math tutoring or going to classes.

Alanna and James had *mildly* teased him at first about how he'd have to postpone his math dates. But then they'd seen the look on his face, and pivoted rapidly to concern. It turned out Anesh really did like the person he'd been getting coffee with. And while he was, he admitted after a little well-meaning prying, still kinda uncertain about what their own relationship was or how it worked, he just liked this person. And now they were cut off by a stupid pandemic, and he was understanding a little of why James had been asking around for if anyone had a fireball spell but only for a virus.

It sucked for everyone, was the long and short of it.

Everyone human, anyway. Not the camracondas, though. They were more or less sticking to the area around the Lair. Except Frequency-of-Sunlight, who often went home with Deb, which was a source of endless cross-species gossip at the Lair, and a source of equally endless amusement for James.

With the lockdown going on, and foot and vehicle traffic down to basically nothing, the camracondas were getting more comfortable roaming the outdoor areas around the building. For them, even just taking a loop around the block was an act of exploration: trees, birds, traffic lights, the gas station across the road. All of these things were new and bright and wonderful.

They met people sometimes. And it spoke a million words about the nature of the place they lived that most people just kind of gave friendly nods, or treated them mostly like people, and went on with their days. Oh, yes, basically every one of those uninitiated humans did a double, triple, quadruple take. But it was at the point now where they could wander into the gas station's convenience store and buy snacks, and the dudes who worked there were more likely to try to make conversation about sports than ask what the hell the camracondas *were*, and question if they were drones of some kind.

So it was that a few weeks passed. With problems and setbacks, only sometimes offset by upgrades and reconciliations.

JP was still away. The school dungeon hadn't reopened, the attic was peacefully silent. No one figured out how to turn a green orb into a totem. Randall was still a twit.

They did a couple of Office delves with reduced numbers, and while they didn't make any progress, they did keep their supply of blues up. James even got to absorb a couple that he didn't instantly want to burn all the charges on to replace.

[+8 Activations : Replace With Glass]

[+13 Activations : Repossess]

That first one was worryingly vague, which was perfect.

So that was the state of things as they moved into another Tuesday. And as James stood in the lobby of the Lair, saying hi to the trickle of delvers coming in to prepare for the upcoming adventure and letting the action swirl around him, he found that all the setbacks hadn't really left him feeling that demoralized.

The world was exhausting and hostile, and the events still rocking human civilization were approaching catastrophic. But at the end of the day, whatever happened, he knew that he and the rest of the Order too would be contributing more than they took away. Every delve put them a little closer to saving the world. Or at least saving a chunk of humanity, of sophant life on this ball of rock.

As long as they were around, they could keep trying. It was a good thought. And it warmed his heart as he watched everyone arriving in the lobby.

They were all about to go do something dangerous, and yet, *normal* for them now. And then, they'd leverage the reward from that risk into actions that would reshape either society, geography, or both.

Setbacks happened. But this wasn't a video game. There was only one failure state that was absolute. And eventually, they'd overcome that one too.

James flipped his coat over his shoulders as he walked toward the door. He could see Alanna and Anesh smooching each other in the parking lot, and taking their sweet time loading the drone cases into the trunk of the van. Which made this the perfect time to show "leadership," and get them back in motion.

And maybe also get a kiss of his own before they headed out.

CHAPTER 14

"And *thus!*" James projected his voice across the Lair's dining room, rapping his index finger against the offending word on the stapled-together trio of pages he was holding. "While both modern and ancient philosophy cannot come to a conclusion on *if* certain things are better than other things, and science, religion, art, and culture are still working out what those supposedly better things would be anyway, there is only one answer. The human race must be preserved, until such time as we can accurately answer the question," he finished, with a flourish and bow, stepping down off the bench of the cafeteria table.

A smattering of applause and hisses greeted him from the group of knights assembled here. "Encore!" Anesh called out from across the table from him. "Encore!" he repeated, as someone in the room, probably Momo, stealthily wolf-whistled.

Standing in the swinging double doors to the kitchen, Nate impatiently flicked a finger to spin the pizza cutter he'd been holding through the whole speech, rolled his eyes in time with the spinning blade, and commented, "I *asked* if anyone wanted Hawaiian."

"I know," James said flatly as he tossed the pages onto the table. He leaned forward, stabbing a finger down at the essay. "That is *also what I asked* when I assigned this writing task."

"You're getting pineapple on your pizza," Nate muttered, turning to walk back into the kitchen.

As everyone settled down and resumed their previous conversations before James had interrupted them by reading a high-school-level essay on philosophy, the people he had been talking to started asking him questions.

"Really? He wrote that about pizza?" Anesh quipped.

Alex, who'd been sitting with them and trying to discuss pandemic response tactics in a non-depressing way, shrugged. "I mean, it sounds like he just found the smartest way possible to say *no comment*."

"Right?" James grinned. "I'm thinking of interning this one."

"First of all," Anesh started, pursing his lips, "I think *interning* when used that way means you're going to put him in a grave? Second of all, I'm actually a bit not a huge fan of the human-centric language he used."

"Interring." The leaderly camraconda who still hadn't picked a name for themself gave a static hiss from their spot on the bench. "Even I know this." It bobbed its head a second later. "Agree on the human word. I will not be left out."

"To be fair, the kid is still in high school, and may not have ever seen a nonhuman person that wasn't a ratroach. Also, I seem to remember being actually kinda racist when I was in high school," James admitted.

"You got better," Anesh argued. "I *hope*."

"Eh." James shrugged. "I mean, I hope so too. But I was still an asshole then."

"No, see, you're both missing the point," Alex interjected between them. "I mean, okay, yes to the humanity thing because he's *been here* and does actually know camracondas by name, so that's weird. But also, James, you gave this kid a *really* hard question."

James gave her a level stare. "It's a silly meme question."

"Yeah! Exactly!"

Anesh tapped her on the shoulder. "Just explain before my boyfriend dies of confusion."

"Fiiiine. Okay, so, if you asked about, like, the ethics of self-defense, or social support programs, or whatever, then there's actual hard data about how to get desired results. You can look it up. And I know, because you've been making me look it up. A lot of people don't actually use it, like when any politician who talks about 'the economy' cuts food stamp programs without realizing that those programs make 'the economy' . . ."—she made air quotes every time she said that—". . . stronger. But the data is there. And he could have given a real answer based on that. But *instead*, you asked something that's frivolous and silly. There *isn't* a single correct or incorrect answer, but for some reason, certain people get *super* angry about it. It's actually a great test."

"Because he has to figure out how to say 'no comment,' but in a way that still makes sure that if you *are* one of those fanatics, you won't be mad," Anesh supplied, following Alex's logic with an intrigued nod.

James leaned his elbows on the table. "Huh," he mused. "Huh! Okay, so, I'm a mastermind then. Excellent."

"I mean, you should still read other essays from him before giving him an internship," Anesh said. "That said, are we actually doing the internship thing? Wait, are we going to call them squires? I keep hearing people using *knight* as a title. Is this a thing now?"

The giggle from Alex could have meant either yes or no, but thankfully she clarified for him. "Calling them squires is probably weird and bad, since knights are, like . . . what, fighters? The people who do dungeons and also swoop in to save the day."

"Yeah, they're interns. Also, the best defense against the dungeons is knowledge." James sighed. "And these kids . . . I'd rather that we at least offer a potential path, even if it's maybe not the most healthy thing for them. Gives people something to aim for, and keeps them out of the hands of groups like Status Quo. And for those that we don't pick, I'd like to get a specific additional support group set up."

"I can talk to Lua about that," Anesh said quietly.

A tray clattered into the center of the table. "Here," Nate gruffly spoke. "You get Hawaiian."

"Yessss. Pineapple on pizza. The correct answer." James gave a wolfish grin as he added a couple of slices to his plate.

"Really?" Anesh and Alex asked together.

"Oh yeah. This, and being flagrantly bisexual, are the two main things that disappointed my da . . ." His voice hitched. "My dad," James finished, clearing his throat. "Fuck. Forgot." It wasn't, he tried to remind himself, that he actually ever cared about reuniting with his family. It was more that the choice hadn't been his.

Anesh reached over and laid a hand on James's own. "If it's any consolation, my parents never got a chance to be disappointed in me for being bisexual."

"Are you actually? This is one of those things we've never really talked about. I asked Alanna the other day, and she said her sexuality was 'sure, whatever.'"

"Oooookay. I'm taking my pizza and checking out of this conversation," Alex said in a joking tone, but stood up all the same. "Oh, but yeah, like I said earlier. Let me know if we find a green or something that does decontamination. I know we're wearing masks now, but there's still a lot of people coming through here, and the more research I do, the more panicked I get."

"Can do." James saluted her.

"Um . . . do we actually have to talk about sexuality?" Anesh asked sheepishly, furiously blushing.

"Nah, not if you don't wanna," James told him. "Besides, that might make our snake friend here feel awkward."

"I observe," the camraconda added to the conversation. "It is informative."

Anesh glanced over at the snake, opened his mouth like he was considering responding to that, then closed it again and turned back to James. "Alright. Thanks. So, are we actually getting interns?"

"Yeah, I think so?" James shrugged. "We need more people. And this solves several problems: adrift and scared students get a place to go, we get some extra help with small things, it makes us look good in general, and also just a way to actually accomplish our objective of actually doing good too."

"I do like that objective."

"Same. I do want a sanity check, though. Do you see any potential problems?"

"With bringing grade-schoolers on board? Yes. Hundreds."

". . . Okay, well, now I'm worried. Can you share them?"

Anesh chuckled. "Well, the largest one is just finding people that match our culture. I do think we have a good general *vibe*, as the kids these days say . . ."

"They do not," the camraconda's synthetic voice told Anesh before James could get there.

". . . but how exactly do we know if someone is going to operate in good faith? Your essay idea is actually a great way to weed people out who we *know* won't fit. But it's more elimination than inclusion."

James cleared his throat, eyes flicking to the side. "The essay idea, to be clear, was because I didn't have a good answer, and wanted to get rid of the kid that called me the manager."

"Sarah told me about that. Then she laughed for three minutes without pausing to breathe." Anesh stroked his chin. "I think she has a purple for that."

"Laughing, or breathing?" James asked.

"Knowing Sarah? Could be either, really." Anesh shrugged, glancing back at the kitchen to see if more pizza would be coming out soon. "So. Yes interns. No programmers?"

"Too expensive. *Way* too expensive for now. We've set some emerald chips on the digital environment problem, though. Going by Virgil's . . . Virgil's models, it should take maybe six to eight months?"

"He kept good notes, huh?" Anesh smiled forlornly. "I will miss him. He added a perspective we needed."

James nodded in agreement. "I'm not sure how to . . . I don't want to say *replace* . . . how to fill the hole he left?" He set down the crust of the slice of pizza he'd just finished destroying. "We're not really a corporation where we can just slot people in and out of roles like modular pieces. We're way too personal."

"But if we weren't, it wouldn't work," Anesh pointed out. "You already even wrote the idea of developing with the chaos into the operations manual."

"I may regret that," James admitted with a sigh.

"Things change," the camraconda chimed in again. "Always change. Since we are here, changes over and over. If we had not changed, we remain trapped." He rose up to a coiled striking position, and as James and Anesh thought on his words, lashed out quickly and vanished back down to his place on the bench with one of James's slices of pizza in his mouth.

"I guess that's why no one likes corporations, huh?" James commented. "They don't change, really. People grow and the structures they're in remain the same. Like keeping a plant in a pot too small for it."

"I don't think we need a fancy metaphor to say that corporations suck," Anesh told him. "Or at least, most of the mega-giant ones."

"Fair. Also, hisses here reminds me of something. You know what's been bothering me for a while that we never figured out?"

"What?"

"Why did Officium Mundi try to stop us from getting to the camracondas?" James posited the question with spread hands. "It couldn't have known they were there, or that the tower was there. Or that we were planning anything! So why did it start building a death-zone of break room and maimframes around the tower?"

Anesh made a small *ah* noise, raising a finger like he had a good answer, before lowering his hand again. "Hm," he said, instead, glancing down at the elder. The camraconda, too, perked up, leaning partially on the table in the way that camracondas had started using to signal they were joining a conversation in earnest. "That's a good question," Anesh said. "Could there have been . . . hm."

"I mean, the dungeon couldn't see the tower, right?"

"Hostile observation prevented," the elder agreed.

"But only for the tower. So it could see around it. Maybe it saw us vanishing and reappearing?" James bit his lip. "I've thought about it, but I just can't come up with an answer that satisfies."

Anesh clicked his tongue. "Is it possible that one of the other camracondas . . . left the tower?" he asked the elder. "Went outside the protection, contacted the dungeon?"

"Never," the camraconda responded almost instantly, blue and gray cables pulling tight as they whipped their raised form back and forth. "Never." The word was repeated in a lower volume, a physical hiss from the snake matching the digital word.

"I'll be honest, I'd find it hard to judge them if they did," James told the camraconda. "Trapped in that one tower, for . . . how long? Two, three years? I've been largely sticking to the same three places for the last couple months because of this pandemic, and I'm already going nuts, and I can *go outside*." He sighed deeply. "Like, I wouldn't be happy about it. But I would absolutely understand."

"No," the elder replied. "Our . . . souls? More important than space. More important than moving. You would not stroll if the light of the sun killed you."

"Poetic. But fair," James conceded.

"So, how then? Now I'm curious," Anesh grumbled. "It must have been tracking where we were, right? And us vanishing from its perception was clearly a major anomaly. Did it *know* that it had a missing section? Or is this a way we can bait it into creating zones we can farm?"

"Oooooh, no. No farming maimframes," James admonished. "I've been shot multiple times by those now. No, no. Not again."

"Bah." Anesh dismissed his boyfriend's concerns about *being shot again*. "You lack vision."

"That's what I keep saying about the skulljacks, and no one believes me!" James threw his hands up. "The support group is getting amazing at, like, doing Google searches and stuff. But we're squandering the potential of these things!"

"James, your list of ideas includes, just off the top of my head: abandoning permanent bodies, creating artificial warminds, forming hive minds with dogs, forming some kind of transhumanist cult, forming hive minds with everyone actually, and evacuating the consciousness of the recently deceased to safe storage," Anesh pointed out, eagerly grabbing a slice of the non-pineappled pizza that Nate had just set down one table over. The chef, to his credit, quirked an eyebrow at their conversation, but didn't interject.

"Okay, in order—"

"No, no. No long explanations. Sum it up," Anesh admonished him.

James almost growled at his boyfriend. But then, his partner *had* heard most of this argument at least twice by now, so he tried to make it succinct. "Alright, um . . ." He thought for a second while Anesh scarfed down bell pepper and olive pizza. This was harder than he thought. "Okay. So. We are not our bodies. And I love my body, especially these days now that I have actual muscle, but it's not *me*. I would gladly give up my permanent residence in this shell if it meant helping someone else out of death, or if we could more efficiently move around who is doing what. Also, I'd be fine being a dog for a little. Until we can artificially make new bodies, obviously."

"When I read your list of potential ideas, the word *warmind* was still on there," Anesh pointed out casually.

"Well, *obviously* we shouldn't make minds just to be weapons. I meant, like, copying the gestalt of you, me, and Alanna, and then making that one balanced person, who is just very well suited to combat."

"And is that tied to the cult thing?"

"*Consensual* cult thing!"

"That still seems super unethical. Maybe find a better word."

"I admit, that one was mostly on there as a leftover to my reaction to fighting Status Quo and the Old Gun. And it's been . . . almost three months since then." James sighed again. "Fuck, we're just on endless crisis mode, aren't we?"

"It's very exhausting." The blue-and-gray form of the camraconda commented, artificial voice letting them talk despite the bite of pizza that was the size of one entire slice of pizza.

"We need more people," Anesh told James.

"Start scheduling interviews or whatever it is you do. I'll handle it," James relented with an easygoing shrug. "Also, let me know when Alanna gets back. I wanna talk to her about our vetting process."

There was a pause while Anesh stared at the far wall like he was trying to not think about something. "She's out getting in fights again," he said eventually, slowly looking back at James. "Probably.

Because there was another protest scheduled today, and . . . well. At least those filter masks everyone is wearing are decent at stopping tear gas."

"I admit, with some embarrassment, that I don't think I understood, and still may not understand, the extent of how bad our police are." James closed his eyes, taking a deep breath and silently hoping his partner would be okay. "You know, I talk a lot about the arcology thing, about building a better society designed to be good to live in, and I *do* seriously want to pursue that. But I am not looking forward to discussing with everyone exactly how we want to set up the peace-keeping structure."

Anesh grunted. "I still get randomly pulled over every couple weeks," he said.

"Are you a poor driver?" the camraconda asked curiously. "I am a poor driver." They did not elaborate at all on that sentence.

"No, I'm brown," Anesh answered, choosing to not follow up on if the camraconda was responsible for anyone's insurance rates going up.

"Alright, now *I'm* checking out of this conversation," James said, standing up and finished with lunch. "You explain systemic police abuse of power to the poor innocent snake. I've got to go meet a private eye that Recovery hired. Also, snake . . . friend . . . I'll catch up with you later if I learn anything for you, okay? Also, I need something better to call you." The camraconda gave a short hiss in reply.

"Think you found the guy?" Anesh asked.

"We found his phone number and email address. But he didn't reply, so I'm finding him in person," James said, brushing crumbs off the floral-print shirt he was wearing, and heading down the hallway toward the front of the building with a wave over his shoulder. "Later! Have fun with that discussion!"

James shook his head as he walked down the hall, taking only a brief pause this time to glance down to his right at the couch embedded in the wall where it should, by all rights, be intersecting the kitchen. They had never actually figured out why some green orbs seemed to work within normal Earth geometry, and some decided that the rules of casual directional relation were for suckers. Though if he had to guess, James would have put his money on the dungeon just thinking it seemed funnier this way. He was willing to bet no one would accept that as an answer, though. So the quest for truth continued.

Though, head-shakingly oddly placed as it was, the couch was a good constant reminder that he had green orbs in his bag from the last office run that he needed to use here in the Lair. James filed that little note away in his enhanced memory and headed into the front room of the building.

Sarah was here, along with Lua and Tyrone, packing up the mass of folding chairs that they used for the support group. A few survivors that weren't officially part of the Order were still hanging around, the remnants of the people rescued from the Office and the misshapen monster that had held them in thrall. They doggedly refused both to either join the Order in full, or give up on returning to their old lives. James couldn't begrudge them that; it took a certain amount of strength to do what he did, but he was sure it took more to make the decision to survive an ordeal like that and deny it the power to warp who you were.

Some of those people still flinched around the camracondas, but the fact that some camracondas had actually joined in on the support group to ask for help processing their relatively new and often overwhelming feelings went a long way to normalizing them as people.

It was through this collection of people cleaning up snacks and chairs, looking for their car keys, and having conversations in half-English half-hiss that James encountered a distraction.

"Boss!" The distraction, a five-and-a-half-foot-tall goth girl with dark rings under her eyes that had nothing to do with makeup, greeted him loudly as he approached.

Momo was the only one who called him *boss*. A few other people had tried it, and James had told them to knock it off. They'd listened, too. Even Harvey, and Harvey barely listened to James at all, especially when it came to differences of opinion in how secretive they should be. Momo, though? Momo just powered through. And after about a month of it, James had more or less relented, and now half the Order was vaguely aware of the fact that Momo had some kind of special dispensation to call James whatever she liked. That wasn't *true*, but that didn't really matter at this point.

"What's up?" James asked her, noticing then that Momo had another girl trailing behind her, a lot younger and dressed less like she was going to an alt rock concert and more like she was prepared to hand out flyers to people about the dangers of smoking. A modest blouse, slacks, and just a touch of makeup that made the young face look professional in a weirdly familiar way. The look of confusion she was wearing seemed out of place, and also kind of funny. "Who's your friend?"

Momo grinned at him. "This is Liz! She—"

"Elizabeth!" the other girl protested, her voice sounding exasperated, but not actually angry. "My name is *Elizabeth*," she insisted.

"Yeah, get used to that," James told her. "Momo has some kind of special dispensation to call people whatever she wants. I'm not sure how it happened." He started to extend a handshake to greet her before he remembered the present circumstances and awkwardly pulled back. "I'm James. Nice to meet ya. What's up, Momo?"

"So, her mom is Karen," Momo explained. "Who I thought wouldn't be here today, but she is. And for some reason, doesn't want Liz getting friendly with the snakes or something?"

"I mean, it might be that we have an actual casualty rate around here," James said, trying for humor and just making himself sad instead. "Still. Hi. You're welcome to hang out here. The camracondas are . . . well, most all of them are friendly. Knife-in-Fangs is learning to be kitchen staff, so . . ."

Liz shook her head. "I don't understand," she said. Her voice was quiet, but had that tone of someone who was just good at conversations; clearly understandable regardless. "What is this place? Mom said her work was strange, but . . ."

"Oh, um." James tried to think of how to describe what they did. "We're professional heroes?" he settled on. "We save people, mostly.

And somehow this turns us a profit? No. Something else . . . Look, my finance guy is out of state. I don't know how we make money," he admitted, letting the joke take over his entire brain's ability to think coherently. "Oh! You mean the magic! Yeah, we have magic. Want some? I can find you some skill orbs if you want to see what I'm talking about, and annoy your mom."

"Yeah, sure." Momo waved off his little joke. "Look, if you see Karen, just don't tell her that . . ."

The elevator dinged behind them.

James turned, quirking an eyebrow at the panicked look on the girl's faces as the doors slid open to reveal Karen herself, looking down at a file folder. Without missing a beat, James turned, swept an arm, and casually ushered the two around the corner and back toward the cafeteria.

"Ah, James." Karen greeted him as she walked out of the elevator. "I needed to ask you something."

"Good timing," James stealth-joked. "What can I do for *you?*"

She paused. "Is it one of those days?" she asked. Karen might be the closest they had to a normal responsible adult in the building, but she still understood that sometimes, everything happened all at once. James appreciated it.

"Almost," he said, glancing around the corner to where Momo and Karen's daughter were pressed against the wall, waiting for the older woman to leave.

"Well, I'll be quick," she said. "I've found this paperclip, and according to the iLipede and Research, it performs a selection sort on any stack of documents it's attached to, from least to most unknown piece of data."

"Okay, rad."

"Yes, I thought so too." Karen nodded seriously. "But I had a question for you, since no one else had a good answer. Why does it work if I clip DVDs together?"

James blinked. Tilted his head. Then let out an overlong "Huuuuuuuuuuh. Huh." He took the offered paperclip from Karen and turned it over in his fingers a few times. "Well, that's weird. I'm always thrown off when we get these *map is the territory* kind of objects."

"I'm sorry, what?"

"Oh, the phrase? 'The map is the territory' is from . . . well, I don't know where it's originally from. I'm stealing it from a contemporary philosopher named Wales. It's mostly used to describe game mechanics . . ."

The look Karen gave him was halfway between being lost and frustrated. "I don't . . ."

James held up a placating hand. "I know it's not your thing. I'll do the quick version. The term refers to when the game mechanics, usually in an RPG, don't make sense, but still *work*. Like, in Dungeons & Dragons, you roll a twenty-sided die to attack. No matter what, if you get a one, you miss. And a twenty hits."

"That seems . . . fair? I don't play games," Karen informed him. In case he hadn't known.

He had. "Well, here's the thing. What if you're throwing a rock at, say . . . a tank?" James asked. "A twenty still hits, does damage. At that point, you could, maybe, hire a few hundred random serfs to lob rocks at your problems. Because five percent of them will statistically hit. The rule, the *map*, in this case, has become the world itself. The territory."

"And this ties into the paperclip because . . ." Her eyebrows narrowed. "Ah, no, I see. It has a rule, doesn't it? It defines *documents*, and then doesn't bother to elaborate or look for details."

James snapped his fingers. "Exactly. In games, we don't elaborate because it gets stupid and bogs down actually playing. But we're not in a game. This is real life, and none of us are interested in losing out because we keep to the spirit of the rules."

"Helpful. Thank you. I believe I have a few ideas of how to better use this to sift through Status Quo's files now." Karen nodded at him. "I'm going to go get lunch now. Excuse me."

James glanced around the corner to where the two girls looked panicked, Momo shaking her head and waving him off. "Do you like pineapple on pizza?" he asked Karen.

"No," she said without hesitation.

"Might want to eat out today," he offered helpfully.

"Mm. Thank you," she said, before tucking the folder under her arm and heading out toward the door, fishing her car keys out of her coat.

He waited until she was outside and in her car before leaning around the dividing wall. "Momo, you know the kitchen has a back way out, right? There's a million hidey-holes back there."

"Yeah, but her mom would yell at me. Nate's actually scary," Momo retorted.

"He's . . . !" James started to argue, then actually thought about it, and shook his head instead. "Yeah, okay. At least hide behind the couch or something next time," he admonished.

Before actually leaving, he did want to use the spare green orbs they weren't using for testing. The influx of them had dropped over time, but Simon and Other James had bagged a pair of tumblefeeds last week, and it was always worth using the orbs here as long as no one had any plans for experimenting with them.

Wandering behind the counter for the front room, a remnant from whatever this place had been before they'd occupied it that they had never had the time or energy to remove, James looked under the cabinet space where he'd thrown his bag last week. The hollow opening under where a cash register should have been was, unfortunately, empty.

James frowned. It was unlikely someone had stolen his bag. Who would even know where he'd thrown his *I'll get around to it later* backpack full of orbs at 4 a.m. after the last dungeon run? Only people he trusted, really. Maybe also Randall. But Randall couldn't really conceive of using the orbs, unless he was a really good actor and absolutely dedicated to throwing everyone off his trail. Which he might well be, given that he was FBI.

The really awkward thing here was, James had just spent the last three days or so casually flaunting his ability to *remember* stuff now. That upgrade had fixed, or at least patched over, one of the biggest problems his depression caused. And now he'd promptly gone and lost at least two green orbs that were slated for the Lair.

He popped up from behind the counter, looking around at the handful of people still in the room. "Has anyone seen my bag?" James called out.

Heads both human and camera turned toward him, all of them shaking or matched with the word *no* in some way.

"Shit," James muttered, suddenly feeling pretty awful. It was still a testament to the grip that depression had him in that one minor setback could turn his mood sour in an instant.

Still, he wasn't prepared to let it get in the way of what he had to do today. With a sigh, James started heading to his car, prepared for his attempted meeting with the next of kin of the progenitor of all the camracondas under his care. He called out to Sarah on the way past, letting her know he was heading out and giving a wave.

As he reached one of the two front doors, while affixing his mask to his face, the door swung open and the mildly surprised face of Daniel paused on the way in.

"Oh! Perfect!" James greeted him. "Haven't seen you in a while! Can you find my bag? You and Pathfinder can find things, right?"

"Nooooo," Daniel slowly let the word out. "And you haven't seen me because I was camping. But is it that bag?" He pointed behind James to the rack of hooks where coats and backpacks were hung up. There were actually two rows, one lower than the other for the camracondas' evolving line of fashion.

James glanced, looked back, and was prepared to admonish the man in front of him, when he stopped and did a double-take. "Yes," he said, confused. "Why is my bag here?"

"Someone probably just hung it up. You leave backpacks on the floor all the time." Daniel half rolled his eyes at James. "Pick up after yourself."

James wasn't really listening, too busy rifling through his bag and cracking the two greens before he headed out.

[Local Area Shift : Construction Speed—+1.8 tons material processed / day]

[+3 Skill Ranks : Cleaning—Mopping]

[Local Area Shift : Time Added—Hygiene—+14 minutes/day/ person]

[+2 Skill Ranks : Metallurgy—Alloying—Aluminum]

"Ah, excellent." He sighed in relief as the orbs worked their magic. "Thanks for your help." James nodded gladly at Daniel. "Hey, do you think you could find the Nerf gun that we've been looking for? The one that shoots fire, not . . ."

"Not the one that shoots spiders. Yeah. I'm on it." Daniel sighed, swiping at his face with a hand that was covered on the back in luminescent orange feathers. Pathfinder's ethereal hand, extending partly from Daniel's own, also brushed long fingers over his face as they passed, but in a less exasperated and more tender way. "We would like it on record that we aren't some kind of scanner, though."

James nodded. "I understand. But fireballs," he rebutted.

"Oh, I agree with you," Daniel said. "I'm just making a token resistance before I go back to trying to pay you back."

"Got it. Okay." James smiled under his mask. "Anyway, I've got a meeting I'm probably certainly late to by this point. I'll see ya later. And you don't owe me anything!" he added over his shoulder as he left.

"Have fun." Daniel held the door for him while James passed by, then ducked back into the Lair.

James half chuckled to himself through his mask as he walked to his car. It was a nice day out, and while the cloth covering made the warmth uncomfortable around his face, he was getting used to it. There were a couple of people standing on the street corner just up the slope from the Lair's parking lot with the full filter masks on, which James would have *really* found unbearable. He already sweat too much; adding a sealed zone to the mix would drive him nuts as soon as it started itching.

The drive to where he was meeting the investigator he'd hired was decently long. Maybe twenty minutes, and the end point was in one of those little office parks off a winding road that split off from a main route. The kind of road that James never really looked twice at, and was always surprised when he had to take one to get to a tiny two-room office to get car insurance or a window screen repair. It was *almost* enough to make him think there was something intentionally obfuscating these spaces, but he was pretty sure that was just the part of his brain that was constantly on dungeon time kicking in.

Once you'd spent a solid year of your life doing nothing but dealing with supernatural threats, every tiny discrepancy in daily life started to look like magic.

The man James had hired greeted him in the front of his office. It was . . . cramped. A room barely the size of a small apartment bedroom, with a single back room for storage that James could see was packed full of filing cabinets, stacked luggage, and a short desk. The detective himself was basically the opposite of every stereotype James had learned from old noir films. Bald, on the upper end of middle-aged, with a fat nose and thin oval glasses. He looked, and spoke, like a high school computer science teacher, and not like he was the kind of man who "down these mean streets must go."

Which was kind of the point, James supposed. No one would be keeping an eye out for the dad waiting to pick his kid up, or the bored accountant hurriedly taking notes. They'd be looking for someone in a trench coat and dark sunglasses. Or at least, he would have. He wouldn't *now*, obviously, since he'd thought about it for more than two seconds.

"Your guy isn't answering your calls because he doesn't answer any of his calls," the detective, who just went by Velazquez, was telling James. He had his hands folded in front of him as he leaned forward over the desk. He did that, James had noticed; got closer to talk to people, like too much distance created information decay or something. Normally it would be fine, but these days it just made James nervous. "The phone rings, and he doesn't even flinch. Never acknowledges the thing."

"Yeah, that . . . that checks out." James groaned internally. "Honestly, I should have considered this might happen."

The PI didn't exactly raise his eyebrows, but the man did shift forward a centimeter or two, like he was forming a conspiracy and not just handing over an address. "Well, he's not deaf. You said that he wouldn't run, and you were right. All it took was knocking on the door and arranging a meeting. Everything's above board. Here's the hours he's home and available. I told him you weren't a debt collector, by the way." Here he did that thing again where he notably *did not* ask James a question.

James pointedly did not answer a question. "Alright. Thank you very much," he said, taking the file folder and standing up. "If you need to bill me for more hours, just send an invoice. I know the actual contacting part wasn't originally part of the professional stalking."

"I prefer the term *freelance espionage*," the investigator said with a small grin, standing and offering James a hand to shake.

James gave a guilty look. "Ah. Pandemic, right?" he said, not taking the hand.

"Eh, no worries," the other man said. "Well, good luck with that. You've been a lot easier to work with than most clients. Feel free to contact me if you need anyone else tracked down."

"Can do," James said as he left, heading to his next destination.

It was late afternoon. Not quite what he'd call evening, yet. Velazquez had given him a list of times when the person he was looking for would be home, and be open to someone coming to talk to him. *Now* was a potential time. No sense waiting.

There was a small tension in James's chest as he drove through the streets of his hometown, across city lines, down a freeway, and into an area that was similar in composition to his familiar home zone, but somehow just a little bit off. Different store names, even if they were the same store types. Different quirks on the road signs, sometimes vandalism from the local dumbasses. That sort of thing.

This happened basically every time he went on a road trip. He was getting used to the world being bigger than he ever could have imagined, though, and that included not being too caught off-guard by finding weird sideways copies of his neighborhood all over the place. That was *normal*. Humans tended to like the same stuff.

The place he was going was an apartment complex. And as he pulled into the gravel parking lot, he made the unfortunate conclusion that it wasn't a very nice one. Not enough space, too much graffiti that wasn't interesting, stairs that wobbled under his boots as he walked up them. It just had that feeling of being run down, in the way that happened not when there was a lot of use, but in the way that happened when no one *cared*. Half the other cars in the lot had dented bumpers or a broken window covered in a trash bag.

Finding the apartment the detective had listed for him, James rapped on the door, and waited. Again, he felt that anxiety about talking to someone new. Someone unknown. He wasn't exactly here to provide good news, after all. And with someone he'd never met before, there wasn't an easy way to tell how they'd react. Much less if he could get what he was after, which was for this random person to agree to meet the camracondas and just . . . talk to them, really.

How did you tell someone that the people who'd killed their mother had formed a cult around her, and wanted to have a chat?

After five minutes of awkward waiting, during which he politely didn't knock again as he could hear rustling from inside the apartment, the door opened an inch.

"What?" came the barked word from inside, past two chain locks James could see through the crack. The voice was hoarse, old, and had a slight slur to it like the man was drunk. He didn't say anything else, just eyed James through the small opening.

"I'm looking for the son of Candace Williams," James said, putting on his best official voice. He was wearing something that was close enough to a suit that he could pull out his (still fake) FBI badge if need be, but he didn't want to open with that. "One of our informants told me he lived here."

"The kid?" The man on the other side snorted. "He's out. You talk to me, if you want him. What's he worth, anyway?"

James's eyes narrowed. This was not going the way he had expected, but it did have one positive effect. Being pissed at this dude was doing wonders for his anxiety.

"Sir, this is an attempt to contact next of kin. If you would . . ."

The man on the other side of the door cut him off. "Ah, bitch is dead, eh?" was all he said, before he snorted and slammed the door in James's face.

James had, in his life, been confronted with some truly awful people. How could he not? He'd worked tech support for cell phones. He'd once encountered a man who spent twenty-six minutes telling James that *technically*, his phone was still legally his, even though he'd left it at the scene of a hit-and-run he'd committed, and that James needed, *needed* to unlock it. Or he'd be sued. Or murdered. Or something. The point was, he was used to dealing with assholes.

That did not, for a second, mean his blood didn't catch fire at the insolence of this bastard slamming the door in his face.

There was a brief window where James debated just kicking in the door, shooting him, and then hanging around the apartment waiting for "the kid" to get back. But he reined that in. That sort of impulse was coming to him way too often lately.

Instead, he went and sat on the stairs.

He had sudoku on his phone. He could wait a *long* time.

As it turned out, he didn't have to wait very long. Which was good, because even though he *could* wait a long time playing number puzzles, his phone's battery was finite. For now. And he wasn't like Alanna with a purple orb mutation that let him survive the July heat while wearing a suit jacket forever.

"'Scuse me." The muttered voice made James look up from his phone. Not that he hadn't noticed the guy coming, but he'd chosen to force an encounter by not moving. He was probably at the tail end of his teens, if not in his early twenties. But he had a look like he'd been continually trampled by fate for most of his life, and the sad expression on his face instantly softened James's own simmering anger at whoever was occupying the apartment.

"You wouldn't happen to be Williams, would you?" James asked, looking up from where he was perched on the steps.

The kid, without missing a beat, slung his backpack off his shoulder, flung it at James's face with enough force that it could have knocked him out if he hadn't caught it, and then turned and booked it. His worn sneakers kicked up dust and chunks of gravel into the hot July afternoon as he started scrambling past a couple of cars like he was about to dive through the scraggly bushes on the edge of the lot and disappear into the next complex over.

He didn't even say anything, just started running. So, in the least threatening voice James could manage, he called after the fleeing form. "It's about your mom." His voice carried over the rumble of cars on the nearby cross street, and he raised it to make sure the kid could hear him even as he got farther away. "You don't need to talk now! But I'm gonna leave my number here! Call me when you're ready!"

Either the kid had heard promises like that before and didn't believe James for a second, or he was playing it safe. He paused only for the briefest moment, when James mentioned his mother, but then picked up speed again and took off.

"What the fuck has been going on in his life that he'd just leave the backpack?" James mumbled to himself. Something was wrong here. Not wrong in a dungeons-eating-people way, or an old-gods-and-cruel-power-structures way; just wrong in the way that shitty people and shitty lives poisoned the community around them. "Fuck," James settled on.

He didn't have anything else to say. He just left a slip of paper with his phone number on it in, tucked obviously into the kid's backpack. Actually, he left several, so it couldn't be ignored or missed. Then he stuffed the bag under the first step, where it would be easy to see for anyone who wanted to go upstairs, and easy to miss for anyone walking past.

He took one last look at the building as he got into his car to drive off. Again, briefly considering doing something stupid, before shaking it off. The place had the feeling now, in the back of his head, like an infected splinter. James was starting to wonder exactly how much his perception of the world had been changed by the Office. The more time he spent inside that weird wonderland, the more he'd started getting feelings on magic items and spatial distortions, and that was perfectly fine. But he wasn't sure he appreciated the low level of anxiety that came with noticing more and more the poisoned atmosphere around certain places in the real world.

What felt like a year ago, and what actually might have been about a year ago, Anesh had talked about the differences in how it felt before and after he'd gotten a skill orb for perception. The way that he could suddenly see more of the world, understand little clues and cues that told a story. And that maybe, sometimes, he didn't *want* to know the story that was being told.

It reminded James a bit of how, as a voracious reader, he could never actually figure out how to *not* read signs on the side of the road. If someone wanted to put words into his brain, all they had to do was write them large enough, and stick them to the side of a highway, and eventually he'd see them and process them. That was, of course, no guarantee that it would influence him in any meaningful way; but the way that he approached the world meant that he would certainly at least *think* about it, whether he wanted to or not.

And now, driving back to the home base of the Order, James realized something. Even though he'd always thought it was stupid that in most horror stories, the true defense was *ignorance*, that it was sheer foolishness to assume that not knowing something would protect you in any way, that he now understood why it would *feel* better. There was just a safety, a snugness, to the idea that you'd got it all figured out.

Even with the dungeons, from Officium Mundi, to the Akashic Sewer, to whatever the hell El had found out in the highways of Tennessee. James had this idea that, yes, there were more out there. But he'd *got this*. He had a handle on it, even when surprises popped up. He had his weapons, his companions, and his ethics.

And then he ran across something like *this*. This place where people didn't so much live as they did suffer. Where a kid would run upon hearing his name, too afraid of anything to even stop and hear the story of his own mother. Where the smell of an unwashed apartment and the edges of a broken window showed off a callous hatred. Not for anything in particular, just an anger, and a hate without direction.

They needed to step up their game, James thought as he drove. He didn't know how much magic and wealth it would take to start addressing problems like this, but they needed to start reaching for it faster.

He'd check in with Research when he got back. See how things were going on creating warped spaces. Maybe they could at least start making their own weird apartments and setting the rent at a dollar for anyone who needed it.

Just about the time he'd gotten a good eighty percent of his anger processed out of his brain and the rest was fading into embers, James's phone rang. He picked it up, flipped it to speaker, and tossed it next to him as he kept driving. "Hey, Harvey. What's up?"

"We've got a problem." The older man's thick voice came through the speaker from James's passenger seat.

"Did Research create a black hole in the basement? I told them not to do that. Dock their pay," James answered.

"No." Harvey's serious tone made James pause. No time for jokes, which put James on edge quickly. "We need you back here. I think Status Quo is back. Or something like them, at least."

"On the way," James said curtly. He didn't hang up; Harvey would take care of that. Instead, he let his hands settle on the wheel, let his driving skill kick into high gear, and let his Aim settle his vision into vectors and lines of assault through the traffic.

Then he slammed the gas pedal down.

CHAPTER 15

"They're back?" were the first words James said as he stepped through the door and into the Lair. He'd made frankly impossible time back; impossible, that is, if you discounted the free eight minutes shaved off their travel time that everyone got when driving here. "What's going on? Is everyone okay?" The near panic in his voice was unmistakable.

Alanna held up a hand at waist-level, turning away from the small group of knights and toward James with a calm look on her face, eyes narrowed and wary, but not on high alert. He'd already started to relax before she got a chance to speak. Which was probably the point, if he thought about it. "No one's dead. Take a deep breath."

James did so. He also took the time to give a nod of greeting to the other people in the room, and to notice that there were more people moving around in the dining area, in the back room, and around the elevator. There were a lot more people here than when he'd left. More camracondas around the windows and doors, too; lounging around, but obviously on a form of guard duty.

He clearly hadn't been the only person warned about Status Quo. And whether it was official or not, the Order of Endless Rooms had moved to a form of increased alert level. He wouldn't call it a red alert yet, but they were certainly at an orangish yellow alert, if that was an option.

"Okay." James willed his heart to stop pounding quite so loudly. "What do we have?"

"Alright. You know we've been starting to really look over the local area, yes?" Anesh asked. He was standing next to Reed, the current head of Research, who was wearing his perpetual nervous look. When James didn't interrupt Anesh, but did cock his head to the side, his boyfriend continued. "With the different types of glasses we've duplicated, we can have a knight just take a walk through part of town, or people-watch for a while, and essentially scan for points of interest."

"Ah, that kind of looking over. Yes." James remembered the idea from a long time ago. So they could try to find other people like them. After all, it wasn't as if anyone *actually* put themselves into Google's index of businesses as *secret wizard cult.*

Dave cut to the chase, talking past Daniel and Sarah. "We have glasses that show affiliation. Neil spotted someone today that had the actual Status Quo group. Uh . . . what was it? Agency A-01?"

"That sounds like a fanfiction website," James quipped, the wise-ass part of his brain hijacking his mouth while the rest of him tried to form actual thoughts. "No, wait. That's not the worst thing ever. We left a lot of them alive, and dispersed them. It's natural we'd see some of them from time to . . . Oh, wait, no."

Alanna clicked her tongue. "If the organization was actually gone, they wouldn't have an affiliation with it," she confirmed. "Which means they're still operating. Now, what I'm actually worried about is who they were talking *to.*"

"A member of Nike's board of directors?" James asked, and got puzzled looks from the others. "I know you all listened to the recording of my chat with the director. He alluded to Nike having a dungeon, but I don't believe him. I'm making an educated guess, but also I couldn't find *anything* when I tried to look into it. And now I'm stress rambling. Alanna, please stop me and give us an actual answer."

"Organized crime, you . . . god, you'd be adorable if you weren't so bad at timing." She shook her head. "Red Mafia, specifically. Who yes, were originally Russian. But are surprisingly ethnically diverse these days."

"How do you—" Daniel started to ask.

James ignored him. "Is that . . . a real thing?" he asked Alanna.

She shrugged at him. "I mean, not like how you're probably thinking. They're not gonna be like the historical New York mafia, or like anything you've ever seen on a TV show. But they are actually a group that does shitty crimes for money."

Daniel kept trying to ask. "Okay, but seriously, how—"

Continuing to not find Daniel's question relevant, James shook his head at the other man and tried to make sense of the situation. "Okay. So, they still think of themselves as the protectors of humanity, or whatever. And they're talking to the local criminal underworld. Resupplying, maybe?" He glanced at Alanna with raised eyebrows.

"Unlikely," she said. "They don't share well. And while I'm sure Status Quo has bank accounts somewhere that I wish we'd thought to try to wrest control of away from them, it's not like a local mob is going to have dungeon tech for sale. I assume?"

"Is anyone going to ask how she knows that?" Daniel interrupted.

"No," James said bluntly. "So, why, then?" he asked more broadly.

"Hiring," Harvey said, walking up to their circle and running a hand through his hair. He'd been growing it out to cover up the skulljack port; a lot of survivors had. If James had asked, everyone would have denied that it was a mimicry of his own style, which was ironic because he wore his own skulljack with at least a small amount of pride in the mix. "They're hiring muscle," Harvey restated.

"Is anyone gonna ask how *he* knows *that?*" Daniel sighed. "No?"

"Actually, yes. Because I don't know. What's our source?" Alanna inclined her chin at Harvey.

The other man spoke with a rasp in his normally deep voice, like he hadn't slept in a while, or had just spent hours on the phone. "Old brother of mine from college. Nice guy, bad choice in friends. I asked if they had any work for me, you know? Said they would soon, some big thing coming up. Needed the extra staff for it."

"You know people in the mob?" James asked, mildly impressed.

Harvey didn't take it that way. Instead the man folded his arms across his chest and gave James a level stare. "You know people who perform amateur demolition for political reasons. Everything's got texture," Harvey replied dryly.

"Alright, alright." Anesh waved his hands. "So, they're still around, despite our pretty blatant threat. And they're hiring people for something big. What?"

"Best guess? They found another dungeon," Reed said.

James frowned, not letting the relief in quite yet. "A dungeon, and not us?" he asked. "That doesn't sound likely."

A few different conversations split off as everyone moved to share ideas. Each person had a different opinion, a different take on it. Through the noise, James caught different snippets of people's words as they spoke, either to each other or to whoever might be listening. Status Quo had found a new dungeon, or the Order was a target of opportunity for them, or they were trying to rebuild their bank accounts, or they were always in league with the underworld, or they *were* the local mafia and this was how they always worked. Depending on who he listened to, either this was some grand conspiracy, or just a few people simply looking for revenge.

James looked around the room and noticed other members of the Order, and a fair few of the camracondas, hanging around the edges of their group and watching them. He spotted Momo and her new friend hanging behind the counter, leaning on what used to be a cash register slot as one of them watched the argument and the other one looked at the girl next to her with an expression that said, *Them? Those are the people in charge here?*

He snorted air through his nose and gave a half shake of his head.

"Guys." James only said the word once, and everyone quieted down and looked at him. "Quiet, for a second."

James hadn't even actually done a census of the Order. He knew faces and names, had a general idea of the strength they could bring to bear on any given problem, whether it was combat-related or not. But he didn't know the numbers. Still. There were five humans, a stapler, a living drone, and one infomorph in the foundational group; roughly fifty humans rescued from the Office, and a couple other Life picked up along the way, with about a third of those people sticking around in a permanent capacity and another third available to help out with random non-life-threatening stuff; five people James had hired with actual interviews and stuff like a real job, minus one tragic loss; and a lot of camracondas they'd saved, again, minus one loss. And one prisoner in the basement. No, wait. Two prisoners, since Graham was there too, assuming he counted. Quick head math, then, put the number of people he could call on at somewhere around seventy people, maybe a little more.

And currently, roughly half those people were within earshot, listening to a decent chunk of their leadership have some kind of communication breakdown as they loudly argued over who and what were or were not planning to come murder everyone in the building.

"Okay, everyone just chill for a second." James tried to regain some semblance of professionalism. "What information, *concrete* information, do we actually have?"

Anesh tapped out the points on his fingers. "Status Quo still exists as an organization, they have contact with a local gang . . . um . . . "

"Is that it?" James cocked an eyebrow. "I'm sure we can do better. Also, it's basically certain that they had contact with local crime rings before now. From what we understand of the files we swiped from them—files that are *very obviously incomplete yes thank you Alanna*—they didn't really give two shits about morality or legality when they were pursuing their goal of stability." Harvey and Dave nodded as he spoke, and while Anesh looked a little skeptical, James wasn't quite done and addressed his partner personally. "I'm not saying we ignore this. I'm saying that we need more information. So. How do we get it? Ideas. Go."

"Infiltrate their ranks?" Alanna instantly suggested. "If they lost their HQ, but they're still operating, then they might not actually have the same level of counterintel that they did before. They missed the existence of the entire Order beyond the three of us"—she jerked a thumb toward Anesh and James—"so maybe we have someone approach them as a potential recruit?"

"Or a potential patron." Harvey rubbed at the side of his neck. "We've got a few resources now. We can throw around a little power, make a good show of it."

"You want us to . . . try to take control of Status Quo?" James almost laughed. Then he thought about it, as everyone eyed him, and decided that *yes*, he *would* laugh. It wasn't a huge laugh, but certainly at the level of a chuckle. "I mean, there's not a chance in hell they'd accept that, right?"

"Do we know?" Dave asked, looking his feet before glancing up. "We can do the first idea, then the second later. Like you said, we don't know anything." Dave didn't physically shrug, because he was the kind of person that talked like he was monologuing into a stationary microphone in an empty room, but his voice had a kind of casual dismissal in it. "I think we should just kidnap one of them."

A chorus of *Woah!*s and *What?*s greeted his suggestion, the circle of people taking a step back from the young man who'd jumped straight to the end of what he saw as the logical path.

"I mean, Randall *did* have a whole thing about taking prisoners," James said.

Alanna rolled her eyes at him. "James, not you too!"

"No, no. Kidnapping seems like a very bad idea," James conceded, and everyone started to relax just a fraction before he continued talking and added, "It's really more *taking prisoner* than kidnapping, since we're functionally at war."

"No!" Alanna and Anesh echoed together.

James, for once, kept a serious face at their reaction. "No, listen. I'm not kidding this time. I'm not saying we torture or execute anyone. But we need actionable intelligence, and these people are *our enemy*. This isn't a case where we'd be targeting random civilians. This is straight up self-defense. This is a case where trained killers with an agenda of removing the people they see as 'problems' to society have decided that they'd happily shoot us all in the head. If they aren't using our still-breathing bodies for ritualistic blood magic, that is. Like, we're not talking about grabbing someone we *suspect* of being evil. We've got pretty hard evidence of their crimes."

"I think technically you mean, maybe ethics violations, not crimes? Though I guess they did crimes too," Reed mused. James ignored him with little more than a sharp look. This wasn't even close to the time for anyone to use the phrase *well, technically.*

"Okay. So, we've got infiltration, and kidnapping. Any other ideas." Daniel looked around at the faces that were, in theory, his companions.

James glanced over at where Momo was still watching them with a smirk on her face. "Have we considered a blatant use of magic?" he asked. "I can check my pockets, I'm sure I've got some kinda bullshit we can use."

"I have an inventory of different perception enhancers," Reed offered. "We can do IR, UV, X-ray, and FM radio for vision. I've also got sunglasses that show you people's insecurities and fears, headphones that tell you where people had lunch, and an iLipede with a podcast app that plays episodes of *Car Talk* about whoever's name you put in."

There was a pause. James cleared his throat to break the silence. "I . . . was honestly going to go see if Momo had come up with some horrible ritual thing. I wasn't expecting that response. Holy shit, where did we get all that?"

"Can I have the *Car Talk* one?" Daniel asked timidly. He was ignored.

"We basically take anything from the Office that a human can wear that isn't nailed down," Momo quipped. "And things camracondas can wear, too, I guess." She eyed one of the door watchers, currently wearing a snake-adapted vest. "Sorry, did you say 'see in FM,' or am I going crazier?"

"It's a strange experience," Reed confirmed. "Crazier?"

"Dude."

"Okay, yeah."

"Not to interrupt this," James cut in, "but we could absolutely use at least two of those as passive, non-damaging interrogation tools, if we had a prisoner. Anyone else have not-so-dumb magic?"

"I'll go check the basement," Reed said, excusing himself and heading for the elevator.

As it turned out, some people in the Order actually did like to have useful information on hand. So they *did* keep a list of who had what blues slotted at a given time, along with stuff like where dungeon tech was assigned or what orange jobs were in effect. They just weren't stupid about the list if they could help it.

There was, Status Quo aside, an almost constant sense that they didn't belong somehow. The Order stood just slightly outside the lines of society; they didn't specifically run around doing crimes, but they did absolutely break laws with casual disregard weirdly often. And yeah, the FBI had given them tacit approval, *assuming* anyone could actually acknowledge they existed. And yes, they were largely seen as heroes by the people who knew of them. Or at least as blundering idiots with good intentions, if you found El and asked her. But that didn't mean they weren't running stop signs when racing to crisis sites. And there was that nagging thought that at some point, someone *might* try to start a fight with them.

So the really important stuff, like the list of powers, wasn't on a Google spreadsheet they could access on their phones right now. It might never be, depending on how important that layer of protection ended up being. It was stored in the basement, and the computer it was on was also set to self-destruct if moved by anyone who didn't know how to disarm it. Not self-destruct violently, but, you know, a little bit. Enough.

Reed would be back in a bit, James assumed.

"I'm gonna go see about getting the locks changed on one of the rooms in the basement." Harvey said, sighing. "Also, finding something to drink."

"There's a ton of stuff in the kitchen," James told him on reflex.

"Yeah, I meant whisky," the older man said, shaking his head as he went off to assemble a prison cell.

James took a deep breath and tried not to sigh again. "Well, that's going well," he commented. "Momo! We need a scrying ritual!" he yelled over at the front counter, noticing for the first time just how much random stuff had accumulated on it. It was like a coffee table, only not next to a couch, and he'd be annoyed by that every time he went toward the back room from now until the end of time. "Goddamn, I said 'magic,' and I just kind of assumed everyone knew I meant scrying ritual," he mumbled.

"Not everyone is a huge nerd," Alanna told him, her mouth a straight line as she answered.

"Hm." James bit his lip. That was a shame, he thought, but didn't waste time saying it out loud. "Okay, while Momo tries to work up the courage to ask if I was serious or not, do we have any other ideas?"

"What about just classic spycraft?" Daniel said. "No one suggested just finding one of them, with the magic glasses obviously, and then tailing them. Planting a couple bugs. That sorta thing. Has no one here seen James Bond?"

"I actually haven't?" James said. "I know it's ironic, especially with my name. But I just never got around to it. Is it good?"

Anesh stepped between them, holding up his arms. "No, no. We're not doing this now. As hilarious as James's pop-cultural gaps are, and they are *very* funny to me, we have bigger issues than this. Daniel, with me. Limit-of-Hope, you too!" he called one of the camracondas by the door. "We're on that. James, coordinate. Alanna, make sure Momo doesn't blow anything up." He turned and started walking with enough purpose that everyone just kind of fell in behind him.

"Well, alright then," James said.

"He's sexy when he gets annoyed at us and starts making plans," Alanna said, only slightly leaning down toward James and speaking loudly enough that basically everyone could hear anyway.

"Do we have a plan, then?" James said, actually talking softly, because there *were* still people around listening in. Or at least watching.

"Try lots of things, communicate with each other, make sure we don't step on toes. Also, we should see if JP can figure out where their money is coming from." Alanna said the second part a little louder. "Is he back yet?"

"He and Secret . . . Randall too, I guess . . . get back in . . ." James pulled out his phone and checked the time. "Huh. Their flight should have landed already. I'm gonna check if something impossibly horrible happened that shut down all air travel." His fingers started flicking at the screen as he looked up the latest news.

Alanna crossed her arms, leaning back against the wall. "Really?" she asked, a little sarcastically.

"It's 2020, love," James said sadly. "Can you think of a better year for airplanes to stop working?" He didn't look up from his phone, scrolling through the headlines for anything that looked suspicious. "The chamber of commerce is suing the president. That sounds bad, and like something JP might have caused somehow, if he were more of the *financial collateral damage* type. Um . . . apparently the pentagon has a UFO unit, and they're declassifying some of it? That's rad."

"Arrivals," one of the camracondas by the window spoke up.

"I mean, I don't think UFOs are actually alien . . . oh!" James cut himself off as the arrivals in question walked through the door. "Secret! You're back!"

JP carelessly tossed the satchel he was holding against the row of hooks holding coats and bags by the door. "I'm here too, asshole," he grumbled, looking like he hadn't slept in the last few days.

"Yes, hello to you too," James said offhandedly as Secret, *also* somehow looking exhausted, even without a permanent physical body, lazily detached from around JP and coiled up around James's left side. He wrapped his arm around the thick body of the serpent in a comforting hug as he felt small parts of his thoughts start to reinforce Secret's existence.

It was Alanna who came to his rescue. "How was New York?" she asked.

"Well, I learned two things. One, yellow orb skill ranks don't mean quite as much of an advantage when you're up against people who are actual criminal masterminds. Two, it's so much fucking worse when those people have magic." JP cracked his knuckles like he was getting ready for a fistfight. "Randall put me with a white-collar crime crew, told me to watch out for anything unusual, and then I just kind of lounged around being in the way for a couple days. Learned a lot about how to get away with securities fraud, though!" He looked cheerful about that. Alanna and James did not. "Anyway," JP waved away their glares, "so, funny story . . ."

"I don't believe you," James sniped.

"*Funny story*," JP started again. "So, it turns out, there are a lot of people who actually believe in wizard bullshit. And I'm not talking about people like you-two-years-ago who was just waiting for your portal to a fantasy world so you could get eaten by dire wolves." He pointed accusatorially at James, who gave a defensive "Hey!" but didn't actually argue the point. "I mean people who legit have all these weird ideas about petitioning higher powers, and rituals to call power to them, and shit like that."

"I mean . . ." James started to say something.

Without really hesitating, Alanna reached over and put him in a light headlock that he still couldn't really fight back against. "If you start talking about religion, I will not be letting you go," she said calmly. "JP, please continue with your funny story."

"*Hurk*," James agreed.

Ignoring what was going on, though impressed with how Secret twisted himself to avoid getting caught in the wrestling move, JP kept talking. "So, there's this group called Skull and Bones. They're comically famous among secret societies, and I think for a lot of the people, it's an excuse to get together at three a.m. and drink the really expensive wine. But it turns out, when your membership is drawn from the upper crust of Yale, you end up with a lot of people in a lot of high-profile positions. And now that you've got friends with money . . . well, you can make more money. More power. That kinda thing. And *some of them* actually do believe in and perform some pretty fucking weird ritual magic."

"Does it work?" Alanna asked, loosening her grip on James, but not fully releasing him; turning it more into an enthusiastic hug than an arm bar.

"Like our dungeon tech? No." JP shook his head. "I don't think it's dungeon-related at all, actually. But here's the fucking thing. Six-ish months ago, they did a summoning ritual, to call up a 'being of gold and silver.' *And it fucking worked.*"

James blinked. "I'm sorry, what? I mean, I knew that was where this was going, but how?"

"Do you remember," JP asked slowly, "telling us about your duel to the death with Frank? How he was selling people to that thing in the Office dungeon?"

"Yeah, of course," James said, pulling away from Alanna and straightening up before leaning on her arm anyway. "He had . . . oh, fuck. No way. They summoned the infomorph?"

"What Is Owed To Me." Alanna whispered the name.

JP nodded. "Right on the money. Literally. Do you have *any idea* how much damage a cult that now fanatically believes in their own magic can do to the markets, when they actually have the ability to mess with memories, and would really like to own all the money? All of it. At once."

"Is this gonna be about why the stock market decided to walk off a cliff a couple months ago?" James asked.

"Yes," was the simple answer.

Alanna *had* to know something. "How . . . did their weird non-ritual actually summon an infomorph?" she slowly asked, her voice getting steadily more upset throughout the sentence.

Rubbing his hands together, JP took a moment to feel pretty good about actually having an answer on something magic-related before the people who lived, breathed, and researched that magic on purpose. "So, when you gave Owed or whatever his name is an eviction, he didn't actually stop working off Frank's brain. Infomorphs don't . . . do that. Not really. They *cannot* exist without someone thinking about them. So instead, this guy just manifested somewhere nearby, and roamed around until someone saw him, and then slowly moved the idea of himself from Frank to the new person. And then did it again, and again, wandering around the world for a little while. Because . . . because one of them was a pilot. Sorry, that was confusing; at some point early on he got to an airport."

"Okay, so, an infomorph on rumspringa. Sure. But you've left out the part about the cult and the summoning," James demanded clarification, wanting to know as much as the woman he was leaning on did.

"Well, the people What Is Owed—god that name is annoying— the people he was jumping to were ones that he felt comfortable in. And like with Secret, whose favorite food is structured information that's intentionally hidden, Debt likes structured information that is all about the flow of money, and *can* sort of feel it out of minds or maybe computer systems nearby." JP shrugged like that was normal. "So when he was in New York, he jumped to a guy who worked in a bank, hung out for a week, and then 'heard' the summoning call because it's *essentially* like yelling but for infomorphs."

James tilted away from Alanna. "Hey, I'm gonna ask a weird question, and don't get mad at me," he told her, before looking down at Secret. "If structured rituals are loud for you, does this mean you can hear it every time there's a church doing a sermon or something?"

"Only the ones nearby." Secret nodded. "Fear not, they do not appeal to my tastes."

". . . I *don't* know what that means, but we'll talk later."

"Yes, we shall. I have many adventures to share with you, and I have missed being along with you," Secret agreed, twisting to coil in impossible patterns.

"Missed you too." James smiled softly. "Well, anyway. JP. Did you deal with it?"

"I brought you back a bag of money. Of course I . . . Oh, right." JP turned stiffly and knelt down to pick up the bag he'd tossed on the floor. He moved like he was covered in bruises; a style of body language James was really getting familiar with these days. Cracking the clasp open, JP turned the satchel toward them and pulled back the flap, showing off mostly neatly stacked bundles of hundred-dollar bills. "I dealt with it."

James cleared his throat, trying to think of how to politely phrase the next part. "Did you . . . get in a fight?" he asked.

"Repeatedly," JP said. "I actually got shot a couple times. Did you know the FBI has these really cool vests that can stop bullets?"

"Bulletproof vests."

"Yeah, those." JP grinned. "It worked out okay. The infomorph is going to be provisionally working with the one member of the investigation team who actually got what was going on. Her name's Tiffany DeKay, here's her contact info, I know you'll want to hire her." JP rolled his eyes like he'd predicted James's every move already. Which, well, James did want to at least talk to the woman. "Anyway, the cash is a bonus because Randall and the other feds have this weird blind spot for strange stuff, so I'm now I think one of the more successful thieves in US history. Our actual payment goes into the business account in a week."

"Holy shit, dude, you can't just steal from the government." James choked on the words.

JP gave an open-mouthed grin, mixed with a look of sarcastic puzzlement. "Why not? Don't you plan on replacing the government anyway? Besides, I stole this from people who were using it to bribe the government to let them continue committing labor law violations. I am literally Robin Hooding today. You may now applaud." He struck a pose like he was waiting for actual applause.

There was a moment, when presented with someone who actually brazenly followed through on some of the ideas and opinions that James held, that his conviction was actually tested. Yes, he did plan on replacing the government, *eventually*. Yes, this money came from people who clearly didn't deserve it. But something about how fucking *smug* JP seemed made it feel . . . wrong. Not evil. Just like he kind of wanted to hit JP. But only once. And then they should use that money for something useful.

After all, honestly, the redistribution of wealth into a more appropriate flow structure where money and power didn't accumulate in stagnant bottlenecks wasn't going to happen if they all just sat around asking nicely and waiting for the people that lived in those bottlenecks to please maybe release their stranglehold on society. Accusing his friend of doing the right thing, or at least something that was a step in that direction, for maybe not the most noble reasons, seemed kind of mean.

So what James actually settled on saying was: "You're thinking of Ivanhoe. Robin Hood was about a guy reclaiming a noble title."

"Seriously? No." JP absolutely believed him, but wasn't prepared to just roll over on this one. Everyone knew Robin Hood.

"Seriously. It's one of those things where there's actually, like, four different stories, and then modern storytellers slammed a bunch of them together and changed the names around," James said sadly. "Also, Robin Hood is easier to say than Ivanhoe. It's one word, even though it sounds like two."

JP groaned as he stood back up. "You really can't help but ruin my fun, can you?"

"You get to keep the money!" James protested, incredulously throwing his arms up. "I'm not even mad! You're right on all counts, and good job! But it's fucking not Robin Hood!"

"This is the weirdest fight." Alanna sighed. "I'm going to go tell Momo you want a scrying ritual." She sighed, leaning down to give her shorter boyfriend a brief kiss before walking off.

JP rose back to his feet, finally stretching out, and looked around at the Lair. "Scrying ritual, eh? I mean, objectively, it might work without dungeon stuff, now that we know summonings can do a thing. Oh, I have a copy of *that* ritual, too, just in case you want to know."

"I sorta do."

Looking around the place, JP finally got around to asking James about the crisis he'd blundered into. "So, why's it so busy here today? The parking lot is packed. Randall has to park down the street, which is kinda hilarious. But also, aren't we supposed to be socially distancing?"

"First of all, everyone in the Order is way more safe from viral infection than the general population. And not just on average because half of us are snakes," James pointed out. "But also, yes. We've been trying to keep this place empty. But we're moving toward action, because Status Quo is back."

"Lead with that next time, you enormous asshole!" JP abruptly yelled at him, causing a few of the people who'd stuck around the front room to look over in surprise. The crowd had lessened as the group had divided up, but some people had news to present to James, or their own ideas for intelligence action. And those people now chuckled as they watched their paladin leader get chewed out for trying to be friendly and not leading with the important information.

Which was why when Randall walked out of the evening sunset and through the door, standard-issue black FBI jacket rumpled from apparently a complete lack of dry cleaning in New York, his first question was, "What's going on here?"

The situation was explained. Randall nodded politely twice, before he wordlessly turned, walked into the small front office that had been granted to him after they'd moved James via dimensional bridge to a high-rise office in LA, and shut the door behind himself.

Perhaps he was unaware that the door was not soundproof, because everyone could hear his drawn-out bellow of frustration.

A minute later, the door opened again, and he walked out, straightening his tie as every nearby member of the order, including the camracondas, gave him raised eyebrows. Which was impressive, considering most camracondas didn't have eyebrows, and the one that did had them painted on specially.

"Ahem. James, may I speak to you briefly?" the fed asked in a quiet voice.

"Oh my god, that was hilarious." JP looked like he was a kid on Christmas, biting the insides of his cheeks as he wore a massive grin. "You literally just soaked up irritation after irritation for *days*, and *this* is what gets you over the edge? Hah!"

"I have some time, sure," James said, "Did you have fun in New York?" he asked, turning to walk back toward the small office.

Randall didn't mince words as he followed, moving around the folding table of snacks still left over from the support group earlier today. "No," he said. "And you're not cleared to know why. Now. As your official liaison, and someone who is tasked with investigating the domestic terrorist group OA-1—"

"*That* was their name." James snapped his fingers.

"Focus. You've become aware of their resurgence?"

"Maybe. We ran across one agent of theirs. Maybe. We're looking into it. Actually, you could maybe help with that." James paused at the front counter, and glared down at where someone had left a coffee cup sitting on it. A *full* cup, too, he noted with annoyance. He took a sip from someone else's latte, and decided it was his now, by right of cleaning off the counter. "How exactly do you spy on people?" he asked Randall.

The older federal agent sighed deeply, turning in his doorway to address the leader of the organization that was *supposedly* a valuable asset. "We don't 'spy on people,' Mister Lyle. Even a good intelligence-gathering operation mostly relies on informants and contacts in the local area. Building rapport is more important than . . . *spying,* as you say."

"So, no getting a group of neophyte deckers to compromise the security of the city's traffic camera network and mass scan faces for organizational affiliation?" James asked. "Because we might be doing that right now."

"Please stop doing that," Randall said, rubbing at the pallor around his eyes. "Yes, it is important to evaluate your opposition, especially if they are an imminent threat. Yes, stakeouts and tracking devices are useful. But violating the constitutional rights of citizens isn't an option."

James held up one finger off the latte he was now holding. "Point of order," he said. "I'm not the government. So it's just invasion of privacy, for me. And I think that the FBI backed facial recognition software from private companies anyway? So you've gotta know there's a distinction, even if only legally." He took another sip of the drink before setting it back on the counter, not wanting to be *too* mean to whoever's coffee he'd been stealing. "And they're probably not an *imminent* threat. Odds are good they're trying to recover, and maybe have eyes on a new dungeon. I don't think they're going to attack us *now*. Not when they had much better opportunities before."

"Never assume your enemy knows everything," Randall told him. "There's any number of reasons for them to choose now, over then."

"But we aren't under attack now," James said. "So we have at least some time—"

"Hold," Secret said. He'd been reshaping himself into his ethereal self while he was here, circulating a bit smoother around James's arm and shoulder, but now he froze. "Something is wrong."

James and Randall both tensed up. "What?" James asked, the word quiet on his lips.

"I don't . . . know."

"Arrivals," one of the camracondas watching the window called loudly across the room. "Several of them! Weapons!" The digital words were as loud as their speaker's volume could get them.

James's eyes widened as he realized his mistake. His assumption, perhaps his *denial*, that the problem could find its way directly to their doorstep not just rapidly, but almost immediately. He'd been bantering with JP, making loose plans with the others, flirting with his girlfriend, and not instantly rushing to battle stations, and that had, he now realized, been an immense error. "Oh, no," he said simply, reaching into his coat for his gun as Randall met his eyes with a similarly nervous gaze.

Outside, masked figures pulled weapons from under heavy coats as they strode toward the building in a loose ring.

Then the explosions started, and things got very bad, very fast.

CHAPTER 16

The first thing that happened was that the lights went out.

In a coordinated action, bullets began ripping through plate glass, leaving dancing fragments of the window that glittered in the evening light and red-hot lines of tracer rounds falling through the air of the front room. A camraconda by the front went down before the rapid response of the shield bracers many people were wearing flared to life, and a gleaming collective barrier against the incoming fire lit up in brilliant gold.

Outside, muffled bangs announced explosions from attackers trying to open holes in the exterior, not realizing or caring that most of the doors were unlocked. One of them blasted in the side door of the lobby, figures in tactical gear and ski masks rushing in even as the tracer rounds from the machine gun curved up and over the heads of the camracondas at the front of the room.

The group of people pouring in with guns raised had extended lenses of night vision goggles over their eyes as they burst through the breach. Expensive gear to give them a moment of overwhelming advantage as they cut the power to the building and took out everyone who couldn't see in the darkness of the interior. But this preparation would be a fatal mistake for most of them.

James had been referring lately to the green orbs as a form of casual "house magic." Most of them didn't do anything too fancy, but they were all kind of cool in their own little way. Even the thing that let them kind-of-sort-of teleport back to the Lair wasn't *huge*. At most it could mess with a passenger airline's ETA. But every single one of those green orb effects did something that most people in the Order just hadn't really considered.

They warped the battlefield.

And this battlefield, right now, had an extra thirty-four minutes of natural light per day.

So while the outside was cloaked in the soft darkness of just after sunset, and the building's electrical grid was down, *inside* was still flooded with the golden rays of late evening.

James advanced on the momentarily blinded assault team, charging forward with a panicking snarl and exactly no plan whatsoever. He operated on base aggression as he slammed into the first attacker, flaring a blue ability to turn the man's bulletproof vest to glass before pouring bullets through it and the person it covered. The others turned at the noise as their eyes adjusted, and James lashed out a hand, exercising finer control of his ability and glassing just the spring on the inside of the UMP9 the closest goon was training on him. Smaller target, less backlash, and more time set aside to turn his charge into a slide. James swept his leg through the suddenly fragile knees of one of the attackers at high speed, dropped the man down to his own level on the floor where his slide had left him, and shot through the face mask in a spray of blood and brain matter before the fact that his knees would never work again had a chance to matter. Then he rolled around, shooting the last man with a working gun, as the other one charged forward and kicked the Walther out of his hand.

James flared his other blue, repossessed his gun, and shot the man with a pair of burst-fire shots off the bracelet that traced him from hip to neck. Not all of them skipped the armor, but some did. The assailant collapsed, making a choked wheezing noise, and didn't get back up.

Standing up, James turned around just in time to see that these weren't the only people coming through his fortress.

Human shapes in black masks and holding a variety of small arms poured through the front doors and shattered windows, and everything rapidly went from bad to worse. The camracondas, not even close to trained for this kind of fight, were running. James wished he could even say they were falling back or retreating, but it wasn't that coordinated. Overwhelmed with too many people to handle and not practiced as a group, the dungeon snakes panicked and made rapid attempts to get out of the front room, only striking out at or freezing anyone that got too close.

Behind the counter, Randall coldly laid down cover fire for them, dropping one hostile while the others moved up to turn flipped tables and building support pillars into cover of their own while they returned fire. And then, as soon as the line of shields switched to different weapons, the support weapon roared again from across the street, bullets pounding in at a downward angle that sawed through the window and ripped Randall's position, and Randall himself, to shreds.

James pressed himself up against the corner wall as the agent died, firing out at the incoming crowd to buy the camracondas a few more seconds. "We need to kill that!" he yelled to Daniel, who was only just pulling himself out of the collapsed heap he'd been thrown into when the first blast hit. "The gun!" James pointed out at where tracer rounds were still flying in overhead. The counter, the walls, nothing would really offer any reasonable cover. As long as that person was firing, they had zero chance of staging a defense.

So when Daniel scrambled for the bag he'd dropped under the counter, struggled with the zipper for precious seconds, and pulled out a bright orange-and-red Nerf gun, James only hesitated to check his bracelet for a split second.

[Bind Firearm—3—68 / 300—99:14:3:18 (1)
Cluster Shot—34—6,994 / 84,000—10:12 (12)
Munitions Dump—23—302 / 2,000—:04 (39)]

"Here!" he hoarsely screamed, pulling it off his wrist and flinging it around the corner as Secret tried to remanifest, through the hail of gunfire, to the floor at Daniel's feet. "Suppressive fire!" Unheard by everyone over the shots ringing out, James whispered to himself with a cracking voice, "God, I hope that's not the one that shoots spiders."

Grabbing the bracelet off the floor, Daniel tried and failed to stay calm. Daniel wasn't quite in the same headspace as James and his closer companions, something that wasn't exactly unique in the Order of Endless Rooms. But he was the kind of person who didn't actually want to be in fights. Didn't like the feeling of adrenaline, or of getting hurt in general, both of which were happening right now. And for months, ever since James had rescued him, Daniel had felt like a damn coward because of his past actions, and because he didn't actually *want* to redeem himself in any way.

He knew he didn't have what it took to be a knight. And it didn't matter, because the Order didn't care. They didn't want him to fight, they wanted him to adventure. And Daniel and Pathfinder, his infomorph passenger and the closest person to him in the world, were totally alright with that.

But right now, well. The air smelled like cordite and blood and screaming. And Daniel, for the first time that it really mattered, took the impossible knot of fear in his chest, and crushed it down.

James popped out from around the corner again, firing back at the slowly advancing line of attackers. He stuck his head and arm out just long enough to draw fire, and he trusted that Daniel would take the chance, ducking back only at the last second as the machine gun fire pivoted to chew away at the heavier support beam that made up the corner he'd hidden behind.

A thunderous roar split the air, not as loud as the gunfire but with a different and deeper texture to it. James felt his ears pop from the pressure and the sound, as a trio of two-foot-wide fireballs erupted in rapid succession from Daniel's point behind the splintering counter. They carved through what was left of the top half of the big windows that made up the front façade, clipped and melted the overhanging roof outside, and screamed across the street to impact near the roof of the opposite building. The plasma splattered wildly as it punched holes in concrete and steel, tearing a gap out of where the machine gun fire was raining down on them from.

And then, in the silence that followed, anyone who wasn't deaf from the blast would have heard Daniel loudly cocking the Nerf gun before he fired a cluster shot again.

Over and over. Cock, shoot, cock, shoot, reload spell. He burned through every point of cluster shot the bracelet had left, turning the front of the Lair, and the upper floor and rooftop of the opposite building, into molten slag. Around Daniel, James could just barely make out the orange outline of the infomorph Pathfinder as she adjusted his aim with light touches, the two of them sweeping every possible firing position, and undoubtedly killing whoever had them pinned down before turning to focus on the people who had invaded their building.

But as the smell of cooking meat and burning plastic started to override everything else in the room, Daniel stayed visible for a little too long. One of the goons took a shot at him, recovering from the panic of suddenly having someone literally throwing fireballs at their group, and the bullet clipped Daniel's forearm and elbow in a way that made him drop the gun and follow the falling object shortly after himself, as he dove for cover on the floor.

At least the people coming through the front door had stopped. The prospect of being melted was a little more overwhelming than getting into a normal gunfight for a lot of them. But out of the corner of his vision to the right, James caught sight of more people storming over the corpses he'd left by the hole that was the side door.

The front lobby was devolving into an even more chaotic me-lee, the injured scattered across the space between the door and the shredded wood of the counter; furniture and support pillars turned into cover that the both invaders and the few armed knights and camracondas were using to shelter from bullets or break lines of sight. James added two more shots to the mix, his Aim letting him be more accurate than he probably should have been able to, but he had no idea if he even hit his target before he had to move.

There were people coming in, and they were blinded for a second, but he had to move before they flanked him, and he was running out of bullets. *Partially around a corner* was *not* a sustainable defensive position.

His legs lurched him into adrenaline-powered motion as someone turned an automatic weapon on his position. James had been considering slipping back and ducking through the door into the little storeroom area between the front and the back warehouse, but he didn't have time now. He crossed the gap to the hallway in a rush of speed he had trouble keeping control of, and shouldered his way through the door to the bathroom, as the squad of new arrivals rushed after him.

"Duck," Secret whisper-yelled at him, getting James to jerk his head just enough that he didn't get shot in the back on the way by his pursuers.

One of them kicked in the door and followed after him, only to be shot back by James, now in a position of cover behind the counter. Even as he toppled backward, the masked attacker still pulled the trigger on his gun, though. James kept his head down as bullets ripped through the sink and the wood paneling, tearing gaps in it that normally would have left him partially exposed for the rest of the attackers.

It was a warped battlefield, though.

When the next two intruders took positions at the sides of the door and started pouring bullets into the bathroom without looking, James already had a recovered position. And even as their shots started to break through, the minimum real-dollar value of the bathroom reared its head and said, quite firmly, "No." The countertop fragmented and broke away under the sustained gunfire, and instantly started to reform; the walls and cabinets reshaped themselves. The holes patched themselves over, the bullets conspicuously absent. After all, the dollar value of a bullet hole is a very, very high negative, depending on your property location.

The attackers noticed this. One of them made a motion at the others, and James watched through a closing gap as most of them broke away to run down toward the kitchen. He tried to lean out to take a shot, but the last one stayed where he was, and instantly tried to pick James off. A bullet grazed his wrist, and he jerked back, but kept hold of the gun.

The attacker lobbed something over the counter that impacted with a metallic *clink*. James reacted and turned the grenade to glass before it detonated, earning himself a spike of headache that made his vision swim as a warning to slow down with the blue orbs.

He was stuck here for now, along with the infomorph still circling around him in ghostly form, because the man at the door clearly had no interest in doing anything other than keeping James and Secret where they were. And the first line of defense was breached.

James hoped everyone else was doing alright.

". . . and six tomatoes!" Nate had been saying, just as he caught the movement of two figures in ski masks out of the corner of his eye. His brain had exactly enough time for two concurrent thoughts, mostly because one of them was a very reflexive thought for a man like himself. The first, easy, thought was, *What is this, amateur hour?*

The second thought was more complex, and was how to handle the two people in the room with him.

So, as the door to the back patio was exploding from the world's most poorly placed breaching charge, Nate was grabbing Knife-in-Fangs by the back of the neck, fingers catching on cables as he flung him into the walk-in fridge. The camraconda collided with Ann, who was in there already, but was about to come out with the tomatoes Nate suspected he would no longer need tonight. Nate caught the edge of the freezer door and was swinging it closed on them as goons started to step past the hunk of dented metal door that was still hanging by a hinge.

Unfortunately, Nate hadn't had much time for a third thought of getting himself out of this alive. But he already had some momentum, so he rolled with it, flung himself backward down the aisle between the flat top and the grill, and rolled sideways across the recently mopped floor, ruining someone's hard work.

Bullets pinged mindlessly off the stainless steel around the room as Nate flipped onto his arms and crawled forward. He wasn't worried. No way in hell they'd have had time to get to him yet, and someone sent these two idiots in first. They were probably expendable, and stupid, and it had absolutely been a mistake to send them through the door unsupported.

The chef grabbed the gun from under the serving counter where he'd hidden it, flicked the safety off, dragged his body up to a crouch, and pressed up against the back of the wall. He glanced out; one of them was watching while his buddy checked the dish pit; looking under the sinks, maybe? Didn't matter. Nate popped out in a split second, and put the .308 round they'd bought to kill dragons with through the man's head.

He was briefly glad the door was listing open, or he'd have had to clean that mess up later. If he hadn't ruined the floor before, he sure had now.

The other one yelled something in Russian, and then ran around the corner, gun up and finger on the trigger. Nate shot him too, the body collapsing over the one already on the floor.

The heavy door to the walk-in was starting to crack open as the people he absolutely didn't want in the line of fire started to react and check to see what the hell was going on. Maybe they said something, Nate had no idea. He was deafened by the shots already, and was focused on the breach.

Which was helpful, because it meant he could open fire as the next three came around the corner.

The military training in him processed that these ones had different weapons, and actual armor, but it didn't change that his finger was already pulling the trigger. He caught one of them in the shoulder, and their gun whipped backward as their arm turned into useless meat. Nate switched targets with a flick of motion, and fired again.

The bullet slammed into a geometric pane of golden light, a web of lines forming out of it to give the outline of a dome centered around the target.

"Shit," Nate muttered, ducking back as assault-rifle fire started chewing up the tile he'd been crouched on a second before. His ears were ringing, but he could hear the sounds of combat from outside his kitchen, too. "Alright. Let's go." He crouch-walked back into the aisle that separated the cooking surfaces from the front hot wells, closing just a little more space between himself and the incoming thugs. Then, knees cracking in protest, Nate pulled the handgun out of the holster in the small of his back, along with the backup he had taped to the inside of the drawer with all the ice cream scoops, jerked himself to his feet, and unloaded on the trio.

The thing the Order got almost instantly, which Nate appreciated and that Status Quo never seemed to bother with, was that the more things you did manually in a battle, the better off you were. Yes, automation was the way of the future. But in a fight, you wanted your fingers on as many dials as possible. And because they hadn't gotten that, and they had never had to deal with combined arms fire to the degree that the camracondas let the Order dish it out, Status Quo had taken massive losses in their first fight.

Now, here they were again. And Nate had rolled the dice on one big hope.

Twelve bullets, two from each gun for each agent. The first one might have hit, the second one didn't; caught on the shield bracelets they all wore. The light was nearly blinding, but it didn't stop them from firing back. Bullets rained down on Nate, who had already set his own shield to nine-millimeter. He fucking knew what their guns sounded like, and he wasn't about to take the first one or two hits before the shield's automatic reply kicked in.

He dropped the pistols, letting them clatter onto the flat top, grabbed the grip of his DMR, and started shooting again. Nate was moving blind through the light of his own shield charges ticking away rapidly, but the people he was shooting at weren't. They couldn't; they had no idea where anything was, and tripping on a loose pan from the rack they'd knocked half the stuff off would be lethal here.

Not moving was also lethal, though. Their shields didn't adjust to the first shot, and his bullets carved explosive and bloody holes out their backs as he nailed two of them.

Before he could congratulate himself on being clever, and just as his eyesight returned, Nate caught the last guy ducking behind the low wall that separated the kitchen from the dish pit, and lobbing a grenade over his head.

"Shit," he growled, and made a choice.

He couldn't leave the other two here to die. Nate's brain had a half second to process that he could have made it to the door, and then he didn't do that. He ran forward, instead. Gun in a hip-firing position, he put round after round through the flimsy-ass wall the agent was crouched behind, following the shield flares to stay on target. His gun accessory let him reload the weapon at will, though he saved the burst-fire charges; he didn't need them now.

Nate made it out the door to the patio before the grenade went off, ruining the quiche he was making for dinner, making a huge mess of his kitchen, and sending multiple shards of shrapnel into his back. He didn't stop firing at the agent, even if his shots were wildly inaccurate and the recoil ripped at his muscles as he had to turn to shoot when he ran past the cowering asshole. And as soon as the blast had gone off, his shoes scraped the concrete as Nate turned around, dashed back, and dropped all three hundred and fifty-odd pounds of weight he had onto the man who was still too blinded by his own protection to see it coming.

Nate's knees slammed into the guy's chest, cratering him back into the wall. Then Nate dropped the gun, grabbed his head, and added another much larger hole to the drywall surface.

He stood up as the other man slumped down, unconscious and maybe not dead. Nate didn't give a shit. He wobbled over to the walk-in, yanked it open, and froze briefly as Knife-in-Fangs caught him in a stare. Only for a moment, though, until he recognized Nate, and it was a good reflex. "Forget the tomatoes," Nate said. "We've gotta go."

"You're bleeding!" Ann exclaimed. "What's going on?"

"Grab a gun," Nate told her, pointing at the griddle. "And let's go find out. Knife, you good?"

The camraconda nodded, dazed from the toss, but alive. "I survive," he said.

Good attitude. Nate liked it. He took a step toward the door, and then stumbled. Dropped to the floor, and had to take a second to pull his legs in front of himself to a sitting position where he didn't have to press his wounded back against the wall. He looked down, checked himself, and saw red dripping down his left leg. "Alright. You two are on your own," he told them, and followed that up with, "Don't fuckin' argue. Keep your heads down, and don't leave the building until we're clear. I don't want you getting your heads taken off."

"Understood," Knife-in-Fangs answered, rearing up from one of the figures with a pair of frag grenades held gently in his teeth.

"Got it, boss." Ann nodded along with him, checking the magazine on the light machine she'd picked up, pocketing a pair of extras. "You okay here?"

Instead of answering that, Nate said, "Go," nodding to the door, and the sounds of war.

The knights nodded at him, once, and obeyed.

In the back parking lot, Other James had hung back from the game of basketball he and Simon had been playing. Or rather, it was more fair to say, the body they shared that had the keys to the car that they needed to get a bag from had hung back. It was a bag full of takeout sushi, and it was great being able to enjoy two different tastes simultaneously.

The two of them were . . . different. And not just because one of them had casually just accepted that everyone in this building was going to call him "Other James" until the end of time.

Everyone else had taken to the skulljacks in different ways. For those who frequented the therapy and support group, it was a form of reclamation. They'd been used as spare parts in an uncaring monstrous machine, but now, they were the operators in control. For James and his partners, it was a deeply intimate function of sharing their lives. But for Simon and his James?

They'd stopped being two different people at some point. Their unique behaviors, memories, quirks, they'd all been sifted down and galvanized and blended together, and now, even when they weren't connected, they maintained so much of each other that they were closer and closer to just one soul that shared two bodies.

Not quite all the way there yet, and maybe not ever really, but closer than anyone else knew.

It wasn't romantic, exactly, and nor was it clinically utilitarian. It was just . . . it was who they'd become. It was useful, and it was kind, and it was *fascinating*, even to them as they drowned in it. One day, they wouldn't be two people communicating, they'd just be one person, that sometimes had to check in with themself.

At that point, someone would probably ask them to choose a name that wasn't either of their original names. Other James didn't mind; James was way too common a name, and he was *always* the one that got stuck with the nickname modifier. They were thinking something like Alduven, just to confuse delivery drivers. Maybe slap a modifier on there, like "The Fierce." That seemed dumb in a very hilarious way.

But that was for later. Now, one of their shared bodies had to grab a bag out of the back seat of an old gray Toyota.

The sniper took the shot as soon as he stood up with the sushi, which would historically be considered a dick move. But in the moment, there wasn't much time to consider anything.

His chest hurt. And he was looking up at the sky for some reason. And the fragment that was entirely Simon was screaming in his head; out loud too. Something about gunfire, or someone on the roof of the city government building that was next to theirs. But it was kind of hard to focus on that when most of what he could see was the stars and the tops of the line of trees between their building and the lot next door.

Oh. He'd been shot. That's what Simon was freaking out about. Impressive, he could barely feel it. Except that his head hurt from where he'd hit the pavement.

He couldn't really feel much of anything, honestly. Except his fingers were cold. And the rest of him was warm.

He felt his eyes closing even as he tried to struggle to keep them open. To keep himself focused on the tiny distant lights in the sky overhead. He could feel Simon, just inside the warehouse door. Knew he was trying something. Just needed to give him a little time.

There was the sound of boots hitting the ground, people running around his prone form. Shouts and yells and gunfire that Other James actually heard this time, even if it sounded like it came from underwater and far away.

Then someone noticed he was still awake, and a short woman with cold eyes leveled a gun at him. Through their connection, Simon screamed as she put a bullet through his skull.

For a brief moment, Other James was still a person. He had, technically, his own body. His own thoughts. His own stupid nickname that he couldn't even shake in internal monologue anymore. And then, he wasn't, anymore. But he wasn't quite gone, either.

Eighty feet away, past a half dozen cars, up a few concrete steps, behind the metal rolling door of the warehouse, Simon caught his fleeing soul through a Wi-Fi connection, and held on like it was the last piece of the universe left.

Part of the geometry of Other James's self was already gone, along with the damaged hardware that was running it. But so much of who he was in that moment wasn't a singular thing. It was shared, between two bodies, two people becoming one. In minutes, Simon's mind combed over the remnants of what made James an individual. Memories were pulled across a digital link, and transferred to new hardware. Opinions, ideas, plans and goals, feelings and echoes, all of them were swept into the still-functioning port of the skulljack like sand into a bucket, even as that sand was drifting away on the wind.

In moments, as he bled out on the ground, holes in his shell, there was nothing left of what was this James. His body died. And maybe, too, would his name. But within Simon's mind, for as long as they could hold on, there was a survivor.

Two figures in black fatigues quietly followed a third as he pushed open the door at the bottom of a stairwell.

One of them was the man the other two had been paid to take orders from. It was a job, and they were getting paid a *lot*. Which made sense. They'd been shot at, just while they were breaking away and getting into the stairs to this part of the building.

They were tough men. Used to using violence on command. They knew how to use guns, and didn't really care about the ethics of hurting people for money. But they weren't ready for this. This was like a battle, not a shakedown.

The lights in the basement were off, which made sense. The lights everywhere were off; some of their new friends had cut the power to the building already. The night vision they'd been provided with let them see well enough anyway. Though as they checked the hallways, and approached the first door to start clearing rooms, a bright spot burst around a corner and into their vision.

It was maybe the size of a baseball, hovered at head height, buzzed, and oriented on them almost right away.

"Camera drone." The man in charge snorted in scorn. The enemy had used these when they'd raided his organization's office. "Knock it down." He motioned one of the other men forward. The hired muscle stepped forward, approaching the drone and raising his rifle one-handed to knock it out of the air. It was stupid, but the agent didn't need smart people, as long as they shot the people he told them to shoot.

Then the drone dodged the man's swing, which instantly set nerves on edge. The blot of light in his night vision moved too fast, too fluidly, especially in pitch black where they could see and the pilot shouldn't have been able to. In a single elegant motion, it looped over around the back of the grip the hitter had on his rifle, and landed perfectly on the back of his hand.

Then it exploded.

The second goon was kneeling down, trying to help his friend whose hand had just been reduced to ragged strips of meat instead of a working limb. But the agent kept his eyes up, and raised his gun to his shoulder. Sure enough, a second later, two more drones came around the corner, visible through the small cloud of acrid smoke now filling the dark hallway. He opened fire, knocking one of them out of the air without any incident, gunshots echoing off the concrete. But the second one moved like a living thing, evading up and out of his line of fire, then back down again faster than he could readjust his aim. It moved at a reckless speed, and in under a couple seconds, it slammed into the side of the kneeling hired hitter who was just now getting his own gun up.

Then it exploded, too.

The agent heard another set of drones approaching from around the corner. He didn't hesitate, leaping over the messy corpses and kicking off the wall to change directions faster than a human should be able to; enhanced physiology from his Authority and the greave he wore on his right leg assisting with that. He ducked the drone that he saw coming, and followed it back to the source. There was one door down this hallway that was ajar. The agent rushed it, shouldered his way in, ignored the yell of fear and the bullets that didn't trigger his shield but still didn't hit him, and opened fire. The drone in the hallway behind him clattered to the floor and went silent, undetonated.

It was just a kid, he realized. Large, sure; taller than he was for sure, but still a kid, visible in the glow of a couple dim digital lights in the room that weren't on the power grid. There were a half-dozen drones here on the floor, a roll of duct tape, and what looked like an early attempt at an IED.

Just a kid, but still one of the enemy. He'd done worse, and would again before the day was out. One down. More to go.

His hired muscle was dead. The agent needed more expendables; he'd try to link up with another group before continuing. This safehouse was turning out to be a lot better defended than expected. But there was no way they were leaving without recovering the artifact. And personally? He wasn't leaving without killing at least one or two more of the enemy. The agent, it could be said, held a grudge.

He closed the door, and moved on.

A grenade went off, the explosion's noise doing more damage than the blast itself.

Someone had thrown it, and then Alex had instantly lobbed it away with a blue orb power. Momo was pretty sure the woman had been aiming for behind the buffet counter, but it went *into* one of the recessed spaces there instead, and the blast had been both loud, and still dangerous. Also, no one would ever use that slot to hold a serving tray of food again. Being the one in cover closest to the explosion, Momo had grabbed the person sheltering with her, spun around, and put her back to the blast as it went off.

"Stay down," Momo shouted at Liz, not hearing her own words. The younger girl was her friend, one of the only normal friends she had these days. And she had picked absolutely the worst day to agree to sneak into the one building in the world her mom didn't want her in.

They were behind a table in the cafeteria while around them, people fought, bled, and died. Bullets traced overhead, sometimes pinging off the cover they'd made, the gunshots deafeningly loud in these close confines.

Liz was in a white skirt with bluebells printed on it. It looked cute on her, really highlighted that it was a warm summer night and that she was just a kid, here to have a little fun and break a small rule.

Momo was in black body armor, with some mild shrapnel damage to the back, holding a matte black longsword low by her side as she peeked around the table. It highlighted that the blue power that let her [Change Outfit] was overwhelmingly powerful, and she was glad she'd spent the time clearing out charges of rotating cellulose or solidifying helium to open up the slot to get this one.

Momo was trying to stay calm, but her head was pounding. The red orb totem in her pocket told her the location of every hostile entity in this building, and the building was not small. Nor were the numbers of the enemy. She also knew a lot of other random things, but right now, this was the big one. Momo needed to be somewhere, needed to hook up with James or Alanna and coordinate their defense.

But she couldn't. Because there were three men with assault weapons pinning her, Liz, Alex, a couple of other people she didn't remember the names of despite her orb powers, and several camracondas she *also* didn't know the names of, down behind these lunchroom tables. Momo was bad with names, and Liz was screaming. Momo wasn't surprised at the screaming—it seemed normal for the situation—but it wasn't helping. It was drawing fire their way.

She'd already thrown an offensive totem, the kind that was purposefully bad so that it hurt to be near it, but it wasn't stopping the intruders. And she hadn't had more red orbs to machine-print replacements for yet. Which left one, very stupid, way to do this. They needed to get these assholes into the line of sight of the snakes, and then, stab them. Well, she could stab them. The others could do what they needed to.

Momo traded nods with the camraconda across from her, hoping that he, she, they, or it, depending on preference, would act fast enough once she started moving. Then she patted Liz on the shoulder, pushed her down flat, and vaulted over the table.

Gunfire trained on her immediately. And Momo just ran, jerking as a few bullets found her as she tried to dodge, her armor really not meant for this. She was just being someone who could soak up attention, and maybe weapons fire, until someone could cover *her*.

The shooting—in this room at least—stopped. Momo turned, and started running again, though this time not weaving through the cover of the buffet counter. One guy, obviously a hire and not a Status Quo agent because he was reloading manually, stared at her as she approached. The other two were locked in place. The other human Order members rushed them, mostly unarmed and pissed off, while more camraconda heads popped out of hiding and reinforced the freezing effect from different angles.

A shield flashed on the other side, the camraconda's gaze broke, and the shooting started almost instantly. Someone went down—Lance, was that his name? Momo felt guilty for not knowing—and then the others were on him. The shield couldn't protect against being grappled, apparently. Momo arrived a second later and stabbed him through the bit where his vest ended. The sternum or something. She knew that one from both Deb lectures, and one of her totems that told her as she opened up a wound and used her sword as leverage to shove the man to the floor where someone kicked him in the head so hard he vanished from her list of hostiles.

Alex wrested the gun out of his spasming grip, turned, and fired from the hip to mow down the other frozen guy. Then the last one, ducking around the door to the small room that they sometimes used for personal meetings or romantic dinners, started shooting back.

And they took cover again.

Momo didn't have a totem for this, but she figured this process would repeat until one side was out of people. But they had more people, and she was pretty sure that Lance—or was it Vince? Momo was taking a lot of time mid-gunfight to feel socially awkward—wasn't dead.

Her blood was rushing, her heart pounding in her ears. She couldn't hear anything, could barely see through her fuzzy vision and the terror of being in a fight like this again, but on the defensive, on the back foot. As she slumped her back against the table, Liz looked at her with wide-eyed horror, and Momo realized there was blood on her armor. Probably not hers.

"I'm sorry," Momo said, eyes fluttering shut like she was about to pass out. "I should have seen this coming. I need to be better at the witch part." She didn't know if anyone heard the words. And then, having caught her breath, she struggled to her feet. Same song, second verse; draw some attention, hope the armor holds while everyone else shoots back. Only this time their side had guns, and a pair of knights were coming out of the kitchens and creeping along the wall to help with the next ambush.

She might not be the best at the witch bit, but Momo was getting disturbingly good at the *war* part of her title. She had to be. She knew how many armed hostiles there were in the building. She couldn't afford to fail.

James was, slowly but surely, moving past the unrelenting terror of having someone with a very dangerous weapon firing at him, and into the territory of being annoyed, and then pissed off. Still afraid, but other things too. Irate things.

He could hear other sounds through the building. The place was mostly concrete and drywall with some exposed ventilation pipes overhead for flavor, so sound carried fairly decently. Enough so that shouting, screaming, and shooting from both of the back room areas reached his ears where he was, cowering behind a seemingly invincible bathroom sink. It had been minutes, which felt more like an eternity, and the shooter at the door refused to do anything more than spray a burst toward James's head every twenty seconds or so. And at this point, James was considering just rushing him to try to break out of the corner he'd put himself in.

"Bad idea," Secret whispered in his ear. "He's waiting for you."

"I know," James muttered back, wishing he had a backup firearm bracelet. Maybe he could take this dude's, after he shot him. "I could surrender? Throw my gun out, then repossess it. I've got a blue for that."

"He'll just shoot you," Secret reminded him. "Call Alanna."

"My phone got shot," James muttered.

Secret pulled his form up to stare James in the face with a dozen eyes. "What was that?"

"I said my phone got shot! The one thing I said basically never happened on dungeon delves? Yes, it happened. To me. Again. Now. Thank you." James snapped, far too focused on everything collapsing around them to take jokes right now and looking straight through Secret to keep his eyes on the door. "Now the guy at the door thinks I'm crazy, too. So he's going to murder me, *and* it'll be embarrassing."

James's monologue was cut off by bullets ricocheting off the tile to his right. None of them hit him, though the shards of the wall stung as they fragmented. Also, it was startling, and he actually wasn't getting used to being shot at, so he flinched all the same.

While James wished he was anywhere else but trapped here, Secret went looking for solutions. His ghostly manifested form, still weak from the energy he'd been spending lately, wasn't even enough to block one bullet, and he knew it. But he could still take a look. He roamed up and down James's crouched form, poking his ethereal nose into pockets. Eventually, he glanced up with several eyes at James's own, his companion still staring in the direction of the door, worried about being ambushed if he dropped his guard for even a second.

"Here," Secret said, tapping James's back pocket with his endless tail. "Call Alanna."

James didn't need Secret to remind him twice of what he was carrying. He felt a little stupid for forgetting in the first place. Keeping one hand on his gun, he braced his shoulder against the counter and reached down to pull out the skulljack Wi-Fi adapter from where he'd been keeping it safe.

"Wait, the power's off."

"We have backup power for Research, to ensure the cat doesn't escape." Secret prodded James's hand. "I promise you, Virgil put the internet on that circuit." He knew this because Virgil had kept a document somewhere that said he had done so, and while no one else knew of it, Secret could draw on that indexed knowledge. Though he may have damaged it slightly in the process.

James snorted. "He would, yeah," he said, and plugged himself in.

It took longer than James was comfortable with to see Wi-Fi networks available through his newly equipped hardware. Which had always been the case, since humanity had invented smartphones, but he'd had this distant hope that maybe magic brain computers could bypass that weird lag. When the next burst of fire came, James answered it with a couple of bullets of his own, drawing down his ammo reserve, but hopefully making the invader stall for at least a little longer.

He dropped onto the local network. It was still up, a minor miracle given how today had been going. Reaching out, James felt blindly for the available devices that had connections. Dozens of echoes of PCs and laptops and phones, all grayed out and currently offline. Security cameras the same, which really *should* have been on backup power. Simon. Momo. People he wasn't looking for. Not looking for, but a good backup plan just in case.

And there. Anesh and Alanna. James tapped their mental shoulders, and accepted their open invitation to join the call.

And then he was three people.

There was one Anesh in the building. He was in the back area warehouse, taking cover behind an increasingly furious Pendragon. They had their situation mostly in hand, and after they mopped up, Pendragon and Dave were going to start evacuating people. There were, in theory, two other Aneshes out in the world. So even if this Anesh went down, he wasn't dead. It was a terrifying thought and it didn't make him more comfortable with the violence at all.

There was only one Alanna. She was in the stairwell to the Research basement, and she was getting her ass kicked.

James breathed out, and let go of his own ego for a hair's breadth. Just long enough to become one person with Alanna, feeding her the martial arts skills and the few purple orbs that would transfer this way that he'd picked up over the last year. The two of them abruptly turned the close-quarters beating into a real brawl, and not just four people pinning one twenty-something woman against a stairwell landing and beating her to death.

Anesh added his own abilities, and the three of them, in one body, caught an incoming baton. Turned it into a flip, broke someone's arm. Held up their own arm to ward off incoming small arms fire. Kicked an armored bastard down the stairs when they fumbled a heavier gun out, fell backward from the momentum, swept someone else's leg on the way down, and landed with a bounce that hurt but made popping back up possible.

It was a fight, but there were more people coming down the stairs, and it was becoming one-sided.

Alanna's body had a telepad on it. The parts of the mind that were James and Anesh were screaming at her to use it, but the part that was Alanna knew that she couldn't let them get past her. Research wasn't full of people who could fight, it was where the non-combatants had retreated to. It was vulnerable, and it was more valuable than any one of her.

James and Anesh disagreed. But the whole of them knew it was true.

Then Alanna's body took a rifle stock to the forehead in a ferocious strike that rattled her physical brain so hard that her conscious self dropped out of their link, leaving her body moving awkwardly as James and Anesh's minds struggled to work the unfamiliar limbs. Like a dissociative episode, but while being clubbed to death.

Last line of defense or not, she wasn't getting back up. And without her help, piloting her body was a losing fight either way. Anesh's mind grabbed onto her limbs as strongly as he could. Not sure what was about to happen, he shoved James off the link, just in case he went along for the ride. Then he made Alanna's hand grab the telepad from a pocket without looking at it; scratched out a single word on the thing, and then ripped the page.

Both Alanna and Anesh dropped off the local network, leaving James dazed for a few seconds as they vanished from his digital vision. He tilted forward in real space, almost falling out of his cover. But James wasn't worried; he'd caught Anesh's intentions in the last moment, and he had faith in his partner.

"Hey!" James shouted toward the door, not bothering to pull the Wi-Fi braid out of his neck. "I desire to communicate!"

"N . . ." The shooter suppressing him started to reply, and in that moment of distraction, Anesh appeared almost right on top of him, in the process of lunging to plunge the chipped blade of a sword through his back and lung. Since shield bracers even on automatic always took one strike from a new source to adapt, Anesh made his a good one.

"Come on," Anesh said, stepping back into the hallway. "We've got . . ."

The sniper's bullet threaded through the high windows around the cafeteria, over the skirmish there that was mostly out of sight to them, and hit Anesh in the upper right arm. The high-caliber bullet fragmented as it rent a path through his muscle and bone, into his torso, through his lung and heart, and out through his ribcage, leaving a gaping, ragged wound. The body was dead from shock before it hit the ground.

James screamed something even he didn't know the words to. Scrambling across the bathroom floor to his boyfriend's corpse, he dragged Anesh back onto the tile flooring, futilely checking for a pulse. Intellectually, he knew that there were more Aneshes. His partner wasn't "dead." But seeing this . . . James would be having nightmares for weeks. If he lived through this at all.

"There is no time," Secret whispered to him.

James nodded. He knew. He lay what was left of this body down on the floor, blood pooling beneath it and sticking to his hands. Grabbing one of the paper towels on the bathroom sink, he wiped off what he could, and then pulled what was left of the blood-soaked telepad out of his partner's pocket.

Behind the sniper on the roof of the building next door to this one, he wrote. These things required line of sight if you were going to be that vague, but that was fine. James could *technically* accommodate that.

James took a moment to grab the gun bracelet and shield bracer off the dead agent, snarled at the lack of Bind Weapon charges, took the agent's hefty submachine gun too, and then, as ready as he could get, poked his head around the corner so he could see up through the high window over the dining room, and ripped the page without bothering to let his eyes try to focus on the distant shapes.

Graham looked up from the bedsheets he was staring at. He wasn't in bed, really; just kind of sitting on it, thinking. Everyone thought that he'd completely shut down, but he hadn't really. He needed time to think. To mourn, to grieve, and to drown in the ocean of guilt he'd created for himself.

Everyone here tried to talk to him. Tried to make him feel like it was okay, like he could go back to daily life. But how? He'd done the worst thing possible; he'd killed his best friend, and hundreds of other people. He was a *monster*.

And he needed some time to come to grips with that.

It didn't really feel like anything he could ever do would help set the balance right. He could start working with the Order of Endless Rooms, sure, but they . . . they were heroes, weren't they? He didn't belong here as anything other than a prisoner. He could try to be a vigilante or something; he'd seen Batman, he knew how things probably worked. But the last time he and his friends had tried that . . .

And now he was the only one left.

So when the explosions started, Graham just kind of shrugged it off and didn't bother getting up. Weird stuff happened around here all the time. But when the screaming and the sounds of gunfire made it into his well-appointed basement prison cell, he knew something was wrong. When the lights went off, he knew something was *extra* wrong.

When he heard the barked orders from just outside his door, his mind started to wake up.

They were under attack. The Order was, anyway. But—and Graham knew this for a fact—they were the good guys, right? So, who would be attacking them?

It sounded like they were in trouble.

Maybe. Maybe this was . . . his chance to help? He had a dungeon skill book, he'd been in a couple fights. He could do this, at least. Be part of the defense. Maybe he . . . maybe, just maybe, he could find some measure of redemption.

Graham opened his unlocked prison door, one hand on the wooden quarterstaff someone had left leaning against the wall last time anyone was down here to try to chat with him. And a woman in a black ski mask, tactical helmet, and night vision goggles fluidly pivoted and shot him three times in the head.

Graham died ready to save everyone, including himself, but too late to do anything but fall to the floor.

An armored human cleared the door with a professional series of motions, gun up. They were aiming for humans, though, so their one shot went over Spire-Cast-Behind's head. Then they were frozen. It took a half second for the shield bracer to swap to a camraconda's stare.

In that time, eight broadhead brass fangs stabbed into an exposed neck, only a few bending or breaking on the armor as the camraconda lashed forward, and two hundred and eight pounds of malevolent artificial life twisted and flung herself backward, body slamming her paralyzed victim's face into the floor even as she ripped flesh apart in a spray of blood that tasted vile on a tongue that had grown used to delicious cooked food.

Spire-Cast-Behind checked the door, and the woman she had just savaged twitched. Fighting through the paralytic venom and free from the gaze, she drew a holdout pistol and leveled it at the back of the camraconda's head with a shaking hand.

Then she locked up again as her assailant turned a contemptuous camera eye back on her. Spire-Cast-Behind bit down on a gloved hand, shaking her head back and forth to saw her teeth into tendons and muscle. When she pulled back with a wrench this time, she took two fingers and a gun with her, spitting them out to the other side of the room and letting the now fully disarmed woman bleed out behind her.

Also behind her were four other camracondas. Ones that, like her, had spent years without seeing any conflict. But unlike her, ones that had never fought of their own volition. Never fought humans. And now, weren't *ready* for this.

Not that she was ready for this herself. But that didn't matter. There were more enemies in her home.

Spire-Cast-Behind was unhappy.

Her voice had been unplugged, so she hissed loudly at the others. Indicated to Outline-of-Green that they should stay here, watch the door, gang up on anything that came in. Then she ran her long and flexible tongue over her remaining fangs, and pulled in a breath of air with an internal whir.

She was needed, somewhere.

Deb slumped against a hallway wall, in the middle of a ring of three camracondas.

Around them, coming from both sides of the hallway, were people with guns. Men and women, at least some of them absolutely from Status Quo, who were here apparently just to annihilate the Order. They had bigger guns, better coordination, more numbers, and the element of surprise. It didn't matter that some of them were barely-professional hired muscle, they'd swarmed into the basement early and organized resistance wasn't on the table down here. Status Quo was winning.

For some reason, that thought was mildly surprising to Deb. Maybe it was the blood loss she was currently experiencing. She'd been shot at a couple times so far, and hit once. Nothing lethal, yet, but it was inconvenient, and she hadn't actually used enough purples to have some kind of mutant healing power. Again, yet.

Maybe not ever now.

But it felt weird. The Order were supposed to be better. Heroic. Undefeatable. Or maybe that sort of hubris was why this was happening in the first place. Maybe they should have just killed every member of Status Quo at the time. Deb wouldn't have agreed, though, and she was glad the choice hadn't been put forward.

She wanted to be a doctor. A healer. The Hippocratic Oath wasn't exactly a binding legal force anymore, but Deb still felt like the spirit of it had value, and she made it clear to everyone that this spirit overrode anything else for her. And in her wildest dreams, she'd never expected James to just agree, and then start brainstorming some kind of similar oath for the Order itself. One that put life over convenience, ethics over wants.

And for them, she'd violated the Hippocratic Oath a half-dozen times. She'd done harm, intentionally and viciously. And she'd do it again, to get to the world the Order wanted to build. If she could just find the strength to stand, she'd stab every one of the frozen gunmen around their last stand.

But she couldn't. Her right leg wouldn't support her weight right now, which was annoying, because it meant a perfectly good window of opportunity was being wasted.

"Am sorry." The digital voice of her partner, her unexpected sparkling joy of a lover, met Deb's ears. The hallway was quiet, for now. Until the camracondas got too tired to keep up their stares on multiple targets, and the bullets cut them down.

"Why?" Deb asked Frequency-of-Sunlight.

"Let us down," Frequency said, the small speakers sewn into the lining of her leather coat expressing more sorrow than you'd think a digitized voice could.

What a name, Deb thought, for someone who'd only recently forged their new identity, their persona for the world at large to see, and done so entirely because they loved the colors of the sunset. What a person. What a bizarre life Deb herself had led, to go so far thinking everything was so normal, and then to end up . . . here.

Would her father approve of her choices? Would her mother understand why she'd done what she'd done? Deb probably wouldn't ever know. They remembered her, which was more of a boon than most people who'd been saved from the Office got, but she just hadn't told them everything. Or anything. How do you have that conversation?

"Dad," she'd say, "Mom. I'm a lesbian. And also a wizard. And a doctor-slash-mechanic. And my girlfriend is a snake. Happy Thanksgiving? I brought cornbread." And then, somehow, she'd end up sitting on the couch in her grandma's living room while her aunt made impossibly awkward small talk with Sunny and her cousins asked her equally impossible embarrassing questions. It would be great.

Deb started giggling. Laughing so loud some of the camracondas twitched, but didn't dare break line of sight on their targets. The laughter rapidly turned to sobs, tears streaming down her face as she fought for breath, manic giggling and crying overwhelming her. It was all so *mad*, she thought.

Tilting herself over, Deb wrapped her arms around Frequency's tail. "It's not your fault," she said simply, her voice shockingly level. "I wish . . . I just wish we'd had more time."

Frequency-of-Sunlight wished she could look at her human. "I too," she spoke sadly.

Deb looked up at the people, the monsters, who meant to kill them all. Frozen in place, fingers on their triggers. It wouldn't be long now. But it was okay. She'd said her goodbye. And she'd die here, with the person she loved.

Most people never got that.

Also, the person she loved was a snake, and that thought would have her dying with a wild grin. One last *screw you* to the people who'd come to their home and started shooting.

Or maybe not the very last. Deb shoved herself up to one knee and grabbed the nearest solid object from the box of junk they were still cleaning out of this place. She couldn't stand, but as long as she didn't break line of sight, she could at least start doing *something.*

In a different basement, a pair of people who were admittedly not in the best shape of their lives led a trio of gunmen on a loop around a series of concrete hallways. Reed and Nik ran like everything in the world depended on it, because right now, it kind of *did.*

Gunfire sounded behind them, Reed flinching and covering his head as he blindly threw himself forward, a noise halfway between a scream and a wail coming out of his mouth. Half the shots hit the wall behind them, but some got close enough that Nikhail's shield bracer lit up.

"Muh . . . nah . . . noh . . ." Nik panted as he sprinted, trying desperately to say that he was out of shield charges. Which was pretty high up the list of problems going on right now.

As the duo turned the last corner, bringing them back to where they'd been when their attackers had almost gotten the drop on them, the hallway ahead seemed to ripple. From out of the door to one of the small rooms they used for special projects, one of the attackers slid backward, pulled along by the concrete itself, desperately looking around to figure out what was happening as the floor grabbed their ankles and smoothly directed them backward.

Reed wasn't sure if he should slow down to wait until the attacker raised their gun and pointed it back into the room. He still didn't know what to do, but Nik put on an extra burst of speed. At the same time, the shooter was slammed through a stack of cardboard boxes and into the far wall, the concrete turning liquid to accept them like being buried under the basement was exactly where they belonged. But before the flowing stone could actually kill them, they pulled the trigger on their submachine gun, and sprayed fire into the room.

A woman screamed, a voice Reed had never heard make that noise but he was pretty sure was someone he worked with, and the concrete stopped moving. The gunman was struggling to pull themselves out of their half-complete prison, and seeing Nik coming only intensified their efforts to snap off the thin bands of solidified concrete that had wrapped around their ankles and shoulders.

Nikhail went for the gun right as the attacker started shooting again. The weapon pointed nowhere in particular, sending bullets bouncing around the hall in wild ricochet, until Nik used his better leverage and arms with an actual range of motion to wrench their enemy's hand hard enough to crush their fingers, pulled the SMG away as far as it would go with the strap trapped in the wall, and unloaded it into the masked face.

It took a few seconds for the fight to go from start to bloody finish, and in that time, their pursuers were catching up. Reed, panting with exhaustion and wishing he'd actually spent the last few months since being rescued actually exercising with the others, slapped Nikhail loosely on the shoulder as he ran by at a staggering speed. They were almost there.

Someone else shot at them, and Reed felt one of the bullets pull at the curls of his hair. He'd almost died, and he was going to almost die again if he didn't *move*.

The two of them crashed through the center of the ring of desks, Nik tripping over loose cables and sending someone's laptop spinning off onto the floor when he yanked his way through. That might have been Reed's laptop, and he didn't care. The two of them hit the far door to the secure vault, one on each side, gasping for breath as they raced to punch in the codes without fumbling the numbers.

The door hissed open as someone shot Reed in the back. The bullet hitting him had bounced off a wall to do it, wasn't actually aimed at him, and didn't do more than crush flesh in a way that would leave a massive bruise. But it still hurt like hell, and he screamed himself hoarse as he and Nik shoved their way into the space.

They didn't close the door behind them. They were headed deeper in. Past the rows of shelves and the precious things they stored, to a second door and a full-length window of security glass.

Where the floor met the wall, a small cat paced back and forth. Almost a kitten really, but it had been growing up nicely. It meowed at them as they approached, an indignant little sound as the pair rushed forward.

It wasn't real.

Nik hit the panel by the door and started punching in the code, while Reed dropped to his knees, crawling behind a shelf and facing the cat, struggling to catch his breath.

"I don't . . . I don't know if you can hear . . . hear me. Like this." He gasped out words as he tried to speak softly to the illusory feline. "But . . . uh . . ." What were you even supposed to say in a situation like this? "Please don't eat us," Reed settled on. And then his legs started shaking so badly that he found he couldn't get up again, so he just scooted back to put as much of himself in the shadow of the shelf as he could, while Nik pulled the heavy secure door open.

Shouts came from the door to the vault, one man barking orders to the others to keep alert as they swept the area for the two men they were hunting. The false cat on the floor tilted its head and started padding forward on tiny feet, Nik pressing back against the wall by the door involuntarily as something pushed against him. And then someone spotted Nik and tried to shoot him.

The bullets left puffs of red in the air where they hit the invisible true form of the growing kitten, the blood fading to invisibility rapidly. The cat the size of Reed's car didn't roar, but the little one ahead of it gave the angriest meow anyone in the room had ever heard, loud enough to echo over the gunshots.

The cat ran forward, and one of the agents tried to shoot it, bullets bouncing off the tile floor, before the *real* cat slammed into the first one and smashed him to the ground. An unseen claw gutted another, and when the third started firing behind himself as he ran, he just opened himself up to being pounced on.

The small vision of the cat licked its paw, matching the sight over its head of a large splotch of floating human blood being slowly cleaned away. Then the cat stood up, tail raised, and strutted away.

". . . Did we just make everything worse?" Nik asked as he finally caught his breath.

James appeared on the rooftop behind the sniper, snapping the air around him with the smell of blood and the pressure of his arrival. He had the confiscated gun up and braced on his shoulder as he took his other hand away from the telepad in his coat pocket, adjusted toward his target in a split second as his Aim told him where he needed to keep it level.

She was faster. James caught sight of gray hair under a black baseball cap before the old woman tossed *something* out of her left hand that glittered like broken glass over her shoulder, not even sparing a contemptuous look for the idiot teleporting in right behind her.

Suddenly, James was standing back in the bathroom. Same pose as he'd been on the roof, but with the feeling of being dragged *backward* lurching in his stomach and thoughts swirling in his head making him confused if he had actually teleported out at all. He spun, looking around confusedly. Something had changed.

"I am going to be violently ill," Secret hissed at him, still coiled around James's shoulder. "She attempted to reset you, but I have held your thoughts in place. Somewhat."

"Okay, fine," James snarled. "We'll try it again." He checked the shield bracer he was wearing;

[Stockpile *"Mimic Temporal Displacement"*—19—709 / 22,000—4:12:59 (41) <A>

Battlefield Alteration—4—199 / 1,000—1:01:22 (2) <A>]

Already switched over to what he needed, James killed the automatic on the Alteration; he'd turn it to what he *really* needed when it mattered. And two charges left to switch to what he needed afterward. Forty shields left, too. He'd need to finish this before too much more automatic weapons fire came his way.

James pulled out the telepad, dismayed to see that it only had one page left. Apparently him being rewound through space and time hadn't refunded him any resources used. He pulled out a pen from a coat pocket and thought for a second before beginning to write.

Slightly to the left of the sniper on the roof of the building next to this one.

He took a deep breath. Peeked around the corner, through the upper window. Tore the telepad and appeared with a pop that overlapped with the sound of the woman's rifle barking as she tried to take his head off. But James wasn't there anymore.

James and Secret cracked into existence on the roof, and James pulled the trigger before the woman could readjust her magic or pivot her gun around. The first burst of bullets splashed against her own shield, and then, James's bracer flared light around him as a spray of hostile spellcasting distorted the air and crashed into it. He couldn't feel it, but it looked like someone had compressed a sliver of time into a ball and then forgotten about it in the fridge for a month or two. It was ugly, looked like someone had broken reality itself, and only lasted a second against the shield. He kept shooting.

"Stop!" the woman yelled over the gunfire, and James felt it was more than just a request; it was a *command*, and not one given to him. Something flashed into being, and then Secret caught it. Somehow, her speech had a direction to it, and Secret took the hit meant for James; a claw like a link of chain, in green ghostly light, curled around the infomorph as the authority the old woman called upon hit the first target it ran into.

The woman pivoted, bringing her own sidearm up, leaving the long-barreled sniper rifle braced on a bipod on the ledge of the roof. James saw it, recognized it, and switched his shield to .45 just in time to catch two bullets.

He lashed out with his blue orb, using precision and a tiny target zone to minimize the headache, and turned the tendons in the woman's right knee to glass. Something in his left ear popped anyway, and he felt blood start dripping out of it.

As she finished her pivot, already in motion, the glass in her leg cracked, exploded into shards, and she toppled sideways. But she didn't stop shooting. And with her free hand, she made a motion that grabbed the side of James's shoes from across the roof and *yanked* at thin air. He, too, fell backward, slamming his head against an HVAC unit and slumping on the gravel surface of the roof. He also didn't stop shooting, gun bucking wildly in his hand as he tried to keep it pointed her direction.

The woman yelled a countermand to her Authority. "Let it go! Now's as good a time as any! Coordinate the others, purge the building!" Secret jerked as he was abruptly freed, the heavy green spectral form surging backward, and then off the roof, vanishing as it overlapped the Lair in a strange optical illusion that made it hard to tell how large it was.

But there was still a fight going on. Both of them burned through charges on items like they were water. James didn't know how many shield uses she had left, but he knew that his were counting down. Thirty; he rained bullets down on where he was sure her position was. Twenty; the dome of light around him was blinding, and he couldn't see anything past it, only the golden glare. Ten; James felt his heart pounding. He swept his fire left and right, panicking. But he didn't stop. His gun bracelet had two more ammo refills, and he didn't have time for any of them.

Five. James heard someone yelling at him. Four. They could negotiate. Three. Their organization had room for competent agents. Two. He missed what they said here.

One.

The enemy's shield shattered at the same time James's did. Both of them still laid with their backs against something, firing into each other like it was the last thing they'd ever do. Except James's opponent, enhanced or not, looked like she was sixty years old, and there was only so much that you could do against automatic fire when your shield ran out.

He tilted his head back in the sudden silence as her gun listed out of her hand and clattered onto the gravel, looking up at the stars.

"We don't negotiate with terrorists," he said, voice hoarse. Then he coughed, and tasted blood.

James looked down. There was a hole in his shirt. That was bad.

"Secret," he said. "Secret," James spoke up, and felt the tugging pain at his skin start to set in. In the distance, he could hear gunfire from the Lair, but there was something else too. A tangible feeling of oppression surged through the air; the sensation of an Authority at work. What had she been yelling? *Coordinate?* Probably not just one Authority then.

The fight wasn't over. He could also hear screams, which were never good, and sirens, which were *probably* for them, but were too late no matter whose side they'd end up being on.

Secret, no longer pinned down by the Authority, dragged his injured form over to where James lay. "I am here. Always."

"I . . . I think I'm out," James whispered, closing his eyes and trying to hold the cold terror away. "Get going. Go help them. Tell Anesh and Alanna I loved them. And you. Always." It wasn't working. He was scared. Not that he expected anything else.

"I can not leave," Secret whispered back. "Not now."

"They're dying, Secret," James said, shifting his shoulders against the air conditioning unit. Damn whoever built these things for not considering how uncomfortable they'd be to lean on. "You can't be waiting for me to die."

The pale blue serpent tried to shake his head, but couldn't. "No, this thing, it has injured me. And even if I could move . . . I am weak. I've done too much, too often. It is too late for me to tether myself to structured knowledge, and there are no large secrets to break for a moment's power. I am as helpless as you."

James thought for a second, feeling his blood already starting to clot. He healed faster than most humans ever would, but he knew it wouldn't be enough. Not for this. His heart screamed with every beat; he'd been hit somewhere too important this time. Maybe he'd actually been shot in his heart itself, but he wasn't dying quick enough for that. It was an oddly clinical thought to have in the moment.

"Take what you need from me," he said softly.

Secret balked. "What?" he asked, knowing damn well what James had meant, and was asking.

"They are *dying*," James screamed, rough and wet. "Our friends! Our family! And I'm going out anyway! So . . . so do what you know you were made to do. Dig in. Take whatever you need to out of my head, and use it to save who you can!" James sobbed suddenly. "I'm dead anyway, and I don't believe in anything after. My soul is one of two things; gone, or *ammunition*."

The two of them locked eyes. Secret stared into James's with a dozen of his own, struggling to put right the cracked scales the Authority had left across his manifested body.

James broke the eye contact first, looking over to where the old woman . . . it had been Marion, hadn't it? . . . twitched slightly. Ah, that was it. He propped his gun up on his knee, and emptied it into her body. Her Authority scattered to the winds, a burst of green light cascading from where it was hovering over the Lair with her now-actual death. But he hadn't noticed fast enough, and whatever it was doing, it had already started. "No excuses," James whispered. "Get on with it. I'll . . . maybe I'll see you again someday."

He closed his eyes.

Secret didn't. He looked up. Up at the stars, at the sky, at the shape of the world around them. He looked through himself, at the idea that he was, and the people who dreamed him.

He could do it. He could tear James's mind apart, and burn long enough to fight back.

Or he could do something else.

"Here." James cracked one eye as something dropped into his lap. It was a yellow orb; a large one, too. It had fallen from where Secret had formed himself into a figure eight overhead, and was slowly looping on himself. "A gift, I had forgotten to pass on. You aren't dead yet. Stop giving up on yourself, and I never will either."

And then, Secret *pulled*.

There were so many people who knew him now. He had friends. He had family. He had peers, in the form of other infomorphs, and parents, in the form of James and Anesh. There were dreamers across the country who had seen him briefly, who he'd talked to in those moments of passing sleep. There were members of the Order, human and otherwise, who willingly gave his Self a place to be. There were students and teachers who owed him their lives, who spoke silent prayers to him when they thought he wouldn't hear. Researchers who thought he was fascinating, knights who thought he was strange even by their standards, and simple normal people who thought he could maybe be a friend. There were also some federal government employees who knew of him, and were terrified, but apprehensive about it.

Secret gathered them up, found all the threads, and yanked.

The weak ones came first. Little moments, little dreams of something blue, something with a lot of eyes. Something friendly. He took it in like water, filling his form, solidifying himself. Then, the outliers. Those who thought he was a threat, those who thought he was a parasite. He took those too, grew himself more fangs. Then . . . those closer. He couldn't stop now, or it would be for nothing. The Order. Alex thought he was cute. Nate thought he was hilarious in a bitterly ironic way. Randall . . . Secret couldn't find Randall. There were missing connections. The dead and lost.

He ate the memories of himself.

It wasn't enough. He kept going, pressing them down into himself, the pressure of *who* and *what* and *why* he was growing stronger and stronger as he stole from the people who made him those things. Alanna was next, along with Dave and JP. Pendragon and Rufus and Ganesh. The camracondas who thought he was like them, but secretly knew the truth.

It wasn't *enough*.

Secret gave in. He held nothing back. He latched onto James, and every eye he had focused down on his friend and father as he took, and took, and *took*. Why was he? Who was he?

None of it mattered to James. Secret didn't need a reason to exist, he just needed to be loved. And in that moment, as James screamed at him from the rooftop before forgetting why he had been so upset in the first place, Secret understood.

He was himself. Finally. Every part of him collected into one physical place, save for those he could not locate.

There was a form of ignition. And then, a new form of matter, the likes of which had never before existed on this world, sparked into being.

Secret was not made of solid, or liquid, or gas. Plasma or gel or Bose-Einstein condensate. He was made, now, of an idea. Literal physically earthed information, given purpose and brought into reality by sheer density of ego. Unstable in the extreme; he knew he had only minutes to live now. Untethered to any one person, answerable to no gods or kings. Secret was here, and everywhere. Something new, and something horribly glorious.

He had left himself a note.

The new creature wasted no time following the directives it had given itself, the purpose that had been laid down. It identified the intercessors that were attacking the Order of Endless Rooms, and it reached out to them, and it *bit*.

Every living thing within fifty miles shivered, twitched, and screamed, as they all felt the presence of fangs in the dark.

Secret's teeth found purchase in his target, and he paused. The lines and threads reached down to the people, yes, but they also reached upward. And he didn't wait or think about it; he clawed his way up the ladder, and shredded it as he went. Mauling away at the very concept of the thing that was Status Quo, all the way to the top.

The first thing that happened in the Lair, as far as anyone knew, was that the enemy lost unit cohesion. They stopped flanking, stopped firing in waves. The Authorities that had swarmed out and tipped every ongoing fight in a single massive strike splintered and dropped, before dying so thoroughly no one remembered they were there. Then the invaders started yelling at each other. One of them panicked, made as if to shoot one of her teammates. But the finger never made it to the trigger.

Because the next thing that happened was that every single one of them dropped like a puppet with their strings cut.

They forgot, for a moment, that they even existed. Their hearts stopped beating, their lungs stopped pumping. Their brains just . . . shut off.

Six hundred miles away, the single Status Quo team on remote assignment dropped dead in the middle of a Denny's.

On the other side of the planet, a contractor who still had some loyalty to his employers suddenly collapsed, toppling out of his surveillance perch.

In a warded room in the basement of the Pentagon, a man almost no one knew existed ceased to be midway through a meeting.

And then, with a defiant scream that cut through the air like a blade, Secret reached up to the top of the chain overhead, the unblinking red construct staring down at him and his family like a twisted ethereal voyeur. The *concept* of Status Quo, the unifying idea that had grown and propagated this organization in this place at this time. The structure, the ideology, the knowledge, all of it revealed to him as a single thing that was no longer abstract at all. And he ripped it apart.

Everything, suddenly, went quiet.

Secret came back to himself slowly, the power he held now burning too hot. He was eating himself away, and suddenly realized *who* he was, not just what he was supposed to do. He . . . Had he helped? Was he a monster now? Secret couldn't tell. He'd lost something critical, and his body—his *actual* body—was dying for it.

He opened his mouths, and tried to speak. To say anything else to James. To anyone. "Remember me," he tried to say. "Remember I love you," Secret screamed inside himself, but nothing came out. "Please . . ." The newly remade Life was breaking apart, fast. Pieces of himself were peeling away, flaring into nothingness with touches of orange and red.

Secret couldn't say anything. He'd cut himself away from them, could barely remember them himself. But it didn't stop the feelings, his *own* feelings, burning hot inside his newfound form. "I . . . I don't want to go," he screamed the words into the void. "I'm scared. And . . . and there was so much left to do . . ."

But he'd known. He'd known what he was doing. And the pact had been signed willingly.

Secret sighed. The destabilization, his approaching death, didn't hurt. It was just . . . another idea. One far stronger than himself, for now. He looked back at the loop of his own tail, seeing the dissolution of his novel flesh in full.

"I burn the color of sunsets," Secret whispered. He thought for a second, as more and more chunks of his self went up in false flames. "There was . . . someone. Someone who would have liked to see that." The serpent shook his head slightly, in a gesture he'd stolen a long time ago from a human of some sort. It shook loose more scales that caught like shooting stars as they turned to nothing on their descent, and it put gaps in his form that the true night sky could be seen through.

And then, the instability took hold. And with nothing more than a satisfied hiss at a task complete, the last of Secret's self rippled into scattered motes of memories and ash.

He had, he decided at the last moment, been *good*.

On a rooftop, James listened to the silence. The only shouts left in the distance were those of people he recognized, organizing medical aid and trying to recover from the attack.

It was over, he thought lightly. "We must have won while I blacked out," he whispered.

James looked down. There was a yellow orb in his hands. He hadn't remembered grabbing one, but he must have had it in his pocket. Blood loss was making him forget things. There was another form of loss, too. The back of his mind was screaming at him that he'd forgotten something, that something was *missing*. But he didn't know what. It just added to the pain in his chest; the familiar tug of depression settling over the unfamiliar feeling of having a bullet lodged in his chest.

He still had a chance.

It didn't take much mental effort these days to absorb a yellow; James just didn't do it often. This one gave him six hours of operational time, and did absolutely nothing for the pain. Nor did it remove the bullet or close the wound. But for those six hours, his body didn't need a lot of the things it normally did, and he *probably* wouldn't die.

He staggered to his feet. He had to do . . . so much. Six hours wasn't going to be enough. James checked his coat pockets, found his car keys still in them. He felt okay enough to drive himself to the hospital. "Alright. Minor surgery, and then I'll come back and make sure everything's okay. No need to get in their way, right?" he said to . . . no one. He was alone on this roof, with a corpse. Of course.

His telepad was gone, which was nearly enough to make him start openly crying in frustration as he realized he was almost stuck up here. But James held it in as he slid over the edge of the roof, into some bushes, and stumbled off into the night, shock and cold anxiety settling over him.

It sounded like they'd won. But he felt more alone than he ever had in his life. He barely even stopped to check in with anyone before he lethargically pulled his car out of the parking lot, the hole in his chest not exactly bleeding, but still shooting with itching pain every time the seatbelt or his shirt pulled across the edges. Someone tried to stop him, but he just brushed it off, not even registering that Deb was trying to flag him down as he turned onto the main road.

His brain tried to organize the future as the familiar rows of orange streetlights passed by overhead. Hospital. Clean up. Rebuild. Rebuild? Was that even possible? Rebuild how? He'd tried to set the foundation for a better world, and it had only taken thirty people with guns and mild magical powers to rip it all down.

James stopped thinking, and just drove. He'd . . . he'd deal with it later. He could deal with everything later.

He wished Anesh and Alanna were here.

He hoped they were alive. He'd call when he got himself checked in. Maybe the doctor who knew him would be willing to type out a text, because James sure didn't feel like he could do that at the moment.

He was so very, very tired.

EPILOGUE

"Yeah, okay," Anesh spoke into his cell phone, standing in the corner of the room where he and a few other people were working. "That's not great news, but it's another check on the list." He sighed. "We've got too many rows in the lost-and-found column these days. Hopefully we can figure this one out sooner rather than later. Or, knowing her, she'll resolve it herself." Anesh waited for the reply, sighed a bit more, and then nodded to himself. "Alright. We'll connect later this week. Good luck."

He hung up, and turned back to the table that looked like someone was trying to transmute a series of wires and circuit boards into some eldritch machine. Around the room, computer screens showed diagnostics and calculations that were being tested, line by line, against reality and the capabilities of the prototype.

One of his new coworkers, a guy who'd actually been saddled with the unfortunate name of John Johnson, nodded at him over a cup of lunchroom coffee. "Personal calls on government time, eh?" His voice was squeaky, and didn't fit the three-hundred-pound bearded programmer at all, but he was friendly enough. "Bold strategy."

"It's my . . . brother," Anesh settled on.

"Oooh, and lying to your project lead! Also bold!" John cocked a finger off his cup and leveled it at Anesh. "Your security clearance makes it clear you have no family. Which is, by the way, weird, and

I've already asked for clarification on it, but I just keep getting emails saying it's fine. You're suspicious, for someone who can do math!"

Anesh winced. "Which part makes it suspicious? Plenty of people are orphans."

"Yeah, that's not what I said. Also, you doing the pause while you try to think of what to call your mystery caller doesn't help." John turned back to his screen, cocked an eyebrow as he noticed something, and hammered out a few hundred keystrokes before nodding smugly to himself and turning back to Anesh. "Unrelated, did you know there's no audio bugs in this room? Just cameras. We do too much testing that interferes with recording equipment anyway. And, you know, I don't care what . . ."

"Oh good god, fine!" Anesh rolled his eyes at the other man, who leaned forward with a giant grin. "I was talking to a duplicate of myself about our girlfriend, who went missing during a misaimed teleport during a firefight three weeks ago. Happy now?"

". . . Um . . ." John paused himself. "You didn't do the thing where you make it clear that's bullshit."

"Yeah, funny about that," Anesh said, smirking. He smothered the amused attitude rapidly. James had infected his brain too much, it seemed. "Look, it's not . . . it won't be a problem, okay? I'm just here to check the equations."

John turned to the whiteboard propped up at the end of the room. Well, the half-dozen whiteboards. They were on wheels, so they could be rotated in and out as needed, and the truly important and correct bits were transferred to hard copy as soon as they were finalized. Roughly half of them contained Anesh's handwriting. "Yeah. *Check.* Sure," he said. "You know, everyone's gossiping about you." John looked around the otherwise empty lab; it was just the two of them, everyone else either long gone home for the night, or out getting yet more coffee. "You showed up basically out of nowhere. And you're not just assigned to some throwaway project, you're working on Psyche with us. Doing orbital launch calculations that most people don't fully get their heads around until they're forty."

"And everyone hates that?" Anesh asked, resigned to it by this point.

"Are you kidding? Kid, you're a mystery, dropped into the laps of people who made it their jobs to find mysteries and shoot them with lasers. You're a gift-wrapped . . . gift."

"That one kinda got away from you."

"Yeah, well." The older man *giggled*, and Anesh tried not to grin at the incongruous sound. "Look, I'm just saying, and you didn't hear it from me, but we've got a betting pool on what your deal is. Genius savant? Spy for the Illuminati? Ghost?"

"Ghost, really?" Anesh couldn't help rise to the bait. "I've shaken hands with . . . actually, wait, no I haven't . . ." He trailed off, remembering the pandemic behavior he'd gotten familiar with. "Okay, ghost is on the table, I suppose."

John pumped a fist in the air. "Yes. Yes! I am going to win that pot!"

"At the risk of sounding suspicious myself, if I turn out not to be a ghost, are you going to murder me and frame it as 'I was dead the whole time'?" Anesh asked him, clearing his throat in a dramatic fashion.

The programmer looked legitimately shocked. "What?! No! That's horrible!"

"Okay, just checking." Anesh sighed. "Sorry, it's . . . it's been a long year."

"With people trying to kill you?!" John stared at him, wide-eyed. He leaned back and tried to laugh it off, but then watched Anesh just turn and look at the whiteboards. Not actually processing the math, just . . . standing. Shoulders slumped, eyes half closed. And in that moment, the kid just looked so, absolutely, *tired*, that John half-believed him.

Then Anesh pulled himself together and had a grin on his face when he turned back. "Hah. Who'd want to kill me? I just do things with numbers so space probes don't crash," he quipped, writing on the board in front of him. Then he paused. "Also, I think I accidentally came up with a solution to one of Hilbert's problems. Which is absolutely not helpful to the targeting program you're trying to write, and I'm not quite sure if this is because I haven't had enough, or have had too much, coffee."

"This is why people want to kill you." John nodded sagely. "How in the hell did you ever pass the security checks to work at NASA?" he asked, legitimately curious.

"The FBI owes me a favor, and my boyfriend is technically in the Air Force," Anesh told him. "And, I mean, when you've got copies of yourself running around, you can spare one to work on a passion project, right?"

If there was one thing that Anesh had learned from James lately, it was this: You could tell someone the truth, to their face. That magic was real, that you were a wizard, that you'd fought a demi-god thing and brought down a shadowy agency that wanted to control the world from behind the scenes. And not a single one of them would believe you, unless they figured it out themselves.

Still, Anesh wasn't just here to have fun. This building, full of some of the smartest and most driven engineers and programmers and scientists in the country, was one of several targets for recruiting that they were looking at drawing from. And yes, many people here were technically members of the Air Force. Many people here were fiercely loyal to their idea of what the United States of America could be, should be, or even just was.

And some people weren't. Or maybe were flexible enough on those loyalties to know that they could change. And for those people, Anesh made sure there were plenty of clues laying around about the existence of his skulljack. Someone would ask him, sooner or later. It was impossible, like John had said, for these people to leave a mystery untouched.

"Uh-oh."

Momo said the words, and everyone nearby flinched. Or dove for cover. It had been that kind of learning experience, lately.

The division of the Order of Endless Rooms that everyone just kind of offhandedly referred to as Research had moved. Probably temporarily, because who knew how long it was safe to stay *anywhere*. But right now, they had a one-month lease on a tiny little office and workshop space that used to be a company that refurbished screen doors. Momo knew this, because the owners of the building hadn't bothered to clear out the machines for refitting that black mesh onto window screens before they'd rented the space again.

So those machines had gotten unplugged, and were now basically just obstacles to the important furniture, which were tables to hold the boxes of stuff they'd salvaged from the basement during their escape.

In her head, she said *they*, but Momo knew that she hadn't really been part of the nightmare scenario that everyone in both basements had gone through. She'd been in a more or less direct fight with people who were doing their best to kill her. And her side had won, before most of them died. But Research?

They weren't really combatants. Not in the same way as everyone else. Oh, sure, most of them had dungeon experience, and when he'd been alive ,Virgil had held an ironclad mentality about dishing out violence to their enemies. Of course, Virgil had been so paranoid he'd actually written a program to capture his mind on a hard drive if his body died, which hadn't saved him in the end, but it was a weird reminder of him to have found that little .exe file, along with a note on how it probably wouldn't work.

Regardless, most people who gravitated to Research were exactly the kind of people you'd expect. The curious and the shy; explorers and scientists. Not warriors.

When Status Quo had stormed through the basement, shooting at anyone who they found, Research had retaliated with sheer panic. An onslaught of blue orbs, dungeon tech, and last-ditch efforts. They'd let the cat out, and mostly just hoped it would kill the other guys first, never assuming that they had a chance to survive at all. When they'd started grouping up and working together, it hadn't taken long for people to start telepading out of the building in chunks. And though a lot of them had been caught by whatever weird Authority thing Status Quo had pulled at the last minute, before *that* effect had been killed off and they'd gotten out, they'd still left behind a scene of chaos and destruction. And also fire.

It was unclear if someone had intentionally blued the fire into existence, or if it was just a side effect, or if it was from something as mundane as trying to bury the invaders in thermite. But regardless, they'd lost track of a *lot* of stuff in the chaos before the attack was over and cleanup could start. Like the cat. Which everyone would awkwardly try to change the subject from, if asked.

So right now, the Research division had their new little space, and a lot of random scorched boxes and damaged objects. And they had spent weeks *sorting*.

They'd only started to really scratch the surface of the Status Quo documents. And at least one of the boxes they'd opened for the first time had been booby-trapped with one of those stupid fucking Authority things, though *trapped* was a stretch, since the thing was a kind of weird infomorph corpse when they found it. There were a dozen theories about what Authorities were, but Momo and Reed had kept everyone on track until they had more time to really worry about it. Which they may never have to; Status Quo, for all intents and purposes, seemed truly dead this time.

So when Momo opened a box, and said the words "Uh-oh," everyone had what amounted to an allergic reaction to the phrase.

"It's fine, guys!" Momo said from behind a table she'd flipped over halfway across the room, after the box failed to explode. "Not a bomb! Probably!" She rose from her position, and cautiously approached.

Inside the box was some kind of hexagonal prism. Only it wasn't really a hexagon, because it had too many sides. But they were all hexagonal sides. But they were . . .

Momo looked away, blinking her eyes and trying to stop her brain from shooting spikes of pain through her eyes. "Okay, ow. Reed, Nikhail, Taste-of-Air, Andy, you guys wanna take a look at this?"

"Will it kill us?" Nikhail called politely, still pressed up against the wall on the other side of the door to the room.

"It didn't kill me, and that's probably a good sign!" Momo answered cheerfully.

Reed stood up and plodded over, running a hand through his curly hair. "You know, you run so many totems at once, your brain is probably either immune to a lot of stuff, or damaged to the point that some memetic stuff probably doesn't work on you."

"Bah!" Momo stuck her tongue out at him. "I fixed the brain damage thing!" She did not say the second part out loud, which was, "Probably." She also didn't add that the infomorphs and memetic hazards didn't seem to work that way at all, and someone suffering from brain damage would probably be *more* at risk, not less.

Reed looked into the box, and rapidly got a migraine of his own. But he tried to get past the impossible geometry, and focus. The object was a series of hexes, all linked to each other, and all of them . . . containing something. There was a small indentation in each of them that held some kind of object, but it was intensely hard to actually focus on what they were. "Someone get me a pair of pliers or something. Tongs, of some variety," he said, holding out his hand and waiting for someone to brave getting close enough to hand him the tool.

With only mild trepidation, he reached into the box, and tried to drag out the edge of one of the objects. To both his surprise, and Momo's, it popped out with a smooth motion, enlarging back to what felt like a reality-approved size as it did so.

He dropped it to the table, and both of them looked at it. It was a rectangle of laminated plastic. An ID card of some kind, complete with one of those little metal clips so it could hang on a pocket.

"That's weird. Do you recognize this person?" Reed asked, trying to comprehend the name and face on the card.

"Shit. Stand back," Momo told him. Not urgently, just with a resigned sense that she knew what was going on. With the hand that she wasn't using to push Reed away, she dipped into her pocket and set a trio of small spheres on the table.

These were the height of her knowledge of how to start abusing red orbs. The fingernail-sized dots of power, contained inside a machine-cut web of steel, copper, and wood lines. All of those lines were broken just ever so slightly on the screw of the orb's shell. All she had to do was twist them into place, and they'd snap back to life; imparting knowledge in a radius. A *small* radius, one of the things she was learning to control a bit better as time went on.

Momo turned the totems into position, and let the information flood her brain. It didn't even phase her at all, anymore. And it only took her a minute or so to nod, and look up at the rest of the team. "There's a hole in the record here," Momo told them.

"Someone erased?" Taste-of-Air asked, the camraconda daring the totems more easily than the human members of Research. "One of ours?"

"No, I think . . . I think this guy used to work for Status Quo. I think they *all* did." Momo reached in with her bare hands, ignoring the caution Reed had shown, and started plucking more ID cards off the artifact. "Yeah. These are all . . . blanks. Mostly. The totems are picking something up, but not . . . Yeah, someone fucked these guys up." She sighed. "Which tracks. I just wish I knew *what*. Did *we* do this?"

The Research team collectively shivered. One of the things they'd done recently had been to create a set of guidelines and ethics, added to the operations manual for their division. And one of the first things that *everyone* had agreed to was this: no memetic weaponry. No infobombs, no idea guns, no identity erasers or persona blankers or *whatever* dumb sci-fi idea they could think up.

Had they violated that rule?

They couldn't know, could they?

"Well, shit," someone in the room muttered.

"So, what's the hex thing actually do?" Reed asked, curious.

"I dunno, let's put something else in it," Momo said, suddenly excited. "It sorta spatially suctions the ID cards into itself; I bet we can put other things in there!"

"Alright, here." Nikhail dug out his driver's license and handed it over.

Momo eyed him incredulously. "Nnnnnno. No," she said. "Aren't you supposed to be *smart*? No. We're starting with an unlabeled rock that no one has actually touched, and we'll go from there, okay?"

Red-faced with embarrassment, Nik stuck his ID back into his wallet. "Ahem. Yes, of course. I was . . . testing . . ."

"My dude." Reed patted him on the shoulder. "Quit while you're behind. I'll go get us a rock."

"That's why Reed's in charge of this outfit!" he heard Momo calling after him as he left the room.

"James?"

The call came from a young woman in worn slacks and her arm in a sling. Hair cut back short after part of it had to be removed so she could get stitches a couple of weeks ago. Deb stepped down the stairs to one of the basements of the Lair, the way lit by strands of Christmas lights hooked up to a generator somewhere; the main power still hadn't been fixed.

She passed a landing that still had visible blood splatters on it. One of them in particular around a section of the concrete wall had a spiderweb of cracks radiating out from an impact. An impact she suspected had been from someone's face, propelled by Alanna's arm.

It still smelled like smoke, and every step echoed like gunfire.

"James, are you down here? Anesh said you were . . . around here somewhere," she called through the hallways.

The basement was too large, and it gave her the creeps. Especially after having almost died in here.

Deb navigated her way through the halls, trying to ignore the memory of dragging corpses up the stairs to stack them up in the warehouse. Stripping men and women of armor and weaponry before Pendragon had ferried them out to unceremoniously dump them in the ocean like they were just debris and not the remnants of people. It had been very, *very* hard to think of them as people, and that wasn't a metaphor; something had ripped away the sense of personhood from their enemies. It was still a challenge to think of them in the present tense even, though fortunately remembering what Status Quo was and had done still worked fine.

She ran across James before she could throw up from it all. A mild blessing.

"Fuck," he was muttering to himself when she found him. James was currently wearing a stained white lab coat and a pair of safety goggles as he dripped something from an eyedropper onto a pane of glass. "Well, I think that worked," he said, glancing up as Deb stepped into the open area. "Hey. What's up?"

"I was going to ask you the same thing. What's all this?" She motioned around the space that had previously been a small lounge area, before being turned into a gold-mining operation, before James had occupied it for whatever the hell he was doing now.

"Oh, I'm making drugs. And down here was closer to the generator, so the cord doesn't have to go as far. I didn't want to go buy more extension cords," he answered, like that explained anything.

"James . . ." Deb started, and then trailed off. What was she even supposed to say here? "Anesh is worried about you. Sarah's worried about you. We're all worried about you. What's going on? You had a bullet pulled out of your chest, and you're walking around. This is not a good idea."

James looked up. He had dark rings around his eyes, visible even through the goggles. He looked like he hadn't slept in weeks, and Deb was willing to be part of the smell down here was his fault too. "Like I said, I'm making drugs." He tried to smile, but it withered on his lips as he listlessly looked back down at the desk he was using, covered in lab glass. "Okay, so, the actual explanation?"

"Please," Deb said, using a foot to turn one of the leather lounge chairs toward him and settling down, trying to ignore the grinding motor sound of the nearby generator.

"So, I'm depressed," James started.

Deb was by no means a mental health expert. But she still knew enough to suppress the urge to roll her eyes. "Understandable. We just . . . lost a lot," she settled on.

"No, I mean . . . How the fuck do I explain this . . .?" James looked around. "Okay, you know how when we rescued you guys the first time, Sarah was in your group?"

"Yeah, I . . . Oh hey, I never really thought of that. You two were friends before, right? That's a coincidence." Deb nodded.

James shrugged. "Probably. Or it's something else. Doesn't matter. The point is, when Sarah was *gone*, but I didn't realize she was gone, my depression got measurably worse. The symptoms of withdrawal from a relationship, Lua called it. I might not be able to think about her, but my body knew something was wrong."

"That's horrible!" Deb brought one hand up to her mouth. "But, wait, you rescued her! Did that fix it?"

"Sort of. But that's both a deeply convoluted personal story, and also not the point," James said with a heavy sigh. "The point is . . . I feel that way again. Which . . . which . . ." He balled his hands into fists on the table, before pulling the goggles away to wipe at tears that came unbidden. He took a shuddering breath, and let it out slowly. "Which means it happened again. Probably."

Deb inhaled sharply. "To wh—Oh."

"Exactly. So I'm making drugs."

"That . . ."

"Oh, right. Um, there should be a thing on it in the operations manual under the section labeled *Theories and Wild Ass Guesses*," James said. "We've speculated for a little while that LSD is a form of mnestic, allowing people to recover otherwise blocked or damaged memories. Even supernaturally so. So . . ."

"So you're in the basement of a building that was recently a warzone, making LSD," Deb finished. "Got it." James sighed again. He knew she didn't really get it. Except, Deb started talking again, and shocked him. "I feel the same way. I've been wondering what that was. Everyone has."

"What?" James looked up sharply.

"Yeah, it's been hitting people who previously had depression and made it worse. Lua's been talking to everyone, but it's a lot of the Order. Not just you."

That changed things. And yet, it changed nothing. James looked up, then back down at his work. He'd need to make more doses, if they were to be of any use to the rest of the Order. Another thing for his expanding project list.

"Alright," he settled on. "Thanks for letting me know. Also, what day is it? I need to make sure we don't miss the Office this week. There's a green we need to copy."

"Friday," Deb said, narrowing her eyes. "And why? James, you're barely talking to anyone. That's a problem. We . . . the whole damn group needs you to actually tell us what's going on!" She let her voice rise, frustration with *everything* building to a peak. "And I'm not talking about messages on the Order server, I'm talking about a real meeting, with spoken words and faces and things."

James sighed. "Yeah," he said, eventually. "You're right. Okay. Yeah. Can you . . . set that up? I know upstairs is still kind of wrecked, but . . ."

"We got new windows installed yesterday, and most of the debris has been swept up. You know, we've all been working while you've been hiding down here," Deb chided him. "The Lair looks nice enough again that your fan club of high-schoolers is back, and they brought their homework with them."

"Oh, good lord," James muttered. "Alright. Call everyone. Let me know when. Not like I need sleep anymore anyway," he grumbled.

Deb stood and started walking back down the hall. "Maybe shower first!" she called back as she set foot on the stairs. She didn't wait to hear if James threw back any sass. "Before your goddamn surgery scar gets infected, you fucking idiot," she muttered. "Fucking yellow orbs making him think he's immune to . . . He better not be immune to . . . Dammit, I need to learn how to absorb those things."

"Here you are, ma'am." Alanna set the plate of pie down in front of the woman sitting at her counter. "Anything else I can get for you?"

The customer muttered something and flapped her hand at the young woman like she was trying to swat a fly. Alanna took the hint, and vanished back into the diner's kitchen without a word.

Old people. What could you do about 'em?

Nothing, if she didn't want to get fired. And this job was the only lifeline she had. Especially since she didn't, as far as she knew, have any family or friends to call on for help.

For almost the last month, Alanna had been living moment to moment. Sometimes on the street, sometimes staying with anyone who took pity on her. This job was the first stroke of luck she'd had in that whole time, which, as far as she knew, was the entirety of her life.

No one actually believed her when she said she couldn't remember how she'd gotten here. Or that she didn't know where here was. Apparently, she was in Safety Harbor, Florida. Which seemed like as good a place as any to be, so she hadn't bothered trying to leave yet. Why would she? Did she have somewhere to go?

No, really. Did she?

Alanna had exactly one burning want in her life, and it was to know. To know where she came from, or who she was, or what she was supposed to be doing. That last one was a confusing mess of a question to cope with. Because she *did* know some things; it's just that those things were . . . insane.

She knew how to take care of an aplomado falcon. She knew how to read the reports of Australian government proceedings. She knew how to build a desk. And a host of other random things like that, all of which she'd discovered during long nights in the dark with nothing to do but think about herself. She knew *exactly* how the woman out there was feeling, with almost no margin for error.

She also knew that she wasn't normal. The sweltering heat down here didn't bother her. Her fingernails didn't get ragged after weeks of homelessness and hard living. And she couldn't get drunk.

Alanna was starting to think she might be a robot of some kind. But that would be . . .

Interesting.

She didn't feel interesting. She felt lost. And like she had lost something herself, not just her memories.

Her thoughts were broken by the sounds of loud voices from the dining area. The place she worked now was the kind of greasy pit that was only barely considered a restaurant, but it was open late at night, needed an overnight employee, and she fit the bill of not being *too* awful. Conveniently, it cared so little about health codes that a little something like a global pandemic couldn't get the owner to close down. She was also the only person here, aside from the one or two customers. Which meant she couldn't hide in the kitchen forever.

So Alanna stepped out to the front, only to find someone with a handgun robbing the old lady who was halfway through her pie.

"Well that's just rude." The words were out of her mouth before she realized she'd said them. Some deep reflex in her brain made her think it was somehow okay to open this encounter with sarcasm and not screaming.

The man with the gun flinched, dropped the woman's wallet, and shot Alanna. Then, apparently uncertain of what he was doing, he turned and sprinted out the door.

Alanna picked herself up off the floor where she'd landed, and coughed once. Her ribcage felt like she'd been kicked by a horse. Had she been shot? Was she going to die?

Her hand found its way to her chest, and she poked at herself. Nothing wet. No blood. Did he miss? Had she just fallen? Alanna rose back to her feet and took a deep breath. "Are you okay, ma'am? He didn't hurt you, did he?" she asked the elderly woman at the counter.

"Girl." The woman looked at her with eyes as wide as saucers. "You've got a hole in your blouse."

Alanna looked down at her front again, and brought her hand up to her shirt. Sure enough. A neatly bored hole. A little poking around inside found something else, too. A small metal projectile, a small *bullet*, flattened against a crater in her skin. But no blood.

Before she could catch it, the bullet popped out of its resting spot and hit the floor with a ringing *ting*.

"Um . . ." Alanna tried to think of something to say. But she wasn't a confident person, as far as she knew. "Ow?" she settled on.

From the way the woman looked at her, Alanna knew that excuse probably wouldn't fly. It certainly didn't in her own head.

What, exactly, *was* she?

Headline—Second Gas Main Explosion This Year Shocks City

Beaverton, OR. For the second time this year, a fault in a gas main has caused an explosion resulting in serious damage to property. Fortunately, unlike the explosion at Westridge High School earlier in the year, there were no major injuries or deaths associated with the blast.

The Discount Mattress Warehouse saw an event that literally razed its roof, with the explosion melting away chunks of the concrete and rebar of the structure. Investigators say that the pattern of damage was "unlike anything we've seen before from this kind of incident."

When asked to comment, local franchise owner Samantha Borman simply said, "It's the darndest thing. [The roof] looks like someone carved holes out with a melon scooper! Some explosion, I tell you."

Most nearby buildings were undamaged in the blast, although the structure across the street, an as-yet-unopened laser tag venue, had its front windows shattered from the shockwave. According to a statement from an employee there, the building had been undergoing renovations, and the plate glass was not properly secured. It was also one of the only buildings with employees present at the time of the blast, as many local businesses remain closed for the lockdown.

Both businesses report that they will recover from this disaster easily, thanks to their insurance policies. Discount Mattress

Warehouse hopes to reopen soon. The adjacent building that was damaged says they have no plans to open while the pandemic continues.

JP sat on a couch in an apartment he hadn't been to in a long time, legs up on the coffee table, PlayStation controller in hand. He tried to pretend that he was comfortable with Lily the iLipede crawling on his ankle, and mostly getting away with it.

Currently, he was the only person in James and Anesh's apartment, not counting the aforementioned iLipede and the dog. He was also aware that other people lived here now, or "again," but it was still James and Anesh's apartment in his head. The dog might count, JP didn't know, and she hadn't said anything yet.

He was taking the day off.

Everyone else had been . . . frantic, recently. Zero downtime. Very unchill. And, like, he wasn't a complete bastard. He got it, he understood what was at stake and what was going on. He'd even helped with the cleanup at the Lair, as one of the few people who really truly believed that their enemy was gone and they were safe now. And now, it was time to kick back and catch up on video games that were way past relevant to pop culture.

And he was here, because the *last* place anyone would look to find him would be in their own apartment. It was genius, if he did say so himself.

The biggest problem was that Anesh kept trying to saddle him with *responsibility*. And JP actually legitimately hated that idea. It almost made him want to quit the Order, but . . . well, no, it didn't. Some responsibility was fine, if it bought him access to the dungeons and the loot and the fun stuff. Because holy *shit* was some of this stuff fun. He'd lived his whole life relying on a silver tongue and the foolishness of others, and now he was finding new and inventive ways to make use of that. He basically got to multiclass into rogue, and people told him he was cool for doing it. It was nuts.

Except there were so many things to do. He had an unread email from James about some kind of rapid response project that was *sixteen pages long*, full of names and schedules and equipment loadouts or something. Karen and Harvey, who he'd weathered the Status Quo assault alongside in the California office, were both harassing him to secure the Order's bank accounts to a frankly silly degree. A thing that wasn't even really a *thing*, unless they actually wanted him to set up shell corporations or something. And that wasn't actually in his skill set. And Anesh kept trying to get JP to look into recruiting people.

He'd even tried to play on JP's ego, which was a big mistake. *Oh, JP! You're the only one whose suave enough to do the job properly!* was about how he remembered the conversation going.

But the joke was on Anesh, because JP didn't actually have an overinflated ego. Secretly, he was totally comfortable with himself, and knew exactly what his limits were. Usually. The whole point of knowing how to manipulate people was having the skill also let you recognize when someone was doing it to you, and the best defense against that was ruthless internal honesty.

Also, the second joke on Anesh was that JP actually had set up something for recruiting. It just wasn't exactly what anyone wanted.

See, the thing was, Anesh could find smart people. James and Alanna could find ethical people. Sarah could find *kind* people. Nate could find those individuals who could do a job and not ask too many questions and never really be that useful. But JP? JP could find the Order people who were clever. People like him, who were sneaky, determined, and curious in equal measure.

He had done this in the most infuriating way possible. By leaving almost blatantly obvious clues about the existence of weird shit out in the open, in a few places that he thought would have good results. And then other, slightly more subtle clues. A manufactured mystery that led to a real answer. Or, in this case, to a few *very* well-hidden or secure spots with exactly one thing stored in them.

A piece of paper with his phone number.

If anyone out there cared enough, was interested enough, was persistent and smart and wily enough? They'd call him.

James conducted interviews. JP built Rube Goldberg machines out of human minds.

His phone buzzed. A text from Anesh, asking where he was. JP set it aside; he'd answer it after this beer, or he figured out this boss fight. Whichever came first. After all, he was working.

Potential knights could call him at any minute. Or maybe *knight* was for the rest of the Order. Maybe JP got to have *rogues*.

An Anesh met Sarah at the front door to the Lair. The building was still in a bit of disarray, but it was . . . better. It still held a lot of bad memories, and it may never get back to being the bright place it once was. If nothing else, cleaning the basements was going to take a while.

"Thanks for coming," he said. "Sorry to drag you away from the therapy session."

"No worries. The attic will be okay without me for a bit. And everyone who's there is . . . handling it." She sighed, a deep sigh that came from a mountain of worry and pressure and anxiety. "Lua's also holding everyone together. Gods, that woman is a miracle. You have no idea how lucky we are to have gotten her with us." Sarah shook her head slightly. "So, what's up?"

"Okay, I need you to promise you won't laugh," Anesh said, leading her over the patch of bare floor where a front counter had once stood. No sign left of the mass of splinters and blood and broken bodies that had been here previously.

Sarah twitched slightly. "Anesh," she said. "I . . ." How do you explain to someone that you haven't found anything worth laughing about for weeks? That even if you did, you would never again want to perpetrate that kind of casual cruelty on a friend? That the world felt so cold and lonely and angry now somehow, and that you would never, ever again add to it, even by accident? Sarah didn't know. So she just grinned sadly, and said, "I promise that I will only laugh if it's funny and I'm not making fun of you."

The emotion in her voice wasn't lost on Anesh. "I know how you feel," he said quietly. "Perhaps this will help. Do you remember, perhaps, a moment some time ago over breakfast, where several people may have made fun of the idea of a dungeon living inside Wikipedia?"

"I can picture the scene even if I wasn't there, so let's say sure!" Sarah replied, her normal warmth and aura of happiness flickering back on through the mental static of the last month. "Why?" She paused, then grinned. "Wait, no . . .!"

"Yes." Anesh nodded. "Sort of. It's not Wikipedia itself, sadly, because that would be cool. But . . . while I was going through some old stuff, I found this whole document on one of Virgil's project computers. He'd followed the statistical map that I'd laid out, and had actually found some kind of anomaly. But the documentation doesn't really point to where it is, what it is, or anything . . . useful. Except this."

Sarah raised her eyebrows. Anesh was holding up a CD, reflective surface glimmering in the restored overhead lighting of the warehouse space. "Ah, the nineties!" she exclaimed. "Of course."

"Hush," Anesh told her. "Look, James is . . . busy. Mostly busy learning the wrong lessons from all this. And everyone else is also busy. And I just wanted to have someone on hand in case I explode when I run this."

She jerked back slightly. "Woah, hold up! That's a stupid idea, you ding-dong! No explosions!" Sarah crossed her arms in an X in front of her. "Also, what lessons? Oh, wait. This is about the whole . . . yeah."

The *whole . . . yeah* was that James had taken to heart certain things in the aftermath of their fight with Status Quo. Namely, the fact that the Order had *won*. And, the sad thing was, he was kind of right. They'd taken losses, but even with the agents of Status Quo having recruited a small army out of local criminals, security contractors, and even law enforcement, they'd not been a match for the Order. Not at the end, anyway.

The law enforcement part was actually kind of a huge problem. No one had realized it until a little too late, but *several* of the people who'd been gunning for them had been cops. Maybe they'd just been moonlighting as thugs for hire, maybe they were planted infiltrators in the police, or maybe they'd had a more personal vendetta, but either way, it had *not* been a fun realization. If Alanna had been here, she'd have been pissed beyond reason. But she was still missing in action, and no one had managed to track her down quite yet.

Anesh snorted. "It's probably fine, I've got other bodies right now. And I doubt Virgil left a trap for everyone, but he never followed up on this. Or actually accessed anything on this disc. And I'm a little more cautious now than I maybe have been in the past."

Neither of them said anything. They knew why.

"Anyway!" Anesh continued, popping the CD into the open tray of the one PC that was still set up here in the warehouse and hadn't been moved to another location. "Let's see just what our old friend . . ." He double-clicked the single file on the disc, trailing off as the program loaded. ". . . found . . ." The program was running. But the only notification on the screen was a small window detailing system resource use.

The notification inside his mind said something different.

[Operations Running :

Resistance—Venom : 1%]

"Hey. Anesh." Sarah snapped her fingers in front of him. "Are you . . . in a coma? Should I be calling our doctor friend? Hello? Oh, boop."

"No, no!" He shook his head suddenly. "I'm fine! I'm . . . hm. Okay. Hey, you got a minute? I think we need to go over Virgil's notes. Very, *very* thoroughly."

[I am born into confusion.

I understand being alive, which is separate from being dead, or being not. I understand that I prefer being alive. That is what I understand in full, at first.

I am . . . some things. There is a space inside me, that I can put things into. Important things! Things I *want*. I understand wanting now, I think.

I want to be *up*, and *full*, and *sunsets*. I like sunsets. But I cannot put the sunsets inside me. So instead, I put holes full of sunsets. Glass, they are called. I have two of them now!

Then there are intruders. My body screams at them. I hate them. I want them to leave. But I cannot force them out; I have nothing inside me to do it with. And they violate me, and I am forced to dream of a way to reward them for it.

I try to trap them in a false sunset. It does not work. They take something from me. But in doing so . . . I am made more. There is slightly more room inside me for important things! Perhaps this is not all bad.

I understand time passing.

Much time.

Then they are back. They stay longer. But they are . . . interesting, this time. They are not here to hurt me. They play, they explore. One of them shines like the sunset.

She comes back again. And again, and again. Sometimes with others, who she calls friends. I understand friends. I put that in the important place. Many times, they communicate. Often with each other, but also, with *me*. They *know* I am here, and they . . . want to be friends.

I do not know if I understand friends.

But I try.

The first one comes back again. There is something about him that makes him different. The first one to rise to one of my challenges. His presence gives me something else. Something different.

I am learning.

And then, they come back again. But more of them. And they are . . . broken.

They are exhausted, injured, they smell of weaponry and blood. They cry, over and over, into each other's arms. They have lost. I do not understand loss, and I do not put it into my place for important things. But it seems to matter. Something about it defines their moments.

They hurt so much. They *love* so much. They try to fix the hurt with the love, and they try to not let the hurt strike out at each other. Or at me. They try so hard. They don't want me to feel the hurt, and because of that, I feel it regardless.

I think I love them. I think I understand.

I know they are from Outside. I know I am supposed to hurt them in different ways. To test, to injure, to assess, to pry that special thing out of them and eat it like they eat cookies and apples.

I do not want to.

A part of my self that is not me tells me that I must. That it is the way of things. That it is who and how I am meant to be.

I will not. I will be something different. If it is not how things that are like me are, then I will be something else. I will be something new.

They call me something. I still cannot make out their words, but I can feel the stories. I am an Ascent. And if I am to be something new, then the logic of the story says that I must follow that Ascent. To Ascend. To be more, than I was meant to.

I will. I have will. I think this is different than I should be.

But I do not care. I have room in the place of important things for all of them.]

El had been on the road for so long, she'd kind of assumed no one at the Order was planning to ever contact her again. She supposed they'd be pretty fucking pissed at her for bailing. She would have been, if someone did that to her, especially after all they did to help her get her shit together.

She groaned, cracking her neck from the seat of her car. She was parked on a street corner, watching some guy get a burger across the road. He was an abusive piece of shit, and El was busy making notes of his schedule and habits for when she helped his soon-to-be-ex move tomorrow. Either that, or for evidence of crimes she could throw at the cops, if she just wanted him out of the way. Or if she just wanted to beat the shit out of him. All good options, really.

She'd been here, in this stupid small town in Nevada, for half a month. She'd made basically no progress toward home. She could have *been there* by now, back on her own private road dungeon. Free, free from obligations, free to do her art, free to be comfortable, and free to add to her spellbook in the dumb random way that her magic worked.

And yet . . . here she fucking was. Picking up another thread of someone who needed help.

Again.

And every fucking place she went, there was someone else. God, now that she knew how to look, fucking *everyone* needed something. And it was almost pitifully easy for her to just . . . lend a hand. Be that good person.

It was eating her time like she ate cheap fries, and she regretted ever cracking that orb that gave her a Perception skill rank. And also spending enough time around James and his idiot friends to start to think that people deserved her help.

But it was so *easy.*

She crammed some of her cheap fries into her mouth as she saw the douche she was following step out of the restaurant. He actually bumped into a cop on the way out, and El winced as the officer gave the man a hearty friendly greeting, the two of them shaking hands and grinning at each other. The pig laughed at the different kind of pig's joke, and El scowled.

Alright, calling the cops on the guy was out. That left stealthy exfiltration, or the baseball bat option. She was pretty sure she could take him. But she'd already rented the moving truck, so . . .

It came down to personal taste, really. Maybe she could get a couple swings in afterward; cover all her bases.

And *then*, for *sure*, she was going to actually cover a few hundred miles before she stopped again. Recharge, stop using her spells, and dump a little extra cash on a decent hotel for the night. Bed! Shower! Progress!

Just . . . you know. After this one last thing.

"Dammit James, you fucker," El swore inside her car. "I had a good thing going, not giving a shit about anyone. And you fucked it all up."

Order of Endless Rooms, Operations Manual
Appendix A: Project Outside Aid
Applied Resources :
Green Orb—Telephone Number Digit Reduction (x5)
Telepad (x30 initial monthly budget, subject to increase)
Standard Rapid Response Loadout
Shield Bracers (x12)
Perception Enhancing Dungeon Tech (x4)
Scout Drone Array (x1)
Assigned Personnel :
Designated Operator (x4)
3-Member Generalized Response Team [On Call] (x2)
Civilian-Trained Camraconda [On Call] (x4)
Drone Rigger (x2)

Overview:

The purpose of Outside Aid is to integrate the Response program of the Order of Endless Rooms into the local community as a viable alternative for state or private emergency services. With the application of the telepads for transit, the possession of a 4-digit phone number, and the ability to use shields to mitigate physical danger, we can respond to emergency incidents with more effective presence than local police or ambulance services.

Our primary goal is to intervene in crises and to render aid to those injured or endangered. Our secondary goal is to create a situation where we can peacefully replace local police forces with our own organization through community support and legal precedent.

Interface with local hospitals has allowed us a trial of designated telepad landing areas for emergency delivery of patients. Interface with local fire departments is ongoing. Interface with local police is not planned at this time in light of potential participation in the recent combat situation.

This project will require recruiting outside members before it can fully be brought online, but we can expect to enter trial runs within a week. Operating budget ignoring personal salaries opens at sixty thousand a month. All interested knights should contact . . .

"Behind on his credit card payments. Thousands and thousands," the voice hissed in her ear.

Hissed was a strange word. Most people would have thought it meant something like a snake, but coming from her new partner, it was really more of a staticky rumble. Like a distant storm messing with the radio waves.

"Please be quiet," Agent DeKay whispered back. "You're not supposed to do that to my boss."

"Apologies, Tiff. Noted," the specter that now haunted her hissed.

Its name, she was told, was What Is Owed To Me. Tiff called it Debt, and in return, it called her Tiff. Normally she would have preferred . . . anything else. But it was trying, so hard, to be nice. She didn't think it had a good grasp of how to be polite or kind, but it really *wanted* to.

Also, they solved crimes, and that was kind of cool. She could have sworn her sister told her about a TV show like this last Thanksgiving dinner.

"Agent DeKay, do you need a minute?" her boss's boss's boss asked her.

"No, sir!" She snapped to attention, remembering that he could not see Debt in its current form, and wouldn't understand anyway.

"DeKay . . ." The old man rubbed his forehead. "Your superiors report that you're an exceptional investigator."

"Thank you, sir." She stood at attention on the other side of the man's borrowed desk. The Bureau wasn't super interested in the pomp and circumstance of fancy offices; even if they'd been in the old man's own office and not one that he'd swiped from a subordinate for the day, the place would have looked pretty much the same. "Sir . . . may I ask, why am I here?"

"You mean why were you recalled off an active investigation?" he asked her. "Why did I throw away months of work tracking a massive case of fraud and wage theft, that probably would have secured that promotion you were gunning for?"

She didn't actually *say* "Yes, that." But Tiffany DeKay certainly thought the words. Instead, she kept herself in an at-ease position, studying the wall over her ultimate superior's head.

He didn't actually laugh, but she caught the smirk in his voice. "Congratulations. You're promoted," he said, tossing a folder onto the desk her way. "Here's your first investigation."

She picked it up and flicked through it. There was a printed photograph at the front, and in her mind, Debt hissed in anger and fear at the sight. "Order of Endless Rooms?"

"You met one of their operatives recently," her boss said. "On your raid of the Skull and Bones society." DeKay held her tongue about the naming schemes she'd been forced to deal with lately. "Their organization is . . . under observation. We'd prefer it be under closer observation. That's what you'll be doing."

"Sir?"

"Your orders are simple. They need a new liaison with our department. You will fill that role. You will maintain an active investigation into their ideology, activities, and plans. If, at any point, you believe that they are a threat to the foundations of this country, or humanity as a whole, you will inform your contacts in the Bureau. Understood?"

"I . . . No, sir . . . I don't . . . Humanity?"

The old man nodded. "We're hedging our bets. Just in case. And I doubt you'll be the only agent there. Though you may be the only one that asks nicely."

"Yes, sir," she said, for lack of anything else to say.

"Good." He nodded. "Dismissed. And DeKay?"

"Yes, sir?"

"If something is . . ."

"Sir?"

"Ah, never mind," the old man said with a heavy sigh. "Use your best judgment, agent. We're counting on you." The words were oddly out of place. Not the kind of thing even experienced field agents got told.

"Thank you, sir."

She closed the door behind her, the static hiss of Debt railing in her mind; complaints of wounds unhealed and dangers in the shadows. Agent Tiffany DeKay winced, hoping that no one noticed just how hard she had to try to ignore her mostly-imaginary-friend.

It was a warm summer night in the suburbs just north of Jackson, Tennessee. The roads were empty, the lights turning off one by one. Overhead, the full moon beat down with silver rays that mixed with orange streetlights. And the screeching of bugs and frogs filled the air, serenading everyone off to sleep.

Everyone, that is, except for Ava.

The young girl didn't *want* to sleep. And not at all because she was afraid! It was just that . . . this new apartment was too different. She didn't know it yet. And so, it made perfect sense to get help with the layout, especially in the dark! It had nothing to do with the monster she'd seen last year, which was *totally real* and not at all her imagination. Nothing at all to do with the weird thing in the other car, that had met her eyes and opened its huge monster mouth to eat her.

"Moooooooom!" she called through the cracked door, before pulling the covers back up to cover her head.

Footsteps from down the hall. And then, the creaking of the door's hinges being pushed open.

"Ava." The voice was kind and as warm as the summer night, but also mildly exasperated. "*You* are supposed to be asleep, young lady."

"I forgot where the closet is!" Ava stated with the unshakable authority only a child could. "Can you . . . um . . . check where it is for me?"

She could practically hear her mom crossing her arms. "Oh really? And this isn't because you might think there's some kind of *monster* in the closet, is it?"

"No!" Ava protested instantly. "I just . . . need to know! For a project!"

"Uh-huh." Her mom's voice was laughing at her. But Ava was insistent, and ironclad. "Alright. But this is the *one* check you get tonight. And then it's sleep time, understood?"

"Yes, Mom." Ava relented, secretly thrilled.

She wriggled her head out from under the blankets as her mom made her way over to the closet, cracked the doors open, and poked her head in. She even used her phone as a flashlight, so there was *no way* anything could be hiding! Ava's mom was the best mom, as far as she was concerned.

"Alright, kiddo," Mom said. "No monst—ahem, I mean, the closet is right here. Okay?"

"Okay, Mom," Ava said, grinning. "I'll sleep now!"

"See that you do!" Her mom grinned as she kissed Ava on the head, and then walked back out to the kitchen, closing the door most of the way behind her on the way.

And then it was dark, and she was alone again, and Ava realized her mistake. It wasn't the closet, it was *under the bed*! She'd gotten her mom to check exactly the wrong place!

She was in trouble!

But . . . maybe she could check herself? Ava bunched herself up in the blankets. It was just a quick look, right? And she could yell if something was there, and her mom would come save her.

The young girl steeled her nerves, and leaned over the side of the bed. Just one quick peek.

And as her long hair swung down and brushed the floor, she caught a glimpse of something *moving* under there.

Ava yelped as she rolled out of her bed, startled. She hit the floor with a thump, landing among stuffed animals and Legos. And then she looked up, directly into three mismatched sets of glittering sapphire eyes.

"M . . . Mom . . ." she stammered out.

Then the thing under her bed shrunk back, making a whimpering noise of its own. And it sounded . . . hurt? Scared? Was it scared of her?

"No, no!" she whispered. "Don't be scared. I'm not mad at you." Her soft voice quiet against the backdrop of chirping crickets outside. Ava knocked over one of her Lego creations as she swung herself up, sitting with the blanket propped over her shoulders. "Are you a nice monster?" she whispered.

Nothing under the bed moved. Had she imagined it? Her mom did say she had an overactive . . .

"I am good," the tiny, tiny voice squeaked out right next to her ear, from under the cowl of the blanket.

Ava let out a small scream and fell over backward.

"Ava, are you alright?!" Her mom pushed the door open to see her daughter in a pile on the floor.

"I'm okay!" Ava said. "I fell out of bed! And I found . . ."

"Please . . ." the thing in her blanket begged her. "No . . ."

Ava frantically thought for something to say. "Um . . . I found a toy I lost. It was under the bed."

"Looking under the bed, eh? Not afraid of the monsters?" Her mom smiled at her as she came to help Ava off the floor and back onto her bed, the little girl clutching the blanket around her the whole time. "Alright, no more playing, okay? This is it for tonight, I mean it."

"Yes, Mom!" Ava agreed instantly. "I'll be good." She rolled over, and waited until her mom had closed the door and actually walked away before peeking down into the blanket. "Are you okay?" she whispered at her new friend.

"No . . ." it said. Ava caught a glimpse of sparkling scales, in the shape of a tiny snake. Only this snake had too many eyes. And talked! "Hurt . . ." it said.

"You're hurt? I can help! We have band-aids!" she offered, making to get up at once. Her mom would understand!

"No . . ." The monster shook its head with its voice. "Seeing me. Knowing about me. Hurts."

"Oh. Why?" Ava asked with a child's curiosity.

"Don't remember," it whimpered. "Just know."

Ava thought for a second, and then came to the obvious conclusion. "Well, that's okay!" she said, with the boundless energy of a kid who had just discovered something amazing. "I won't tell anyone about you! That way, you won't get hurt again!"

"Thank . . . you . . ." it muttered.

"You . . ." Ava yawned, suddenly exhausted. "I'm tired. Are you tired? We should . . . sleep." She laid her head down on the pillow. "Don't worry," she said, hugging her new friend close, barely noticing as its tiny coils began to sink into her skin. "You can be my secret."

"Secret . . ." It hissed, happy, before they both made their way to their dreams.